LITHIUM FIRE

Liam Taliesin

BookLand
press

Published by
BookLand Press Inc.
15 Allstate Parkway, Suite 600
Markham, Ontario L3R 5B4
www.booklandpress.com

Printed in Canada

Library and Archives Canada Cataloguing in Publication

Title: Lithium fire / Liam Taliesin.
Names: Taliesin, Liam, author.
Series: Modern Indigenous voices.
Description: Series statement: Modern Indigenous voices
Identifiers: Canadiana (print) 20230513891 | Canadiana (ebook) 20230513905 | ISBN 9781772312249 (softcover) | ISBN 9781772312256 (EPUB)
Subjects: LCGFT: Novels.
Classification: LCC PS8639.A45 L58 2023 | DDC C813/.6 – dc23

We acknowledge the support of the Government of Canada through the Canada Book Fund and the support of the Ontario Arts Council, an agency of the Government of Ontario. We also acknowledge the support of the Canada Council for the Arts.

This novel is dedicated to my wife, Joanne Tessier, whose love, support, and endless patience sustained me throughout the process of writing it and, without whom, it might never have come into being. I am infinitely grateful to her for her grace as my muse. Merci, Joanne.

*"The child who is not embraced by the village
will burn it down to feel its warmth."*

~ African proverb

Table of Contents

The Heart of the Continent

Smoke and Ashes

City of Ghosts

The Heart of the Continent

Prairie Sunsets in the Blood

The editorial committee was trying to decide if it would accept the grant. Midcontinental was a mobile, tactile gallery, with art coming off on the reader's hands in smudges of ink, and according to the McDermott Street Manifesto, the tabloid was supposed to remain independent, free of outside pressure or interference. Was the committee willing to compromise its creative integrity to secure community credibility? Debate was fierce and the meeting went on too long. It deteriorated when Karmin lunged at Furnace Face, dragged him to the ground, and pinned him between her thighs. He seemed to enjoy his predicament a little too much until he started turning blue. Scott Kostyk moved they adjourn. Furnace Face seconded from the floor.

At two AM everyone went over to the Lithium Café to hear Terminal Jerks. Kostyk stayed behind to lock up, stack chairs, and put away the coffee machine. His breakup with Svetlana had been an undercurrent at the meeting all evening but the others were too polite to say anything. Canadians could nice you to death.

Apocalypso was just starting band practice up on the fifth floor as Kostyk left the building. The sound of a booming bass guitar shot down rickety stairs, shaking the walls and vibrating on the handrail he gripped, the sensation trembling through his fingers and into the rest of his body. Next to the stairs sat an ornate brass cage holding the guts of an ancient elevator that was lovely to look at but precarious to ride. On the third floor he saw light under Dick Costello's door. The writer was either working late or living in his office. The Bate Building with its cheap rent and character to burn housed a dozen artist studios.

Kostyk walked down to the Lithium Café located in a largely abandoned warehouse just down the street. At the door, he spotted a strange man loitering in the lane, his face illuminated by a cigarette. Kostyk ran inside the building and the stink of steam heating and mould hit him. Loud music at the other end of a dark hall muffled the creak of the wooden floor under his feet. Laughter split the air like the crackle of small arms fire as he moved toward the light. It was Svetlana.

The Lithium was brightly-lit, buzzing with caffeinated chatter while new wave shamans decked out in ecclesiastic black oozed carefully-cultivated despair. A homeless man, huddled on a stool at the lunch counter, was sound asleep. Sebastian had created a genuine counter culture in the Lithium Café, turning a decrepit greasy spoon into a post-depression psychedelicatessen. The interior was decorated with curios he liberated on late night garbage runs in the city's back lanes. Paintings by future art stars hung on the walls, obscure acts were offered an intimate, but viable performance venue, and quality grub was provided at decent prices to poor artists.

Terminal Jerks had set up by the kitchen at the back. Digger was belting out 'I Wanna Be Your Bully Boy Billy Boy'. The band was getting better. It was when they concluded in a clap of musical thunder that Svetlana swept into the café from the back like the Russian aristocrat she claimed to be. She said her family fled the revolution and bragged of Mikhail Bulgakov being a great uncle. She hated Kostyk teasing her, calling her Svetlana Stalin. She was waving a cigarette like a baton, working the room, and drawing otherwise intelligent people into the vortex of her personality. Then she saw him. Her eyes were black stars. She was very stoned. Svetlana strode over to him, a nasty grin going up one side of her mouth, down the other. Her voice was shrill.

"Scott Kostyk is the master of angst. He thinks so hard his face hurts."

The crowd was amused. Some laughed. Others clapped. With a single remark, she'd made him the entertainment. Kostyk had to retaliate and levelled his own cutting comment. The insults began to fly. But Scott had an advantage. He was straight. Svetlana realized he was winning and went white. She slapped him across the face and flounced back out to the kitchen, where Kostyk assumed another snort waited for her.

Scott Kostyk despised drugs and had tried to tell her it was because they bought bullets and cattle prods in third world countries. She never listened, always laughed, and called him silly.

Suddenly, there was a woman standing by the front door and screaming.

Frozen in place, Kostyk didn't move at first. Smoke billowed, quickly filling the room, his nose, and his mouth. He couldn't breathe. Angry heat was pressing into his chest and throat and lungs. He charged through the thickening fumes, stayed close to the floor out of instinct, tripping over things. A voice inside told him to keep moving. He bumped into tables, chairs, other fleshy objects. Another voice cried his name. Don't stop the first ordered. He burst from the building, coughing and blinking icicles. The wind was a cold fist slamming into his face. He fell, his lungs a bellows, forcing in fresh air, pushing out poison. He wasn't sure how long he lay on the ground breathing hard before a blanket was thrown over his shoulders and he was led to a bus where he took his place among ghostly, gaunt figures. Someone pushed a hot mug into his hands. He peered down into the cup. Flashes of red, blue, and yellow light skimmed the liquid surface.

◆   ◆   ◆

The fire eight nights ago had spread so fast. He was at the meeting one minute, dashing down a dark, smoke-filled hall the next. Scott Kostyk was lucky to be alive. It could have been his body dragged from the debris; his corpse lying on a slab under a coroner's indifferent scalpel. Everything had started to slide sideways since then. He didn't want to see anyone or do anything. He hid out at the gallery, living like an urban hermit, sleeping on the couch, eating leftovers from the fridge, washing in a bathroom sink. It would have been easy to slide into apathy, align with a legion of lazy vagrants living downtown.

But Kostyk didn't want to surrender to some stumble-bum existence, stay in a place where dreams went sour. He decided to go, gather supplies, and get a little fresh air. He bundled up for the winter weather and set out to find a store. Yet, his feet pulled him in another direction, down the street, toward the scene of the fire a few blocks from his gallery. Why was he back there? His mind raced with questions that had no answers. What in the world did he expect to find here; an explanation, a reason for what happened, some absolution? When does colour leak from a life he wondered? Kostyk had taken it in directly as a kid, eating his crayons before discovering a better use for them. He learned to draw and paint and ended up in Winnipeg after leaving Grand Forks. He met Svetlana, a confident, capable artist with strong, calloused hands, clay embedded in her fingernails, her skin perfumed with paint and linseed oil. She encouraged him to stay, saying the light was good for painting. He was charmed. They were a couple.

Standing in front of the burned-out shell of the building, the smell of smoke and tendrils of charcoal snaked into his nostrils. His nose throbbed; itching like it was on fire. He was too frozen to scratch. Kostyk couldn't feel his feet or hands or face, despite wearing a balaclava, wool mitts pulled on over leather gloves, a warm winter coat, decent boots, and an extra pair of heavy socks.

They say exposed flesh will freeze in two minutes when the wind-chill hits fifty below. But it wasn't the crazy cold of a Winnipeg winter that held him now. It was beauty, producing sharp pain and piercing his defences. The rhythmic sweep of fire hoses across the limestone structure eight nights earlier had woven a tapestry and transformed the burning building into a shimmering cathedral of ice. Dangerous spikes drew his eyes down into devastation, silver spires lifted them again. The scene was both surreal and banal with police barriers, bits of fluttering yellow tape. Kostyk wished for a moment he had his camera with him to take pictures of this. Then he shook his head to try and clear it as a wave of shame swept through him.

Three people were dead; Svetlana, Oscar, a homeless man. Stark images popped in his brain like exploding flash-bulbs, bursts of jagged light, and fragments of colour. He inhaled a sharp spear of ice. Nobody sane was out tonight. His body was numb and he had to get going. It took forever to extricate his stiff frame from its frozen position, to propel it back down the dark street.

He stumbled through a surrealistic landscape, passing by a car that had mutated into a Dali sculpture coated in thick, pearly ice with its wheels fused to pavement. Opaque telephone wires sagged with the weight of wintry teeth hanging between poles. It was the year of Orwell in a city so damned cold even Big Brother didn't bother with it. Winnipeg was at the drop-dead center of North America, more hamlet than metropolis when Kostyk arrived from North Dakota ten years ago. It was in the middle of the country, the middle of the continent, and the middle of nowhere; a flatland where planes of sky and earth extended forever until they coalesced at the curved edge of the world. The rows of deserted downtown warehouses hid this view from the urban eye but couldn't obscure the sense of relentless, empty space which permeated the city's soul, sucked out the marrow, and opened minds and hearts to the hope of infinite possibility before crushing them with claustrophobic weight.

Svetlana had said Winnipeg was a manufacturing hub at the turn of the century with a large concentration of factories and warehouses. But a railroad system bulldozed into being by money-grubbing politicians from Ontario had been abandoned, collapsing the city's economy. The smart money fled, eviscerating a downtown already overrun by lowlifes and bedbugs. Artists attracted by inexpensive, abundant studio space gravitated into the area. Bookstores, theatres, art galleries sprouted up along with small, funky businesses like a vintage clothing shop called Walk Around Time. Before long, sleazy power-brokers claimed the neighbourhood, re-branding it The Exchange District, and johns chasing hookers were joined by real estate hustlers cruising deals. It's hard to shake a bad reputation and a half-century of neglect wasn't undone by throwing money at it. The tourists from Transcona didn't see much difference between pushing dope and peddling dreams.

As Kostyk walked along the slippery, subarctic street back toward Confidential Exchange, Svetlana's face loomed up, locking his brain in neutral. There were no degrees of separation. Yet he couldn't feel her death, touch it, or get a hold of it in some way to grasp the thing. It was too unreal. Kostyk couldn't wrap his mind around crazy thoughts spinning in his head; corral them into a manageable construct, something that made sense. Did Svetlana know she was going to die or think of him in those last minutes? The gallery was just a half block away now but he had to get warm.

A neon sign flickered up ahead. The Royal Albert Arms Hotel was legendary in the city. It boasted a red-tile roof facade, wrought-iron balconies on two of its four stories, and an enormous arched window with a provincial insignia and the hotel name chiselled in stone over it. The hotel had offered respite against the elements to itinerant salesmen and actors decades earlier. It was a dive now but had a reasonably comfortable bar which would be warm.

A large fan braced to the ceiling blasted hot air into the lobby. Elements of former elegance were still evident; dark-wood wall panels and a once gorgeous but now crumbling front desk. Cowboy stood behind it, wearing a bolo tie, a black leather vest with a sheriff's badge pinned to it, and his trademark Stetson. The front lobby of the Albert was frequently the flash-point where the street collided with the bar and nightmare scenarios fermenting in the hotel rooms sometimes spilled. Cowboy managed these converging energies, greeting customers with a smile and riding herd over unruly drunks. He kept the peace, cajoling and threatening if necessary, defusing tense standoffs. He had the ability to turn angry antagonists into good buddies who would leave the bar laughing and clapping each other on the back.

Kostyk only knew the second man standing in the lobby by reputation. Tony Bender was a notorious pusher who controlled most of the criminal activity in the neighbourhood.

They were both staring at him, Cowboy stroking a nic-otine-stained moustache, studying him from under the brim of his hat, Tony glaring with cold, steely eyes, cigar smoke curling around his head. Kostyk remembered the ski mask and removed it. When he did, the two men turned away and resumed their conversation.

"Don't know where fuck-head digs up these bands," Cowboy said. "Lethal Spit and the Thundering Sighs; should be Motor Mouth and the Might-Have-Beens."

"Zoltan's a zero," Tony Bender said. "A one man circle jerk only concerned about cash, coke, and cute bums wrapped up in tight jeans. What happened with Boyko?"

The desk clerk took a deep drag of his smoke before answering.

"You know Boyko. No bells and whistles. He tried start-ing a fight with the band; the guys backed off. Not the singer. The lip on this chick; real toilet mouth. Four-foot-fuck-all she puts up her dukes. Boyko's a pig; think nothing of decking a dame. He takes a poke at her. So she ducks, plows him in the belly, and pops him on the nose when he folds. Then she's all over him like a two-by-four. Wham! Bam! Thank you, ma'am! Turns out she's a women's boxing champ. If I'd a known, I would've taken bets. Broad has balls but the music is still shit. Sorry, Tony."

"Not a problem. Just means we tolerate their noise a while longer. That Boyko is a waste of skin though. Need to do some-thing about him. You hear more about the fire down the street?"

"Nada," Cowboy said. "Nightmare is all I know."

"Any messages I'll be inside," Tony said and headed to the bar. Kostyk started to follow him and Cowboy barked.

"Whoa! Where the hell you think you're going?"

"Need a drink."

"Cover charge for the band," Cowboy said, jabbing a thumb at a cartoon of him holding a six-gun with $5 written underneath.

"I don't hear music," Kostyk said.

"Torture commences at ten. We start charging at nine. Now."

Arguing with Cowboy about cover was a tradition at the Albert. But Kostyk wasn't in the mood. He fished out a five and forked it over.

"You draw this?" he asked, pointing at the cartoon. Cowboy smiled. "I'll publish it if you do a strip about the characters around the Albert."

The desk clerk tucked the five dollar bill in a vest pocket.

"Got too many friends here," he said just as three bikers swaggered into the lobby.

"How's it hanging, Cowboy?" the tallest one asked, tossing his long red hair.

"Good, Eric."

"Nobody's cut it off yet, eh?"

His friends laughed. Cowboy didn't.

"Long way from home, Eric," he said. The biker leaned over the desk.

"How is that any of your fucking business, goof? I'm here to talk to Tony."

The biker turned and walked to the bar with his buddies.

"How come they don't have to pay cover?" Kostyk asked.

"Who's gonna argue with that much leather," the desk clerk said and Kostyk held his hand out for a stamp.

"I'll remember your face," Cowboy said. Kostyk had no doubt of this.

The bar was busy despite the weather. Punks swaggered around the pool table brandishing cue sticks like erections. Broken-down booze hounds nursed their drinks and foul moods while the staff loitered by the bar, smoking cigarettes and chatting. Scott found an empty table and settled into a chair, his back to the wall, leaning into the shadows like he'd lived his life in them. The L-shaped bar was divided in two sections. A narrow stem ran parallel to the lobby with the bottom half of one wall covered by wood panels and mirrors above them. The other wall had a bank of windows that looked out onto the lobby. Tables and chairs fleshed out the area. The wide base of the bar held the heart of it; a service bay with stools for customers, washrooms, a pool table, juke box, video games, and two exits. One door led to a small café, the other beside the washrooms opened on a parking lot behind the hotel. At the apex of the bar, there was a dance floor in front of a small stage with risers, black curtains, and theatre lights that gave it the feel of an intimate performance space. The bar's most attractive feature was over the stage; a vaulted, stained-glass skylight on the ceiling Zoltan paid a fortune to restore. The Albert was a cut above other neighbourhood hotels. Everyone was welcome, whether leading citizens or losers. There was no pressure to perform a particular way, meet any expectations, or remain conscious; and when the mix was right and the music tight, the bar shook with frenetic fusion as students, hipsters, artists, hoods, hookers, bikers, and undercover cops all rode the same funky beat to the end of the night.

Kostyk and his friends often went to the Albert after an event or a meeting to unwind and soak in the atmosphere. The hoods didn't mind the artists being in the bar as long as they stuck to their own business and the two crowds tolerated the idiosyncratic nature of the other. The tough guys gave the bar bite, the bohemians lent it colour. Kostyk knew nothing about the regulars and the anonymity of being among these familiar strangers, but not of their company, was especially comforting tonight. It offered refuge, some respite from thoughts eating away at him. He could relax a little. He desperately needed a drink. An angel in blue jeans arrived at his table, balancing a tray of bottles in one hand. He ordered two glasses of beer. When the waitress returned, the whisper of denim pulled Kostyk's gaze up into ebony eyes shot through with green and gold. She placed the beer down in front of him and he thought that he could paint this woman.

"What's your name?" he asked.

"Velvet," she said.

"Nice."

"Nice what?"

"Name," he said. She sighed, collected his cash, and strode back to the bar. Kostyk shoved his wallet in his shoulder bag. His hand struck something. He took out the volume of Haiku he'd bought Svetlana as a parting gift when they split up. Svetlana hated Haiku.

He and the others had jammed the Misericordia ER following the fire. In the morning, he sat in a chair while a buttoned-down kid barely out of school, but already puffed up with self-importance told him Svetlana was gone. He started muttering platitudes. Kostyk walked out.

The hospital wasn't far from where he and Svetlana lived before the break up. He still had a key. He walked over to Wolseley and let himself into the apartment, tripping over her hot-pink rubber boots parked in the front hall like exclamation points.

Svetlana hadn't finished packing. Half-filled boxes littered the floor. The stereo was still hooked up. Kostyk threw on Cabaret Voltaire and 'Ghostalk' hammered the air as he drifted from room to room like some alien being, a space invader, sneaking among her things. Despite the growing animosity between them, maybe because of it, careful diplomacy had been required in the disentangling. It was a difficult process, frequently painful, securing the return of music the other had appropriated, negotiating the release of books taken prisoner in earlier skirmishes. He wandered in the space they had shared and kept expecting her to come walking through the door, stamping snow off her boots. She would fix herself a cup of tea while wiggling to The Specials, stretch out on the couch, and read the latest issue of Prairie Fire as rainbows from a prism in the window danced on her throat. Svetlana violently vomited paint, a drum banged in his brain, and he was back in the bar at the Albert. His thirst had no bottom. He drank his beer, gripping a glass like a lifeline and choking it back, spilling half on his clothes. Kostyk chuckled at it being cheap cologne and ordered two more.

Bright flashes flared on the big screen TV hanging at the back of the stage. Robert Palmer was so cool, wearing an expensive suit and crooning with a chorus of brunette clones, all lips, legs, and mascara dancing behind him. The light spiralling from the screen was transformed into a mass of luxuriant blond curls framing Svetlana's face. Kostyk cursed. He didn't feel anything, couldn't stand the sight of her even dead. His grief lacked grace to temper it. He pulled a pen out of his bag and started scribbling on a napkin.

> *Bright moon floating fire*
> *Frozen colossus dark ghost*
> *Dawn opaque dream cold*

He sipped his beer and examined his first creative effort in forever. It wasn't bad. Kostyk continued to drink and write, crawling through a crack in space, barely aware of the bar except for the occasional caterwauling and shadows corkscrewing on his table. Beer flowed in, poetry out. He would stop periodically and attempt to decipher the conga line of squiggles dancing on the paper without success. It didn't matter. He was making art.

Shouting startled Kostyk, shaking him from his reverie. The biker, Eric, was raving and waving a fist at Tony Bender. The pusher didn't move a muscle. His face was a grim mask. Eric stood and stormed out. His biker pals followed him. Tony turned to a big man sitting beside him. Jimmy Jazz was built like a box, massive and square. He had enormous arms and shoulders, but was tiny from the waist down with pencil-thin legs. He waddled like a duck walking out after the bikers. Kostyk doubted anyone ever dared tell him this.

He lifted a glass of beer to drink but it felt funny. He held it up to the light and watched the amber liquid sway like honey. The beer looked fine. He set the glass down next to another and realized they were not the same size. Zoltan was obviously introducing smaller ones to boost his profit margin. But his minions had neglected to remove the large ones. Kostyk couldn't help but let out a loud laugh. Heads swivelled in his direction, regarded him for a moment, and, satisfied he wasn't about to go crazy, returned to their drinks. Tony Bender's eyes had locked on him though. Kostyk didn't care. He was a psychic gumshoe prowling the city streets and probing its grubby underbelly to unearth secrets. He held the glasses up to show the pusher the discrepancy, drained both, and ordered two more. He went back to writing and time dissolved.

When a shadow lingered too long over his table he looked up, squinting into the light at the dark shape hovering there. Karmin Magis was the poster child for punk militancy in her leather jacket, loose-fitting khakis, and shit-kicker boots. She was the brightest of her bunch and the grappling-hook of her intelligence was an aphrodisiac, evoking the easy, unearned confidence of Kostyk's youth. Karmin was aware of his attraction and tried to leverage it a few times. It wasn't necessary. The carnal was never a factor in his decisions. Her work had impressed him the first time she'd marched into his gallery clutching a portfolio of stark, black-and-white photographs that spoke their truth without bullshit or bluster, much like the woman herself. And since the fire, sex was the farthest thing from his mind anyway.

"We've been worried about you, Scott," Karmin said and rested a hand on his shoulder. It was this scenario he'd been trying to avoid. His friends would be reliving that night, expressing their grief about the fire, and expecting him to do the same. Neither his tears, nor theirs, would facilitate healing if the scab was being ripped off. Besides, Kostyk couldn't discuss his feelings when he had so few. He had to understand what happened with his head, not his heart; process Svetlana's death on an intellectual level, not an emotional one. His remorse ruled out any easy answers. There was something else nagging at him too; something he could barely acknowledge to himself let alone share with his friends. In the last ten years, he'd acquired a reputation as a creative midwife; a gallery owner and grant-getting wizard; a confidante, teacher, arts advocate, and political animal. But what people knew about him was stripped-down; a polished persona, not the painter he was. How could he explain the Lithium fire had lit another inside him? He was alive and filled with an urgency to paint again. Was that right?

"Fire marshal wants to talk to you, Scott. You're the last person he has to interview. He's a real Colombo type, keeps coming back with the same questions. Why was the door unlocked so late? What were we doing in the building? Was someone hanging around? Your disappearing act has only made him more suspicious."

Kostyk knocked back his beer, swallowing it down in great gulps. Karmin groaned.

"You're drunk," she said and her voice ruptured. She seemed older, the fault lines of her face ready to crack. Tears were pooling in her eyes.

"I am not drunk," he said, slurring his words.

"This is hard for everyone, Scott. Fuck your Slavic stoicism."

She wheeled away from his table and strode back to sit with the others he'd been dodging. There was no escaping them now. Kostyk was surprised at how unsteady he was collecting his things. He reached for the volume of Haiku and it scuttled to the other side of the table. He managed to grab it and stuff it into his bag. But his pen was doing the Red River Jig. He took a breath and then snatched the pen before it danced away. He staggered over to his friends, leaving the coins lying in puddles of beer for Velvet.

At their table, Lethal Spit was sitting beside a cute kid she'd blow off the nanosecond he bored her. She was a flapper punk and her rock star persona had traction. A five foot, hundred and eleven pound phenomenon with large almond eyes, hair clipped in a pixie cut, Lethal Spit wore a leather skirt and fishnet stockings strategically ripped at mid-thigh to reveal her pale skin. She was the love-child of Betty Page and Betty Boop with a D-ring at her throat and handcuffs hanging off the belt around her waist. It was her fake drama that pissed him off though; the black armband and a devastated look that lacked sincerity. Lethal Spit was nowhere near the Lithium the night of the fire. She jumped to her feet to hug him, but sensing his anger sat down again, a smirk replacing the sad look.

"Sit, Scott. You're wobbling like a tourist with his hard-on hanging out."

"Nice of you to notice, darling."

"Don't call me darling, dork."

"Stop it," Karmin snapped. Kostyk shrugged and sat. Furnace Face was at the table too. He had a tendency to hang on every word Karmin uttered, follow her every move with submissive eyes. Did she find that attractive? His name was Howard Storm. He hailed from East Braintree and had moved to the city to become rich and famous. He bugged Kostyk about selling his work, a derivative, pedestrian pastiche of bad drawings, forties-style cartoons, and magazine clippings he arranged in collage. But he was likeable in his way, so Scott gave him work and three days a week Furnace Face answered the phone, booked meetings, and swept the floor at the gallery.

"Where you been, man?" he asked. "Günter's show is supposed to load in next week with a vernissage on the twenty-first. You need to give me some keys, Scott."

The kid had been dropping by the gallery every day since the fire, hammering on the door, slipping notes underneath, leaving messages on the machine. Kostyk didn't tell him he was going to cancel Günter's show and keep Confidential Exchange closed awhile. He had little enthusiasm left for shilling art; wrangling artists, coddling collectors, or pampering critics. Besides, he might lose the gallery. It was haemorrhaging cash. Still, Furnace Face was probably hurting. The gallery was his only source of income. Kostyk would shoot him a few bucks; help him get through this rough patch. This proved unnecessary.

"Guess what," Furnace Face said. "A few days ago, I broke down, got a real job at Bonar and Bemis. I now ride a plastic bus to the factory where I stack plastic bags onto a pallet, eat plastic cheese sandwiches at lunch, and listen to co-workers yak about the plastic toys they've bought with plastic money. It's depressing but pays four times what you do, Scott."

The guilt trips were starting and Lethal Spit picked up the baton next.

"You missed Oscar's funeral," she said.

"Anyone attend the homeless man's funeral?" Kostyk asked.

"His name was Arnold Sinclair, a veteran of the Korean War," Karmin said. "He had a military burial. I was there."

Kostyk wriggled in his chair. Lethal Spit cleared her throat.

"My book dedicated to the Lithium Three is back from the printer," she said. "For Svetlana Bulgakov, Oscar Lehman, and a homeless man. It's too late to add his name."

She dug into her bag and plucked out 'Pickled Peter'. The cover featured a picture of her in boxing gear with the gloves up.

"Read something," Karmin said. Lethal Spit opened the book.

> carbohydrate mama
> ironing board thighs
> knows a hard rain is gonna fall
> peel skin off faces
> pop cans of worms
> star fucking celestial zits
> my winnipeg
> an old grand dame left behind
> made dizzy by the swirl of history all around
> my winnipeg, the blanche dubois of canada
> does this make toronto
> stanley kowalski

Furnace Face lightly applauded and Lethal Spit took a bow from her chair.

"Don't knock the Poles," Kostyk said. It got a laugh.

"Good one," Lethal Spit said, scribbling it down in a notebook.

"Consider it a gift," he said.

"Listen, Scott," Karmin said. "We're planning a Benefit and silent art auction to raise some money for Sebastian and Terminal Jerks. He lost everything, the band their equipment. So far we have Apocalypso, Royal American Retards, the Citizens Band from Hell, Spit and the Sighs, and the Jerks playing. I'm contributing a few signed photographs, Furnace Face a collage he did, and Spit two copies of her chapbook. We need a space. You've always been ace at venues."

"I'll talk to Zoltan about getting the Albert," Kostyk said. "He's usually in a good mood in the morning before his day goes south. I'll hit him up then."

"Mind if I tag along?" Furnace Face asked.

"Meet me on the corner tomorrow at eleven." Scott said. Velvet brought a round of drinks no one had ordered. As she was replacing empty glasses with full ones, Prince slithered into a seat beside Lethal Spit.

"I took the liberty," he said. Kostyk despised the pusher. Svetlana might still be alive if not for him. His partner, Billy Triangle, was dragging a chair from another table.

"Hey!" the bartender shouted. "Wanna pick that up?"

Billy jerked the chair over his head and the bartender ducked. Billy lowered the chair. The bartender went back to wiping down his counters. Prince smiled, his eyes psychedelic pinwheels travelling the table in a slow, predatory arc taking the measure of each person's discomfort before settling on Scott.

"The man of mystery has risen from the dead and deigned to grace us with his presence,"

The others enjoyed his arcane musings, but Kostyk couldn't stand his oily, cloying manner. He was a dilettante, a two-bit hustler who'd managed to insinuate himself into their circle. Prince was more pusher than painter, Charlie Manson without the charm.

"What are you babbling about now?" Scott snarled.

"I bring tidings. Oberon smashes skulls for pleasure while Babylon burns. The Lithium fire was arson."

"You're crazy," Kostyk said, his mind flashing on the sinister figure that had been lurking in the shadows before the blaze. The bells on Billy Triangle's buckskin jacket jangled as he was reaching for his hunting knife. Prince grabbed his wrist.

"No, Billy," he said. "The scuttling churl must be commended for finding its bark, its bite, its snap. But where will the next snap be — the fingers, legs, or twisted coil passing for a spine? Crazy is for confused, incontinent fools dribbling in their soup, Kostyk. I am mad. I know what I'm doing. You weren't aware the fire was deliberate? You need to turn on a TV, a radio, answer the phone, or talk to your fucking friends. Otherwise, where will you be when the flying saucers land? Just another galleon grounded in the asteroid belt. Rest in peace, earthling."

"Hey, I want what he's smoking," Furnace Face said, laughing.

"And you shall have it, my son," Prince said. "I am the river on which good things come to this cosmic way station."

Prince and Kostyk stared at each other, becoming oblivious to everyone. The bar vanished. The silence lengthened. A sense of danger deepened. But who was predator, who prey? Kostyk wondered how far they could push this confrontation without risk and then he realized, it was all risk, every moment of every day. Lethal Spit stood up and it broke the spell.

"Time for our first set," she said. Prince turned. His eyes burrowed into hers, hand snaking out to stroke her thigh through the tear in her stocking.

"The leather collar and handcuffs—fashion statement or lifestyle choice?"

Lethal Spit fled to the stage. Kostyk had never seen her so shaken. When the band started, she screamed the lyrics of 'Kick Start' and stomped up and down on the small stage like it was an enormous one in some arena. The music blasted white heat while teen-age peacocks covered with sweat and spittle collided on the dance floor, preening and posturing, a pantheon of prancing young gods.

Prince put his arm around the Face's shoulder, a commiserating ghoul, listening to the poor kid babble and cry about the fire. Jimmy Jazz walked by them, pointing and laughing.

The fire was arson. Maybe whoever set it was in the bar now. Kostyk didn't want to think about it or his failure to save Svetlana. He didn't want to be conscious so grabbed a glass of beer. Karmin slapped his hand away. It was hers. Kostyk picked up a different glass, drained it, then another. He kept drinking, gulping down glass after glass until he had entered the realm of the truly smashed. His friends were lit up with abandon and edging toward amnesia as their bobbing cartoon faces shifted shape, acquired fox ears and owl eyes, other animal attributes creasing their features in a bizarre parade. The bar became a soft blur and Kostyk was the axis around which it spun. The air was still and sticky, swirls of hot smoke freezing in the haze. He couldn't breathe and banged his glass down. He had to get out of there. He stood, pushing passed people, going through the front door, and ending up on the street, howling at the black sky until his throat was ragged. Then he started to stagger toward Portage Avenue.

A voice shouted his name and he spun around. It wasn't Svetlana.

"You forgot your bag," Karmin said, banging it into his chest and looping her arm through his. They leaned against each other, holding each other up as they walked down the street.

◆　◆　◆

Kostyk woke with a bad case of cubism. Graceful hieroglyphs and geometric lines churned all around him, luminous threads shredding the substantial, weaving it into a tangle of spinning spheres, squares, oblongs, and octagons. It made him dizzy. He wanted to vomit. He closed his eyes instead and submitted to the sizzle of brain cells in his skull. He shouldn't drink. He wasn't used to it. He swallowed and opened his eyes again. The planes of the room were still tipping precariously, but had stabilized enough to restore some equilibrium. Every object, each article of furniture, the odds and ends had recovered their normal shape. Black-and-white photos hung on plum-coloured walls. Unvarnished hardwood floors smelled of cleaning products. Kostyk realized a hand with long, elegant fingers was tethered to his. He turned to her, sleeping with the covers up to her chin. Her features weren't typical of a traditional beauty. Her nose was too large, green eyes too fierce, short, spiky hair too severe. But Karmin had an alluring warrior spirit that was tempered by a quiet vulnerability, a bohemian charm that undercut her brittle exterior. She was strong, yet managed to exude empathy and tenderness, a quality of mercy. Kostyk was too old for her and as invisible to her as she was transparent to him. She was awake now and pulled her hand away from him. He dived deep into her eyes.

"Don't," she said, throwing back the covers and jumping out of bed. Kostyk wasn't sure if he was more amused or disappointed by the flannel pyjamas with the pictures of Pooh she wore. She started pulling open dresser drawers and slamming them shut again.

"What are you looking for?" he asked. She froze, holding a black leotard in her hand. Her gaze was a delicious burn on his skin.

"I need to shower," she said and disappeared into the bathroom. Kostyk slipped into his jeans. He had never seen Karmin's apartment and was surprised by the lace curtains and scented potpourri. It was a side of her he hadn't known before. In the living room, he perused her record collection, predictable fare: New Order, The Cure, Human League, and Wall of Voodoo. But her books were a revelation; Joseph Campbell's 'Inner Reaches of Outer Space', Jung's 'Man and His Symbols'. Kostyk was browsing a volume of Man Ray photographs when she emerged from the shower, looking like she had just stepped from the pages of the book with an enormous black towel throwing her china-white skin into relief. He closed the book and suggested breakfast.

"I'm buying," he said.

Outside, the cold snap had lifted. It was only fifteen below. Kostyk had lived his entire life in the North Country, first in Grand Forks, now here, and he was still amazed at how quickly the weather changed. Karmin lived in the attic of a house on Gertrude Street, two doors down from where Marshall McLuhan grew up. McLuhan once claimed the wide open western skies were a canvas on which you could paint dreams. It was true. You got prairie sunsets in your blood.

The Osborne Village, on the other side of the Assiniboine River away from downtown was where Svetlana had her hippie experience before the bohemian ghetto fell under the wheels of commerce. A book store, one for music, a pool hall, and the head-shop where witches would buy their potions and incense were gone. Yet even with fusion restaurants and trendy boutiques the area remained a gentle ruin. A Chopin concerto spilled onto the air inside Basil's while they waited by the front. The morning sun revealed dust on the leafy fingers of perennials in macramé plant hangers. Basil strode over, menus and coffee pot in hand and steered them to a table by the front window, prime real estate with lunch hour looming.

"Good to see you," he said. "I am truly sorry to hear about Svetlana and the others."

"Things so bad you're waiting tables?" Kostyk asked; the quip more reflex than wit.

"You just can't help yourself, eh Scott? Always have to be the funny man. Helen is in back prepping for the lunch rush, assuming we have one. Whatever you want, it's on me."

"I'll have my usual, a Denver omelette," Kostyk said. Karmin ordered brown toast.

"Toast," Basil noted.

"With strawberry jam," she added.

"Nice touch," Basil said, leaving for the kitchen. Karmin lit a cigarette and the restaurant owner returned, topping up coffees they hadn't touched yet.

"We're non-smoking now," he said. Karmin exhaled a grey cloud in his direction and Basil retreated. She stared out the window.

"You okay?" Kostyk asked. Karmin took a drag of her cigarette, not answering right away.

"Sometimes I handle my feelings. Sometimes they handle me," she said. "I mean, it's all so fucking arbitrary. We drift through each day, distracted and disconnected, thinking nothing bad will ever happen. You know, the night of the fire Svetlana ran out of the kitchen, crashing into Oscar climbing out from behind his drum kit. They both went down, a pile of arms and legs. She called out to you. Svetlana's family took her home to Toronto for the funeral."

"What about Oscar?"

"He was buried in St. Boniface after being cremated."

"I suppose there is some symmetry in that."

"Fuck, Kostyk. Do you ever just listen? Get things out of here?" she asked, tapping his temple with a finger.

"Ouch," he complained.

"That didn't hurt," she said. Silence hung over them now, a devastating emptiness Kostyk felt an urgency to fill.

"I first connected with Svetlana here, at Basil's. I grew up in Grand Forks. My parents had a corner store my mother still operates. I worked there after school, stocking shelves and bagging groceries, making deliveries. But I never felt like I fit in, that a proxy self was standing in for me. The people baffled me and I wanted to understand what went on behind the smiles and the small talk. So I turned the store into my lab. I studied the customers, dug into the minds of neighbours to try and crack the code, discover who these strangers were, determine what puzzle lay behind the faces I only knew on the surface. Do you know what I learned, Karmin?"

"Tell me please."

"There are no secrets, just wrong impressions. If I could keep my personal agenda out of the equation, didn't allow a need or desire to obscure my vision, the truth was all too obvious. I was able to read the signs; what a raised eyebrow indicated, the significance of a curled lip, the meaning of a smile. I started drawing faces as I saw them, as they really were, free of the masks people wore, stark, honest, true. I believed my work would be appreciated. I was wrong. People were upset, even angry. I had to get out of Grand Forks. Armed with a BA from Bemidji State, I applied to the Art Institute in Chicago. I was accepted. Before moving to that windy city though, I decided to visit this one. I wanted to see my old college buddy, Zoltan Kisich, in Winnipeg. He was running the Albert for his parents and let me crash in a room at the hotel while I was in the Peg. One evening he dragged me to a community meeting where an obnoxious politician was at a podium babbling about the prohibitive cost of the social safety net. A stunning blonde stood to challenge his assumptions. She spoke with passion, conviction. The politician was dumbfounded. I was smitten. Zoltan introduced me to Svetlana. The three of us came here for coffee and dessert and discussed art and politics late into the night. Ten years ago and I'm still here. But she's gone. Something is burning!"

Kostyk's head started spinning in circles, his eyes darting around the restaurant.

"It's my toast," Karmin said. She crushed her cigarette in a coffee cup while the waitress watched in horror. Kostyk smiled at Helen. She smiled back and left.

"Don't mime apologies for me," Karmin said. She bit into her toast, tossed it aside. "Tastes like ash. I need another cigarette."

She went outside. Kostyk decided he wasn't hungry either. He left Helen a big tip. Karmin leaned against a building as morning sun poured dandelion wine down Osborne Street. The light was pretty and yet harsh, hurting his eyes.

"You're pissed about finding me in your bed this morning," he said.

"Fuck!" Karmin said. "Nothing happened, Scott! It was freezing out last night. You were loaded and refused to go home. So I hailed a cab, took you to my place. You broke down there, blubbering. It was the most honest I've ever seen you. Then you called me Svetlana. I won't be a stand-in for her ghost."

Karmin flicked her cigarette butt away and stormed off, a lanky tempest striding down the street. Kostyk's breath, an empty thought bubble, leaked loss, regret. The slender heat of a winter sun almost seemed warm to him and he decided to walk downtown, tramping over the Osborne Street Bridge, remembering when he and Svetlana were still in love. They would drink red wine at sidewalk cafés under powder-blue Magritte skies and talk about the beautiful art they would make together, her with chisel and stone, him with paint and canvas. They embarked on a fierce, creative frenzy. She had integrity and her commitment was complete, greater than his. Svetlana turned her back on all the parties, politics, and social gatherings, not leaving her studio for days, sleeping and eating there, emerging covered in clay and marble dust, hair a mess, body ripe. But integrity doesn't buy groceries or pay rent. Kostyk set aside his own work to open Confidential Exchange, stealing the gallery name from a defunct theatre troupe that took it off an old sign in the building where they rehearsed. He had done a little work with the group before it fell apart and felt it was fine for him to use the name. Growing up in a grocery store, he had learned to balance the books and count pennies. The gallery prospered. Kostyk kept busy filling out grant applications and attending meetings. Artists sought him out for professional advice. Bureaucrats press-ganged him into sitting on committees, being on boards, giving lectures. He was consumed by minutiae. His days often involved doing an end-run around tedious people waving pamphlets, petitions, working papers, and project proposals. He tried stealing time to paint, sneaking into the gallery early, staying late. He and Svetlana seemed happy. But after he sold one of her pieces to a movie star, he realized the global village had put him in the same business as his parents. He operated a corner store, hawking art instead of bread and milk. Svetlana's output remained prolific, his anaemic. Maybe it was why they drifted apart. She disdained his mercenary dealings; he envied her success. It dawned on Kostyk they had never really understood each other and only touched the surface, never the depth, mistaking routine for intimacy. He was better with the idea of a woman than the reality and always seemed to be chasing something missing; without love he hoped, with it he suffered. He had tried to break down the walls between them, work through the isolation and disconnection. He failed. They began a slow slide into indifference punctuated by angry outbursts of malice and bile, usually over something meaningless. At one stage, Svetlana ran off to Toronto with a jazz musician but was back six months later with a black eye, swollen lip, and the knowledge her new beau didn't just like to beat on his drums.

Things were good between them for a while. It had all came crashing down three weeks ago when he discovered cocaine hidden under her spoken word poetry. After that, they fought every day and couldn't even stand to be in the same room. When it finally ended, it was less a breaking up than a letting go. Her death was a grim postscript condemning both his profound failure as a husband and his paralysis the night of the fire.

He no longer knew if he had stayed in Winnipeg for love or for light.

A woman banged into him halfway across the bridge. An office worker from Great West Life heading over to Osborne Village for lunch, she didn't apologize or acknowledge him and just kept walking.

Svetlana's hard work had paid off. She was regarded as brilliant. It was said a piece by her possessed both gravitas and delicacy; embodied movement and stasis equally, was weighty yet light, earthy but ethereal. These tensions lent her sculpture resonance, vibrancy difficult to resist. Observers were challenged to think and simultaneously compelled to submit to the apprehension of beauty. Why did he know more about her work than his own? Because her work soared while his tanked. Expressionist art was in vogue. His impulse lay elsewhere. Kostyk didn't care about the fashion and painted realistic portraits of people with eyes and noses where they belonged. He considered post-modernism the last refuge of a failed imagination. Unfortunately, critics conferred that dubious status on his painting. It meant the last seven years he ran a gallery filled with work he despised, deluding himself into believing he was making art by dealing it. He didn't want to be an art pimp anymore, another anarchist afraid of growing old alone.

The Lithium fire had proved life was short and capricious, every day above ground a good one. Kostyk longed to put the beauty of this one on canvas; paint cerulean-blue smoke billowing from rooftop chimneys, capture the colour of a small, black dog yapping at a door vibrating with cadmium yellow. He yearned to record the inclined figure of an old man wearing a green parka and scraping ice off a silver car; the postal worker in regulation blue, a fugitive from Van Gogh straining under the weight of the day's mail; the young mother bustling past, pulling a sled piled with blankets, a tiny face with a pink nose and cherry cheeks peeking from its center. Endless subjects filled the streets; a thousand sublime miracles crowding into his head, calling to him as colour permeated every crevice of his brain with bright bursting yellow and bloody oozing red, melancholy blue seeping into each pore and flooding his bloodstream. Rainbows shot from his fingertips. His hands ached for the feel of a brush.

On the other side of the bridge, he walked down Assiniboine Avenue. His lungs filled with fresh air, his step lighter.
He felt fantastic for the first time in ages. He had to harness
this energy, apply paint to canvas, and toil in the trenches
of art again, resurrecting the delicious derangement of his
youth. He had no romantic notions about what this meant.
There were no health benefits or pension plan for artists. He
would have to live on peanut butter, give up his new apartment. He'd continue staying at the gallery. Zoltan would let
him wash up at the hotel. His friend was good that way.

Kostyk walked around the corner of Notre Dame onto
Albert Street to find Furnace Face waiting outside the Chambers Building, smoking a joint. He stubbed it out when he saw
Scott. Going to the hotel, they went by a new gallery opening
soon. Kostyk knew the owner. He was an unscrupulous huck-
ster who wrote poor contracts, peddled McArt, and sported
a leather bag made from the skin of painters. His presence
would generate outrage, take some of the heat off Kostyk.

Zoltan was sitting in the bar, drinking coffee.

"Hookers on Albert Street," he said, shaking a newspaper at Kostyk. "You have hookers on Arthur, Princess, McDermott, and King Street but I have a hotel here so it's hookers on
Albert. I wish we were back in simpler times, Scott, when you
designed the set and costumes for 'Waiting for Godot' and I
played Estragon. Believe me, I would love to Gogo now, man
and leave all this wonderfulness behind."

Velvet arrived. Scott and Furnace Face each ordered a
glass of draught.

"I'm buying," Zoltan said. They asked for two. "You're
hard to reach these days, Scott. I've been trying to get a hold
of you for days to see how you are. I still can't believe Svetlana
is gone. Anything I can do, you let me know."

"Actually," Kostyk said. "We're planning a Benefit for
those burnt out by the fire and need a venue."

"You think the Albert? I don't know. Business is bad.
Not sure I can afford a night without any cash coming into
the bar.

"You bitch about bad press, hosting this Benefit will generate positive spin. If nothing else, it can be your good deed for the year."

"Suppose one night of lousy liquor sales won't kill me," Zoltan said. He bellowed at the desk clerk standing at the other end of the bar. Cowboy waved a cue stick.

"It's my day off. I got a game going."

"Never mind playing pocket pool. I have a glass of rye with your name on it."

Cowboy materialized at the table.

"If you're buying, something big is brewing, boss."

"Don't try to be smart, Cowboy. You'll hurt yourself. Scott and Furnace Face are holding a Benefit for the victims of the blaze down the block. I figure a Friday night will work. They'll get the cover plus ten per cent of liquor sales. My donation, so I expect a receipt from one of those charitable thingies you operate, Scott."

"Have you fucking flipped?" Cowboy cried out. "You wanna let your fruity friends have the bar on a weekend? They don't drink. We won't make any scratch."

"Give him a mile, he takes an inch," Zoltan said. "Not everything is about cash, Cowboy. You can hammer the details out with Scott. I got places to be. The afternoon is on me, boys."

He slapped Kostyk on the back and left. Scott was glad he had caught Zoltan early because he wouldn't darken the door again all day. Tony Bender was staring hard at Kostyk like he had the night before but got up and left the bar, something he rarely seemed to do.

"Hey," Cowboy said agreeably now that free booze was on the table. "Why they call your buddy Furnace Face?"

"Because he's always blasted," Kostyk said.

Rusty Nail Reflections

Cocaine was opening doors all over town for Tony Bender. When Buck Tamblyn, this big shot restaurant guy from River Heights, was looking for a connection six months ago, Zoltan introduced him. Three weeks ago Buck asked him about torching a white elephant he owned. He planned to use the insurance money to build condos on the lot and offered Tony eleven thousand dollars to do the job. It was a sweet, easy score. Tony shot his brother, Bernie, a grand to set the blaze and said he would top up his stash of bennies in perpetuity. But the dream job had gone bad. Nobody was supposed to be in the building. Nobody was supposed to die.

Buck only had to clear the warehouse of tenants and Bernie do a clean job. But they both screwed up. Buck failed to evict the hippie diner on the first floor and Bernie was sloppy. Now, fourteen days after the fire, instead of a fast peek by a friendly fire marshal, Tony had to navigate a full-blown arson investigation, which would involve an inquest, maybe manslaughter charges if Bernie was busted. His little brother was normally a good producer, but unpredictable when he was stoned, less criminal mastermind than career convict. He must have been blitzed burning down a café crammed with people. Bernie also had a tendency to run his mouth, brag about his exploits to the waitresses and strippers he liked to date. It was how he first ended up in the joint and every other time after that. Bernie had escaped from Stony Mountain awhile back and Tony tried to help him, throwing him cash and a little work. Tony had never done time and wasn't about to now because of these clowns.

Bernie was crazy. All Tony's brothers were, three doing long stretches in the can and the youngest, Donovan, squirreled away in Selkirk. He was being released soon, so as well as fallout from the fire Tony had to deal with him being back on the street after five years on a forensics psych unit. Donovan was a spinner. Anything could set him off. One wrong word or a funny look from someone, he would go ballistic, smashing whatever, whoever got in his way. There was never any warning and no stopping him when he lost it. Stick a knife in Donovan, he didn't feel a thing. It was like he was on angel dust.

Tony had been at war with the Curb Stompers when Donovan drifted into one of their bars. Two bikers jumped him in the parking lot. He killed one and put Eric the Red in traction, then rehab for a year. Eric had already been around, sounding off about putting Donnie in the ground. Tony wouldn't let it happen. The MC President, Rusty Decker, didn't want the peace to unravel because of some beef between Eric and Donovan either, so was keeping Eric on a leash. But that might not last. Tensions were high.

Buck was late. Tony should be back at the Albert by now handling business, not sitting in a bar on the skids, chewing his last ice cube.

He hadn't been to the Paddock in years, not since he was eleven when Whiskey Jack took him to see the ponies run and watch chumps lay down hard-earned cash on the slim expectation of winning a few bucks. After the races, the old man always dropped by the Paddock to put away a drink or three. The horseshoe-shaped bar would be flush with high rollers, bookies, and jockeys getting smashed and swapping stories. Tony would sit on a stool, slamming down pop while the old man did shots. After that, whiskey, cigars, and horse-shit smelled like money to Tony. But the track moved south and a mall stood where it had, six lanes of traffic zipping along Portage Avenue, leaving the Paddock in a time warp with its chipped linoleum floor tiles, torn bar stools, and the stink of piss and beer.

Tony cracked his humidor and a tart cedar tang blended with the full-flavoured scent of his signature smoke, teasing him like a talented peeler doing a pole dance. He had the Juan Lopez Seleccion Two imported from Cuba, a superior cigar rolled just right, not too loose, not too tight, the pull perfect, the taste mild but with a sharp edge. Tony knew all the sweat and hard work that went into making each hand-rolled cigar and it only increased his pleasure in smoking them. He snipped the end off one, set it on fire, and took a deep draw. The bartender finally acknowledged his existence. A good cigar made a statement.

"Another," Tony ordered. "Put the premium scotch in this time."

He was on his fifth Rusty Nail when Buck finally showed up with a goofy, got-the-world-by-the-tail grin Tony wanted to slap off his face.

"You're late," he said. Buck shrugged.

"Gonna break my legs, Tony? I have other business needs my attention."

"With those pricks in Tuxedo think they run this town."

"They do, Tony, despite any fantasy you entertain."

Tony grabbed Buck's scarf, yanked his head to the bar, and held his eyes until the rabbits there darted for cover. The old man always told him respect was equal parts fear and love. Tony found fear more productive.

"I can run a fuck of a lot faster mad than you can scared, Buck."

Tony released him, told him to pay the tab. The fool shot the bartender a fifty, waving off the change. Put the pinhead in pain, he still plays big shot. No wonder he was broke.

In the parking lot, Buck pointed to an old, beat-up Renault. Tony crawled in the passenger side, kicking away beer cans, fast food containers.

"Your car is a piece of junk," he said.

"Gotta maintain a low profile in this town, Ton," Buck said. "Don't dress fancy or flaunt your wealth. It's the way to get along. Nobody will take my baby; if they try, I keep a shotgun in the trunk."

Tony lit another cigar.

"What happened at the border, Buck?"

"Oh man, whadda cluster-fuck. Sailed through the Yankee side but at the Canucklehead, some snivelling servant sniffs around the car like I took a dump in it. She asks if I got anything to declare. I say nothing but a hangover and empty wallet. Next thing I know she has us inside and strip-searched. It was fucking humiliating. Tony, I didn't know the chick you set me up with was carrying. She was cool though, said I didn't know about the drugs so they cut me loose."

Tony was surrounded by idiots and assholes. Micheline was his best mule going down to Minneapolis to pick up a package. Tony figured the trip could do double duty, give Buck an alibi the night of the fire.

"Where's my bread?" he asked

"Glove compartment."

Tony removed the envelope, counted the cash, and stuffed it in a pocket.

"This is a little light. Take me to the Albert."

Buck put the car in gear. He was quiet now, his head tilted at a reflective tilt as his brain ran laps. He licked his lips, strangling the steering wheel. Tony let him twist and smoked a cigar, watching high-rises fly by with windows lit like neon teeth. Buck finally found his nerve.

"This was what we agreed on, Tony."

"Before the job went bad. Arson is one thing. Murder another."

"It was your man fucked up."

"He can do the time, Buck. Can you? Staying out of prison will cost you twenty per cent of the insurance money, five percent of every condo you bring on line."

"Tony, there may not be any cash or condos if they decide I set the fire."

"I'll make this easy for you then—another twenty grand by Monday."

"I don't have that kind of cash."

"Borrow it from your buddies in Tuxedo."

"I had to fight with my investors just to get this. They didn't want to pay a dime. Even if I can find it, I need time. You have to be patient, man."

"Patience is for pussies. In two weeks you meet me at MAC's bowling alley on Selkirk Avenue with the cash."

"You gonna drag me down to the North End?"

"Drag you down to it or around it, you decide. My pet pyromaniac wants to burn down everything now, Buck. You have a lovely home in River Heights, a nice family."

"Jesus, Tony."

Buck drove the rest of the way to the Albert in silence, dropped Tony at the door, and sped off as fast as his little Renault could carry him.

Cowboy was at the front desk, half-hammered as usual. He was Tony's eyes and ears at the hotel with an inside track on every intrigue hatched in every bar in a six block radius. But if he wasn't talking to you, he was talking about you. It was going to burn him one day.

"You look thirsty, Cowboy. Call the bar," Tony said. The other man beamed and complied. Velvet brought out his rye then vamoosed. She knew Tony would take care of her later. The pusher waited until the desk clerk had the drink to his lips before dropping the zinger.

"Jimmy Jazz saw you at the Charlie last night with Sawchuk and he was buying."

Cowboy's zip took a nosedive. He hit the yammer-hammer.

"That cop ain't a pal of mine, man, just a pipeline. He spilled more than I shared."

"For example."

"Fire dick is taking a hard look at that blaze, interviewing survivors. He talked to them all but the skinny guy with wire-rim glasses, scribbling in a notebook in the bar."

"The narc I saw you drinking with this morning."

"He's not a narc, Tony. I would know."

"Tell me if he starts mouthing off about the fire."

"You got it," Cowboy said. "There is one other thing. Dude claiming to be your uncle been calling all day. He left a number."

"Get him on the horn; patch it through. I'll send out another drink for you."

Jimmy Jazz was holding things down in the bar. He took his coat off Tony's chair. Tony had first met Jimmy Pringle at the Vaughn Street Detention Center while he was there bailing out Bernie. Jimmy was just a kid parked in a hall on a bench between two beefy cops giving him grief. He was a speed freak looking at hard time for pulling B&Es in the wrong end of town — the good end. His head bobbed as he bopped, running jazz riffs he heard in his head. Tony saw something in him though, found him a lawyer, got him out of the jam. Jimmy had been a loyal soldier ever since. People often thought he was a Bender. He was proud of that. When the time came he would run the front end for Tony. Jimmy Jazz was worth his weight in pharmaceuticals.

"Not much happening," he said. "Too cold for the weather wimps."

Velvet brought Tony's scotch, Jimmy another rum.

"You seen Eric since he was around raising hell?" Tony asked. Velvet was in tight with the bikers.

"Rusty sent him to Thompson to visit affiliates. He'll be out of town awhile."

"Middle of winter, guess he took a bus, eh," Tony said.

"Funny," Velvet said. Bikers. They had no sense of humour about weather. Still, Eric being out of town was good. It gave Tony time to deal with Donovan.

Jimmy sipped his drink through his teeth, an irritating habit he had whenever something bothered him.

"Just spit it out, Jimmy," Tony said.

"Screws snagged Ferret and his wingy cousin at the Charlie this aft."

This was critical information Cowboy had neglected to share. He was either slipping or holding back. Ferret didn't know much but enough.

"Call Wolch, arrange bail; then you find them and finish them," Tony said. The phone at the bar rang. Velvet answered and nodded to Tony. He picked up the receiver, knowing who was on the other end.

"Been awhile, loser," he said.

"Fifteen years, you're still pissed, Tony?" Just Joe said. "Need to do some growing, boy. You know I had to get out of the game. Ticker couldn't take it no more."

Just Joe was the old man's brother and they'd run a bootlegging operation together. The two brothers had a deal they'd take turns doing time when the joint was raided. But Just Joe's spin of the wheel came up and he walked, leaving Whiskey Jack holding weight. He resurfaced a few weeks later and announced he was getting out of the racket. The old man did six months in Headingly Jail. When he got out the business was in the toilet. Whiskey Jack drove a taxi now, sold the odd bottle out of the trunk. Tony wasn't going to let this cracker keep yakking crap. He told Joe to get to the point although he knew why he'd called.

"Need your help, Tony. We just got back from a month in Florida."

"Go-cart business must be good."

"Not bad. They robbed us while we were gone, man. Buggers even took the fucking dust bunnies. Willa is going bonkers, blaming me saying it must be somebody from the old days. I have no idea who did this. I'm out of the loop. Wouldn't even know how to find these guys."

"How much you got tied up?"

"Five hundred thou in furniture, clothes, jewellery, art."

"Art?"

"Willa loves that shit. Neighbours say two guys in white overalls showed up in a moving van, figured we were staying Stateside."

"And give up your health-care?"

"Couldn't be many crews pulling this kind of caper, Tony. Can you find them?"

Tony took a long pull on his cigar and let his uncle dangle.

"They sound like pros," he finally said. "Good thieves don't stick around."

"How much it gonna cost me, Tony?"

"Ten percent of the retail on everything they took."

"Kind of steep."

"They'll have expenses."

"Gonna really stick it to me, eh?"

"You want your shit back that's the price."

"Screw it. Do it. Benders gotta stick together."

Tony hung up. He would let Just Joe stew in his juices before calling to say he'd found his stuff. Bernie had pulled the score for Tony before torching the warehouse. At least, he'd got that job right. Whiskey Jack would get a kick out of it when Tony told him about this and handed over a cut from the cash he got from Joe.

Jimmy Jazz was wrong about the cold keeping people away. Cabin fever was kicking in and it was getting busy. Velvet and Fran raced like roadrunners between tables as rounders bawled at each other across the pool table and brain-dead punks pumped quarters in pinball machines. But when business was good for Zoltan, it was lousy for Tony. Junkies hated a crowd.

Scott Kostyk was still in the bar, sitting with Itchy Dick and Big Ron after a long day of drinking. He was smashed but taking in the scene, just like a narc. Prince was by the bar with Billy Triangle. The arrangement Tony had with him had been profitable until recently. Tony dealt speed and pharmaceuticals. As long as Prince paid for the privilege, Tony allowed the punk to peddle his psychedelics; pot, hash, mushrooms, and acid. The downside of cocaine coming on the market in town now was Prince wanted a piece of that action. It was another hassle Tony had to handle.

Cowboy banged through the door in a dizzy state, landing at his table.

"Zoltan is in the restaurant, looking owly. He wants to see you, Tony."

"One of my regulars shows up; tell them I'll be right back, Cowboy."

Zoltan was smoking a cigarette, and staring out a window in the dark café. He was startled when Tony came in. The hotel owner was jumpy. Good. The pusher sat down and lit a cigar.

"You have to smoke those?" Zoltan asked.

"How you doing?"

"Street is quiet."

"It has been for awhile, Zoltan."

"Nothing to do with the fire down the street, eh? I knew two of the people died — Svetlana Bulgakov, the sculptor, Oscar, drummer for Terminal Jerks. They play here sometimes."

"Your stash is low."

"You have a lightening grasp of the obvious, Tony."

"And you owe me a serious chunk of change."

"Temporary cash crunch I shall soon resolve."

"I can help you clear your debt, Zoltan, put some real money in your pocket."

"We've had this conversation. I won't rent you rooms in the hotel. Don't want any junkies shooting up here. I run a clean place; seniors live here, old men on their last legs, young ones just starting out."

"Everybody in town thinks you rent by the hour."

"I can't help that. I don't control what people think and may not be able to keep the pimps, punks, prostitutes, and pushers out of the bar, but I will not allow them upstairs."

"Only have to hope the firebug who lit up that warehouse doesn't strike again," Tony said. Zoltan danced in his chair.

"You do malice well. You're a medieval man in a modern world, Tony."

"Your credit is good, Zoltan. See Jimmy Jazz. He'll take care of you."

Zoltan went vertical and lurched out the door. Tony smiled. Medieval man my ass.

Enemy Outpost

The prairie landscape looked like it was ready to snap, explode into flying pieces of dirt and debris. Siren drove the bus down a treacherous two-lane, head tilted back like a baying dog, belting out obscure doo-wop tunes at the top of his lungs. The day before Doctor Lawler had told Donovan he was being discharged. Siren had been parked on a pyramid paperweight, cackling and drooling all over the shrink's desk. Lawler didn't notice. Donovan didn't say anything. He hadn't told a soul about the hallucination hounding him. He might be crazy but he wasn't stupid.

The ride from Selkirk into Winnipeg was short and the bus wheezed and groaned, slipping into an empty slot behind the station. It lurched to a stop, opened metal jaws, and spit Donovan onto the sidewalk. He hauled a suitcase into the bus depot under the watchful eye of a rent-a-cop with a nasty German shepherd at his side. When he left the hospital that morning the staff gave him a brown-bag breakfast with an egg sandwich, a juice box, and an apple. Donovan tossed it in the trash going out the door. Never knew what kind of rat poison was in it. He was hungry now.

The greasy spoon in the bus depot was mostly deserted, a few drunks, night shift workers on the way home. The guy on the grill looked grim, slopping coffee into a cup stinking of javex. The vegetables being held prisoner in metal trays behind the counter screamed at Donovan and he decided breakfast could wait. He snagged a corner booth to have his coffee, do a little reading, and kill a few hours. He had a long day ahead. The rent-a-cop came into the cafeteria, stood by the cash register, and eyeballed him. A small pellet of rage dropped into Donovan's gut. He had to leave. He didn't need trouble his first day out of hospital. He stashed his suitcase in a locker and cold air slammed into him when he pushed through the door of the bus depot.

Donovan rode the North Wind down Portage Avenue toward Main Street, inhaling fresh ice crystals, exhaling stale institutional stuff. Cabs idled at the curb, the ghost faces of the drivers reflected in dim light as they dozed or read dime novels. Everything seemed to be the same yet different, slightly off-kilter as if reality had shifted a degree or two, distorting this dimension and twisting the frame into another shape. At the corner of Kennedy, Donovan waited for the traffic light to change, rocking back and forth and stamping his cold feet in a primeval winter dance. He felt the cop car before he saw it. The cruiser slipped out of the shadows and stopped in front of him. When the window whirred down Donovan stepped to the curb. He knew the drill.

"Where are you going?" the cop asked.

"Just walking," Donovan said.

"Don't get smart. Lemme see some ID."

Donovan fished out his wallet and waited while the cop studied the contents.

"Donovan Bender, any relation to Bernie?"

"He's my brother."

"You see him around lately?"

"No. I've been in hospital."

"Oh, you're that Donovan Bender. Keep moving and stay out of trouble."

He returned Donovan's wallet, rolled up the window, and put the cruiser in gear. The cop car crept back into the early morning darkness.

"Fucking pig," Donovan muttered. He turned up the collar of his leather jacket, lit a smoke, and took a drag. He didn't need this aggravation, couldn't wait to get out of town and start fresh somewhere else, among picture-postcard-mountains, where nobody knew the Bender name. But his bus connection to the coast didn't leave until eleven PM, sixteen hours from now. He would have to keep busy somehow while avoiding his old haunts.

Up in the sky, dawn edged a narrow strand of light along the horizon, revealing low-hanging clouds. It smelled like snow.

Donovan's first stop was the Garry Street Salisbury House where he had his first decent breakfast in five years. The Sals had the best back bacon in the city. He almost pasted some guy bugging the waitress. She was an easy target, one of those terminally-cheerful types dispensing coffee and warm smiles to ungrateful slobs. Donovan wrote her a poem while scoffing down his bacon and eggs, but decided not to leave it when he split, slipping a buck under his plate instead. Cash would be more useful to her than poetry.

Almost eight o'clock. The bar at the Woodbine would be opening soon.

At Portage and Main, Donovan encountered the first real change in the city. Barriers had been erected, blocking the intersection. Pedestrians had to go down to an underground concourse to get across the street. He was standing on the southwest corner, the Woodbine on the north. A stairwell in a business tower led him to a dark, cave-like area with low ceilings and deserted storefronts. Winnipeg Square was a circle and he followed it around trying to find the right way back up to the street. The only open place was a clean, well-lit drugstore, where a cashier was counting her morning float. Two kids came flying downstairs, one of them holding a paper bag to his face. Donovan could smell the airplane glue from across the hall. When they danced toward the drugstore, the clerk picked up a phone.

Donovan climbed the nearest stairwell, exiting a concrete bunker to find he was facing the Richardson Building on the northeast corner. The Woodbine was still on the other side of Main. From here he could walk one block to McDermott and cross at the light. Before that though, he leaned against the office tower and lit another smoke. The street was starting to hum with the rattle of day-people walking by him and pretending he wasn't there. Siren's head bounced along the sidewalk then bolted into the sky, soaring in a delicious trajectory. Donovan stared at the sun, a ring of pale, frozen fire, took a short, sharp drag of his smoke, and flicked the butt at a passing suit who shot him a dirty look but had enough sense to keep moving.

The bar in the Woodbine Hotel was the last of the men's beer parlours; no jukebox, dance floor, women, or fights. It was warm inside except for a corner where wind blew through a crack in the wall. A lime-green carpet was pock-marked with cigarette burns and beer stains. On top of a bar greasy garlic sausage was basting in its own fat in a rusty rotisserie. The numberless initials of nameless drunks craving immortality was carved into tables. A single customer was in the place, an old bum muttering into his beer. Donovan could handle this for a few hours, then cruise a couple of coffee shops, maybe hit another bar later. Someone behind him touched his shoulder and he flinched.

"Easy there tiger," the waitress said. "So, I imagine the sudden jaw drop is due to finding a female shackled to a tray in this fine establishment. Well the Woodbine has gone coed. Welcome to the eighties. I'm Darla. What can I get you?"

Donovan liked Darla right away despite her abrupt manner. She had kind, blue eyes, a sprinkle of freckles across her nose, and dirty blonde hair cut in a bob. Her figure was boyish but womanly too. Donovan hadn't been with anyone for ages. The nurses in Selkirk were sensual but aloof and the succubae teasing out his dreams at night ultimately unsatisfying.

They didn't sell Jameson so he settled for bar scotch that burned going down but did the trick. Donovan wasn't supposed to drink. Lawler had been adamant. His discharge depended on taking meds, keeping appointments, and abstaining from alcohol and drug use. If he violated any of these conditions he would be readmitted to a more secure facility.

Lawler was a quack. He played the sideways game, inserted acute angles into Donovan's brain, probing and prodding with dull questions and sharp needles, sometimes resorting to bug juice, fogging Donovan up so bad some days he could barely tie his shoelaces. Lawler stole his poetry, promising to give it back. He never did, putting it in his chart instead. It took three years to convince Lawler he didn't represent a danger to society and another eighteen months to win discharge. The shrink would never consider him cured though. Being a head case was terminal and would follow him into the ground.

The old drunk at the other table burst into hysterical laughter. He had a crazy, cracked face and pointed at the chair across from him.

"I'm a hero, Sam! You're a zero!"

The bartender barked at him and the bum went into damage control.

"It's all copacetic, shareholder. We're ready for another round."

"These are the last two," Darla said, placing the beer on his table. "Four dollars."

The bum pushed a bottle across the table and nodded at the empty chair.

"Your turn to pay, Sam," he said. Then his smile dropped. He started digging around in his pockets, fishing out a few coins. Darla separated them from strands of tobacco and toilet paper.

"You're two bits short," she said. The old man muttered, rummaging through his pockets.

"Never mind," Darla said with a sigh and walked off.

"You embarrassed me, Sam," the bum shouted. "Fuck you! I always buy!"

He rose in a rage, swept the bottles and glasses off the table and jackknifed out the door. Donovan decided it was time he left too. Darla, stooped over to pick up broken shards of glass, gave him a forlorn shrug.

The day was still young, a long time to eleven. Donovan spent the rest of the morning and half the afternoon walking, avoiding certain streets, going down one block, flipping over to the next, and then the next. Eventually this got boring. He collected an hour's dust hanging in a coffee-shop then grabbed lunch at the Windsor Hotel, choking back another bad scotch. At the end of the day, he went to Eaton's and walked around the store, checking out the merchandise. He was in the library by five, scanning newspapers and magazines, tearing out an article about medical students in the UK caught playing football with the head of a cadaver. It seemed like Siren was everywhere.

Donovan cracked the book Suzie had given him before he left Selkirk. She was the nicest of the nurses and always made time to talk. Sometimes though, it seemed like she was trying to pry the lid off his head to find out what was inside. Did she really believe he would ever spill his guts? Fuck her fake Florence Nightingale act. He fell into the book, letting the 'Strange Life of Ivan Osokin' carry him away from Winnipeg to Moscow.

It was after seven o'clock when Donovan resurfaced from reading. Another four hours, he could split town. Outside, it was dark. The days all end early in January with the temperature dropping drastically when the sun goes down. Donovan jammed his hands into his pockets. He should have boosted a pair of gloves in Eaton's. He darted across Portage Avenue, dodging cars trying to nail him while Siren sang 'Eve of Destruction'. On the other side of the street, Donovan didn't see the old man standing, his hand out, and almost knocked him over. The drunk sputtered and cursed then recognized Donovan.

"Spare a little change, shareholder?"

Donovan kept walking. The bum grabbed his arm.

"They'll find my dead and frozen body behind a dumpster. It'll be you to blame," he said. Donovan whipped around and the fire went out of the old man when he saw the ice in his eyes.

"Four bits won't kill ya," he said, a toothless grin creasing his face. "I ain't ate in days."

"You'll just buy booze with it," Donovan said.

"Fifty fucking cents! A tad delusional, don't ya think, shareholder? But takes one to know one, I guess."

"I'll spring for a burger at the Sals."

"You're not one of them crazy characters butchers old guys for kicks?"

"If you want a bite, I'll buy. If not, fuck you."

"Blunt! I like that in a benefactor."

The Salisbury House at Notre Dame and Albert was a fluorescent glass cage with people penned inside. Donovan pushed a tray with two cups of coffee down a counter to the cash register, the bum following.

"How can I help you?" a weary waitress asked.

"A beer would be nice," the bum chirped. She scowled.

"We'll have a Mr. Big and a double-cheese burger with bacon," Donovan ordered.

"That'll be a Mr. Big nip and a double-cheese nip," she corrected. "Take a number. I'll bring your food when it's ready. And Tommy, you be good in here!"

The bum ignored her and pushed passed Donovan.

"Let's sit by the window, watch the buggers go by freezing their balls off."

Burrowing down in the booth, the old man produced a tobacco pouch and started rolling a smoke. Donovan offered him a tailor-made and the bum's eyes widened. He pulled a cigarette from the pack and held it high, turning it between his dirty fingers.

"A thin white duke is perfection," he said with Siren's voice. "Set me on fire, shareholder."

Donovan retrieved his lighter. The old man took a few puffs and when the waitress brought their food, he stubbed out the cigarette, stuffing it into a pocket.

"It's a city bylaw. Light up, they bring your grub. I'm Downtown Tommy. Friends call me DT. Ha-ha right?"

"I'm Donovan."

"'Sunshine Superman,'" Downtown Tommy said. Siren hummed the song while the old man attacked the burger, licking the plate clean when he finished and patting his belly. He pointed at Donovan's food.

"Go for it," Donovan said. Downtown Tommy snatched the burger, wrapped it in a napkin, and shoved it in a coat pocket.

"How about another cancer stick?" he asked. Donovan pushed the pack over to him and Downtown Tommy helped himself to several. He guzzled down his coffee, slammed the cup on the table, and suddenly grabbed Donovan's wrist, becoming the crazy man from the Woodbine again, his bird head jerking.

"Hear the buzzing drills, the grinding gears, and pounding hammers." he muttered. "Aliens are building an enemy outpost in the next dimension. Have to have a certain way of seeing, twist your head this way and tilt it at the right angle to catch them."

Donovan's stomach was a whirling pinwheel with Siren doing the backstroke in his coffee. He wrenched his hand free, stood, and spun out the door, staggering down the street not knowing or caring where he was going.

When he stopped to catch his breath, his eyes darting, he saw the sign. He'd managed to avoid this place all day. But he was here now and might as well go into the Royal Albert Hotel for a drink.

Siren's thin frame wrapped around the clock on the wall in the lobby and he lapped at dust particles with his long tongue. Cowboy was at the front. He was the desk clerk, doorman, lobby manager, and bouncer and hadn't moved an inch in five years. He was busy with a strawberry blonde and didn't see Donovan at first.

"What you think?" she asked, holding her coat open and swaying. "The blouse was pricy, but I needed a little pick-me-up."

"You look great," Cowboy said. "If you haven't heard from the cops yet, I gotta friend on the force. He can find out what's up, Fran."

"That would be sweet, Cowboy. You know, it was nice being robbed by pros. They broke into my place, scooped up valuables, and left without smashing up any of my furniture, breaking windows, or punching holes in the walls the way kids will do. They were tidy."

"I'll tell Sawchuk to watch out for neat thieves."

Fran kissed him on the lips and Cowboy saw Donovan.

"Jumping Judas! Tony told me to keep my eyes peeled for you. When they cut you loose?"

"This morning."

"And you're just coming around now? Where you staying?"

Donovan shrugged and Cowboy threw a room key on the counter. The blonde gave the desk clerk another quick peck on the cheek.

"I need to let off steam, do a little dirty dancing," she said and walked to the bar.

"Whoa, check out that rear end suspension!" Cowboy called out, smacking his lips, and she laughed. He lifted a glass from behind the counter, drained it then looked at Donovan.

"Where's my manners," he said and turned to the switchboard. "Hey Rambo, still quiet in there? Why you think I want something? I'll have my usual and a beer for my buddy. Of course, I will pay her."

Velvet marched out from the bar.

"Six fifty," she said, placing both drinks on the desk. Cowboy went into his routine.

"Catch you later, babe. Got people coming in owe me cash."

"No way, this came out of my pocket."

"You mean Rambo made you pay up front?"

"Never mind the doubletalk."

"Swear by the end of the night."

"Before closing time, Cowboy. I gotta get back inside."

Right after she left, the bar door banged open and a small man exploded into the lobby like a shotgun shell. He started screaming at the desk clerk who listened with a sly smile on his face. When the bartender ran out of steam, Cowboy leaned forward.

"Never mind the drinks," he said quietly, winking at Donovan. "We gotta real problem. A hit may go down in the bar tonight."

The bartender slipped from Rambo to Tinkerbell.

"Maybe I should bring my shotgun down from my room," he said.

"We don't need no gunslinger convention here, man. These dudes will take that shotgun and ram it right up your ass. Best you be cool. Not get in over your head. Course, anything above five foot is over your head, Rambo."

"Stop calling me that!"

"Short?"

"Rambo!"

"It's your handle, son. Get used to it."

"Why does everybody in this town have a nickname?"

"You have any idea how many Johns I know? Big John, Little John, Square John. So while you're out here ragging on me, the regulars inside are robbing you blind, Rambo."

"Shit," the bartender shouted and ran back to the bar. Cowboy laughed. His folksy charm hid a mean streak and he loved making people squirm.

"Tool doesn't have enough brains for a headache," he said. "Gunslinger Convention is a Montreal band plays here sometimes. I'm sick of him bragging he served in Vietnam. If he did, it was boiled potatoes and rubber steaks in the men's mess."

"I'll pay for the drinks," Donovan said. His sawbuck barely touched the counter before it disappeared into Cowboy's vest pocket.

"I'll see Velvet gets it," he said. The front door opened. Siren started jabbering and flying in circles on the ceiling. Cowboy's hand slipped under the counter to the baseball bat he kept there. Two hippies entered the lobby, not flower-children, but brooding lowlifes. Prince had long black hair and piercing eyes. Billy Triangle was blonde, all bone and sharp angles with bells jingling on a buckskin jacket.

"I see the tourist bus from Uranus is back in town," Cowboy crowed.

"Don't be a twit, old man," Prince sneered. "Make way for the new wave."

"The lavender wave," Cowboy barked. He heard bells whisper and whipped around to face Billy Triangle who was gripping a knife; glaring at him and slapping the baseball bat against his thigh. Donovan sighed at the alpha strutting. Prince turned to him, his eyes narrowing.

"Who is this divine, rockabilly boy-chick? I am Captain Trips and will attend to your every yearning; mushrooms, acid, girls, boys. Ask and you shall receive."

"Zoltan don't allow dope dealing in here, Prince," the desk clerk said.

"You're such a coy-boy, Cowboy," the hippie said.

"This is Donovan Bender."

"Oh, so you're the famous Bender, prettier than expected, almost elegant," Prince said. He blew Donovan a kiss, draped an arm around Billy's shoulder, and led him to the bar.

"Don't tell people I'm a Bender, Cowboy," Donovan said.

"Ain't exactly a state secret, bro."

"Lotta new people around here."

"The faces change but the lives remain the same."

A door behind the false wall going to the rooms groaned and a grubby man waltzed around the corner, wearing a yellow shirt with dark stains, no socks or shoes. What little hair he had was greasy and long at the back.

"The things you see when you don't have a shotgun," Cowboy said.

"Gotta smoke?" Itchy Dick asked.

"What does the thing dancing between my lips look like?"

"A smoke."

"Then I guess I got one."

"Bum me a butt, man."

"Listen, I give you one, I gotta give Donovan one, then the next guy, and the next. Pretty soon I got none left."

"It won't kill ya."

"Are you really this stupid or do you sit up in your room at night and practice?"

Itchy Dick turned to Donovan.

"Gotta smoke?"

"Where'd you like me to mail your nose?" Cowboy exploded. Itchy Dick laughed.

"Whadda cutup. How about it, man?" he asked again. Donovan sighed and gave him one. It was the only way to get rid of these guys. Itchy Dick lit the cigarette, took a drag, and peeked at Donovan from behind bushy eyebrows. Then he strolled to the bar. Cowboy shook his head.

"I swear they're gonna carry that clown out in a butterfly net or a body bag. Itchy Dick, big time DJ at some primo radio station until cocaine took him from prime rib and party girls to hotel droppings."

"I'm going inside for a drink," Donovan said.

Siren splayed across a mirror behind the bar. Velvet sat on a stool, smoky coils of rage curling around her head while Rambo ate her up with his eyes. Donovan paid her for the drinks she'd taken to the desk. They both knew it was the only way she would ever see her money. She smiled when he ordered a Jameson.

"Didn't strike me as a beer man," Velvet said as she studied him. "You've been inside. Welcome back to the real world."

"Is that what it is?" Donovan said. They both chuckled and he walked away. He'd spied an empty table by the back exit. It was perfect. He could get out quickly if Tony showed up. His big brother was the last person he wanted to see. Tony always worked the angles and Donovan's discharge would be just another one to exploit. The Benders were the toughest family to come out of the North End in twenty years. Tony worked this to his advantage. The other four brothers were all doing serious time because of him. For years Donovan had tried to escape the family rep but never succeeded. Wherever he went whispers would start. Why was he here? Who was going to get a beating? Some in the crowd would cower, scared or fascinated, while the creeps sucked up, hoping hanging with him would enhance their reputation as tough guys. There was only ever one exception to this; Banjo Bob Holiday, a decent guy without an ounce of BS, no agenda, axe to grind, or scam to run. All Bob ever wanted was to share a brew and a song. Donovan relaxed around him.

It wasn't long before Cowboy bounced into the bar rubbernecking, head bobbing, eyes roving. Tony and Jimmy Jazz strolled in behind him. They took up a perch at their usual table where they could see everything and everyone who came and went in the bar. Donovan slipped out the back door before they spotted him and went around to the front of the hotel. He'd missed his bus but had the room key Cowboy gave him. He could hide out upstairs for the night and try to get some rest. He was too tired to go anywhere or do anything else and there would always be another bus tomorrow.

The second floor of the hotel stank of stale beer, tobacco, unwashed old men. Room 211 was at the top of the stairs. When Donovan unlocked the door and saw inside, a deep sigh rocked him. The sink was browner than white, the mirror hanging over it murky. A narrow bed had thin sheets and a dark stain on the carpet looked like dry blood. The room had a single saving grace, a private bathroom. In the morning, he could freshen up and shower without using the public one down the hall.

A sudden loud thumping detonated under his feet. Guitars shrieked and a woman started to screech like a cat being strangled. The walls shook. The sink bounced. His room must be over the stage in the bar. He collapsed on the bed, pulled a pillow over his head, and covered his ears. Sleep was rarely a refuge for him but where Siren orchestrated his nightmares and the ridiculous ripened into the incomprehensible. But it had been almost twenty-four hours since he rested and not even this rock and roll thunder kept him awake long.

Donovan flew too fast toward the wall. He was going to smash into a million little pieces when he hit it. Siren's voice vibrated on the air.

"You can fly, you can go through the wall," he said so Donovan did. But now he was stuck inside the wall, a prisoner plunging down a bottomless, black pit.

"You can fly into a wall, you can come out the other side," Siren crooned. Donovan did and was awake, lying on a bed, in a dark room. For a moment, he thought he was back in the hospital. But it was the Royal Albert Arms Hotel. He lifted his head, looking over at the pencil-thin line of light along the bottom of the door. It was supposed to be the point of demarcation where his private space was separated from the world. A shadow bobbed there, Siren mewling, a desperate voice, whimpering in a suicidal litany.

When Donovan had come upstairs earlier, he'd seen the area surrounding his room was a dumping ground for all the loud, heavy metal machinery used to run the hotel; an ice-maker, the soft drink machine, a decrepit elevator. But he missed the fucking payphone. Now, in the middle of the night, a creep was calling home, crying the blues about not being able to hack it in the city and how he might end it all. Donovan's toes tingled, the sensation working its way up his body, quickening every nerve ending, burning his skin. He gripped the sides of the bed's metal frame, his knuckles white, his fingers stiff as he resisted the urge to run out into the hall and pound the miserable, fucking shadow into powder. But finally, the loser ran out of steam and tears, stopped wailing, and shuffled down the hall to his room to either sleep or hang himself.

It was quiet now, except for the radio somewhere playing 'Classics Till Dawn'. Donovan crawled out of bed, went to the sink, and splashed cold water on his face. Siren stared back from the mirror, his moon-face beaming in the dark.

"Welcome home you schizophrenic son-of-a-bitch," he purred. Donovan didn't know if the voice was coming from the mirror or inside his head. He went back to bed, fell asleep instantly.

He wasn't sure if cold or the ringing phone woke him. It was Cowboy on the other end, wanting to go for breakfast. Donovan's throat was dry, his mouth sour. Gray light seeped into the room through a window covered in ice. He washed his face and combed his hair. Siren was gone from the mirror. Downstairs, Zoltan Kisich was at the desk laying out bills in neat piles.

"Heard you were here," he said, acknowledging Donovan. "You look like hell."

"Thanks, Zoltan."

"How you fixed for cash?"

"I'm broke."

"Of course," Zoltan said, peeling off ten twenties and pushing them across the counter.

"What's the catch?" Donovan asked.

"It's a loan. Pay me when you can. We'll work out the room later. But keep it to yourself. I got enough deadbeats hounding me for bread."

Zoltan dropped the other bills into a strongbox and slammed it shut. He bummed a butt off Donovan and studied him while fighting for the first, scalding sips of coffee in a paper cup.

"What do you want from me, Zoltan?"

"You are astute. Cowboy is dipping sticky fingers into the till. The man's a liar, thief, and third-rate thug but I rely on him. He works the desk six nights a week, watches the door Sundays. But there isn't much juice left in those old bones. Handle the front a few nights a week, give him a break. Then he can go drink somebody else's rye for a change. Don't decide now. Think about it for a day or two."

Zoltan slid out from behind the front desk and headed upstairs to his office.

The smell of bacon led Donovan back to the Salisbury House where he'd bought a burger for Downtown Tommy. It was only last night but seemed longer. Siren scuttled in an alley between the Sals and the Oxford Hotel then vaulted into a dumpster. Cowboy waved to Donovan from a window and flagged down a waitress flying by with a coffee pot when he joined him.

"Need another jolt of java to jumpstart my happy face this morning, darling. Bring my buddy a cup too, silver plates. I already ordered breakfast, Donovan. Couldn't find you in the bar last night. Where you go? Get any rest in that room?"

"The band was loud."

"Sorry about that. It was the only room I had available."

"Some goof got on the payphone at three AM and started bawling about killing himself."

"That's all we need, a stiff stinking up the hall. Happens again, feel free to kick the shit out of him."

"Don't need your permission, Cowboy."

"Right. Course not, bro. So, I put a bug in Zoltan's ear about bringing you on. I can use you in my corner."

"I'm leaving for Vancouver."

"Aw, you'd hate it in a week, yahoos wandering around like they're wading in maple syrup. It's not rain falling there but Valium. Besides, you don't know a soul and it ain't cheap in my hometown. Stay awhile. Sock away some scratch and you can leave with a decent stake."

"There are some people want me gone."

"Eric the Red?"

Five years earlier, Donovan had been half-hammered and stumbled into a bar, forgetting it was a Curb Stompers hangout. An unwritten rule was the bikers didn't wear colours in Winnipeg bars. It started fights. But a couple dozen characters were wearing the same red-and-black plaid lumberjack coats in this one. Donovan got the drift and left but not soon enough. Two Curb Stompers cornered him in the parking lot. Donovan clocked their every move, every look they exchanged, calibrating each twitch of their bodies, their breathing and beating hearts, clomping boots and clanging chains. Slow motion ramped up to warp speed and he flew at them with blood roaring in his brain as he punched and kicked and bit. It took four cops to pull him off them. One of the bikers was dead; the other, Eric the Red, close to it.

"Earth to Donovan," Cowboy said. "Don't sweat it. Tony has Eric under control."

"What's this to you, Cowboy?"

"I'm just trying to keep the peace, man."

"So then you're a peace officer."

"Do not even joke about that shit."

Breakfast arrived. They ate in silence. It was true Donovan didn't have a dime saved and Zoltan's two bills wouldn't last long in Van. Maybe he could cope with Winnipeg a little while, squirrel away a few bucks, make his first shrink appointment, and throw Lawler off his scent. He just had to avoid Eric the Red.

"Okay, I'll stay, Cowboy."

"That's the spirit, bro."

Siren had nestled on Donovan's eggs. He poked at him with a slice of toast. Siren jumped off the plate, ran around the table. Donovan banged his fist down but missed. Cowboy watched quietly, drinking his coffee, waiting for Donovan to finish.

"We should tell Zoltan before he takes off," he said finally.

◆　◆　◆

Fierce muttering penetrated every part of Donovan. He took a slug of rotgut directly from the bottle and got lost in luminous, bobbing particles flooding the room. The booze burned going down, searing his insides. He climbed off the bed, crossed to the sink, and yanked a towel off the mirror. Siren's saucer-blue eyes stared back, scalding, silently scolding. Siren had always been amorphous before, hovering on the ceiling, needling Donovan, nagging him; or surfacing like a cockroach caught in sudden light, scrambling across the floor. He would float on ice cubes in Donovan's drink or park beside cherry tomatoes on his plate. The one constant was Siren never stayed. He came and went, leaving an oasis of calm, at least for a little while. But the apparition was stuck in Donovan's mirror now, plaguing him without respite. Unable to see his reflection in the mirror, Donovan shaved by touch, dragging the blade up his throat and opening bloody tears.

At eleven, he was a Rembrandt with the razor, slicing fine lattice-like threads in his skin, creating designs up and down his arms. They caught him in the washroom at school and thought he was trying to kill himself so sent him to a shrink. They didn't understand cutting took away the cold, allowed him to feel something, anything.

Siren was starting to shape-shift in the mirror, the hollows and creases of his face squeezed like clay between unseen fingers. Donovan towelled his face dry and darted from the room, slamming the door. He heard restless scratching in the hallway and spun around, lifting his foot to squash Siren under his boot. It was Itchy Dick, rummaging in the trash. His face lit up when he saw Donovan.

"Hey man, you gotta — "

"No!" Donovan shouted.

"No problem, pal. Catch ya later," Itchy Dick said and wandered away, scanning the floor for treasure.

It had taken Zoltan a whole week to arrange his training on the desk. Donovan still had an hour before starting and went to the small café off the lobby. Bertha wasn't thrilled when he only asked for a coffee. She brought him one and thumped to the other end of the dining room where she collapsed in a chair and started thumbing through a magazine. She hadn't left any cream. He waved. She slammed down her magazine and ambled back over, her wide hips rolling like ocean waves. He explained. She cursed in Ukrainian, went to the kitchen, and brought back a container of cream. She tossed it on the table and waddled off. He poured the contents into his coffee. The cream curdled. He lifted his hand again. Bertha returned, snatched his cup, and brought another coffee. She forgot the cream. He decided to drink the battery acid black.

Bertha's Place looked out on the street through three enormous windows. Large flakes of snow were starting to fall, turning Albert Street into a snow globe. It was pretty yet sad. A pale apparition floated by the window. Donovan's insides bucked and kicked. Bernie waved, came inside, and sat down across from his brother. Donovan touched his thin cheek.

"It's really you," he said. Bernie laughed.

"Good to see you too, Donnie. How goes the battle? Tony told me you were out."

"But you're in prison."

"Busted out, bro. The River Heights High School had a drug prevention program, wanted trained seals from Stony Mountain to tell the kids how drugs made them do terrible things. I had to volunteer. Never expected they'd pick me. The school had big-ass signs saying ESCAPE. I figured they were trying to tell me something. Screw with us was too busy impressing the young chicks with his big night stick so didn't see me take a hike. Wild being back on the street. First few weeks,

I would stand in front of doors waiting for them to buzz open and couldn't remember how the payphones worked. Tony helped, shooting me gigs and keeping me in speed. I'm getting low on bennies but he is pretty pissed at me right now. I'm not supposed to come around. Maybe you can talk to him for me."

"Your nose looks like somebody took a hammer to it, Bernie."

His brother laughed.

"Been busted so many times, it's like rubber, bends anyway I like. See? Man, I've missed you, Don. Remember the Bender holler? You hear it, run like hell to help your brother."

Bernie cupped his hands over his mouth, threw his head back, and bellowed. Dishes crashed in the kitchen. A cook cursed and Bertha barrelled around the corner but Bernie was already gone.

"Crazy person stuck his head in here, yelled, and took off," Donovan explained. Bertha grabbed his cup.

"You go too! Enough coffee!"

The day woman on the desk turned a tired face, wrinkled with worry, on him. Cowboy was late to relieve her and she wanted to leave. Something else was bugging her.

"Zoltan wants to know when you plan to pay for your room," Maggie said. It was typical, Zoltan telling him not to worry about the rent then having her nag him.

"I'll talk to him," Donovan said. "Where is he?"

"Bar maybe."

In the bar, Rambo was filling beer fridges.

"You see Zoltan?" Donovan asked.

"Try Bertha's," the bartender said dismissively. Donovan went back to the café through a side entrance at the end of the bar. Zoltan wasn't there. In the lobby Maggie had left and Cowboy was behind the desk, listening to a thickset man with his back to Donovan telling a story.

"Idiot pulls a score, snatches a lousy grand. I haul his ass in, run the gun, and learn it was last registered in 1947. This piece has passed from punk to punk for almost forty fucking years. Should have seen the look on the loser's face when I told him it was an antique worth a hundred grand. He actually started crying."

"Funny," Cowboy said without conviction, concentrating on Donovan who was staring at the cop's back. Sawchuk turned around and laughed.

"Whadda we have here, another Bender on the loose?"

The cop's reputation rivalled the Benders. He was military police in the army — a meathead. Overseas, a young Korean kid shined shoes through a fence by the base. After he had polished Sawchuk's shitkickers, he wanted Yankee greenbacks and not Canadian scratch. They argued. The kid put his paw in a shoeshine box. Sawchuk blew him away. They sent him to DC after that to drive bigwigs around the city and provide security. He was on the town one night, hoisting a few and got into a beef with a local, putting a bullet in the man's brainpan. They retired his ass and Sawchuk joined the Winnipeg police force. He had buried a few bad boys along the airport road but no Bender. He'd busted them all though, except for Tony and Donovan.

"I best boogie, Cowboy," he said. "I got places to toss, punks to roust. You see that little shit Bernie, call me."

Sawchuk glared at Donovan as he left. Cowboy lit a smoke and shrugged.

"You ready to learn the ropes, son? It's time to lower the lights and raise the prices."

In the week Donovan had been staying at the Albert, he had managed to avoid Tony and dreaded running into him in the bar now. It was just Jimmy Jazz inside though and the big man nodded to him. It would only be a matter of time until Donovan had to deal with Tony.

Cowboy fiddled with dimmer switches while Rambo punched in evening prices. Regulars groaned and a few left but an artsy fartsy type remained oblivious to this activity as he scribbled in a notebook. Back in the lobby, Cowboy gestured expansively.

"This is the nerve-center, Donovan, the frontal lobby-otomy. You never know what will sail in off the street at you.

Last week, a guy come in with an axe looking for his girlfriend because she'd been cheating on him."

"What did you do?" Donovan asked. Cowboy chortled.

"I told him she wasn't here. Citizen's Band from Hell is on tap in the bar tonight. Singer teaches school by day, plays rock star by night. His little teenage groupies are going to try to sneak inside, which means we need to check IDs. The sweet spot is that this prehistoric baby here has Alzheimer's."

Cowboy patted the side of the large, clunky cash register.

"It has no memory, no printout, or record of sales which means the cover is tax free cash for Zoltan. We can nibble at it a little as long as we don't take any big bites. Now we sit back and wait for the party to begin."

"Nobody seems to be exactly breaking down the doors."

"Don't sweat it. This crowd hits the bars late."

It was slow for awhile but then the lobby went from comatose to crazy as a steady stream of swaying drunks and obnoxious punks with rainbow-coloured hair and bad attitudes poured into the lobby. Cowboy handled them all with finesse, cheerfully collecting cover, the odd five dollar bill finding its way into his pocket. Periodically, he dashed to the bar, returning with rye for him and beer for Donovan.

When a young woman plunked down cash too quickly, Cowboy asked for her ID. She was indignant, banging her purse on the desk.

"It's how they get your name and address," the kid behind her said. "Should go and get a gun, fix 'em good."

"You out!" Cowboy barked at him.

"Hey man just kidding," the punk whined. "I'll pay the cover."

"Leave before I call the cops."

"Fuck you!" the kid screamed and thumped out. Then the desk clerk turned his attention back to the young woman and smiled sweetly. She sighed and showed him ID. He motioned to the bar. She yanked her purse away and went inside.

"Not a day over seventeen," Cowboy said. "But as long as she has the paperwork if the liquor inspector shows up."

The band arrived with guitars and girlfriends in tow. The singer, an Alice Cooper clone with long, dark hair and mascara on his eyes had one arm draped over the shoulder of a sweet young thing who observed Donovan and the desk clerk with distaste.

"Nobody's gonna pay five bucks to get into this firetrap," the singer complained. Donovan tried to imagine him teaching high school math.

"They will to see you," Cowboy said.

"True."

"And it keeps out the teenyboppers."

"But they're so cute."

"Jailbait, my fine-feathered friend," Cowboy said. The singer grabbed the key to the band room and led his little troupe to the elevator.

They didn't start until eleven. When the phone in the bar rang around midnight, Cowboy answered and then hung up.

"Over our seating limit," he said. "Have to hold the horde back a bit. Liquor inspector is looking for an excuse to shut us down."

Cowboy put up a Full House sign and a group just coming in the door groaned. A line formed quickly, the lobby buzzing with conversation as loud music spilled from the bar. A giant man staggered in off the street and the crowd parted for him like the Red Sea.

"Big Ron!" Cowboy yelped.

"Not so loud," the man grumbled. "I gotta seven hundred dollar hangover,"

"Look who's here," Cowboy said. Big Ron saw Donovan and came to life, darting behind the desk and lifting him off the ground in a bear hug.

"You look great!" he cried out. "A little thin but you always been a bone-rack."

"How do you have a seven hundred dollar hangover?" Donovan asked. Big Ron's smile went south.

"Had to get bent out-of-shape. Vera dumped me for a weasel," he said. Big Ron's old lady worked the street and he stepped up when she had to intimidate a john. Ron was a party animal and a softie but had size. He only needed to stand there looking heavy.

"Sorry to hear," Donovan said.

"If Loopy Larry's inside, he'll spot me a few bucks to buy a brew and my lottery ticket. I carried him a few times."

Big Ron walked toward the bar. The kids waiting in line went crazy.

"Alright, I'll let ten inside," the desk clerk said. They threw down their cash and bolted to the door before he changed his mind. Cowboy shook his head.

"Burns me seeing Big Ron on the ropes," he said. "Stayed with him last time Vera was in the can. We ate pizza, quaffed a few, and smoked a little dope. But he visited her regular as my daily dump. You know she carries a piece now, Donovan? It's been a real shitstorm on the street since that fucking fire. Tell you how I would fix Colin though, that Toronto turd. I'd slip behind him real quiet with my baseball bat and crack his head open like an egg."

The phone rang again. Rambo was screaming so loud, Cowboy held the receiver away from his ear. He dropped it on the desk.

"Sounds upset," Donovan said.

"I better go tend to him before he blows a gasket. You'll be okay here."

The shelf under the desk held another cartoon sign, an empty shot glass, and the baseball bat. The lobby was quieter with Cowboy gone. The door creaked open and a crackpot cultivating desperado airs like he was some kind of hard case crept passed the crowd. He looked like an East European pimp with his long leather coat and matching fedora. Donovan had seen tougher dudes cry like babies while picking up what was left of their faces. Cowboy told him later that his street name was the Midnight Jeweller and he hawked cheap junk to hookers who promised to pay later and never did. He leaned on the front desk, removed his fogged-up glasses, and wiped them.

"You seen Diane, working girl with long legs?" he asked. Donovan recognized the voice. It was the clown who had cried about killing himself on the payphone. Then Donovan smelled the cigar smoke.

"What would Diane want with a stick like you?" Tony asked.

"She owes me for a ring and I'm gonna collect one way or the other."

"You mess with Loopy Larry's lady; they'll bury you in a thimble. Beat it, Bruno."

The Midnight Jeweller limped upstairs to his room. Tony turned to Donovan.

"It's been a long time, little brother," he said. "Lotta blood under the bridge."

"Life is a series of near misses and close calls; you get good at dodging bullets."

"I have no fucking idea what you're talking about. You've always been the creative one, eh, a whack job, writing poetry, cutting like a little schoolgirl."

"I stopped doing that."

"Writing poetry or cutting? You look like crap."

"Shrink's trying to bomb me back to the Stone Age with his meds but you know that, don't you, Tony? Lawler tells you everything."

"Stop taking your pills, you gonna start poking holes in walls and people? Either way, I'll take the Ritalin off your hands."

"You selling kiddie cocaine with sets of Talwin, Tony?"

"I'll shoot you two bills a month, let you run a bar tab."

"Why so generous?"

"Because you're my brother, asshole; and you can give me a room key."

"Zoltan would freak."

"Fuck him. He only thinks he runs the Albert."

It was true. The hotel was Tony's turf, not Zoltan's. Everyone ended up at his table. You needed something or someone done, you talked to Tony.

"I could use the extra cash to get out of town. I'm moving to the coast."

"Yeah, I heard that was your latest fantasy. The old lady knows you're out. I was at their place earlier trying to keep her from losing her mind. Stop ducking family, go see her. You break the old lady's heart again I'll break you in two."

Tony strode to the bar.

"There's a cover charge!" Donovan shouted.

"Shove it up your ass, Donnie," Tony said, disappearing through the door. But the crowd didn't protest this time, intuitively sensing that if Tony was a hawk, Donovan was a loon.

"How much is the cover?" a soft voice asked. Donovan looked down into the doe-eyes of a young woman with an angelic face, a shaved head, and a swastika carved into her forehead.

The Golden Boy

Zoltan Kisich was surrounded, plants, hand-crocheted doilies, and bric-a-brac everywhere. Ma was the queen of kitsch. She had knick-knacks up the yin-yang. These family dinners were dismal affairs, Ma cooking too much food, Pa bugging him because business was bad at the hotel. Tonight, it was worse. The folks were leaving for the old country soon and the golden boy had deigned to descend from his perch on Olympus to grace them with his presence. Nicolai was making a fortune selling million dollar properties to movie stars in California and lived among them in a palatial estate. He could do no wrong. He was even sitting in Pa's place at the head of the table with his tan and smug smile. Zoltan wanted to punch his caps out. He picked at his plate instead. Ma had to lighten up on the portions. Twenty pounds overweight, she still complained he was skinny. The wine, however, was excellent.

"Zoltan!" Pa shouted at him. "You eat like a pigeon, drink like a pig! What kind of son is this Nicolai? I never should have let him go to school in North Dakota. What do they have there we don't here? He wants to be an actor, he says. What kind of work is that for a grown man?"

Pa never understood Zoltan's passion for theatre, the delight of digging into a character's psyche to discover the contradictions, unearth complexities. It allowed him to touch secret places inside himself and explore madness without consequence. Pa was right about one thing though. It was no way to make a living, looking for work every few months, kissing the ass of every tin-pot director in the country.

"You had it too easy," Pa said. "I swam a river to escape Tito, worked day and night to get a start in this country. We slaved so you could have everything and look at us now; six houses, two hotels."

"The houses are dumps and the hotels dives, Pa," Zoltan said. "We're slumlords, saloon keepers. That's not progress."

"See what I mean, Nicolai? He doesn't run the hotel like you did. Should see what he lets in the bar. Kids with purple hair, nose rings. It's disgusting. I don't know how many times I have to tell him. Head-bangers don't drink, but Indians do!"

"Fuck!" Zoltan cried out.

"Watch that mouth of yours in front of your Ma."

"You need to stop spewing these old-world prejudices of yours," Zoltan hissed. "You have no idea about this place. Winnipeg is where the Red and Assiniboine Rivers converge. It was an Indigenous meeting place long before we arrived and started squatting here. Their roots run deep and what we're witnessing today is a real renaissance; a revolution and rekindling of their ways as they move back into this city, bringing their culture, music, and art."

"Bullshit," Pa shouted. "I know what I see and hear and I say what I think. What you and your hoity-toity pals gonna do? Protest, take me to court, or toss me in jail? You are running our business into the ground. I have half a mind to go down to the Albert and check the books."

Zoltan placed his glass of wine on the table and stood up.

"Where you going?" Pa asked.

"To call Cowboy, find out how it is tonight so I can report back to you."

"Make it snappy."

In the small front hall next to the stairs, the telephone sat on a side table smelling of lemon polish. Cowboy was slow picking up.

"Joe's Garage. You jack 'em, we hack 'em."

"Stop answering the phone like that."

"Hi Zoltan."

"How are things?"

"It's slow, man."

"Patch me through to the bar."

"Can't talk," Velvet shouted over the noise. "It's too loud in here."

"So it's busy then. Gimme the desk again," Zoltan said. "Cowboy, I expect six hundred in the till come morning."

"Zoltan, the cash just ain't there. I can't charge the regulars. Those boys will drop a cool hundred bills on booze but won't give you one thin dime for cover. They'll just go drink down the street at the Charlie or Oxford. Meantime, half the punks you let in, sneak through the back door while their buddies are bitching at the front because the band begins so late."

"Tell the rock star to start earlier then. No. Don't. I'm coming down. I'll tell him."

"Zoltan, you'll just piss him off. You gotta way of aggravating these guys. Last time you did, Terminal Jerks pulled the plug and we almost had a riot in there."

Zoltan hung up and went back to the living room.

"I'm leaving," he said.

"But I made palicenke," Ma insisted, pointing at the dessert plate.

"You made it for Nicky," Zoltan said. "Coming to say hi to Cowboy, Nicky?"

His brother practically leapt from his chair as Ma protested.

"I would love to stay, have some of your delicious strudel, but I'm stuffed, Ma."

"Smooth," Zoltan muttered.

"Besides, I wanna see how Zollie is doing at the hotel."

"Lousy," Pa snorted.

"Maybe I can give him a few pointers," Nicky said. Zoltan had to admit his big brother knew how to sell. But Ma wasn't buying it this time.

"You're thin," she snapped. "That fancy wife isn't feeding you. Where is she? Why didn't she bring my grandkids? She too good for us now, her husband is a millionaire?"

"That isn't fair, Ma. The kids have been sick."

"Because she don't cook proper," Ma said. She collapsed on the couch, the plate of pastry in her lap, and started to cry.

Pa threw his hands up. They followed their sons to the door, Pa still bitching about the business, Ma moaning in a singsong voice it was nice that her boys found time to visit. Zoltan and his brother wriggled around them in the narrow hall, wrestling into coats and boots. After much hugging, kissing, handshaking, and handwringing, they managed to make it out the door. Nicolai shivered next to Zoltan while the car warmed up.

"Fuck, its freezing," he complained.

"Thirty below zero, but a dry cold," Zoltan said.

"Born and raised in this icebox, I never could hack winter. Thanks for getting me out—"

A sharp rap on the window startled them. Pa stood outside in his slippers, slacks, and a sweater. Zoltan rolled down his window.

"You're gonna catch pneumonia, Pa."

"Me and Ma talked, Zoltan. We want you to stay at the house while we're gone."

"That's six months."

"Neighbourhood is full of thieves and drug addicts."

"Always has been."

"It's getting worse."

"I've offered to help you find a place in a better part of town, Pa."

"But we love it here!"

"Who will look after my condo?" Zoltan asked.

"What's his name—the bastard. Who has a roommate at his age, Nicolai? Almost forty, no wife, no kids, maybe he's a gearbox, I tell myself."

"Oh, for Chrissake, I'll watch the house," Zoltan said, putting the car in gear. As he drove off, Pa was still standing in the middle of the street, hands cupped around his mouth, shouting.

"I forget how crazy they can get," Nicky said. "How you doing, Zollie? Squirrel away any cash for your great escape?"

"I have a few coins stashed."

"Headbangers still pony up, pay without too much complaining eh, put a couple grand a week in your pocket. That cover provided the scratch I needed to get started in LA."

"Pa wants me to drop it, says it scares off the drinkers. Now he's talking about a fucking audit. I'm worried."

"You'll figure something out, Zoltan. You're creative. But you need to consider what will come after the Albert. Save a few shekels, join me in Cali. I'll get you started in the real estate racket. Nothing sweet as selling to those who can afford to pay the price. You must get tired of peddling booze to losers."

"Thing is, they're my losers, Nicky. In Winnipeg, I'm a rich man; stateside, just another schmuck with a pocketful of cash to burn."

"Don't know what you're missing, man; warm weather, friendly women. Heather can set you up. Who knows? Might meet somebody, get married, and make the folks happy."

"Please. I somehow doubt it," Zoltan said sadly.

"Don't tell me you're still chasing Sarah Grant around? You haven't had enough yet? She has had your nuts in a vise for years and I bet you still haven't poked her."

"It's not like that, Nicky."

"It's always like that, Zoltan. Hey, drive down Memorial Boulevard to the Legislature."

"You ask me to do that every time you're in town."

"The Golden Boy reminds me of my youth. It's like when I hear Herman's Hermits on the radio or catch a whiff of an old girlfriend's perfume. Stop here, so I can get a good look."

Zoltan waited while his brother admired the seventeen-foot, gold-plated statue on the dome of the Legislative Building. The Golden Boy was a gift from France, a naked Hermes holding a torch in one hand, cradling a sheaf of grain in the other.

"Looks like he's freezing his balls off up there," Zoltan said and his brother laughed. He had a warm, infectious laugh Zoltan had always hated. Now he realized he envied it.

They spent the rest of the night drinking at the Albert, only stopping at dawn when Nicky took a taxi back to his hotel. Zoltan crashed on his office couch. In the morning it took every bit of energy he had to climb off it, his head spinning one way, the room another. He had forgotten how Nicky could put away the booze. The bastard even did that better.

Zoltan found a cup of rank, ice-cold coffee and forced it down in fast gulps to complete the circle of humiliation. It was early. A vagrant sun peeked out from behind storm clouds, leaking dull light into his office. The window was filthy. He should get it cleaned. But if he did he would have to get all the hotel windows cleaned, and paint the frames, then the doors. Where would that madness end? Gritty wind-devils whirled down Albert Street. It was cold out which meant the bar would either be dead or crazy busy.

Zoltan's eyes drifted to the incriminating document on his desk with its blur of dancing digits. He didn't need to read the bank statement. He knew the numbers were bad for the third month in a row. Bar sales were plummeting, the return on rooms negligible. The Albert had not always been a financial sinkhole. At one point, it had cachet, the bar a funky nightspot, the hotel practically running itself. Zoltan only needed to drop by for a few hours in the morning, dip his bucket in a money-river, and he'd be done for the day. But the bucket was coming up light and Pa was asking questions. It wasn't Zoltan's fault that business was bad. The neighbour-hood reputation had been deteriorating the last few years. It was a disaster with people thinking it was dangerous, especially now after the fire down the street.

The week following the blaze, there was a small one in the garbage can up on the second floor of the hotel on a busy Saturday night. Nobody in the packed bar was aware of it until they piled out at closing time to find the lobby full of firefighters and hoses. All Zoltan's hard work was unravelling and he no longer measured success by momentum but survival. He had to distract Pa from doing this damn audit.

He had another hit of terrible coffee and called downstairs. Maggie picked up on the first quarter-ring. It would be okay as long as she didn't get too stupid. The poor woman had a drab personality and gray hair that an overzealous stylist had permed into submission. But she was reliable, loyal.

"Royal Albert Arms Hotel, Maggie speaking."

"The switchboard light tells you it's me and that I am calling to talk to you, Maggie. Therefore it follows you know I am on the line and I must not only know who you are, but where you are."

"Yes, I know it's you, Zoltan and I know you know it's me. I'm just being professional."

"Tell Cowboy to get up here with my coffee," he said, hanging up. There was no point in arguing with Maggie. He didn't have the energy to ream her out.

The desk clerk waltzed in with two Styrofoam cups.

"I have coffee for your high-ness," he said. "Drink it fast you won't taste the cyanide."

"What did I tell you about knocking? Liquor sales were lousy last night, Cowboy."

"No surprise the way you and Nicky were putting it away."

"The bar was short two bottles of rye. You drink it."

"So does half the fucking city."

"Half the fucking city doesn't work in my hotel. I am on to your game, Cowboy and I am going to catch you at it one of these days."

"No, you won't, because there is no game, just my life."

"What have you heard about the fire?"

"Not a thing."

"Hard to believe."

"I wouldn't lie about that kind of shit, Zoltan."

"What kind of shit would you lie about?"

"Lighten up, you're giving me your headache."

"Gimme a cigarette."

"You gotta start buying butts, boss."

"I quit smoking."

"You quit buying."

"Time to shake things up around here, Cowboy. I need to make changes."

"Nothing too drastic I hope."

"It depends. I haven't had any rent money from you in years."

"Our arrangement is you pay shit, ergo I get the room gratis."

"Starting February, you fork over five hundred a month."

"That's in two weeks."

"Cry me a river."

"If I had any brains I'd blow this pop stand."

"You have the lips for it."

"Har-dee-fucking-har."

"Never mind that, we have a more serious problem. Pa plans to check the books. So the feeding frenzy is over for awhile. And someone has to take the heat for thieving, throw Pa off the scent. You're a prime candidate."

Cowboy gulped down his coffee, the windmills of his mind spinning at double-time.

"You tell your Pa I'm skimming, he'll kibosh the cover charge and kill the goose."

"What about Maggie then?"

"Even if Saint Margaret of the front desk was capable, she wouldn't dip into the till. She is too honest. Your Pa knows that. Besides, the room rents are chump change. The real money is in the bar. Maybe it's Rambo with his hand in the register."

Zoltan hated the idea of burning the bartender. They'd been friends since they were kids. But Cowboy was right. The bar was where the haemorrhaging of cash would be obvious and he could convince Pa he'd solved the problem by firing the culprit.

'Who would run things inside?"

"You have to ask?" Cowboy said.

"I will only let you do it until I find someone I can trust."

"Good luck with that."

"Get out. Go gather thine evidence," Zoltan said. Cowboy leapt to his feet, slamming the door as he left which did nothing for Zoltan's headache. He unlocked a desk drawer, removed a leather pouch, and laid out several lines of coke. He'd dealt with one disagreeable issue and now needed to figure out how to get Tony Bender off his back. He had hoped helping Donovan find his feet might buy some goodwill with the pusher. It didn't. He had another pressing problem on his brain though. Something Nicky had reminded him of last night.

Zoltan had been eight when he first saw Sarah Grant and her sister playing on the sidewalk outside his parents' home in the North End. Everyone said Emily with her pale, plaster skin, blue eyes, and blonde hair was the pretty one. But he was more enchanted by Sarah, her mocha flesh deepening to coffee in summer and dark, piercing eyes that were mysterious puzzles. Zoltan was almost twelve when Pa moved the family out of the North End after a break-in down their street, two six-year-olds burning down the house. His parents became refugees again, this time fleeing the North End to Winnipeg's West End, although not fast enough to escape the spreading slum. But Zoltan had never forgotten the shy little brown girl and the longing she stirred in him.

They were in their early twenties when their paths crossed again. Socials were a common event in the city. Couples raised money for their wedding by getting a liquor license, renting a hall, hiring a DJ, and selling tickets to the bash. The pair having this particular social had organized several of them but never got married. It was a scam they used to make some fast cash. Nobody seemed to mind. It was always a good time. Zoltan hadn't recognized Sarah right away, but a bolt of ardour shot through him, overriding his usual reserve. He asked her to dance and the connection was instant. They spent the rest of the night outside walking and talking. They started hanging out together — watching fireworks as a light rain fell, leaning into each other with their hips grazing or sitting on a kitchen floor painting with oils, his poor effort giving them both the giggles while, the whole time Zoltan was applying colour to canvas, he longed to kiss Sarah. He never did. He never had the nerve to tell her how he felt. She had a fierce pride inflamed by deep anger and Zoltan couldn't push passed her rage. They never touched, only talked. He listened as she complained about this boyfriend or that one and how she maybe hated men, a sad litany that shut him up and shut him down, rendering his heart inarticulate. Their time together turned into an erotic tease that played out on a visceral level. They were constant companions for awhile and then had no contact. In the last two decades, they had gone through periods of seeing each other, then stopping, starting, stopping again. From the unpractised perspective of his youth, her chaste manner seemed like a manifestation of some ideal, perfect love, not a perverse, tormented desire fuelled by denial and paralysis like Nicky insisted it was.

The last time Zoltan had talked to Sarah was only a few nights ago and his heart had done somersaults when she answered the phone. Her voice was cold though, like river ice cracking in spring. She said she had an eight-year-old daughter and was living with someone then hung up. It was seven days after the Lithium fire now; he had to hear her voice again. Zoltan was done with reticent fumbling, clumsy deference, and his downright cowardice. He'd held his tongue too long and was going to tell Sarah how he felt at last. Life was short and he was determined. Zoltan did another line of coke and dialled her number.

Closer to the Bone

Willie Nelson's fractured voice normally gave Sarah Grant a good feeling. But at the end of a long difficult day that began with her world being shattered, she felt only heartbreak as that melancholy 'Stardust' melody spilled from the car stereo and lacerated her insides. She turned off the tape and banged her bandaged hand against the dash. It hurt like hell. She'd been unable to concentrate or stop thinking about her problem in school and became so distracted she almost cut off her thumb with a band-saw. The nurse patching it up eyed her suspiciously as though she had done it deliberately for the pain meds. She told her to take two Tylenol and sent her back to class. Sarah had been dealing with her type since she was little and didn't let the bitch bother her. Besides it was no time to let her emotions flare up and dominate her thinking. She needed to find a solution.

The morning began well enough with Brad leaving early for work. It meant she and her daughter could enjoy a quiet breakfast without having to listen to his constant complaining and criticizing. But when Amy started smacking her cereal with a spoon, splashing milk, Sarah was sharp, barking at her to stop. A strange thing happened then. Amy's brown eyes opened wide and a plaintive moaning spilled out of her, becoming louder and more intense until it was a terrible shrieking and she was sobbing uncontrollably. Sarah felt cold fingers jam into her stomach and squeeze hard.

She'd sensed something was wrong for awhile. Amy was acting odd, talking to invisible friends, wetting the bed. Sarah was going to get to the bottom of this now. She was patient and reassured Amy, calming her while gently probing. Amy slowly opened up. As she did, Sarah's dread grew, first turning to disgust then anger. Her daughter was sharing things no eight-year-old could possibly know except through experience. It all became so obvious to her; Brad's teasing, the tickling and the touching, his fucking eagerness to babysit when Sarah had to go somewhere. She never should have left them alone. They finished breakfast quickly then Sarah packed a bag and took Amy to her mother's place. Amy loved to spend time with her kokum and they could stay there as long as they needed. Sarah still had to go to class at Red River Community College though. She had an exam she couldn't miss if she was going to get her carpentry papers. In her haste to get them both the hell away from that creep, she forgot important documents in the bedroom; health cards, birth certificates.

So now, here she was in the parking lot, outside the apartment building. The exterior of the piss-yellow building seemed so ordinary; no hint of the horrible things that went on inside, yet Sarah could feel misery seeping out through every stucco crack. Sarah never liked living there. Brad didn't let her paint the walls, put up pictures, or even burn sage. He was against her taking a carpentry course too. She didn't need a trade. He made more than enough stacking beer cases at the brewery to take care of them. He didn't want her to buy the beater either, despite the Dart saving her and Amy long stretches of waiting in the cold for buses that always came late and sometimes never did. After what Amy had told her though, the car was more than a convenience. It was a necessity.

Brad had seemed like a good guy in the beginning; a decent man with a paying job, never in trouble with the law. But he'd proven to be a possessive, passive aggressive son-of a-bitch. Growing up in the North End, Sarah had always avoided rounders that spent half their life in jail, the other half in a bar or beating their women. But none of those tough guys would have ever done what he had and would kill anyone who did.

Sarah was reluctant to go up to the apartment but had to get those papers. It was only five o'clock. Brad worked until eight, usually went out with the boys for a beer after, and had started walking home to lose a little weight, which meant he often got back around ten. It gave her time to run up, grab what she needed, and get out before he came home. Sarah killed the engine.

The elevator opened on the third floor. A TV blared all the way down the hall. Brad was home early. Sarah stopped by the door, heard loud snoring. He was likely drunk and passed out. When he came home half-hammered, he always turned on the boob tube, and fell asleep in front of it. If she was quiet she could do this. Sarah turned the key carefully, crept inside, and slipped to the bedroom. She found the paperwork she needed and was halfway out the door again when the phone rang. She ran to the kitchen to catch it before the asshole woke up. It was Zoltan. He'd popped back into her life a week ago, calling and bugging her, whining about how he wanted to get together, his voice dripping with desperation. The terrors of his soul were hardly her concern, especially now.

Brad stirred in the other room. Sarah wanted to just drop the phone and run, but it was too late. Still, he wouldn't know she and Amy had bailed yet. She shucked off her coat, grabbed a pot, and filled it with water. Zoltan ranted in her ear while she put the pot on a burner and let the water boil. She was pouring pasta into it when she felt Brad's bad breath, stinking with the sour smell of stale beer, on the back of her neck. He started stroking her hair, nuzzling into her from behind. Sarah gripped the handle of the hot pot.

"How is my brown-eyed brazen doing today?" Brad mumbled into her neck and she tried to wriggle away. Her squirming only encouraged him to grind his pelvis into her and push his fucking point home.

"Stop that!" she shouted, banging the phone down, cutting Zoltan off in midsentence.

"Lemme guess, it was the idiot calling again," Brad said.

"Zoltan is my friend."

"He just wants to jump your bones, babe."

"You're home early."

"Deliveries were done so they cut me loose. Where's Amy?"

Sarah bristled but kept her cool.

"I have to pick her up at my mother's."

"We're having pasta again?"

"I'm tired. It's fast."

"Quit school then. You'll only have calluses as a carpenter and I don't really want rough hands on my body."

"I've wanted to work with wood since I was Amy's age," Sarah said.

"Bet you were just as cute too," he said. Sarah's insides curdled and she lifted the pot of boiling water, turning toward him. It was as if Brad intuitively guessed her intention. He flipped away and fled back to the living room where he almost immediately started snoring again. Sarah grabbed her coat and got out before doing something stupid.

Days later, she was nursing a cup of cold coffee, clenching her hands in her lap, resisting the urge to clean the table. Bertha's Place was filthy. A cigarette butt was stubbed in the ceramic sugar container; a long, black hair embedded in grunge on a napkin holder with smears of soya sauce finger-painted on the side. Zoltan's hotel was the last place she wanted to be. But she had to act before Brad did something crazy. The last time she had talked about leaving him, he broke down crying, saying he would kill himself before turning nasty, threatening to call up Children's Aid, report her for being a bad mother. Sarah was worried about Amy. She wondered how long her daughter had been keeping this secret, a few months at least. Now she'd crumbled and shared it, she could crash and take years to get over what happened. Sarah was furious but would never go to the cops, not after all the crap she and her brothers suffered at their hands; and no way was she going to let some goody-two-shoes social worker or a greasy doctor prod and poke her little girl. After a day of tormented brooding, the answer popped into her head on its own. Brad Hunter had to die.

Some people would say what she wanted was revenge, not justice. It was neither. When a plant is sick you prune it, cut away the diseased part to protect the whole, drain the poison to stop the infection from spreading. Sarah had no qualms about carrying out this crime; she didn't fear any possible consequences. But after considering the various ways she could commit the act, she decided against doing it. She had to be there to help Amy heal and couldn't do that from prison. Sarah had to find someone to kill Brad. Zoltan would know if a capable person hung around the hotel. So here she was at the Albert, waiting for his lordship to show up.

A man with a beard and moustache stained yellow sauntered into the café. He stood in a corner by the door, his eyes crawling all over her body like bedbugs and started stroking himself through his pants. Sarah glared. This only seemed to further excite him, encouraging him to fondle his crotch even more vigorously. Sarah wanted to stride into the café kitchen, grab a rusty butter knife, and disembowel the bastard. She turned away instead and stared at a grease spot on the table. Suddenly, a big man barrelled into the café, pulled the pervert outside, and tossed him in the street. Sarah hadn't seen Jimmy Jazz in years. If he was here, so was Tony Bender. Zoltan finally showed up, late like always, sporting a smile, spouting apologies.

"I got tied up at the Marble Club," he said.

"By a blonde or a redhead?"

Zoltan laughed.

"It's good to see you, Sarah. I've wanted to get together for ages and couldn't put it off any longer. You may have heard there was a fire down the street not far from here a few weeks ago. Three people tragically died and it made me realize everything is so tenuous and we can't afford to waste our time. We have to share our feelings, express our needs and desires."

Zoltan took her hands in his soft, plump ones; pink roses he only used for counting money. He looked heart-broken when she pulled away. Sarah was aware of his attraction to her. Zoltan could be charming and even generous, but he wasn't right for her. He was too self-absorbed and self-indulgent, an inconsistent friend.

He abruptly leapt to his feet, ran around the corner to a side door leading into the bar, and started shouting.

"How many times I have to tell you to stop spying on me?"

He threw his hands up in frustration when he returned.

"What was that all about?" Sarah asked.

"The desk clerk, Cowboy is a pain," he said. "So you finally called me back, said you had something to talk about."

Sarah's voice was flat, her eyes hard as she told him in plain, simple language what Brad had done. She spoke with determination, not allowing any emotion to enter her voice or show on her face although she was near tears. Zoltan listened attentively, his expression grim, grasping her seriousness, while she explained what she wanted.

"Brad has to die. You know people who can make it happen. You need to put me in touch with them."

Zoltan didn't respond right away and she watched him struggle with the words.

"I don't know."

"You need to be convinced?" Sarah snapped. "Just before you arrived, this clown strolled into your little café, stood by the door, stared at me, and started playing with himself. You don't understand what my life is like. I can't walk down the street, even during daytime, without being hounded by jerks yelling from car windows, calling me names, sometimes throwing things. I've put up with that shit since I was little. Things will be different for Amy."

"Sarah, I would do anything for you," Zoltan said at last. "But there's a line I can't cross."

He was gawking at her with pathetic longing, making excuses. Sarah stood up and threw a dollar on the table.

"For the coffee," she said. Zoltan called to her as she walked away, but didn't follow her, either out of courtesy or cowardice.

The Dart took time to get warm and Sarah fumed while she waited. Zoltan was weak. She despised his illusions and comfortable lies, the not-so covert love he came close to confessing in the café. The door of the hotel swung open and she steeled herself, preparing to give him a piece of her mind. But it wasn't Zoltan. Tony Bender headed over to her car with the swagger of a man used to getting his way. He tapped on her window. She rolled it down partway. His unapologetic eyes traveled deep into hers.

"It's been awhile, Sarah. I gather your boyfriend didn't come through for you."

"Zoltan is not my boyfriend."

"Good."

"What do you want, Tony?"

"I will do what Zoltan won't."

"I have no idea what you're talking about."

"Don't waste my time, Sarah; I won't waste yours. If you want this creep croaked, meet me, ten AM tomorrow at the Windmill. You know where it is."

Tony turned away and went back into the Albert.

The Windmill was across the street from the Merchants Hotel. Sarah parked on Flora and walked around the corner to Selkirk as the full weight of the North End dropped back down onto her. She hadn't been to the old neighbourhood in years. Nothing had changed. That wasn't true. It had gotten worse. Empty lots filled with garbage and beer bottles sat like broken teeth between the buildings and sad houses stood vacant with paint peeling, porches collapsing. Gaunt shadows shuffled on the street clutching plastic bags of stuff, eyes fixed on the ground as if it was rushing up at them; younger, virile ghosts, still proud and angry with heads held high, glared at her as she passed. The hollow feeling Sarah believed she'd banished for good swept through her, bringing back memories of making do with little; the thieving and screaming and fighting that went on all around her. She remembered crossing the street to avoid having to go by Eddy's Pool Hall and Pauline's Restaurant in case someone flew out the door at her; the deviants and degenerates from other parts of the city cruising the North End in cars, harassing her and her friends, trying to pick them up. But Sarah had managed to get out, lose the walk and the talk, the bowed head, averted eyes. She wanted a better life for Amy and herself; now, she was back in the North End, nursing the hope she could preserve what was left of her daughter's innocence.

The Windmill's lunch counter ran along one side of the interior with booths on the other. Tony was sitting in one near the kitchen while a woman leaned against a stool at the counter and talked to him, flashing a little more leg than necessary. When Sarah joined him, the waitress gave her the once over.

"Take this coffee away, Gladys," he said. "Tastes like turpentine."

"Didn't stop you from drinking three cups," she said.

"We'll have chips and gravy," Tony said. Gladys went to the kitchen to holler at a cook.

"She seems to know you pretty well," Sarah said.

"I live nearby, on Scotia Street, across from St. John's Park," he said, flipping through the pages of a jukebox on the wall, pressing buttons. 'White Rabbit' boomed into the restaurant.

"Sounds like they haven't changed the music in years," Sarah said.

"That's one of the things I like about this place. Crispin St. Peters 'Pied Piper' is next. The Windmill was my home base before I moved it downtown. Your brothers would come in, sell me what they scored pulling a B&E or rolling a drunk leaving the Merchants. They never wanted me to pay them with booze or drugs, always insisted on cash. They were smart."

Sarah's brothers were brown too and treated like trash in school, on the street. But at night, the North End belonged to them and their friends.

'They're doing well now," she said. "Sam teaches; Rick owns a small insurance business."

"Good for them," he said. Gladys brought their order. Tony drowned his chips and gravy in salt and ketchup then stabbed a fry.

"Besides reminiscing, what are we doing here?" Sarah asked.

"Straight to the point; something I've always admired about you," he said. "The years fell away when I saw you in Zoltan's joint. You were never like the other kids, defined or limited by the shit and abuse. It was obvious even then you would get out."

"Now, here I am, waiting for you to answer me."

The pusher laughed. It was a quiet laugh, gentler than she'd expected.

"Touché," he said. "I hate skinners, Sarah. I've seen the damage they do. They deserve to die. But what you want isn't cheap. A professional pulling a tough job on a leading citizen can cost ten to twenty grand. Fortunately, your needs are modest—an uncomplicated hit on nobody special. Talented amateur could do it for a couple of Gs."

"That's still a lot of money. I would have to pay over time."

Tony laughed again.

"What's so funny?" she snapped.

"It's been awhile since I was asked to work on credit. I don't do instalment plans, Sarah. Collections are too messy. There is another option though. I'll take care of this goof and even cover the cost in exchange for a consideration that won't require any cash from you."

"That sounds fishy."

"It isn't. Have dinner with me."

Sarah's fork slipped from her hand and fell against her plate. Nobody in the Windmill seemed to notice the noise. Gladys was smoking a cigarette and listening to a Baba babble in Ukrainian by the front.

"That's a little strange," Sarah said.

"Not really. After it's done, you join me for dinner. We enjoy an excellent meal in a fine restaurant and that will be the end of it. You go your way. I go mine. No strings."

"What's the catch?"

"I see something in you I want to know better. Down the road, if you feel my company is not too obnoxious, we can get together again; decide otherwise, I am out of your life forever."

"You're terribly confident or totally crazy, Tony."

"I'm practical. If one evening doesn't convince you, then nothing will. I believe in first impressions, Sarah. Everything else is just hopeless longing."

If anyone was capable of killing Brad it would be Tony Bender. But Sarah shuddered at the thought of having dinner with him. How could she trust him? Still, if she took enough care and exercised caution, she could maybe manage this and have Brad eliminated. She would make sure her mother knew where she was and with whom. Sarah agreed reluctantly. Tony took down her telephone number, telling her he would be in touch after he had dealt with Brad.

"How about giving me a lift to the Albert?" he asked.

"You don't have a car?"

"Who needs one in a city full of taxicabs," he said.

After the overheated restaurant, the air on the street was refreshing and it was warmer out with some people passing them even smiling. It hadn't been all bad growing up in the North End. There were good times. The North End was a people place with a sense of belonging. Neighbours were friends, not strangers. There was even a little fun; Saturday afternoons at the Palace Theatre with three movies, six cartoons, and a small prize for each kid through the door; family dinners with a ton of food and fiddle music, dancing and singing and laughter. Sarah had been able to spend time with her three aunties, Poppy's sisters; strong, smart, and funny Métis women who taught her to make bannock and told her stories about the way things were before the dark times. Sarah straightened her spine as they walked to the Dart. She was bound to these streets by blood. Brad had taken her away from the heart of the North End but driven her closer to the bone.

Closing Time

Darla Jones heard a sound; a scream, siren, or maybe nothing more than her own fevered imagination. It didn't matter. She was awake now. The black ink, so absorbing and absolving in sleep, spilled into space, becoming a deep, impenetrable darkness saturated with bright points of light like dancing stars. Darla had no idea where she was, even less how she ended up there. She began to explore her surroundings, taking a tentative inventory of it in tiny increments. A fabric swaddling her naked body was familiar, the down-filled comforter her mother had sent her for Christmas. She was in her own bed. Darla inhaled and relaxed, flinging her arms to the side, then recoiling when her hand hit a fleshy bump. Her heart thumped like a butterfly in a jar. Someone was in bed beside her. She fumbled for a flashlight on the nightstand and shone it on a sleeping face. She had no idea who he was. She switched off the light and lay perfectly still, not moving a muscle or daring to breathe, attuned to every subtle shift in the shadows while she attempted to connect the dots.

The fog eventually lifted. Darla recalled she went to the Plaza the night before to catch the farewell performance of Tomahawk Trap, the last of the acid bands that played a unique blend of psychedelic jazz. Darla sometimes hooked up with Deed, the drummer, so went early to snag a table near the stage. But as the bar began to fill she counted six of his former lovers in the crowd. During the course of the evening, Deed dropped by only once to say hello and after the band's last encore, slipped out a side door with the blonde bimbo he'd been banging lately.

There was a half hour to closing time. Darla ordered another scotch. Then a stud, prancing like a war pony by the bar, threw her a hopeful glance. She lobbed a smile back. He sent a drink over, a predictable ploy by a predictable boy. But when he plopped down at the table and offered her a line of coke, the die was cast.

Later, he proved to be a lemon in the sack, pumping with excessive enthusiasm, a tortured expression on his face. Worried he would hurt himself, Darla faked the orgasm he was trying to coax from her. His hips stopped rotating and he removed his sagging piston, collapsing on top of her, mumbling about her pixie lips before passing out.

This was the first time she had blacked out. She had to quit partying so much, stop bringing home strange men, like the albino stripper with the crazy eyes she screwed in the bathroom at the Swinging Gate. Darla liked men. They liked her. But the sex was incidental, the yielding never to the man or devices of love. A greater urgency was at work, a longing that was never satisfied and an unfulfilled emptiness, an interminable yearning with no bottom.

Sparrows chirped a clear morning song outside as Darla ran her tongue along her teeth. Her mouth tasted like a toilet and her stomach was spinning on a bed of nails. She slipped out of bed carefully to not disturb her late-night Lothario. She went to the bathroom, locked the door, and ran a hot bath, settling in for a long soak in lavender-scented water, placing a damp cloth on her face. Maybe Romeo would sneak out like the other weasels had. But no; he was rapping on the door, disturbing her reverie, his thick, sensual voice vibrating through the door.

"Need someone to scrub your back?"

"No!" Darla snarled. She knew he would regard the slightest kind word as reassuring and it would only encourage him. She ran more hot water into the tub and spent another forty minutes in the tub. When she finally emerged from the bathroom, she expected him to be gone. He wasn't. He was sitting on the couch in his underwear, feet on the coffee table, eating one of her green apples and reading her Toronto Star. Darla snatched the fruit away.

"Eve reclaims the apple," she growled, grabbing the newspaper next. "You have to leave. My mother is coming over."

He stumbled into his clothes and pulled a plaintive, puppy dog look at the door.

"My name is Coil," he said.

"Goodbye," she said and pushed him out. Darla slammed the door, twisted the latch, and relaxed when she heard the satisfying sound of the chain lock sliding into place. The man had seemed harmless enough. But what kind of name was Coil? Now she had reclaimed her domain Darla needed to dance, recharge her batteries, and reconnect with a positive energy that never failed to lift her spirits.

She slipped off her robe and dropped to a sitting position on the floor, stretching long legs in front of her. Being on her feet all day carrying trays of beer kept her trim and her legs strong, but her neck and shoulders were chronically stiff. Darla took a few deep breaths, did a neck roll, and tightened her stomach muscles. She stood, bent her knees in an awkward plié then pushed one leg out behind her, executing a dismal lunge. She had to get back into shape.

Darla got dressed, put on coffee, and put two slices of whole-wheat bread into the toaster. She cut cheese and apple slices to make a sandwich and listened to some early morning Mozart on CBC radio while she ate. It had been a long time since she'd done any real dancing and it was beginning to show. As a young girl, the films of famous hoofers, Fred and Ginger, Cyd Charisse, and Shirley MacLaine had lit a fire in her. Darla had been determined to dance, believing she had the talent and the drive to make a life of it. She'd begged her parents for lessons and started class at the age of six. Two years ago, she arrived in Winnipeg just another smashed kid from Toronto, eager to apprentice with the Resurrection Repertory Dance Company. It was Canada's premiere contemporary troupe with an international reputation for fresh, innovative work. Back home, her friends had called her crazy wanting to go to a cultural backwater like Winnipeg. Darla wasn't motivated by big bucks or being discovered though. Dance filled the empty places in her. It was her refuge and her rapture, raising her to a higher plane. When she landed in Winnipeg, she quickly learned the city wasn't desolate at all, but a cultural oasis containing a crucible of creative energy where the rich, black, prairie soil seemed to possess some primeval, elemental power. Sadly, her tenure with the dance troupe turned into a bust. They put her to work, teaching little girls and middle-aged women, without any compensation and she never got to perform with the Company. She had to waitress to pay the bills and became lethargic, losing what discipline she had left. She went nowhere fast, drifting farther from dance. Winnipeg had a ton of talented people, but little access to larger markets. The city's two main exports were grain and artists.

The phone rang. It would be Carlos calling from the Woodbine. She should be on the floor by now serving the morning crowd. Darla didn't pick up. She didn't want to go in today. Yet, she couldn't leave Carlos in the lurch.

It was warm enough to walk to work with the Woodbine twenty minutes away. Darla loved living downtown. Everything was handy and her funky apartment on the top floor of a four-storey walk-up on Assiniboine overlooked the river from the back porch. A small battalion of boys selling their bodies down there during the summer were a noisy nuisance sometimes. Darla didn't mind, but her neighbours called police. The young hustlers could smell a cop car coming a block away though and were always gone before it arrived. As Darla strolled down the street on this day, a gray, claustrophobic sky folded her into a mute despair, an acute awareness of absence. She missed Toronto's frenetic, big-city buzz with its psychotic traffic and sickly streets; the incessant noise, stylish strutting, and chattering coffee klatches. It was a long time between things happening in Winnipeg and maybe she should be in Montreal or New York.

It was starting to get colder. The wind drove her into the Convention Centre at St. Mary's where she took a shortcut, weaving her way through a network of skywalks and tunnels that were a winding labyrinth threading through the downtown area, connecting buildings. Darla paused at the Eaton's overpass on Donald and watched people below bustle by on the sidewalk. It was the end of January, 1984. She was twenty-nine years old and tired of soul-sucking, dead-end days and nights. It was time to get her act together. Back out on the street, she tramped along Portage Avenue passed the video arcades, music shops, and sex boutiques. She spotted the new Shirley MacLaine book on display in a store window. She was Darla's hero, a writer, actor, and singer, still hoofing at fifty. The woman was an inspiration, a tonic touching Darla's soul. Maybe there was hope for her yet.

When she arrived at the Woodbine, Carlos was spinning in circles, bolting back and forth between the bar and the tables while the old men hooted and hollered at him. He stopped to stare at Darla standing in the doorway, sun streaming in behind her. Then he started screaming at her. Darla turned around and spun back out. She crossed Portage, headed down Notre Dame, and turned onto Albert Street. She knew where she was going, what she had to do.

She was having coffee in Bertha`s Place when Zoltan came dancing down the street. He did a sloppy arabesque around a drunk sleeping on the sidewalk, pirouetted passed a panhandler, and tap-danced up the single step into the hotel. He saw her in the window and took a bow. They went upstairs to his office. The stink on the second floor was worse than the one you would find in a dancer's dressing room. Zoltan fell into a chair.

"Grab a seat, gimme a coffin nail, gorgeous," he said. "Cowboy smokes shit. You know, standing there, hands on your hips, you look like Emma Peel, only lacking the leather jumpsuit and whip."

"You need to get your chin on the curb and your mind out of the gutter, Zoltan."

"Care for a snort?"

"It's a little early in the day," she said. Zoltan shrugged, winked, and did a line of cocaine.

"Could have used you in my corner last night, Darla."

"I was busy."

"What's his name, what's his game? It's always rock stars, hockey players, and bad boys with you."

"I didn't come here to discuss my love life or participate in a party, Zoltan."

"What then?"

"I need a job."

"You have one."

"I quit."

"When?"

"Ten minutes ago."

"I dunno, Darla. Business is slow."

"After a year of hounding me to work here, you say that?"

"Well, that was then. This is now. Things have really gone down the tubes since that fire. It could happen here too. I have to be on guard all the time."

"It's a short trip from vigilance to paranoia."

"But am I paranoid enough? I suppose I could cut the other girls back a shift each. It would give you three. Don't look disappointed, Darla. You'll make more in one night here than a month in that other dump. You can start tomorrow; take today off and celebrate with me."

He waved his leather pouch, laying out several lines. Darla decided one hit wouldn't hurt.

Her first night working in the bar at the Albert got off to a rocky start. Halfway through her shift, Zoltan's promised riches hadn't materialized yet. Her only customers were a small knot of hardcore regulars who'd taken up permanent residence by the pool table. They were the demon-seed of the drunks at the Woodbine, but not a real problem. Darla just had to laugh at their stupid jokes and straddle the fine line between being friendly and flirty. The other two waitresses barely acknowledged her presence, simply pointing when she asked where something was. Darla could hardly blame them. She was not only taking a bite out of their income but was the boss's friend too. Who knew what stories she would carry to him? Velvet was riding herd over a wild bunch and Darla saw two of her customers with empty glasses. Maybe she could generate a little good will by getting them their refills.

"You have good taste in cigars," Darla said. Tony Bender glared. "My father has a smoke shop in Toronto. Can I get you a fresh drink?"

"Velvet will take care of us," Tony said, dismissing her and Darla returned to sitting on a stool at the bar with nothing to do. Finally, a familiar grandfather Goth straggled into the bar and sat in her section. Darla had seen him around at various opening nights, a few of Zoltan's parties. She didn't really know him, but normally Scott Kostyk was insufferable with a glib, hipper-than-thou attitude. Tonight, all the smugness seemed to be knocked out of him. He ordered one beer, drained it, and ordered another. Before long, two anorexic kids who could pass for twins joined him. Wearing leather jackets and long scarves they looked like World War I flying aces down behind enemy lines. They each ordered a single glass of draught and took measured sips when they arrived. It was going to be a long night.

But business picked up after the band arrived. By eleven the bar was packed with punks flinging sweaty bodies and money around and bellowing over ear-splitting music as the singer shredded her vocal cords. Darla hadn't worked in a busy bar in ages but it wasn't long before the tricks-of-the-trade kicked back in and she was clearing a path through the crowd with her elbows, matching the other two waitresses drink for drink.

After last call, Darla was cleaning her section as any remaining dawdlers cleared out. An apron bulging with cash hung off her hip. She'd made a serious chunk of change and it cheered her up. She was unloading a tray of empties behind the bar where Cowboy was pouring himself another rye. He'd spent more time carousing with buddies in the bar than minding the front desk.

"Leave that for now," he said. "Let me buy you a drink, Zoltan's treat."

"Double scotch neat," she said.

"Oh, you're a serious drinker. I like that in a woman," he said, handing her a glass. Darla went to sit with the others. Fran raised a gin in salute. Velvet, sipping ice water, simply nodded. They were still wary but she'd proved her mettle on a crazy night and they respected that. Darla removed a wad of bills and a mountain of coin from her apron and started to count it. Cowboy came over, a glass in each hand, sipping first from one, then the other. He sat beside Fran and kissed her on the cheek.

"Where was Rambo tonight?" Velvet asked. "Dork or not, we could have used him."

"Oh, you haven't heard," Cowboy said. "Dickless wonder came down from his room this morning, tossed his keys on the desk, and took a walk. He decided to bolt before Zoltan fired him for thieving. Means we need to bring in some fresh blood to tend the bar."

"We?" Velvet asked.

"Zoltan is putting me in charge," he said.

"Did you know this?" Velvet asked. Darla shook her head. She had no idea. Fran had finished counting her tips first and stood up to stretch. It was no wonder she'd made a bundle. Fran was a statuesque, strawberry blonde with a low-cut blouse and flawless breasts that looked like they'd been carved by a Renaissance master. She also seemed to have a sweet, unassuming disposition which didn't hurt either. When she sat down again, she leapt into Cowboy's lap and his hands started to cruise her curves. Fran banged a fist into his chest.

"Don't. I've turned over a new leaf," she said, doing up the top buttons of her blouse in a reverse striptease. Seeing Darla's confusion, she explained she used to be an exotic dancer.

"Best boobs in the biz," Cowboy crowed as if the achievement was his.

"I'm a hoofer too," Darla said. "Although not in your line."

"No, you really don't have the right equipment, sweetie. No offense."

"None taken," Darla said. "I am a mammary midget, a mere titular figure beside you."

"Hey, you're pretty funny," Fran said. "What sort of dance you do?"

"Jazz, modern, took a little tap in Toronto."

"I have ten years of tap, used to throw it into my routine, drove the guys wild."

With the ice broken now, Fran and Darla discussed their mutual enthusiasm for dance then exchanged numbers.

"We can work out together sometime," Darla said.

"Absolutely," Fran agreed.

"Whoa," Cowboy cried out. "Did you just make a date with my girl?"

"Who says I'm your girl?" she said. "I do have other admirers."

"Who?" Cowboy asked. Fran either missed or ignored the quiet warning in Velvet's eyes.

"Eric the Red is one."

"Is that freaking biker bugging you? He's bad news, babe."

"He's a hunk."

"He'll be a hunk in chunks when I'm done with him," Cowboy growled.

"Don't mess with the Curb Stompers, Cowboy," Velvet said. "You aren't so tough, riding your rice rocket like a little European school girl."

"I gotta rocket for you right here in my pants," Cowboy said, cupping his crotch. "Change my oil, babe, I'll be good for another hundred miles."

"I've had it with this boys' club shit," Velvet said, dumping her ice water in his lap.

"Holy Mother of God," Cowboy yelped, jumping up and doing a jig while dabbing at his pants with a rag. The women laughed but when a door creaked open, his improvisational dance routine came to an abrupt conclusion. Cowboy grabbed a beer bottle by the neck. They had been closed for an hour. Nobody should be coming into the bar now. An oddball stood by the door, his spindly, white legs peeking out from under a moth-eaten robe and a big toe sticking out a hole in his slipper. He had icicles in his beard and moustache and hanging from his nose.

"We're closed, Boyko." Cowboy barked.

"Don't hassle me, man. I just walked over from my room at the Charlie. It's freezing out there. Where's Itchy Dick? Gave the fat fuck five bucks to get me smokes two hours ago and he never come back."

Cowboy jumped forward, moving faster than Darla had thought him capable and grabbed the character by the throat, banging him back out the door. He returned in a flash to sit with Fran. Darla was done counting her wealth and downed her drink.

"Time for Cinderella to hit the road," she said.

"We can share a cab," Velvet said. "What about you?"

"Call your sitter, Fran," Cowboy purred, kissing her neck.

"I'm staying," she said.

"Phone Duffy's, Darla," Velvet said. "Tell them it's for staff, they'll come faster."

Darla was on the payphone in the lobby when a man came downstairs from the rooms. She had seen him before but couldn't remember where. His sleep-tousled hair gave him a dishevelled look and the features of his face seemed to shift between sensitivity and strength, depending how the light hit him. He was only wearing jeans and had broad shoulders, a narrow waist. Tiny scars covered his arms in ragged rows from his wrists to his elbows. He was a wild-eyed, mystery man holding out a twenty dollar bill.

"Got change?" Donovan asked.

"It's your lucky night," she said, heaving her purse onto the desk to count out quarters.

"Can't believe the cost of smokes these days," he said. "Be glad when they finally bring out those dollar coins they keep talking about."

He collected the cash, crossed to the cigarette machine, and started pumping quarters into the coin slot, his body tensing and coalescing into a singular mass as the muscles in his arms and his back flexed and his ass tightened. Darla had a thing for edgy, intense men. As a young girl in Sunday school she had poured over the provocative pictures of a near-naked Jesus pinned like a butterfly, longing to take Christ off the cross to heal him with her kisses. She'd never shared this peculiar flight of imagination for obvious reasons, but here she was, fantasizing about peeling this man's jeans off like the skin of a grape.

Velvet tapped her on the shoulder. Darla turned and scanned the lobby.

"He's gone back to his room," Velvet said. "Kind of cute, eh?"

"I suppose the Neanderthal has his charm."

"Donovan Bender is no ape-man, Darla. Trust me. He's actually sort of sweet if you can get near enough to him. I like a little sweetness in my men; not too much, but some. Our taxi is waiting outside."

They settled into the back of the cab as a gaggle of drunks staggered by shouting.

"The anarchists are working late tonight," the driver muttered. "How was it in the bar?"

"Crazy busy with the winter blahs kicking in," Velvet said. "Great for making money but not so hot for riding my Harley."

"Know what you mean," the driver said. "I gotta '68 Triumph Tiger gathering dust in a garage in Steinbach."

He and Velvet started talking about motorcycles, dropping Darla first. She paid her half of the fare and the cabbie waited until she was inside the building before he pulled away. Upstairs, Darla changed into PJs, lit a joint, and made Jasmine tea, remembering where she'd seen the guy in the lobby before. It was two weeks ago at the Woodbine, the same day Downtown Tommy lost his drinking privileges.

So his name was Donovan Bender.

Taking Care of Business

First, he let his left arm and leg fall back behind his body then he leaned forward, swung the arm, and released the ball with a flick of the wrist. It slammed into the pins. Another strike. Tony Bender appreciated the art and the science of bowling; the geometry of applying a precise angle to obtain an optimal result, the physics required to achieve the necessary momentum for maximum impact. It shared attributes with some other activities he enjoyed, shooting pool and preserving his position of power. Even the hard plastic chair he was sitting on had some value. It kept him sharp and alert to developing issues. Dreaming was for half-wits. There were plenty of those floating around to provide fodder. Tony became adept at the skills he required to access his authority at the age of eight while playing on the Aberdeen School playground, separating rocks by colour, shape, and size to build a city of stones, scratching out roads and streets in the dirt with a stick, when a gang of older boys approached him and demanded cigarettes. He didn't have any. The biggest kid slugged him in the head and his friends found this funny. Without thinking, Tony picked up a large rock and smashed the bully in the face, braining him. The kid started bawling. His buddies backed off. After this, Tony pounded any potential rivals into a bloody pulp and as his reputation spread, he acquired notoriety. People deferred to him, looking to him for direction, allowing him to easily dominate the weak, which happened to be everyone.

MAC's was noisy, filled with teenagers on a hormone high, part of some keep-the-kids-out-of-trouble Christian bowling league. Good luck with that. Tony picked up a pencil and tore a sheet off the scorecard. He wrote down some names, listing them in order of priority, culpability, expendability. Sarah Grant`s goof would go first. The hit would need somebody who wasn't too sloppy, certainly not Bernie, considering how he'd screwed up the fire. Things were unsettled on the street and around the Albert because of him. Bernie broke the seal on a basically calm scene, putting everyone on edge. Tony needed a stable environment to operate his business. But maybe opportunity lurked in the chaos. Perhaps, he could turn a precarious state of affairs to advantage and use it to consolidate his position. He still had to eliminate a few loose ends. He looked at his list of names. While Jimmy Jazz could handle Sarah's skinner, he was a bull. He had no finesse. Tony didn't want Sarah upset by any unnecessary drama. The job required a more subtle touch, someone with a sense of its weight. Donovan was no enforcer, yet his experience with skinners meant he was capable of snuffing one. It might even be therapeutic for him. Tony pressed the pencil into the scorecard and put a question mark beside the second name. The Curb Stompers were keeping Eric the Red on a tight leash. He could skate for the time being. As for Prince and Billy Triangle, if they became serious competition for the cocaine trade, they would be history. Zoltan might be toast too if he didn't get the message soon. Then, there was this Scott Kostyk character, assuming he had spotted Bernie the night of the fire like Cowboy said. So, that was his list for the time being. Tony would wait to see which losers had to go. He could be patient.

Buck Tamblyn wasn't late today. He even showed up early. Tony told him to get a pair of bowling shoes and Buck looked at him like he was crazy but complied. Tony almost broke out laughing when the big man waddled back like a drunken penguin.

"They don't have anything in my size. These shoes are too small," Buck complained.

"Let's have a game," Tony said. Buck's play was predictably half-hearted, either out of disinterest, ineptitude, or fear. He lobbed one gutter ball, took out two pins with the second ball, and snagged a single pin with the third. After bowling a few bad frames and watching Tony get six strikes in a row, he threw up his hands and collapsed in a chair.

Buck hadn't seen Bernie strut into the bowling alley and sit at the lunch counter. He didn't know Bernie or that he'd set the fire. But Tony's little brother was showing off, conspicuously parading around like a movie gangster in a long leather coat. Buck slid an envelope across the small table to Tony.

"It's all there, down to the last fucking penny," he said. "I busted my butt pulling the cash together. Does this mean we're done?"

"We're good for now. If there is anything else, I'll let you know."

Buck left the bowling alley, still limping from the shoes. Bernie popped over. Tony hadn't seen him for a few weeks and he didn't look good. He couldn't keep still, his knee pumping like a piston. He was hurting.

"Eat something, Bernie; I'll get you a sandwich from the lunch counter."

"Food ain't what I need, man. Was that the chump from the fire?"

"Not so loud."

"I snatched the shotgun from the trunk of his car like you said, stashed it in my hidey-hole. Bet he was too scared to tell you it was missing, eh."

"Where did you snag that leather coat?"

"Took it off some pinhead giving the working girls on Albert Street grief."

"The Midnight Jeweller; you aren't supposed to be in that part of town, Bernie. You need to stay out of sight, stop fucking freelancing."

"Gimme a break, bro. I'm a little short, if you know what I mean."

"Jimmy Jazz will drop by, top up your stash, and nab the sawed-off tomorrow."

"How you know the piece is sawed-off?"

"I know you, Bernie. You left your calling card the night of the fire."

"No way; I only stuck around a little while to watch it flare up. Man, that blaze was a beaut though, went up so fast, Might have been my masterpiece."

"Someone saw you."

"Who was it? I'll kill 'em."

"No need. The sad sack is on my list."

"You gotta list now? You're a riot, Tony."

"You need to be good, Bernie. I have my hands full between the fire and Donovan being back on the street."

"Yeah, he's at the Albert. He looks pretty good."

"Never mind. You keep it together. Don't lose any more marbles than you already have."

"What you gonna do, Tony; toss me out a car like you did when we were kids?"

"Your laugh was irritating me."

"It was nerves, man. Whiskey Jack was so drunk, driving all over the road, and I thought he was gonna kill us. Spot me a few bucks till I see Jimmy."

Tony peeled off two bills.

"Keep the party down to a dull roar until the heat lifts, Bernie."

"Don't sweat it, bro. I swear, you're like Donnie and the old lady sometimes, the way you worry. Thanks for the cash."

Bernie bounced out of the bowling alley. Tony wrote his name down, put a question mark beside it. He had the kid at the front call him a cab and tossed him a tip, telling him to call the hotel when he was ready for some real work. The punk was smart but not too smart. Tony waited outside and smoked a cigar. Selkirk Avenue was quiet as a bone-yard on a weeknight.

Buzz was behind the wheel when the cab showed up. Whisky Jack must have taken the night off again. They zipped up Salter Street to the Albert. Buzz didn't bother with the meter. Tony stepped out of the taxi in time to catch Cowboy firing a hammered Hutterite into a snow bank, the drunk flying one way, his hat the other.

"Next time, you come here sober then get drunk," the desk clerk barked, reaching behind his back to retrieve a mickey of rye tucked in his belt. Tony followed him to the lobby. Cowboy was a clown who thought he was a maestro, turning the secrets of others into currency while he shielded his own. But he was transparent and his face fell when Tony explained how his new role as the bar manager was going to work. In the bar later, Tony sent a drink out to him in the front. Keep the old bugger happy for now.

Tony's table had good sightlines. Through the bank of windows on one wall he could see anyone coming into the hotel. When they walked into the bar, his table was what they faced first. It allowed him to eyeball them, let them know who was running the show. Otherwise, his view took in the entire expanse of the bar, including the washrooms and the rear exit to the parking lot. He could catch anyone coming in or going out that door too, long before they saw him. By the pool table, Big Ron leaned on a cue stick, looking lost. Velvet brought Tony's scotch and he told her to take Ron a drink, tell him to see him after his game. Big Ron was no pit-bull, no Jimmy Jazz, but he had size. It wouldn't hurt to have extra muscle. Scott Kostyk always seemed to be in the bar these days, drunk and buying booze for his new buddies; Cowboy and Itchy Dick. While the desk clerk reported that he blubbered about his dead wife but said nothing about the fire, his eyes never seemed to stop moving, scanning the bar, and checking things out. He could well be a problem. Donovan wandered into the bar. Tony arranged to meet him the next day somewhere to avoid Cowboy's satellite ears.

The next morning, Donovan was waiting by the Timothy Eaton statue, rubbing the left toe.

"For luck," he said.

"Fuck luck. You have me. Let's walk. I wanna smoke," Tony said. He stopped to light his cigar between the inner and outer doors. Some broad in a fur coat strolled by, sniffed the air, and shot him a dirty look. Tony hooked her eyes and held them until her boot heels click-clacked at double-time into the department store.

"You scared the poor woman, Tony," Donovan said and both brothers laughed, something that didn't happen often.

Out on the street, Tony jerked his head toward Graham and they hustled away from Portage Avenue, neither of them speaking. The crowd thinned out by the library.

"I gotta job needs your special touch," Tony said. "Bernie is good at kicking down doors, beating people up, starting fires, but he don't use his head. You do—sometimes too much—but that is another story. This is right up your alley, pays a grand. I got a skinner needs croaking."

Tony gave him a bowling alley scorecard with the information he needed. They hung a left at Broadway and headed toward Main Street.

"Lemme think about it," Donovan said.

"Don't take long. I need this done fast. Fuck walking," Tony said and flagged down a taxi. Donovan didn't get in with him.

"I'm meeting my buddy, Banjo Bob, at the Westminster," he said.

"It's awful close to Curb Stompers territory, Donovan."

"Don't worry, Tony, no bodies; I promise."

"Just the one I'm paying you for. Let me know when it's done."

Donovan turned onto Broadway and walked toward Osborne. Tony crossed the first name off the list as his taxi shot down Main to the Albert.

The Public Safety Building

Scott Kostyk placed his Pentax on the desk and watched the banker's eyes bulge. Nothing airy-fairy about a five hundred dollar camera. He explained he expected an arts grant to come in the mail any day now and the loans officer nodded sympathetically in that accommodating way they have when they want to lend you money. Kostyk's claim was a lie. He had no cash arriving in the foreseeable future. He might even lose the gallery if he didn't find the rent soon. Any guilt he had about duping the banker dissolved when the man agreed to increase his overextended line of credit, driving him deeper into debt. They were both just thieves conspiring in the collective dance of deception quickly bringing society closer to collapse. He might as well enjoy the ride while it lasted. The loans officer was doing the paperwork when a disturbance broke out at one of the wickets. A native man was becoming angry, trying to get through to a teller asking him confusing, condescending questions. Another bank employee was on the phone probably calling the police. Kostyk thought he should do something, maybe even close his account in protest. But instead he waited to sign the papers as the cops were handcuffing the man and leading him out.

The contract was complete, committing Kostyk to five more years of financial bondage. He could keep Confidential Exchange alive another six months without selling a single piece of art. But his first stop after the bank wasn't to see the landlord. The burning need to create something overwhelmed him. He couldn't waste another solitary second. Despite the depressing rebuke of the cynics, not everything had been said or done. Kostyk had already started to rise with the sun to sketch, write, and take photos, sometimes wandering the streets for hours to find the perfect subject and take the perfect shot. Certainly, painting couldn't be far behind.

Kostyk walked over to the Art Emporium to purchase oils and palette knives, long-haired brushes — bristles, filberts, and sables that would hold their shape better, lasting longer, and not leaving hair in the paint. He chose linen canvas over cotton and stretched it back at the gallery, constructing a fifteen by thirty-six-foot blank slate on which to paint his masterpiece. Once this was done, he fiddled with the canvas until he could drum his fingers on the surface and feel the bounce in the fabric. Then he put a palette together of burnt sienna, cobalt blue, cadmium yellow, and ivory black. He was ready. Kostyk waited. Nothing happened. The untouched canvas taunted him. The possibility his earlier paralysis might have become terminal unnerved him.

He went to his desk and started absently rifling through drawers, not looking for anything in particular, just feeling the need to do something. Under a pile of papers; grant applications, collectors' correspondence, and reviews by art critics, he came across the letters he wrote to his mother. She'd sent them all back unopened with return-to-sender scribbled across the front of the envelopes in her old-world scrawl.

Kostyk's father had died five years after he left Grand Forks. He went back for the funeral with Svetlana. His mother was happy to see him, less so when he told her he wasn't staying. She accused him of choosing his Canadian bitch over her and hadn't talked to him since then. Kostyk could imagine her now, still working in the store, wearing widow's black, bending over the cash register, counting out money while the neighbourhood kids robbed her blind. Kostyk found a letter from his old friend, Hayden, who, unlike him, had actually made it to the Art Institute in Chicago and taught there now. His letter had arrived three weeks ago, on January twelfth, ten days before his birthday, and just one after the fire. Kostyk hadn't read it yet and tore open the envelope.

Hey Kos, still lurching around on the muskeg eating fish-
eyes? After my vernissage last week I had a heavy date and she
brought a friend we sadly bundled off in a taxi because my wingman
is MIA on an ice floe. Best get your butt stateside, man. A whole
retro-realism thing happening here that is right up your canvas.
Come back before I drown in paint and pussy. Hayden.

The letter was filled with his friend's usual provocative
prattle. Hayden hadn't changed in ten years. But there was
something in what he was saying. Why was Kostyk hanging
around the Peg like a puppy tethered to a pole? He touched
his finger to the weigh scale on his desk, a gift from Svetlana
for his thirty-third birthday. She gave it to him early after
their last fight. She had screamed until hoarse yanking the
scale from a hiding place, flinging it at him, and saying it
was the perfect present for an Aquarius with a Libra Rising
whatever the hell that meant. Then she'd walked out of his
life, apparently forever this time.

The gallery lay in darkness except for the area
surrounding his canvas. He didn't need light to make his way
around. He knew the exact position of every single piece of art
having placed each in precise proximity to the next in order
to achieve an aesthetic balance; this was his unique gift. But
these stern shadows — the paintings, sculptures, and mixed-
media installations — were postmodern dreck, black holes
pulling him away from his own work. There was Sylvester
Eleven's 'Louis Riel' an abstract, mottled construction, more
moon rock than sculpture, another gigantic, raven-type thing,
perching in a corner of Confidential Exchange waiting for
something to die. Some days Kostyk wanted to take a chisel
and chainsaw to the lot. The single exception to this tedious
muddle was Svetlana's 'Red River Rusalka Rising'. Kostyk
went to one of the large windows overlooking Albert Street and
opened the curtain to reveal her work. Svetlana wrestled with
the sculpture for two years, chiselling and hammering and
sanding until three willowy black-marble figures rose above
a granite base of jagged waves. She would hunch over the
piece, skin glistening with sweat, muscular fingers, arms, and

shoulders poised to strike as she would focus, concentrating on the position of the chisel to determine how hard or gently to deliver a blow, and then there would be a sharp rap and a section of marble fall away. Svetlana finished the sculpture six months before the fire. Kostyk ran his fingertips along its smooth, sensual surface, feeling the flow of lines, the cruel curves, and the edges articulating lives cut short.

Svetlana massaged the Ukrainian myth of the Rusalka to depict the lives of young women slain down by the river in recent years, thinking to honour their spirits with her work. The reviews of it were mixed. Some critics lauded the work as a significant, meaningful achievement; others claimed she was exploiting a tragedy and appropriating pain that wasn't hers. Still, there was no disputing the raw power of her piece. The sinuous, writhing shapes of the Rusalka seemed to strain against definition and the form she'd imposed on them. Had Svetlana elevated or exploited them, reducing them to prisoners of the marble and her genius? The three figures reached out to the observer with tormented faces and flailing limbs. Kostyk could feel the tug of the Red River pulling him under and hear the muffled screams, a banshee wail more angry than mournful, more punk rock than lament. The sound dug deep and emptied him of everything except lingering, sad longing. Svetlana surfaced now, forgiving him for leaving her to die and for living. Yes! He was alive! He could still feel, even if it was only a hole inside him. He yearned to flow out of himself to embrace Svetlana, touch her ethereal shape as she flirted with him, floating farther off, waving disintegrating fingers as her flesh fell away and she slid back into formlessness. Kostyk closed his eyes and surrendered to an intense palette of colour, a drizzle of fireworks popping in his brain as fierce tears pounded him with their force, rubbing one raw nerve against the next. He had lost Svetlana, not once or twice, but three times. He wouldn't lose her again.

Seized by sudden desire, Kostyk leapt to his feet, lunged at all the other drapes, and opened them, flooding the space with light. He pushed aside the furniture, shoved canvasses into corners, and dragged sculptures to the edges of the gallery, gouging deep scratches in the hardwood floor as he converted Confidential Exchange into a studio to trade body blows with his creativity.

The process of painting begins with prowling and Kostyk stomped back and forth in front of the virgin canvas, not concerned with content, or constrained by concept, but submitting to impulse, allowing intuition to dominate. Finally, he dipped a brush in colour, attacking the canvas, flying from one end to the other, flinging icy blue and burning vermilion with abandon. He took a tube of ivory black, squeezed thick, creamy paint on his fingers, and pressed it into the fabric, rubbing Rorschach blotches of swollen texture into the weave. Pinching a dollop of burnt sienna between his fingers, he lavished it onto the surface, tweaking and squeezing and kneading it into shapes; pretzels, circles, and triangles. The dark of night came early in January and he closed the curtains again but continued to work, drinking in the magical fusion of light and shadow like a fine, chiaroscuro wine. At the bottom of the canvas, the figure of a naked woman was taking shape, stretching across the length of it to form a devastated horizon. Kostyk rummaged through his photos, smudging them with colour, until he found a picture of Svetlana he'd taken when they first met. He cut off her head with a pair of scissors and pasted it onto the emerging body of an indigo-blue earth-mother. He added more photos of her, some happy and smiling, some not, and daubed an angry, crimson crown around the many-headed goddess taking shape as the surface of the fabric burst into a spontaneous combustion of colour and collage he created from the parts of other pictures — newspaper clippings, theatre tickets, and fragments of poetry. Kostyk was on fire now, a conduit, arms flapping with the cheerful slap of paint on canvas, body flushed as he bent and crouched and stretched. Fuelled by cigarettes, coffee, and smoked meat sandwiches, not sleeping, washing for days, or even thinking, he painted. On the seventh day, Kostyk crashed. Twelve hours after collapsing among the half-squeezed tubes of paint, dirty plates, and empty soft drink cans, Kostyk woke to find his skin stained with color, Confidential Exchange a chaotic rainbow of crazed splatters. The voluptuous odours of oils and turpentine intoxicated him. He was no longer a pretentious dilettante or art dandy but a practicing painter.

Kostyk hadn't left the gallery in many days and realized if he could smell his own stink, others would too. He rose from the floor to freshen up in the bathroom sink. He could shower, get some food, and maybe grab a drink at the Albert. He decided to drag his camera along and, filled with energy, took the stairs instead of the elevator, flying down eleven floors. On the street, a bright morning sun almost knocked him over, but he swallowed fistfuls of frozen air and strode to the hotel with a light step.

Bertha's Place was deserted as usual. Kostyk had no idea how it managed to stay open. Over the last couple of years, several owners had tried to make a go of running the café, each convinced they could prosper. Some offered substandard food, thinking they would make some easy money. They went broke. Others sold overpriced, elaborate fare, entertaining the unrealistic expectation of providing a fine dining experience, despite the café being a dive, they also failed. The current occupant, Bertha Lobchuk, had managed to prevail though. He took a table near the window and watched her vigorously shaking her hips as she shimmied to a sultry Sarah Vaughn version of 'Black Coffee' blasting on the stereo. Then she saw him, stopped dancing, turned off the music, and approached him, accelerating until it looked like she was going to roll right on by his table. But Bertha reared back on her heels and pivoted toward him like a burly ballerina. She was pleased when he ordered a plate of pierogies. Her specialty was not as good as his mother's but passable. While he ate, Kostyk scanned obituaries in the newspaper; it was not something he normally did. Bertha cleared away his dishes after he was done. He asked for a beer and started drawing on a place mat she left behind, not stopping to study what took shape, allowing his hand to freely scribble while he looked out the window at fluttering snowflakes like albino butterflies covering everything in white. Familiar faces filled the window. Kostyk dropped the pencil and cursed. So far, he had managed to avoid his friends, mastering the art of hiding in plain sight, exploiting the hotel's maze of exits and entrances. They would walk in one door and he would leave by another. But they'd seen him this time and there was no escape as Karmin, Sebastian, Sylvester Eleven, and Lethal Spit piled through the door and sat at his table.

"Well, if it isn't the wasted wonder of the western world," Lethal Spit said. "Buy you a beer, man?"

"Where's Furnace Face?" Kostyk asked. "Gluepot never misses a gathering of the troops."

"He's in hospital," Karmin said. "He got jumped heading into the Bate for a meeting. They broke his nose, jaw, three ribs, and a leg. He has tubes coming out every hole in his body and may have to wear a colostomy bag for the rest of his life. You should go see him, Scott."

"What's happening with your buddy, Zoltan, man?" Lethal Spit said. "He still hasn't given us a date for the Benefit. He's behaving kind of like you are, Kostyk — doesn't answer the phone and is never around when we try to see him. You two shacking up?"

Kostyk knew Zoltan was a friend of the arts, allowing writers on the ropes to stay at the hotel, feeding poor poets, and lending money to out-of-work musicians and actors. But he didn't like to commit to anything and could be evasive, especially if he was dealing with a cash crunch like now. Still, guilt always worked wonders with him.

"Don't worry, I'll get a date for you," Kostyk said, "And besides that, I have a piece I want to present at the Benefit."

"Don't say, you're dabbling in masturbation and madness while missing in action," Lethal Spit said.

"The queen of glib strikes again," Kostyk snarled, snatching his bag. "Have a nice day, if I may leave on a platitude,"

"As long as you don't live on one," she shouted as he banged out the door.

It was still early and the bar was empty. Kostyk ordered, telling Velvet he wanted to talk to Zoltan. She crossed to the bar and made a phone call. Not long after, Zoltan cruised in through a side entrance. At first, he tried to dodge the subject of the Benefit but Kostyk didn't let him off the hook and Zoltan finally agreed to contact Karmin with a date. Then he put an arm around his friend's shoulder.

"Listen, while I appreciate the small spike in liquor sales your presence represents, you need to give the bar a break. You are out of your element, a deep man in the shallow end, and I do not want to see you drown. Stay away awhile. Okay, I gotta boogie."

Zoltan scooted out the back door to the parking lot, looking over his shoulder as he left. Velvet dropped a drink on Kostyk's table.

"Take this slow. It's sipping whiskey, Scott."

"You know my name?"

"I know the names of all my regulars."

"If I'm a regular, can I run a tab?"

"Now you sound like Cowboy, but cute for a deadbeat."

"I'm not a deadbeat. I'm an artist."

"Sure you are. You didn't get all the paint off," she said, licking her thumb and dragging it down his cheek before returning to the bar. Velvet's touch ignited something in Kostyk. He lifted a glass to his lips. Velvet was right. Hennessy was sipping whiskey. He took his time, savouring the cognac's taste and texture. Karmin barged through the door and stormed to his table.

"What's wrong with you, Scott?" she asked. "You're being a jerk. Spit can be an ass, but you never let her bother you before."

"Treat me like an idiot, I'll be an asshole."

"You've changed so much, become antisocial."

"I have a rich inner life."

"I miss the old Scott Kostyk."

"I am he, Karmin. Ten years ago, when I first came to this city, I was full of piss and vinegar. I had no patience for any of that nihilistic navel-gazing or the self-righteous, new wave Nazis brandishing condescending comments and raised eyebrows instead of baseball bats and broken bottles."

"You're talking crazy now."

"When all else fails trot out the straitjacket," Kostyk said, sipping his cognac.

"And you're drinking too much."

"Have one with me."

"You're hurting, Scott, but so are the others. They aren't just intellectual constructs, chess pieces you can shuffle around in your brain."

"Last week, I was in a coffee shop, Karmin. I saw a decrepit woman sitting at the counter, one of those sad, broken women you see around. I could smell her halfway across the room. You know why old people always smell bad? It's because they're rotting inside. We're all decaying."

Karmin stood and left. Kostyk raised his glass and drained it. He had travelled far from his friends in the three weeks since the fire. They were still locked in an absurd paradigm, mistaking posture for performance and self-indulgence for expression. He would present his new piece, a brilliant, outrageous work at the Benefit and challenge them to recognize that art wasn't a vehicle for their vanity but a provocation.

The bar was starting to pick up with people coming in for a quick drink and the ninety-nine cent lunch. A few wouldn't go back to work after, but spend the rest of the afternoon and half the night drinking. Besides his gallery, this was the only place Kostyk felt comfortable these days. The crowd was down-to-earth and their cacophony calming. He didn't need to talk or think, just follow a simple formula — buy a round, make a friend, repeat as necessary. Itchy Dick was right on cue. He materialized from out of nowhere, picking his nose with one hand and scratching his crotch with the other. The man had a real talent for sniffing out the soft touch but was easygoing and unthreatening, uncritical company. Kostyk invited him to sit down and bought him a drink.

"You're a bud," the moocher said. "Overheard your babe there; not cool considering what you've been through with the fire, your wife being dead and all. Arson is so heavy, man. Those poor people didn't stand a chance. Who would start a fire like that you think? And why?"

Kostyk shrugged. Itchy Dick stopped prattling and didn't push or probe any further. Before long, Cowboy joined them.

"Gimme five," Itchy Dick cried out.

"Take ten," Cowboy grumped. "I need a good stiff one."

"Hard getting hard at your age," Itchy Dick cracked.

"I am gonna hammer you, Dick," Cowboy warned, his voice low and intense.

"You're so freaking melodramatic, man," Itchy Dick said.

"Nothing mellow about me," Cowboy mumbled then cupped his hands around his mouth and hollered. Velvet didn't respond. He bellowed again. She took her time getting to the table.

"Keep barking orders, you'll be putting what teeth you have left in a cup at night. Can't believe Zoltan is letting you run the bar."

"Lighten up, baby and bring us a round," Cowboy purred. "Put your wallet away, Kostyk. It's on the house. So, you and your pals still plan to bring five fucking bands into my house on a Friday night? Boss hasn't said another word, but I assume it's still on and I got a real bad feeling in my bones about it."

"Maybe it's your arthritis acting up," Itchy Dick said.

"How you know I got arthritis?" Cowboy snapped. "You better stop bumming booze and bugging people around here; keep putting your brown nose where it don't belong, someone is gonna lop the fucking thing off. And quit all that scratching! I swear to God, you bring bedbugs in here, you're a dead man! I will personally fumigate your ass."

A pale kid scuttled into the bar, pivoted by Tony Bender's table, and knelt there, bouncing up and down on the balls of his feet. It was bizarre, intriguing behaviour. He had no meat to him and his face was a sunken mask, his eyes receding into the sockets. LOVE was tattooed in ink on the fingers of his left hand, HATE on the right. His loud voice squeaked.

"You somebody what helps them zigzagging with their state-ability, Tony. Gimme two sets today, I'll pay tomorrow."

The pusher turned to Jimmy Jazz who was suddenly airborne, jumping up from his chair, grabbing the speed-freak by the throat, and firing him out the door. There was a loud bang in the lobby and the thin echo of a scream being choked off. Other than Itchy Dick, whose head bobbed like a prairie gopher, everyone else in the bar was acting as if nothing happened.

"Never thought I'd live past thirty," The moocher said, shifting gears. "Now I don't know what to do with myself. It's all valves and vents eh, openings and closings."

"See what comes of doing too much acid," Cowboy quipped and ordered a round.

"I hate fucking birds, man," Itchy Dick said.

"Then don't fuck 'em," Cowboy said.

"I don't fuck 'em, fool! I feed 'em! Least, I did till last summer. I was in the park, sharing my muffin with a panhandling sparrow. He started to peck at what I was putting in my mouth so I shooed him away. Next you know, bird goes gangster, flies in a tree over my head, and shits on me. Happens all the time now. I sit under a tree, a bird poops on me. They must have a telegraph line or something to tell each other."

Kostyk enjoyed this banter and the more mindless it was, the better. Cowboy invited two other men Kostyk had seen in the bar before over to their table. Donovan Bender was a fifties throwback with a ducktail, not one of those wannabe greasers like the crowd that Combo Combo catered to when they were grinding out rockabilly, but the real thing with a scar below his left eye running down to his upper lip and the hard edge of a man marinated in misery. His travelling companion, Banjo Bob Holiday, was a short, scruffy relic from the sixties with a shaggy mane and gentle, round face that held no malice or menace. He looked like a half-frozen lawn elf in his toque and shabby parka torn on one side. He didn't wear a scarf or gloves and gripped his banjo case with beet-red hands, revealing a deck of half-rotten teeth when he smiled.

"Play you a tune for a drink," he said. Kostyk said he would pass on the music but spring for a beer. This seemed to mollify the geriatric hippie. Velvet had cut off Cowboy's free drinks and so he was appealing to Fran.

"I can't afford to keep you in booze," she said. "My heating bill is crazy this winter."

"Just one drink, sweetie," he said. "You know I love you."

"Tell you what. Itchy Dick has been drooling all over me lately. Get him the hell outta here, I'll buy you a double."

"I'll fucking kill him!" Cowboy cried out. Fran sighed.

"I don't want him dead; just gone."

The desk clerk jabbed a thumb at the door and Kostyk was surprised when Itchy Dick left without complaint.

"Something seriously wrong with that character," Cowboy muttered. "Takes goofy to a whole other level. I haven't figured out what's going on with him yet, but I will."

The door swung open and Eric the Red strode into the bar with two buddies. He nodded to Tony, went to stand by the bar, and glared at Donovan. Fran placed a Southern Comfort in front of him. He downed it. She poured another.

"That's my girl," he said, looking Fran up one side and down the other like a side of beef. Cowboy was fuming, a veil of cigarette smoke curling around his head. Eric turned to Donovan. Their eyes locked and a channel opened up between them, flooding the bar with hostile energy.

"Donovan Bender, big man on the straightaway, chicken-shit on the curves," Eric said. But Velvet intervened, topping up the biker's glass.

"Better put your peckers back in your pants before you go off in each other's face," she said and Eric laughed, wagging a finger at her.

"Only you could get away saying that, darling," he said. He shot Donovan another dirty look, winked at Fran who smiled back, and left the bar without paying for his drinks. Donovan went out after the bikers did and Jimmy Jazz followed him. Cowboy seemed to be upset. Kostyk decided to dissolve the black cloud.

"The sycophant and art dealer are dead!" he exclaimed. "Long live the paint-slinger!"

"You're drunk, man," Cowboy mumbled. "Hurts my head listening to you."

"Let's have another drink then. I'm buying," Kostyk said.

After a few rounds of booze and Bob strumming his banjo, the wheels of conversation were greased and a gregarious Cowboy started to tell tall tales about his youth. He was the only child of a single mother who read him the classics; Nabokov, Fitzgerald, and Virginia Woolf. He shared stories of working as an orderly in a psych hospital and a fishing guide in the Northwest Territories. Kostyk was inspired by all this and reached for the Pentax, started taking pictures of Cowboy doing his Marlboro Man act, snapping shots of him grimacing and grinning, winking at a woman leaving the bar then wiggling his tongue at her retreating back. Kostyk sought out other subjects. Fran offered her profile, thrusting her upper body forward, her bottom back. She was a living, breathing French postcard, sultry and curvaceous with a Botticelli figure. Svetlana would have loved to sculpt the woman, Kostyk to paint her. Velvet placed a drink in front of him.

"Your peepers are popping out, pal. Put the camera away," she said but the warmth in her voice trumped any warning. Kostyk aimed his camera at her and Velvet walked away before he could take her picture. He angled the Pentax at the regulars playing pool and a mirror behind the bar, reflecting liquor bottles lined up like religious icons. He snapped a shot of some customers coming through the door. The flash of the camera startled them. They turned around and walked out. Kostyk took photos of the stained glass skylight, the stage, jukebox, Jimmy Jazz, and Tony Bender. He focused the camera to take another when a black blur blocked the lens, obscuring his view. He looked away. Jimmy Jazz hovered over him. The big man snatched the Pentax, turned it over in his massive paws, and tossed it in the air. The breath went out of Kostyk. But Jimmy Jazz caught the camera and set it down again. He leaned in close, clamped Kostyk's jaw in one hand, and twisted his head up.

"Gimme a cigarette or I'll break your fucking arm," Jimmy Jazz said with a laugh. Kostyk chuckled. He knew Winnipeg humour when he heard it.

"You think Jimmy Jazz is a joke—flaunting your little bit of knowledge, playing big shot, buying drinks, and taking pictures of people? You're lucky I don't smash that camera."

Jimmy Jazz took several of Kostyk's cigarettes and went back to sit with Tony Bender. Velvet slammed her tray down and told Fran to watch her section. She yanked Kostyk to his feet, pulled him out the door and into the street. She wasn't wearing a coat but the cold didn't seem to bother her as the wind splashed her long, bone-black hair against a blue sky.

"Where is your gallery?" she asked. Kostyk pointed. They ran to the Chambers Building. In the lobby, Velvet stopped to stare at polished granite walls, mahogany veneer, marble floors, and bronze cage elevators.

"I walk by here every day, had no idea it looked like this inside," she said. Kostyk wasn't surprised by her awe. Eight years ago he'd opened Confidential Exchange on the eleventh floor. Colleagues were sceptical; convinced he was crazy putting a gallery on the top floor. Ground level, second storey, third at most, was de rigueur for an art gallery. But Kostyk secured a good deal on the lease and the Notre Dame Chambers was well-maintained during its lean years. The building boasted exterior terra cotta walls with vertical columns that had six thousand light bulbs embedded in them offering a dazzling display at night. Kostyk was convinced that word would get out and collectors would be charmed with the journey to the eleventh floor of the Chambers Building becoming an integral element of the Confidential Exchange experience. And it worked for awhile, until the novelty wore off.

"Come up with me for a minute," he said. Kostyk unlocked the door and the smell hit him first then the mess. He'd forgotten he was camping out there. He made a quick effort to clean as Velvet wandered around. She stopped in front of his painting.

"It isn't finished," he explained. She nodded and moved on, this time pausing in front of Svetlana's sculpture.

"You do this one?" she asked.

"It's my wife's work," he said. Velvet studied 'Red River Rusalka Rising'.

"Life is sad. Art lifts the burden for people of feeling," she said. "The fact you're shocked I know Flaubert isn't flattering. I read, knit, ride my Harley; don't do drugs, drink, screw around."

"I just thought the observation was astute; I wasn't judging."

"Yes, you were. Listen to Zoltan — stay out of the Albert, stop hanging around the bar, and definitely don't bring a camera into it."

"I was only taking pictures."

"You need to get a grip and stop shovelling clouds. That warehouse was not torched by kids on a spree or some homeless guy trying to get warm."

"You seem to know a lot about this."

"There you go — thinking and not thinking. You aren't as clever as you think, Scott. I need to go back before Fran gets slammed. You be good, you hear me."

Velvet took his face in her hands, kissed him with the softest lips he'd ever felt, and then was gone. Kostyk didn't move for a long while then decided to clean more to take his mind off things. He soaked paint brushes, scraped pigment off the palette, and washed the floor. But his efforts were half-hearted. He was avoiding the obvious. He hadn't taken a good hard look at his canvas since starting it and was still reluctant. Yet, he wanted to see what Velvet had. He needed some fortification first, found a bottle of red wine left over from a vernissage, and took a few deep swallows before facing his work. It wasn't like anything he'd ever done; not a landscape, portrait, or still-life, but something else, something hideous.

Paint had been hurled at the canvas, leaving craters of colour and crudely executed shapes, strokes reminiscent of Beardsley, Bosch, and Munch. Flames poured from wide-eyed windows, wreathing the warehouse in frozen fire while smoky, wraith-like ravens clamoured along the edges of the fabric, waiting to consume carrion. Thalo-green pus oozed from the perforated organs of stick figures scorched scarlet as they ran across the shuddering surface of the reclining earth mother and Svetlana's moon-face beamed from multiple heads. In one corner, Oscar and the homeless man had plaster faces with lips and cheeks rouged as they lay in snug coffins like caterpillars in cocoons. Kostyk contemplated the canvas while chewing on a brush then realized he was eating paint. He threw the brush at the piece tearing the fabric then heaved the bottle of wine at it, baptizing the painting in red. He lit a candle, held it close to the canvas and watched smoke darken around the burning building as the paint bubbled up. A small black hole appeared and Kostyk pulled the candle away, not wanting to start a fire. Still, the ripped and charred areas lent the painting depth it hadn't possessed before. He snatched a utility knife, slashed Svetlana's pelvis. The incision added texture and he set to work again, a candle in one hand, a knife in the other, going crazy, sketching cartoons of Cowboy, Itchy Dick, and Jimmy Jazz. He brought the anaemic speed-freak to life under the watchful eye of Sauron veiled in cigar smoke. After he had developed the pictures he took today, he would incorporate them into the work. But something was missing. Kostyk knew what he needed to do and grabbed his camera.

At the far end of Albert Street, he smelled smoke still clinging to the air three-and-a-half weeks after the fire. In the harsh light of day with much warmer weather, the terrible beauty he'd witnessed on a brutally cold night weeks ago had disappeared. All that remained now were piles of filthy, broken brick and charcoal-smeared concrete. He started to take pictures, stepping over the debris, walking around barriers to get inside the building. Kostyk kicked aside rubble; coiled wire, sticks of furniture, and broken glass. He was setting up a shot of the scorched Lithium sign when someone tapped him on the shoulder. Kostyk spun around to face a cop who looked far too young to be carrying a gun; yet there it was on his hip. His nose and cheeks were red and he was shivering. Winnipeg's cold weather was an equalizer.

"You can't be here," the cop said. "This fire is under investigation."

Two squad cars roared up. A husky gym rat popped out of one of them and a woman, who seemed to be in charge, from the other. She asked for his ID and the camera.

"I know my rights," Kostyk said.

"Alright then, we'll continue this conversation at the Public Safety Building," she said. The stance of the first cop shifted as he spread his legs; the gym rat's puffed-up chest swelled larger. They yanked Kostyk's arms around his back and handcuffed him, while she secured his camera.

The police station with the Orwellian moniker occupied a whole city block at Princess and William. Giant cement slabs had long, narrow windows that gave the building the look of a large jail cell. The interior was equally intimidating with a zigzag array of cubicles and pugnacious fluorescents. The cops went through his pockets, took his wallet and belt, and fingerprinted him, saying he was being held for questioning about the fire. He threatened to call the media and sue them if his camera was damaged or film destroyed. He was taken to a cell with graffiti-stained walls and reeking of urine. In his thirty-three years, Kostyk had never been in jail before. But it somehow seemed like an appropriate initiation into the new world he had entered.

The Doris Papers

At the end of a very long series of thoughts, Doris Bender started retracing them back to the first, attempting to anchor her heart and stop feeling. Sleep came in thirty second snatches, voices mumbling about her condition in the dark room, barking orders at aides. She felt tubes in her nose, arms, and down below. She tried to lift her head but it flopped back on the pillow and when she tried to scratch an itch, she couldn't. Her hands were tied to the bed. Doris had done the ghost dance for years, letting it take her one piece at a time. Now, it was catching up to her, carrying her away, and shutting her down. Life was spilling out of her. She longed to feel the cold, yearned to leave her burning heart behind with a short, one-way trip from intensive care to casket; no lingering in a geriatric hell where even instinct would fail. Death would end all the wondering, the waiting, and the worrying. But, in fact, she wasn't there—not yet.

She was at home with her husband snoring next to her in the bed. The way he honked, it was a wonder he didn't blow his brains out. Whiskey Jack was most charming unconscious. He had been the man of her dreams in 1944, striding a Norton motorcycle, wearing a leather jacket, his handlebar moustache hiding the knife scar above his lip. The old biddies said they wouldn't last six months. Forty years later, Doris wondered if the two of them only stayed together to spite them. She watched him sleeping so blissfully and unaware. She believed him when he told her he didn't dream. Jack didn't think. How could he dream? He was a blank slate, an animal, and a sex fiend. Because of his bottomless desire, Doris banged out a son a year for five until she cut him off when

Bernie was born. Afterward, she was sad all the time, bawling like a junkie who needed a fix of tears. It was the only way she felt alive, knew she had any feelings. Whiskey Jack called her crazy. A shrink agreed, diagnosed her as a manic depressive. They locked her up, pumped her full of lithium, and dulled her senses with shock treatment. Light leaked out of her like a sieve and when she was worn out from crying, had no tears left, she stopped feeling. Back at home she took her meds with a gin chaser. Six years passed and, in a moment of weakness, she gave in to Whiskey Jack and Donovan was born, the last of her sons, her favourite.

Whiskey Jack had beaten his boys bloody. He'd mellowed the last few years, not because his heart was softening, but because his head was. The boys were bigger too, capable of taking him. He tried to fight off the creep of age and was losing; his bones groaning, his heart skipping a beat or two, his mind drifting. Now, he lay in bed with weather-beaten skin stretched tight over his skull, erosion carving crevices in his rock-hard features. If she set him on fire, his face would lose its shape and start melting, the flesh dripping off as it collapsed. She lit a smoke. Whiskey Jack snorted. She could feel his brain spinning like it held an idea.

"Smoking in bed again?" he asked.

"You have a lightening grasp of the obvious, Jack."

"What the hell does that mean? Anything? You'll burn us out one of these days, woman."

Doris climbed out of bed, went to the kitchen, and poured a gin. She took it to the living room, sat in her chair, and sipped the drink. It was still dark out on the street, the first miserable day of February. The snow had come early in late autumn and would stay long. Doris sensed the storm clouds gathering, trouble brewing with her boys. She knew she would probably put one in the ground before she went under. All her sons had filled her heart with grief but Donovan broke it. Her glass was empty. She went to the kitchen for a refill.

"Hey, Dor," Whiskey Jack called from the bedroom. "Fix me one too."

She pulled his bottle of rye down from a cupboard and started pouring, kept pouring until whiskey was slopping over the side of the glass. Jack came into the kitchen in a scruffy robe, his hair sticking out in every direction, and exploded.

"You fucking crazy woman," he shouted. He snatched the bottle away from her, dropped a dishrag on the counter to soak up the booze, and wrung it into a bowl before siphoning it back into the bottle. Doris had to admit Whiskey Jack could be resourceful when it came to drink.

They both drank in silence in the living room and she was thankful for this respite. But he couldn't let it rest, or allow peace to reign for long. He rattled the ice cubes in his glass.

"What you do all day here alone?" he asked.

"Besides screwing boyfriends, nothing," she said.

"You need to get out more, babe. Take a walk, have tea with the ladies at the legion."

"There are no ladies at the legion."

"Don't be that way. Some of those old broads ain't bad company."

"How do you know that, Jack?"

"Don't provoke me, woman. You're trying to start a fight and I'm not in the mood. "

"You never are."

"Guess I'm just a happy guy."

"Wish I was like you, never sick, eating whatever you want, seeing things simple. You'll probably die in bed with a bottle in one hand and a fancy woman in the other."

"Who thinks that far ahead?"

"I wonder sometimes who will go first—you or me."

"Don't matter. Dead is dead. Wondering don't make it less so."

"We're alcoholics, Jack. You hear me?"

"I always hear you, Dor. What time is it?"

'Two forty-five."

"Good lord, I gotta be up for work at six."

"Go back to bed," she said and he surprised her by listening for a change. Doris turned on TV. 'Barnaby Jones' should start soon. Instead of her show, the screen was filled with fire trucks and police cars. She turned up the sound to hear the announcer.

"This is Steve Brogan reporting from Flora and Andrews in the North End where a tactical team in the house behind me waits for orders."

"Jack!" Doris cried.

"Would you mind having your nervous breakdown a little more quietly, Doris? I have to be up soon."

"The police are at my mother's place."

"What else is new?"

"It's on TV, Jack," she shouted. This brought him to the door. "My mother needs me."

"No, she doesn't. That battle axe hasn't talked to us in eighteen years. I'm going to bed."

Doris stared at the TV after he was gone. She wondered if there had been a break-in or fire. Last year, her mother's friend Annie had been beaten to death with a hammer by two kids. Doris never found out how her mother dealt with that. There had been a time they talked on the phone for hours every day. But the old lady refused to talk to her after their fight over Donovan. When Bernie went to reform school for torching the Trick Shop, Donovan stopped talking. Of her six sons, he and Bernie were the closest in age and grew up together. For some reason, her mother had decided Donovan would be better off living with her and launched a custody battle. She lost and hadn't spoken to Doris since. The woman could cut you dead if she thought you crossed her. The last time Doris saw her, she was in hospital after a stroke. She'd sat tall in the bed, grinning at the nurses and doctors, her only regret missing the Battle Royale at the Winnipeg Arena with twenty wrestlers in a cage match. Being sick agreed with the old lady.

Doris had to see her. She didn't want to go to the grave without reconciling. The house on Flora was only twelve blocks away. Doris put on her slippers, grabbed her gin, and sailed out the door. She didn't feel the cold until a sudden surge pressed into her chest. She couldn't breathe and stopped. Gripping a chain-link fence, she sipped her gin and waited until the greyhounds galloping in her head settled then started walking again.

The scene at her mother's house was a wild pinball machine with flashing lights spearing the sky. Doris stood by the fence, frost in her hair curlers, glasses fogged-up. She pushed on the gate but a cop in a buffalo coat blocked her way. He frowned and shook his head.

"It's my mother place," she said. He went inside the house. Time dissolved and Doris lost track of it. Her gin turned into chicken noodle soup warming her hands, steam curling up from the cup and sliding into the street to become winter fog, then speech bubbles over the heads of firefighters and police. Why was she in the back of a cop car? Did she throw a brick through Mischa Pollock's store window again or go after Whiskey Jack with a pair of pinking shears? No, she hadn't killed her husband, a part of her happy she hadn't murdered him, another part disappointed he was still breathing.

The cop dived into the front of the car and turned to face her. His snowy eyebrows and moustache made him look like an arctic troll.

"Your mother doesn't want to see you."

"Is she okay?" Doris asked. He laughed.

"She's in her glory, running around the kitchen making cookies and coffee for the guys."

"Sounds like her."

"A neighbour is holding his wife and kids hostage down the street and we can see into his living room from the upstairs window of her house."

"You're Indian," Doris said.

"Cree," he said.

"Never seen no Indian cop before."

"There aren't many of us. I'll take you home," he said. A crowd gathered on the street tried to get a peek at her in the back.

"Don't look like much," one said.

The Cree cop drove up to Selkirk Avenue and then towards Main Street. It was quiet in the cruiser except for a squawking radio. Doris felt his eyes on her in the rear-view. She figured he had seen women like her before with javex-stained skin and booze eating them alive. She stared back. He returned to his world, leaving her to hers. He hung a left at Charles and tore through the intersections — Pritchard, Manitoba, Magnus, Burrows, Alfred, Aberdeen, and Boyd. He pulled over at College and unlocked her door. Doris got out. The morning air was chilly. She tapped on his window. The frost had melted off his face and he was more St. Bernard than troll now.

"Thanks," she said. He nodded and pulled away.

Hints of shrivelled pink hung at the edge of the sky and a swollen dawn was beginning to bleed light, spilling it down the street like cheap red wine. The high rise loomed in front of her. Jack would be gone to work but she still didn't want to go up to the apartment. Main Street was a half-block away and empty except for two taxis parked in front of Kelekis for breakfast, maybe one of them Jack. Crossing Main a bus almost creamed her. She walked to the Redwood Bridge, stopped halfway over and stared down into the Red River, still covered in ice in February. In the summer it would be more brown than red; nothing red there but blood. Sadness drenched Doris as dread and desperation coalesced in an irresistible, delicious sensation. If she jumped, they'd find her body sprawled on the filthy ice, broken by its rough surface, a public display, not a dignified death. In June, she could slip under the cool, muddy water and be carried off by the current.

She walked back to the apartment building and went down into the basement where she hid her journal in a locker. Upstairs, the telephone was ringing off the hook and sounding pissed. She didn't answer, making a drink instead. The ringing stopped; it started again. She sat down in her chair, sipped her gin, and lifted the receiver.

"Where the hell you been?" Whiskey Jack bellowed. Doris hung up. The phone rang again. She answered.

"Don't you dare hang up on me," he cried. Doris placed the receiver in the cradle. It rang a third time. She grabbed it and spoke before he did.

"I'm tired, Jack. I need to rest."

"No point arguing with you when you're being this buggy. I'll call in an hour."

"Make it two," she said. Doris hung up and pulled the jack from the wall. She washed her lithium down with gin and opened her journal. It had been awhile since her last entry and the tear stained pages surprised her. She hadn't realized she had any left in her. She started to write:

> *Dear John,*
>
> *Don't know how long I will last here. The lithium makes me so drowsy. You said you got to hide your love away but I still want to tell you about my baby boy. Donovan is back after five years in the loony bin and hasn't been to see me yet. I don't think he will come now. I feel cold. I may never get warm again. More later, love, Doris.*

The Prejudgment Day Blues

Backstage at the Winnipeg Folk Festival, Banjo Bob Holiday was basking in the glow of a marvellous ambiance, breathing in the perfume of the sultry summer air. A truant sun, absent all day, had emerged at dusk from behind dark clouds that fractured and blossomed into silver-black dragons boasting a dazzling display of solar spears. Meanwhile, a full moon, pregnant with light, rose simultaneously in a deepening night sky. It had rained all afternoon but the downpour didn't dampen the crowd's enthusiasm. They were there for him.

He waited patiently while the poet, Zookey Zachariah, regaled the crowd with rhymes, his shrill voice ringing out as he pranced on the stage, looking like a cross between James Joyce and Peewee Herman in a tight, black suit and large glasses.

"She feeds me tea and oranges that come all the way from Safeway," he finished. "Now, it gives me great pleasure to introduce a musical legend, Canada's folk ambassador to the world, Winnipeg's own, finger-licking, banjo-picking, Banjo Bob Holiday!"

Banjo Bob stepped into the light. The audience went wild. And although he hadn't finished composing 'The Prejudgment Day Blues', he strummed the opening on the banjo and they roared their approval, the handclapping and cheering becoming louder and more boisterous. A sudden discordant snare drum began to bang in his brain, distorting the melody, derailing him, and disrupting his reverie. Someone was slapping the back of his head. Banjo Bob opened his eyes. Ernie stood over him scowling. The bartender was usually cool, a good egg as long as you didn't provoke him.

"What's happening, man?" Banjo Bob croaked cheerfully.

"This is the third time I've had to wake you," Ernie grumbled. "Time to go."

Bob peered around the bar. He had dropped into the Aberdeen for a quick brew, bumped into some buddies, and stayed longer than planned. His friends were long gone now but he was still thirsty and reached for a glass of beer on the table. The bartender sunk his meat-hooks into Bob's shoulder, pulling him to his feet.

"Where's Jedidiah?" Bob bawled, starting to panic. Ernie jammed the instrument case into him. Bob's equilibrium was largely restored with the banjo in his hands to provide ballast and he only wobbled a little as he left. He stopped in front of the steep stairs leading to the street. It was a long way to fall if he lost his balance. He gripped the rickety railing and worked his way up slowly, taking his time to reach the top. There he peeked out a dirty window where a nasty wind whipped trash around like a surly cop wielding a baton. It looked bleak and a little brisk. Bob dug into his pockets, producing a small collection of coins — a few nickels, dimes and quarters, a number of pennies. Banjo Bob counted the cash; it was enough for a six-pack of beer or bus fare but not both.

Sheila was going to be pissed at him, considering how late he was coming home. A peace offering was definitely in order. So he went around the corner to the vendor and bought the beer. Before stepping into the cold to begin the long walk home, Bob looked for his gloves and patted down his body several times before giving up. He'd obviously lost them. It wasn't long ago he'd found them in a phone booth where someone left them. Now, they had passed on to the next soul who needed them. This was how it went and always would on the whirling cosmic wheel. Bob slung the banjo case across his back, hoisted the six-pack under the crook of an arm, and jammed both hands into his coat pockets. He pushed the door open with a shoulder and stepped out into a freezing Winnipeg winter. As he booted it up Graham, a cold wind drove needles of ice into his face. But Bob didn't mind the inclement weather. It was an elemental prairie reality that allowed his spirit to soar. Caustic outsiders called the city Winterpeg, the armpit of Canada. Bob loved the town though. He was a maritimer by birth but a flatlander by choice. He'd been living in the Peg so long people thought he was born there.

Bob was fifteen when he ran away from home to avoid another beating from his father. He barely had time to grab his clothes before the fists flew and dressed on the porch, realizing he'd forgotten his socks and shoes. It was the middle of the night in the middle of winter but Bob had no intention of going back into the house for them. He walked barefoot on the pavement, trying to avoid the snow as much as possible. He ended up with frostbite and lost all ten toes. He never walked right again after that. He stayed in Halifax five years, panhandling, crashing on the floors of friends, and sleeping in doorways. One bright February morning with the sun in Aquarius, he spotted the banjo in a pawnshop window. He went hungry several months to cobble together the coin to buy it and finally acquired the banjo in June. It was the summer of love on the east coast of Canada and Bob sat in the park day and night practicing, learning to play. He named the banjo Jedidiah and started busking—it beat begging—and eventually earned enough for train-fare. He planned to go to Vancouver where it was warm all year. He wouldn't need a winter coat or much money and could live in Stanley Park.

When the train had a two-hour pit-stop in Winnipeg he got off. He ended up in a little vinyl place called the Swinging Gate where he hooked up with a gang of musicians and jammed with them into the wee hours. He missed his train and wound up staying in Winnipeg. His new friends formed the Flats Wobble Jug Band and though he was disappointed they didn't ask him to join it, he was happy for their success when the group started to take off. Banjo Bob crashed on Howie Hardy's couch for a year until meeting Sheila McSweeney. He could make her laugh and it lifted her up, lighting up her face and letting her beauty shine through. Banjo Bob moved into her place and Sheila became his inspiration. They found a way of being together, getting along without rancour during any difficult times.

Banjo Bob was eager to get home to her now. He cut through Hudson's Bay to shake off the cold creeping into his bones. It meant dealing with hostile, dirty looks from the plastic people and wage slaves who were just jealous of a lucky man with a cold six-pack in his hands, a warm woman waiting for him at home, and a song in his soul. A security guard trailed him until he left the chilly warmth of the store at the Memorial Boulevard exit. Back on the street, he pressed a button at the pedestrian crosswalk and watched six lanes of traffic stop for him. Then he ambled across the street, cheerfully waving to drivers as the growling, grumbling demons that confined and defined them were held at bay by the spell he'd cast. It was the way of the wizard.

A few blocks later, at Broadway and Young, Bob paused in front of Wheatsong Bakery and peered in the window at a loaf of bread and carrot cake. They looked scrumptious. But he wasn't taken in by the trickery. He'd belonged to the collective that ran the bakery before it went broke. And now, free enterprise types had transformed the community based business into a profit-center to rake in the bucks. Banjo Bob decided to go inside, give them a piece of his mind, and get warm.

A small bell tinkled overhead when he opened the door and the tantalizing aroma of freshly baked bread filled his nose. He imagined a delicious crust of it slathered in melting butter and his stomach growled. But he resisted the dizzying, deceptive allure of this and looked around the small shop. A glass display case of cookies and cakes was prominently positioned by the cash register along with a jar filled with business cards. Posters for various cultural events, including next summer's folk festival were plastered on the walls and a bulletin board by the door held announcements for garage sales, ads for babysitters, cleaning services, and music lessons; Bob could probably make a few bucks teaching banjo. Well, at least, the new owners had maintained the neighbourhood feel of the bakery.

A tall dude wearing a baker's cap tilted to one side waltzed out of the back kitchen and startled him. Bob recovered quickly. He looked the man up and down like day-old bread and grilled him about the ingredients they used, the price of bread. The man was unfazed, answering politely, explaining they used all natural ingredients and their prices reflected the increasing cost of production. But when Bob told him there was a boycott being planned, the baker's smile went south. He leapt from behind the counter and loomed over the little man— six five to Bob's four seven. Looking up, Bob could count the baker's nose hairs. He smiled, holding up the six-pack.

"Care for a brew?" he asked. The other man's face softened, his anger fading as fast as it had flared. He led Banjo Bob behind a beaded curtain. Bob hadn't picked up any of his volunteer shifts with the collective and never been in the kitchen before. The heat was stifling, even with the rear door cracked open to let in cold air.

"I'm Banjo Bob Holiday," he said, handing the baker a beer.

"Dave Ledoux. They call me Greasy Dave on account of being the Brylcreem king."

The baker removed a well-lubricated cap to illustrate the point.

"You're old school, like my buddy, Donovan," Bob said, watching Dave's Adam's apple bob like a harbour buoy as he chugalugged the beer then banged the empty bottle on the table, raising a fine mist of flour. The baker wiped his mouth with a tunic sleeve, belched, and nodded at Bob's banjo case.

"You play, Bobby?"

"Folk music is my forte."

"I can introduce ya to Gemini Joe McIvor if ya want. He runs the Winnipeg Folk Festival."

"Cool," Bob said, his heart flipping around like a fish in a feeding frenzy. "You too?"

"I was lead guitar for Gutter Vermin until we broke up. Never heard of us, I bet. We did all the rock classics, some blues, and a little soul."

"No such thing as a little soul," Banjo Bob said.

"Hey, you're alright," Greasy Dave said. They ended up talking about music and drinking beer until Bob realized how late it was.

"Best bolt before Sheila thinks I got hit by a bus," he said. Greasy Dave slapped his back.

"You almost did, son," he said. They went around to the front and the baker pressed a date loaf into Bob's hands, making him promise to come back and buy bread next time.

While a cold wind still blew, Banjo Bob felt fine tramping up Broadway. He was stoked and couldn't wait to tell Sheila about Greasy Dave knowing Gemini Joe. Bob had been trying to crack the granola ceiling for ten years. Maybe eleven would be his lucky number. It just went to show everybody in Winnipeg was only a drink away from being a friend.

The apartment building where Bob and Sheila lived was a firetrap, paint peeling off paper-thin walls, erratic steam heating. He climbed the stairs, not sure what kind of reception to expect. He was really late and the six-pack he'd bought was a two-pack now. Inside, a party was in full swing with Sheila's friends, Tim and Terri, nursing beers on the couch as she paraded around in her housecoat, praising the lyrics of Tom Waits while shouting over them. She beamed when she saw Bob and turned down the stereo.

"The prodigal paramour returns!" she cried out and wheeled over, planting a sloppy kiss on his lips while ash fell from her cigarette. She didn't ask where he'd been or why he was late.

"Your hands are so cold. Where are your gloves? Did you lose them already? Never mind, the boys brought a two-four."

Banjo Bob held up his modest offering and the others laughed.

He woke up the following day on the living room floor. Sheila was snoring in the bedroom, a sound he found curiously comforting. Bob had a two-minute wash and a ten; today he opted for the two. In the kitchen, he put the kettle on for tea and opened a tin of cat food, scooping out the coagulated slop. It didn't smell half bad. He lifted the spoon to his lips. There was a low growl at his feet as the cat glared at him and he banged the gruel into a bowl. After his tea steeped, Banjo Bob dropped a dollop of honey into the cup of steaming mead. He sat at the kitchen table where he could enjoy the ethereal morning calm, listen to the heating rads hiss, and watch sunlight leak light across a salmon-tinted sky as it painted gleaming gold clusters onto the silver whorls of ice gracing the window surface. Bob touched a finger to the cold pane to trace the weave of frosted flowers. It had snowed overnight. Cars, houses, and trees outside were air-brushed white with city grime scoured away.

The toilet flushed. Sheila stumbled into the kitchen, eyes heavy with sleep, hair a jagged tangle. Bob smiled and pointed to the tea. She lit a cigarette.

"I wish you wouldn't smoke, Sheila."

"Bite me, Bob," she said and walked over to the fridge. She reached behind it, pulling out a handful of greasy dust bunnies. Wiping them on her housecoat, she went to the stove, repeating this with the same result. Finally, she stretched a long arm around the back of a door where their coats hung and Bob heard a familiar clanking as she fished out four bottles of beer.

"Knew I hid them somewhere safe," she said, handing him the bottles. "Open me a beer, Bob. What's for breakfast?"

"Toast and peanut butter."

"Really?" she purred, sliding into a chair beside him and placing a hand between his legs. Banjo Bob wriggled. The thought of an erection gave him an erection.

"How do you want your eggs done?" he asked.

"Same way I like my men—over easy," she said, removing her robe and Bob followed her to the bedroom.

A half hour later Sheila watched him make breakfast, slicing, dicing, and then scooping eggs from the frying pan onto plates with a panache he otherwise rarely displayed.

"You could probably find some work in a funky little bistro," Sheila said, washing her eggs down with a beer. Afterward, he collected the dirty dishes and dropped them into a sink that was heaped high with accumulated dregs, where Bob was convinced a sludge-soaked demon lived.

"I'll wash these when I get home," he said.

"You always say that but never do."

"Wouldn't hurt you to get off your ass and help for a change," he said.

"What?"

"Nothing."

"That's what I thought. How many times do I have to tell you that there's no point in doing anything with the world in this sad state. I plan to sit in my room and wait for the apocalypse."

"You've done that for five years; the apocalypse still hasn't come. You're smart, educated, and talented but waste your time doing crossword puzzles. It's a form of mental masturbation."

"You trying to be clever or crude, Bob; because you don't have the backbone or the bile for either."

Sheila was gearing up for a fight but he wouldn't be drawn into it. She thrived on conflict and chaos, no gathering ever complete until she eviscerated some poor soul with her acid tongue and spilled red wine on a carpet. People avoided her. But Banjo Bob understood her. Sheila was not easy in the world; she was too weary and wound too tight. Black skies were all she saw with every little thing eating away at her — a late bill, an eviction notice. Bob tried to make peace.

"You're my Taurus touchstone," he said. "My moon, my Venus, my muse."

"You mismuse me, Bob."

"Every night is Saturday night with me, sweetie. Things are beginning to look up. I met a cool guy with folk fest connections, practically guaranteeing me a spot next summer."

"Somebody is stringing you along, Bob."

"Greasy Dave is alright."

"The name sounds familiar. Maybe I met him some place."

"He runs Wheatsong Bakery."

"That must be where then."

"He's a tall, rugged looking dude, a poor man's Kris Kristofferson, if you like the type."

"Who said I did?" Sheila snapped.

"All I'm saying is things are getting better, despite Unemployment being on my case and threatening to cut me off unless I find something. But I better start my famous job search."

"Thought you did that yesterday."

"I got derailed. You got any cash so I don't have to walk downtown?"

"Take in the empties."

"Brilliant," he said, trying to kiss her. "Dodging the bullet, babe?"

"Back off, Bob. I am not in the mood."

Going into the kitchen, Bob counted the beer bottles and came back doing a dance.

"Baby, I'm a rich man," he sang. "Enough there for bus fare, coffee, fries, and maybe a beer, not necessarily in that order."

Bob packed up the cases and lugged them to the vendor at the Westminster Hotel around the corner.

"Just the coin today, Jake," he said. "I gotta go down to the job bank."

"That time of year already? Daphne has draught on sale, Bobby. You could pop in for a few, still have enough coin for the bus."

"Cool," Bob said and flashed his friend the peace sign. Bob was shocked to find everything inside the bar had changed. Two years earlier they removed the dance floor to stop the fights. It didn't. Now the dance floor was back, along with the last gasps of disco — a DJ booth and glitter ball. Bob would not return until after the next reno. Still, Saturday night fever had not kicked in this early in the day so he could still have a quiet brew among other fugitives from this current, crazy age; time bandits congregated at tables, commiserating and guzzling down cheap beer like it was going out of style, which it was. Jagger was wailing you can't always get what you want on the jukebox. It carried Bob back to 1969 and the Digger pad at 655 Broadway. He had sworn then to be the last man on the planet with long hair. Now, it was 1984, the house was bulldozed into a parking lot like the song said it would be and Bob had a spreading bald spot on top of his dome. Howie Hardy slipped into the bar, head bobbing like a prairie dog. Bob cupped his hands and called him over.

"Not so loud, man," Howie muttered, sidling up to Bob's table. "Don't want anybody to know I'm here."

"But you are here, man."

"Brilliant, Bob. Need to find someone to float me a loan. How you fixed for cash?"

"Hey, you know me, Howie. I'm broke."

"Yeah, but I had to ask," Howie said. "I got myself into a real jam with Jimmy Jazz and owe him serious money. I gotta split. Anyone asks you ain't seen me."

Banjo Bob hated seeing his friend in this fix. Jimmy Jazz had a heavy rep and was no joke. He and Howie played a few gigs together when there were still gigs to be played. The man could set his fiddle on fire when he got in the groove. But he became a speed freak, his gift failing.

"You a musician?" The waitress asked, a late-blooming flower-child and kind of cute. Bob lifted Jedidiah from the case, offering to trade a tune for two glasses of beer and she agreed.

It was late afternoon by time he got to the job bank. While he waited to see a counsellor, he trolled the listings. There was nothing in his line of work. He either didn't have the skill or the education. It took a long time before his name was called but he was used to it. There was never any malice in the hearts of cashiers, clerks, waitresses, bus drivers, and bureaucrats who made him wait. Money can't buy love but it will speed up the pace at which a person is paid attention. Bucks bought service and Bob had none, so was perpetually last in line. His strategy for dealing with this was to take a book everywhere. He was reading 'Lord of the Rings' for the eighth time. Sheila often called him Banjo Bilbo or Bilbo Bob. His sweetheart was silly sometimes.

When a counsellor did deign to see him, she was nasty, browbeating him and complaining she could smell the beer on his breath. Bob felt an unfamiliar undercurrent of rage. He wanted to snap back it was easy for her to scold, sitting in a comfortable office with a good government job. Instead, he smiled through the inquisition and this seemed to irritate her more than anything else. After he enduring her tongue-lashing, he felt the need to shake off the negative energy and decided to go for a drink. He was all tapped out. But the Albert was nearby and Donovan would spot him a beer.

Bob wandered into the bar and saw his friend sitting alone. Donovan didn't smile often but when he did, he was a different dude, his grin like a big scar slashing his face and allowing any distress to fall away from him. People were always warning Bob Donovan could flip out in a flash and to be careful around him. But he had only ever seen Donovan's sweet side. His buddy was a good guy with a good brain and shared his love for music. They'd met twelve years ago in a poetry workshop at the Free University. Bob wanted to write lyrics. He didn't have the gift but Donovan did and they'd penned a few numbers together.

"Thanks for the beer, man," Bob said "Been ducking the landlord for weeks. I'm looking for work but no luck so far."

Itchy Dick joined them and then Cowboy.

"Just had a liquid lunch at the Ox with our fearless leader," Cowboy complained. "Numb-nuts fired my night cleaner. No warning. Nothing. Now, I have to find a new guy. I'm so fucking mad I could hammer someone."

"How about me?" Itchy Dick sang.

"You I will gladly hammer."

"I mean hire me. It's tough trying to catch a break in this town. You have to inherit a job practically. But hey, I ain't gonna slash my wrists about it. Be harder to get a job."

"I'd never hire you, Dick."

"Why not?"

"You look in a mirror lately?"

"No."

"I rest my case."

"Banjo Bob is looking for work," Donovan said. "He doesn't have a single sleazy bone in his body and will keep his nose clean, mind his own business."

"Your word is good enough for me," Cowboy said. "Be here tomorrow at midnight, shorty. I'll show you the ropes. Zoltan don't pay shit but it's under the table and you can keep whatever you find on the floor."

The rest of the afternoon and most of the evening was spent drinking on Donovan's dime. When Banjo Bob finally headed home, he was feeling no pain. He was eager to tell Sheila about finding work. Problem was she hated the Albert. He would need some backup to soften the blow. Greasy Dave was charismatic. Maybe he could be enlisted to help Bob out. The baker was happy to escape the oppressive kitchen heat of Wheatsong for awhile. He grabbed his coat and guitar and suggested they drop by the Westminster to get some beer. Bob's new friend was a saint and easily alleviated Sheila's anger. He opened her beer and assumed a position, but not too close to her on the couch. While she was impressed with Dave, she wasn't with Bob's new job.

"They're burning down that part of town," she said.

"The Lithium fire was blocks away from the Albert," Bob said.

"Open me another," she said. Bob went to the kitchen and dawdled there, draining a beer before going back with hers.

"What took you so long," Sheila snapped and snatched the bottle away. "I hate slowpokes. But then Dave doesn't want to hear about our sex life."

"Break out your banjo, Bobby. We can bang out a tune or two," Dave said. It was the first time Bob heard Dave play and was mortified to learn banging was exactly what Dave did. He was no ace on the axe, his fretwork lacking finesse as he pounded on the Gibson with a ham-handed whacking, playing with plenty of passion but little love or precision. Still, they partied all night and it was late the next day when Bob woke up. The last thing he remembered was singing love songs to Sheila with Dave mangling the chorus. She seemed to enjoy it anyway.

Bob dragged his butt into a dark bathroom. Still not ready to face the light yet, he wrapped his knees around the porcelain toilet bowl, carefully aiming until a satisfying splash confirmed his accuracy. He hit the handle to race the flush to the finishing line. Then he jumped at the sight of a silhouette bobbing in the mirror, only relaxing when he realized it was his own reflection. Banjo bobbing! He could use that in a song. He decided to take a bath before going to work and hit the switch, braving the light at last. He eased into the tub, a cold beer in one hand, a hot cloth in the other. Placing the cloth over his face, he instantly fell asleep. When the phone startled him, he whipped off a now cold rag.

Sheila scratched the vinyl taking Rambling Jack off the stereo. She would never learn. She was mumbling into the receiver. Bob climbed out of the tub and tiptoed to the door, pressing his ear against it. He couldn't make out what she was saying. Some of her friends were jerks, always putting him down, saying she was wasting her time with him. He went back to the mirror, pulled in his gut, and puffed out his chest. No Adonis but not bad. He had great legs and a nice ass from all the walking he did. He swung the door open and strolled into the living room naked. Sheila didn't notice. If he'd fallen getting out of the tub and left blood and bits of brain on the tile floor, she wouldn't know. She was reclining on the couch, head down, eyes closed, ear to the phone, totally unaware of little Bob waving in her face until she opened her eyes.

"Put some clothes on!" she screamed then spoke quietly into the receiver. "Sorry but if you had seen what I just did."

Sheila was off the phone when Banjo Bob came back dressed. He fell into an armchair and then bolted upright at a hideous howling. The cat dropped from his chair to the floor, flouncing from the room, holding its tail high, and contemptuously wiggling its butt at him. Bob scrambled after the beast, chasing it out of the room.

"Leave the cat alone!" Sheila shouted.

"I'd never hurt the damn thing," he said. "I can't even catch it. Who was on the phone?"

"Dave. He's coming over and bringing Chinese food."

"He was here half the night," Bob said, his eyebrow arching up in a question mark.

"All night," she said. "After you passed out he fell asleep on the couch and left just before dawn. I don't want to be alone while you go off to this job of yours. He'll keep me company. Get me a beer."

A twinge shot through Bob, shrink-wrapping his insides, but he let it go. Jealousy was too proprietary and not like him. Sheila accepted the bottle he offered.

"Where's yours?" she asked.

"I put on some coffee. Don't want to be half-hammered my first night at work."

"How many brain cells do you need to mop a floor, Bob?"

He shrugged and watched her drink while she did a crossword puzzle. Then Greasy Dave showed up and shoved the box of beer and a bag of Chinese food into Bob's midsection. Banjo Bob put the beer in the fridge.

"Careful where you walk, Dave!" Sheila bellowed in the living room. "That black stain on the carpet is where the gnome lies to watch the tube."

Bob brought them each back a beer.

"I'm gonna leave early, take two egg-rolls to munch along the way," he said. In the hall, he wriggled into his damp boots. He forgot to put cardboard inside them the day before to cover the holes in the bottom. His socks would be soggy by time he got to the hotel. But he could probably hang them on the rads in the bar to dry. He was just about ready to leave when Sheila hollered at him and came to the door. She wrapped her arms around his neck and ground her pelvis into his, laying a soulful kiss on him and hitting him with the full experience, hoovering his tongue down her throat. Bob didn't know what brought on this sudden passion after months of nothing but he liked it.

"I have something for you," she said. "I went down to the lost and found at Transit Tom's yesterday and got you some gloves. I told them you left yours on the bus. They showed me four pair. I picked out the nicest. Go before you say something stupid like thank you."

On the street, Bob felt his spirits lift. He was on his way to earn a little scratch with a new pair of gloves that had fur lining and fit well, proving Sheila cared. It was a gorgeous night with the wind whistling a sweet melody and the crisp, even snow crackling like cornflakes under his feet. Instead of hanging a left to head downtown after he passed the Granite Curling Club, Banjo Bob went to the right, halfway over the Osborne Street Bridge, to take a peek at the Assiniboine River. Snowmobile tracks crisscrossed the ice below and their engines shrieked in the distance. It was starting to snow, the flakes big and sloppy like Sheila's kisses. A tune rippled through Bob; a tender melody he would call 'Sheila's Song'. He had no pen, paper, or tape recorder to get it all down and it was too cold to take Jedidiah out of the banjo case. Bob dashed back over the bridge, heading toward the hotel, tapping out the tune's rhythm with his feet, rocking his head from side to side and up and down in time to the melody. He had to get to the Albert before the music was lost. The front end slipped away then the middle started to go. He walked faster but by time he reached Portage Avenue, the song was gone, not a shred remaining, and his pace slowed.

At Memorial Boulevard and Portage, by the bus depot, he heard a bloodcurdling scream. Stark terror scorched his insides, scouring away any lingering sadness over losing Sheila's song. A native woman stood at the corner, crying hysterically and howling. Banjo Bob rushed to her side to find out what was wrong. She didn't seem to see or hear him and kept sobbing. A police car pulled up beside Bob. A cop rolled down the window.

"Get her off the street," he growled and drove away. Bob didn't know how to help her and walked away.

Friday night on Albert was a medieval bacchanalia with staggering drunks, working girls, and cars cruising on the street. When a BMW stopped, a woman stepped to the curb, and a lively discussion ensued. She shook her head and the car tore away, tires squealing indignantly.

Inside the hotel, the lobby was deserted. But the scene in the bar was right out of the Rocky Horror Picture Show with a crowd of punk rockers banging beer bottles on tables as Apocalypso cranked out a tune. The chick singing had a great set of pipes and other fine features too. Zoltan was standing at the bar, drawing a line across his throat. The band kept playing. He stormed out in disgust. Cowboy waved Bob

over to the table where he was sitting in the middle of the action and bought him a beer. Once the bar had cleared out, the
three waitresses joined them. Bob had seen them all before
but never met them. They counted their tips, finished their
drinks, and got ready to split. Cowboy had Bob walk them to
the front, telling him to give the door a good pull once they
were out to make sure it was locked. Bob spotted two kids arguing by the used rag shop across from the Albert. Otherwise,
it was quiet. He went back to the bar. The lights were turned
low now and Bob jumped when a door opened and Cowboy
popped from the shadows.

"Come with me," he said and led Bob through a side
door at the back of the bar to Bertha's Place where pockets
of light streamed in through the four massive windows that
looked like a big TV screen. Country music was playing on
the stereo and two full glasses sat on a table.

"Have a brew, Bob," Cowboy said. "See those punks
outside? I bounced the one in leather out on his ass earlier.
Now he's back with his girlfriend, boyfriend, whatever. We'll
wait, see what they do."

"Shouldn't I start cleaning the bar?"

"Only takes five hours. Don't tell Zoltan or he'll want to
pay you even less than he already plans. I need you for backup right now. You have to be careful in this shack, Bob. We get
scum from all walks of life coming in here—hipsters, fashion-
able drunks, sleaze slumming for tail, and rubes cruising on
remote; then there's the winos, hookers, hustlers, hoods, and
punks who don't need a reason to shiv ya. Few years ago they
brained the night guy and he's part of the produce section at
the Health Sciences Centre now. Someone gets in your face,
you back off, but never back down."

"What's the diff?"

"Backing off is negotiated, an easing away from confrontation with body language, tone of voice, and eye contact.
But you back down, show fear or weakness, you lose face,
teeth, maybe more. Pity will not prevail. They're making their
move!"

There was a loud crash and one of the enormous windows shattered. Cowboy jumped up and ran out to chase the kids, shouting back at Bob to call the cops. When the police arrived, he went out, explained the situation, and pointed down Notre Dame in the direction Cowboy went. The cop car took off. Bob tried to get back into the hotel but the door was locked. He decided against going through the broken window. He had no burning desire to be impaled on the sharp glass. He gave the door one last good tug and it opened easily, not much of a security system. In the café, Banjo Bob nursed his drink while he waited for Cowboy to return. His first night on the job had certainly started with a bang.

Black Ice

Donovan Bender went down to the bus depot to retrieve his suitcase before they decided to toss it. Out of hospital two weeks now, he wouldn't be leaving town anytime soon. He needed to be there for his brother. Bernie was doing too much speed after his prison break and had pissed off Tony. Donovan was five years younger and they'd always been close, the only two living at home after their older brothers all moved out. They would lie in bed late at night when they were little, Bernie laughing and babbling about his plans to make it rich. He protected Donovan from Whiskey Jack's beatings and kept him out of trouble on the street, steering him away from kids who wanted to fight a Bender and creeps who would try to take advantage of him. Now, it was Donovan's turn to support Bernie through a tough time.

He was lugging his suitcase down the street and didn't see the black ice until his feet flew up from under him. His head cracked on the pavement and he lay on the ground, not moving a muscle as he assessed his condition; was he dizzy, bleeding, or dealing with a broken bone. His time in hospital had taught him a few things. A woman walking by him stopped.

"Are you alright?" she asked.

"Fuck off," Donovan said and she hustled away. He got to his feet, still sliding around, and headed down Ellice toward Albert Street. Siren was perched on a telephone wire, giving a raven the evil eye. The bird lost its nerve first and flew off. Siren squealed like a caterwauling cat.

The suitcase was heavy and Donovan could use a drink. The Captain's Corner was close. He'd never been there before. One glass door led into a hotel, another into the bar. He dragged his suitcase inside. Nobody seemed to notice or care. He liked that. It was a cozy, old-style pub smelling of pipe tobacco and popcorn. A piano near the front window had stools around it so people could sit and drink while listening to someone play. A huge compass and a ship's wheel hung on one wall. A glass case on a stand in the middle of the bar held a replica of an eighteenth century schooner and a table of old hippies was singing sea shanties. Donovan would definitely drag Banjo Bob down here for a drink; he would dig it. He took a seat next to a table where a brainy chick was lecturing her friends.

"Strindberg was a misogynist. He exploited his wife, using her as a creative crutch. There was nothing benevolent about keeping the poor woman a prisoner at home."

The waitress taking his order smiled at Donovan, tilting her head toward the other table.

"University students," she said. She was nice, but not in some come-tip-me way. She was genuine. He asked for a Jameson then read a few pages of the 'Strange Life of Ivan Osokin'. He was struggling with the story, trying to make sense of it and coming up empty. Besides, Donovan had other things on his mind and couldn't concentrate.

Donovan had gone to see his grandmother earlier in the day after he heard her bragging on 'Beefs and Bouquets' about receiving flowers from the chief of police. For fifteen minutes every morning, just before the eight o'clock news on CJOB, Red Alex listened to the babas that turned garden hoses on bible-thumpers and salesmen, who came to their door, complain on the radio. So why did the cops send his grandmother flowers? Donovan took the Selkirk bus to her place in the early afternoon. The bus was crammed with drunks, swerving and swaying in the aisles, clinging to handrails, as it rolled down the street. They laughed and yelled to each other across the aisle, talking too loud, stinking of tobacco and cheap wine. Some ass sitting behind Donovan blew sour Paraldehyde breath onto his neck. His roommate in hospital, Furry Felix, had been on the med. The two of them had the same shrink.

Lawler liked high profile patients; Furry Felix certainly quali-
fied. He was a serious head case who had picked up a guy
at the Woodbine Hotel, chopped him in pieces, and stacked
them in the bathtub of his room at the Albert. They never
found a few of the victim's parts and figured Felix ate them.

Donovan got off the bus by the Merchant's Hotel and it
rattled off, spewing diesel fuel in his face. He crossed Selkirk
and walked down Andrews to his grandmother's house on
the corner of Flora. He hadn't visited in years. He and Bernie
had spent summers there when they were kids so Whiskey
Jack and the old lady could party. Then, a green veranda had
run along the length of the front of the house and Donovan
tramped up and down it from one end to the other, acting
out childhood fantasies. Sometimes, he would crawl underneath and be immersed in a subterranean world of insects.
Diamonds of warm sunlight would leak through the lattice
while the adults on the porch above said things they didn't
when young ones were around. The veranda was gone now,
along with the wooden siding of the house and the picket
fence. Three enormous elms had been a shady refuge in the
front yard. His grandmother had chopped them down. They
blocked her view. She couldn't see what the neighbourhood
kids were doing on the corner or catch drunks staggering
home from the Merchant's Hotel who pissed on her fence and
threw beer bottles in her yard. Nana made one improvement
every year until the house was reduced to a stucco bunker in
a barren yard surrounded by a chain-link fence. Donovan remembered her calling 911 to scream murder after some kid's
ball broke her window. Six police cars had roared up to the
house, cops jumping out, guns drawn. They almost charged
her with mischief then, but had sent flowers now. Obviously,
fences had mended.

Donovan slammed the gate. A dog in the house went
berserk, howling and throwing his body against the front
door. Nana peeked through the curtain.

"Shut it, Major! It's Donnie!" she shouted, unfasten-
ing the locks with sharp, staccato snaps and then flinging the
front door wide open. Major started going crazy in the hall

and Nana waved an axe handle at him. The dog growled, baring his teeth. Donovan figured it could go either way. But then Major collapsed on the floor in a heap of resignation, Nana attached his collar to a chain on the banister, and returned the axe handle to its place by the door.

"Don't just stand there! Get in here!" she cried, thundering down a dark hall to the kitchen.

"Should I let Major go?" Donovan asked as the dog's rear end wagged its body.

"Leave him! Mutt's getting too big for his britches."

In the kitchen, Nana raced around, putting on the kettle and placing a cup, spoon, and jar of instant coffee on the table in front of Donovan.

"I'm not thirsty," he said. She didn't seem to hear him.

"Are you hungry?" she cried, not waiting for an answer. She jumped from her chair to turn on the stove, crack open a cupboard, and pull down a frying pan. Then she darted to the fridge, grabbed a plate of pierogies, and dropped six in the pan. She was a tiny, tight muscle of gleaming light in the shadow, four foot tall and gaunt in a pair of sad, shiny slacks, an old army shirt, and a red babushka to hide her thinning hair. She was the lady of perpetual motion and had two speeds, fast and stop, talking while she cooked, telling him all about her recent adventure with the police using her house as a command post while they negotiated with a hostage taker down the street. A powerful smell of pierogies and onion sizzling in bacon grease filled the air. Nana made the best pierogies on the planet. While he wolfed them down, she switched off the ceiling light and sat in a chair by the window. Although it was still the middle of the day, a dim bulb over the kitchen sink was the only illumination. She parted the curtain, pulled up the blind, and peered out, her neck stretching one way then the other, head poking the air like a bird, her eyes shooting from the street corner to a truck mirror bolted outside the window so she could see both ways. She dropped the curtain, lit a cigarette, and gulped at her coffee.

"Damn kids are always up to no good. I knew you were hungry," she said. "How are you doing, Donovan? It's been a long time since I seen you."

"I've been in hospital, Nana."

"That would never have happened if they hadn't pumped you up with pills when you were a boy. Your parents are idiots. When the cops were here a few weeks ago your mother showed up wanting to bury the hatchet. I'll bury it right in her head. Best you stay away from the whole bunch. You're the only one that's any good, Donnie. The other boys are all bums, robbing stores, beating people up, Bernie setting fires, and Tony dealing drugs, playing the big shot. He showed up here on a motorcycle one time, bragging how the cops couldn't touch him, like your old man used to do. They caught your father. They're gonna get Tony too. He has one life. Police have forever. Meanwhile, he has to watch over his shoulder, waiting for that knock on the door and wondering when it's gonna come. It's no kind of life."

"I gotta go," Donovan said, standing up.

"Where?"

"I have a job tonight."

"Is it legal?"

"I'm a hotel desk clerk."

"Oh, that sounds nice. You need some money?"

"No, Nana, it's okay."

"Hang on, I'll be right back," she said and was up and running again. "Let Major go!"

Donovan walked down to release the dog as she rummaged through a dresser drawer in her bedroom. Major had been a calm lump until then, but turned into a Tasmanian devil and strained against the leash, pulling it in the opposite direction while Donovan tried to undo it. Once he was free, the dog tore up and down the hall in triumph, only stopping to jump up onto Donovan and slobber all over his face with a foul-smelling tongue. Donovan went back to the kitchen. The dog charged up the hall like a bullet before bouncing back, scurrying under the table, and burrowing his head between Donovan's legs, instantly covering his clothes in dog hair, several in his mouth. Nana bounded back to the kitchen and placed a twenty dollar bill on the table.

"What's this?" he asked.

"Take it. Don't argue. I'll give you some real money next year if I'm still kicking around."

"Don't talk that way, Nana."

"Why not? I could be dead by then."

Donovan had slipped the twenty in a pocket. It bought him a drink at the Captain's Corner. He sipped his Jameson now, removed a pad from his suitcase, and wrote down the first words to come into his head. They didn't make sense. It didn't matter. They took him out of his head for a little while. The waitress brought another drink and waved it off when he tried to pay, nodding at a man stumbling toward him. Donovan had seen this character hanging around the Albert, one of those arty types who thought they were better than him.

"Scott Kostyk," the drunk said, dropping a camera on the table and sitting down. "Met you a few nights ago I think. Mind if I join you?"

"Looks like you already have."

"I just got out of jail. Cops held me two days without pressing charges. I didn't know they could do that. Seems my crime was witnessing the Lithium fire a few weeks ago."

"I was out of town when that happened," Donovan said.

"Well, I wasn't," Kostyk said. "I was there and probably saw the arsonist according to the police. They wanted to know if I got a good look at him. I dunno. It happened so fast. Cops told me the firebug was sloppy, splashing gasoline all over the floors, walls, and outside the building behind the Lithium kitchen. They said he likely soaked his clothes and it was just dumb luck he didn't set himself on fire, burn to death like my wife, my ex-wife. A few days ago, I went to the burned out building, saw the chalk marks, the personal belongings, and debris. They arrested me because I was taking pictures. They wanted to see what I had on film. This morning, I spent forty minutes, dealing with bureaucratic red tape and bullshit, to get my camera back. I guess I'll find out what I have when the film is developed."

Kostyk's head was bobbing. It dropped to his chest and he started to snore. Did this clown have pictures of Bernie setting the fire? Donovan reached for the camera but the drunk woke up. He was disoriented with a thin line of drool leaking down his chin like a zombie in Selkirk as he fiddled with a coaster and started to babble, rambling and jumping from one thing to another.

"I spent two fucking days in a cell stinking of piss and puke, trying to shut out the banging doors, prisoners screaming and singing and yammering nonstop. I used to think jail would be a quiet place to paint and write without distraction. But it is the noisiest, craziest environment I've ever experienced. My father used to call me a bum because I wanted to be an artist. If he saw me now would he be proud? I am a publisher, poet, photographer, and political roustabout—famous in a four square-block area of downtown Winnipeg and cruising on the increasingly thin charm of my reputation. But I'm making art again now—painting and taking pictures, writing. Recently I penned my first Haiku—it's a kind of poetry."

"I know what Haiku is," Donovan snapped. He opened his suitcase, removed a shoe box, and lifted out a sheet of paper, passing it to Kostyk.

winter mists cloak night concealing patient predators
wind a masquerade of ghost whispers and stolen kisses
time a sorry construct a clumsy ledger

"You write this?" He asked. Donovan nodded. "And you keep your poetry in a shoebox. How cool is that? Let me buy you a drink and read some more of it."

"I have to go."

"Maybe next time then, at the Albert?"

Donovan gathered his things and went back to the hotel. It had actually been nice to have someone take his poetry seriously. Besides Banjo Bob and Susie at the hospital, nobody he knew could care less about art or poetry. Back in the North End, the other kids made fun of his writing until he beat them up and his shrink in Selkirk only wanted to stick it in his chart.

Cowboy was on the desk at the Albert, studying a woman using the payphone. Vera had beach-bunny blonde hair, Geisha makeup, and wore a fur coat over a fur coat to stay warm. She had no intention of freezing to death servicing the men of Winnipeg. She finished her call and Cowboy called her over. Vera strolled to the desk like a queen.

"Whatever you want, Cowboy, you can't afford it."

"You should talk to Big Ron, Vera. He is fucking lost without you."

"He was fucking lost with me, Cowboy. I'm warm now and going back to work."

The desk clerk shook his head sadly. Donovan shrugged, hauled his suitcase to his room, and checked the time. It was only nine PM. He had time for a quick drink before heading out.

Jimmy Jazz nodded to him in the bar. Tony wasn't around. His brother was spending less time there lately and was likely off plotting the overthrow of the government or the destruction of the universe. Banjo Bob was sitting alone, looking dejected, and sipping a glass of draught. He brightened when Donovan bought him a drink. Bob was Donovan's touchstone. He could tell a lot about people by how they treated his friend.

"You hear the latest Emmylou Harris?" Bob asked. "The woman has a voice like silk and honey. I got a mad musician crush on her, man. Just don't tell my true love."

"Sheila will understand," Donovan said. Banjo Bob chuckled.

"I mean Joni. Hey, listen to my latest Winnipeg tune," he said and placed the banjo on his knee. As he played, Donovan floated on an easy cloud, forgetting where he had to go, what he had to do. He heard the bells before Banjo Bob did. Billy Triangle stood by the bar glaring with Bruno Pelechaty grinning beside him. The two men flanked Prince and the pusher lifted his wine glass, pointing it at Bob.

"Bozo Bob is a happy, little dwarf star radiating nothing, isn't he? No banjo picker but an ass licker, a perplexed cockroach lacking any cogent thought. If the Antichrist has Alzheimer's, I have clarity pills that will augment the smoke Bruno sold you yesterday, little man."

"Leave, Bob—now," Donovan growled. Bob gargled down his beer and bolted.

"Another mind done in," Prince cooed. "Well, he didn't need it anyway. I am a Scorpio-blaster conducting a reconnaissance mission in the lower stratosphere and eradicating trash from Venus. I zap you from my movie, greaser, so you are no longer in a state of agonization, hopped up on bugjuice, no longer bearing your little cross like a skinner lurking under the Salter Street Bridge, baring his to squirt stars in your face. Hostility sings through your skin. Smiling amoeba crawl up your spine, singeing your flesh just as mine almost was on judgment day at the Lithium, where I saw heaps of ash as God and another Bender tried to send me back to my ancestors."

Donovan wasn't about to let Prince goad him into some kind of beef. He had no time for the grade school politics of this third-rate manipulator. But he wouldn't back down either and stared at the pusher, no fear or anger showing on his face; nothing, not even Siren shrieking. A slow sliver of realization was starting to dawn on Prince as he recognized the absence in him. His bravado shrivelled and he blew Donovan a kiss, leaving with his two toadies. Donovan felt strong fingers squeeze into his shoulder from behind and spun around. Jimmy Jazz returned to his chair. Velvet was on the phone at the bar. She hung up and brought Donovan another drink.

"Tony is on his way," she said. Donovan quickly swallowed the Jameson and headed out the door, hiking over to the Disraeli Bridge.

It was perfect. There was never foot traffic on the bridge at this hour, especially in winter, and definitely not with the streets so slippery because of black ice. Five years ago, when he spun out on the bikers, Donovan had put Eric the Red in traction and snuffed his buddy. Tonight was different. He was completely in control now, his fury focused, and the fire in him frozen to a crisp. Tonight was about righteous retribution. Skinners were the lowest of the low.

The goof walking toward him on the bridge was lost in his little world. He had no size, but it wouldn't have mattered if he did. These creeps always went soft in the end. Sure enough, when he saw Donovan taking up the whole side- walk, he went stiff, turning his head from side to side, trying to find a way to get around him. There wasn't one, the river on one side of the footpath, a railing next to the road too high to jump on the other. The skinner's walk slowed to a crawl, his mouth heaving ragged clouds as he squeezed his shoulders tight together and angled his body to avoid bumping into the other man. Donovan leaned in toward him hard, knocked the goof off-balance, and whirled around.

"What's your fucking problem?" Donovan snarled.

"Hey man, I don't want trouble."

"You calling me trouble?"

"No, no, I just..." the idiot whined, holding his hands high, flapping them in the air. It was what Donovan needed. He hammered the skinner who fell hard and curled up in a ball. Donovan booted him in the gut, pulled his head back, and broke his nose with one good shot. He hit him over and over, kicked him in the balls, the head. The sad sack of shit went limp. Donovan lifted him up and dangled him over the side of the bridge.

"I'm too young to die," the goof moaned.

"Nice shoes," Donovan said. The other man looked hopeful. Donovan yanked the shoes off his feet and let him go. He sailed away screaming, Siren's mouth a nice, round O in the middle of his face as he fell to the ground below.

Smoke and Ashes

Dinner at Dubrovnik's

The house near the river on Assiniboine Avenue was not far from the legislative grounds, a stately old thing with a high, wrought-iron fence framing the yard and falling snow lending it the look of a winter postcard. Back in the North End, it would either be some rich person's mansion or a rooming house with a dozen tenants on welfare living there. This was the second time in as many weeks Sarah was sitting in her car, gripping the steering wheel outside a building she was not eager to enter. Tony had called her two days ago to tell her he'd made the dinner reservation. After twenty years of working hard, keeping her feet on the ground, head out of the clouds, and heart in check, she'd had to handle one crisis after another lately, first Brad, now Tony. Still, she did agree to this unusual arrangement; she would honour her end; get through the night, and never have to see Tony again, assuming his word was good. Then she and Amy could get on with life.

The front gate of the restaurant was open and there was plenty of room on the lot. But she decided to leave the Dart on the street rather than park it beside a BMW. At the door, an elegant, well-dressed Maître D welcomed her to Dubrovnik's, greeting her like she was visiting royalty. Sarah found it disarming. She wasn't used to this treatment. But after he helped with her coat, passed it to a cloakroom attendant, and handed her a receipt with a smile Sarah relaxed. Tony hadn't arrived yet and their table wasn't ready. Sarah rarely wore dresses; she didn't like how they looked on her. But she was glad she had tonight as the Maître D guided her toward the bar through a dining room where a woman in an evening gown was playing a piano while tastefully clothed couples were drinking red wine at candlelit tables. None of them noticed her or sniffed at her being there.

At the bar, she ordered beer from a bartender with perfect teeth that practically glowed in the dark. After he poured the contents of a bottle into a glass, Sarah stared at the label. She had asked for the beer out of habit. Brad always insisted they drink Blue because he worked at the brewery and she'd always gone along to keep the peace. But there was no peace to keep now.

A week ago, Brad's body had been discovered at the bottom of the Disraeli Street Bridge. When the police showed up at her mother's house, they questioned Sarah, wanting to know why she left him and if he was suicidal. She explained they'd had some issues and he had threatened to kill himself before. She wasn't lying. Because there was alcohol in his system, the detective-in-charge concluded Brad had either jumped or climbed up on the railing, slipped on the black ice, and fallen to his death. The one odd thing though was they never found his shoes. But, as far as the cops were concerned, the case was closed. Brad's mother didn't agree, telling police she suspected foul play, suggesting Sarah was somehow involved. She had never accepted Sarah and blamed her for ruining her son's life, claiming he never should have got involved with an Indian woman who had a child. It didn't stop the bitch from trying to bully Sarah into attending Brad's funeral. Sarah refused to go, yet spared his mother the unvarnished truth about her precious boy. She called Sarah vindictive. The woman had no idea.

"Something wrong with the beer?" the bartender asked.

"Don't feel like one after all."

"Let me fix something for you then. I know just the thing."

Sarah sipped her first margarita, savouring the taste as she peeked around the bar. It had a warm and comfortable environment with a working fireplace and mellow jazz flowing from wall speakers. A businessman, down at the other end of the long bar, was chatting with a woman who looked like she'd just stepped out of a fashion magazine. No one seemed to even be aware of her, but Sarah couldn't shake the feeling they all knew why she was there — dinner with a killer — it sounded like the detective books Poppy read. Well, Tony couldn't pull any funny stuff here and she could easily slip away after the evening was over.

Sarah felt a hand at her elbow and turned to see him for the first time since they met at the Windmill. The gangster was gone, disappearing inside an expensive double-breasted suit with a red silk tie. The only remaining trace of the North End tough guy was Tony's silver ring. It had a large lion's head with sharp teeth and Sarah suspected it had left its mark on a face or two.

"You're in a different uniform," she said and he smiled. Tony had a broad, open smile that softened the lines of his face, causing them to crinkle at the edges of his mouth and eyes. Even his voice was warmer.

"You like the suit? Nice to wear it for something other than a funeral. Our table is ready."

Tony was a gentleman and held her chair for her. He ordered a bottle of red wine and she scrutinized him as he studied a menu. He had a firm jaw yet delicate almost feminine features. From a certain angle, in a particular light, he was handsome in a Humphrey Bogart sort of way.

"I'm having a tiger shrimp appetizer and filet mignon, medium rare," he said. "You can't go wrong at Dubrovnik's, Sarah. Everything is good. Why don't you try the smoked Winnipeg Goldeye salad and grilled bison?"

The wine arrived and Tony declined the taste test. The waiter poured them each a glass and left the bottle. Sarah took a sip of the wine, a warm, spicy explosion in her mouth. She smacked her lips. Tony grinned. Did the man miss anything? The waiter brought the appetizers and topped up their glasses. Tony speared a shrimp while she picked at her salad. Neither of them spoke and Sarah was grateful for the silence. Tony finished his plate, pushed it aside, and peered into her eyes.

"Your family used to live on Flora, a half-block from my grandmother's house," he said.

"All the kids despised her," Sarah said. "She was mean."

"She still is," Tony said. "So, it was just you guys and your mother at home?"

"She did the best she could after throwing Poppy out."

"Whiskey Jack kicked me out on my sixteenth birthday. He sat in an upstairs window with a glass of rye in his hand and yelled down at me standing on the sidewalk in front of the house. He said he'd taken care of me long enough."

"That's terrible."

"Actually, he did me a favour. I was better off on my own."

Dinner arrived. Sarah's bison was delicious, tender and juicy. Tony cut into his filet.

"This certainly beats North End steak," he said.

"Do you mean fried bologna or Klik?" she said. Tony ordered another bottle of wine. Sarah would have to pace herself. She wasn't fooled by his attempt to charm her. Born and raised in the North End, she knew all about the notorious Bender brothers and Tony was the worst with the nastiest punks in the neighbourhood congregating around him like cardinals around a pope. Then he did something unexpected and started to open up to her, sharing details about his family.

"I was the oldest of six boys with the baggage that comes with that — being both the golden child and press-ganged into babysitting. Whenever my brothers did something wrong, it was my fault. At Christmas time, our old lady cut stars out of cardboard, glued silver paper onto them, and hung them everywhere. Then she went nuts, losing her temper over some little thing and tearing them all down again, screaming at us the whole time. We never knew when she would explode, so eventually stopped celebrating holidays and birthdays. Family isn't really about blood anyway but a way of being with people. How is your daughter doing?"

Sarah didn't answer. She hadn't talked to anyone about what had happened and certainly wasn't going to discuss it with Tony. He didn't press but changed the subject.

"What kinds of music do you like, Sarah?"

"Hank Williams, Patsy Cline, Willie Nelson," she said and he didn't roll his eyes or make a smartass comment.

"I have an extensive collection of vinyl, mostly Americana, incorporating classic country and fusing it with jazz, blues, folk, and rock."

"You're actually pretty smart, considering."

"Considering what?" he asked. "Well, I'm not offended by that, True, I never finished high school but an education is no guarantee of intelligence. Tough doesn't have to mean stupid."

"I did six months at the University of Winnipeg," Sarah said.

"That was a short sentence — get out early for good behaviour?"

"It was nothing but a bureaucrat and fuck factory. I was sitting in an empty classroom one day and imagined piling all the desks in the middle of the room and setting them on fire. Figured being a carpenter made more sense."

"It's probably more practical than a pyromaniac."

"So the killer is a comic," she said. "I used to dream of being an artist and after I find work and a place to live, I may take some lessons, learn to draw. I've never been to the Winnipeg Art Gallery and would love to go, maybe take my little girl. Amy is an Aquarius."

"I don't know what that means."

"It means her ninth birthday is next week and I need to find helium balloons. Don't look at me like that. Balloons are important when you have children. She has some good days, some bad ones. When Amy was born, I believed a time would come when I wouldn't have to worry about her. But that isn't true. A mother's job is for life. I spend as much time as I can with her to prepare her the best I am able before losing her to the world. But it feels like every moment I take for myself is stolen from her. She was upset I went out tonight."

"She's lucky to have you," he said. It turned out that Sarah and Tony both knew some of the same people from the North End and he had funny stories about them. She still wasn't ready to let down her guard but was feeling a little more at ease. Their waiter was attentive but discreet, doing a lithe dance, seeming to know what they needed before they did, lifting and sliding dishes away when they were done with them, bringing fresh bread and garlic butter, refilling water and wine glasses. Sarah barely noticed he was there until some fresh delicacy magically materialized at the table. The dinner at Dubrovnik's ended with dessert, chocolate cake layered with white cream and sprinkles of cocoa and cashew, the most delicious thing Sarah had ever tasted. Tony ordered them each a coffee and cognac. Sarah shot him a dirty look.

"Don't worry," he said. "Like I told you, this dinner has no strings."

"Why do I not believe you?" she asked.

"Let me explain, Sarah. There are fifty year old boys; weaklings who lack self-control and are incapable of restraint, grabbing at things, acting on every desire and fantasy — men like Brad Hunter and Zoltan Kisich. But disciplined and focused men can be as young as eleven and not need to pick a flower in the garden to appreciate its beauty. I don't get close to people by design. My ends often require distance. But you have qualities that speak to me, strength I recognized even all those years ago on Flora Avenue. But I am perfectly capable of keeping my distance. You are safe with me."

It was after one AM when they finally left the restaurant, the last two customers closing it down. They'd had a fair amount to drink and Tony insisted Sarah leave the Dart at Dubrovnik's for the night. He called a taxi, took her straight home. At the door of her mother's house, he gave her a quick peck on the cheek and pressed a slip of paper into her hand.

"I won't phone you, Sarah but I've never been to the art gallery either. When you decide to go, call me if you want company. Nobody else has my private number, even family; just one last thing. Your lilac perfume is lovely."

Tony stepped away, got into the waiting taxi, and was gone.

Everyone was asleep in the house, her mother softly snoring in her bedroom at the end of the hall. Sarah grabbed a glass of water in the kitchen, went to the living room, and sat on the couch. She listened to the grandfather clock tick and the furnace hum. Despite her initial dread, dinner at

Dubrovnik's had gone reasonably well, passing in a warm wash of food, drink, and pleasant conversation with a man who shared much of the same experience as her. He was white but seemed to sense what she'd been through in life. And Tony had been true to his word too. He wasn't inappropriate, rude, or offensive. It was a refreshing change. She studied the note with his number written down on it, the firm press of the straight digits. Now she had fulfilled her part of their bargain, she could trash it; never have to see Tony again. She tried to imagine this ruthless tough guy studying paintings in the art gallery and realized how ridiculous the prospect was. Yet, she folded the slip of paper in half and put it in her purse.

Morning light was starting to peek through the curtains when Sarah climbed the stairs to the room she shared with Amy. She undressed quietly, slipping into bed beside her daughter. When Amy turned toward her in her sleep, the muscles in Sarah's heart pulled and tightened. Amy looked so much like her father. Sarah never told Max she was pregnant. He was sweet and kind but an immature kid, incapable of committing just like Poppy. Her father had been a free spirit, gentle and giving and enjoying a good joke, a glass of wine. After her mother kicked him out and went to work cracking eggs at the Winnipeg Cold Storage under the Salter Street Bridge to keep the family together, she complained he was the chief architect of their misfortune. Sarah didn't get the chief joke until she was older. It was Poppy's Cree blood singing through her skin, not the Scots. Sarah had been his favourite. He'd sneak over Saturday mornings and her mother would pretend she didn't know he was in the lane playing with the kids despite the restraining order. Puffing on a stogie, he'd pick Sarah up and spin her around, hugging and kissing her, his hair and clothes smelling of cigar smoke and cheap wine. His deep laugh always lit a fire in her and she would get drunk on him, never wanting him to put her down or leave. But he always did, dancing down Flora Avenue toward the Main Street bars, while she stood on the sidewalk bawling, afraid he would never come back. Then he didn't and it opened a hole in her. She was sad after that and the other kids called her melancholy baby. She was sixteen when her mother told her what had happened, how Poppy fell asleep on the tracks behind the Occidental Hotel and probably didn't feel a thing when the slow-moving freight train rolled over him. The dreams started after that. Sarah would imagine him waking up to a bright-eyed monster bearing down on him with its shrieking whistle drowning out his screams. Sarah started to control her feelings, choking off the pain to cauterize the wound. Then the kids called her a cold fish. It had been a very long time since she'd trusted her feelings. Amy wasn't anything like her. She was tender and trusting like Poppy and Max. Sarah didn't want her daughter to lose those vital attributes or become an empty shell. Amy was safe because of Tony Bender and Sarah knew he would never allow anyone to harm her again. Tony came up hard like her and done what he had to do. Still, his swagger hid a deep hurt. Sarah watched Amy sleep and longed to reach out to hold her but didn't want her sweet baby to see her crying.

The Starlight Tour

The hours fell away as Tony swam lengths, gliding from one end of the pool to the other like a metronome, his muscles tensing, limbs stretching. Later, when he was done and washing away a chlorine stink in the shower, he mulled over his dinner with Sarah two nights earlier. He hadn't seen her since they were kids. What he had admired about her back then was still intact. Sarah was a strong woman with a fierce, tenacious spirit, certain in her views and no pushover, not likely to tolerate any deceptive attempts to dazzle or manipulate her. She would require a great deal of time and might still not come around. Patience was the key to unlocking the enigma of Sarah Grant, but not the patience of some pining, lovesick puppy tethered to unrealistic hope. Being poor could breed a penchant for pipe dreams or a pragmatic nature, seldom both, and Tony had learned a simple formula for acquiring things. Gauge the possibility of success against the measure of time required to obtain a positive result and achieve the outcome he desired, then determine when to act, when to wait, and when to walk away. Tony hustled, worked hard to get a decent place to live and gain access to the creature comforts. So far, he had lived his entire life alone without any distress; he could easily continue to do so if things didn't work out with Sarah.

February was cold in the Peg and although it was thirty below, Tony waited outside for a taxi. The Pan Am Pool was built for the '67 games in the Brutalist style with four plain concrete walls, narrow windows. The building was ugly but broke the wind while he lit his cigar. Duffy's came fast, Buzz behind the wheel, stoned on speed, and wanting to chat.

"I can drive all the way from the North End to St. Vital without turning a corner, Tony. Street changes names six
fucking times—Salter becomes Isabel then Balmoral, Colony,
Memorial Boulevard, Osborne, Dunkirk. It has seven names.
Wonder why?"

"So they know what part of town you're from. Stop
talking, Buzz. I need to think."

Tony relit his cigar. The fire was a month ago. Buck had
eventually come up with the coin he owed and the investigation was all but dead. The fire marshal sniffing around was
from Transcona. Turned out he'd dealt a little dope as a kid.
Jimmy Jazz knew him from the old days and got in touch to
reminisce; it put an end to his questions. Arson was a chronic
problem in the city anyway and the poor guy probably had a
heavy workload.

Tony had to deal with Prince now. Strike one for the
psychedelic pinhead was his trying to compete on Tony's turf
for the cocaine trade. Strike two—conning Bruno Pelechaty
into stashing shit in his room and peddling it at the Albert.
Strike three was when he hassled Donovan in the bar by saying a Bender started the Lithium fire. Tony had something
special planned for him that would send a message to any
other loser considering a move against him, whether it was
Zoltan, Scott Kostyk, even Bernie.

Cowboy was at the front desk, jumping around like a
fart in a wind storm. In the bar, Big Ron was sitting with Jimmy Jazz and acting squirrelly too. Good. Tonight, he was going to earn the scratch Tony had been fronting him. Donovan
was at a table, pouring over a book with Scott Kostyk. Tony
had to talk to him about hanging around with that crackpot.
Velvet brought him his scotch and departed. She might not
know the details but sensed he was getting ready to drop the
hammer. Tony sipped his drink, watching the lobby through
the window. It didn't take long for Bruno to show up, coming
downstairs from his room and starting to clown around with
Cowboy. Tony sent Big Ron out the back door to get the Buick
and go pick up Bernie. Then he signalled Donovan to join him
and Jimmy Jazz. The three were heading to the lobby when

a bent, half-paralyzed man banged through the front door of the hotel. Bruno pointed at him and laughed.

"Look out, Cowboy, it's Lurch!"

"Don't taunt the poor bugger, you tool," Cowboy said.

"What's the gimp gonna do; beat me to death with a leg brace? Killer's so fucking crippled he can barely put one foot in front of the other."

"It's 1984, numb-nuts. Killer ain't fucking crippled, He's fucking physically challenged."

Killer's angry eyes bored into Tony as he walked to the bar. The pusher nodded to him and Killer nodded back as he muttered.

"I'll kill 'em. I'll fucking kill 'em all."

Bruno still hadn't seen the three men behind him, but Cowboy did and went into his spiel.

"You got any of that good smoking dope you been pushing for Prince?"

"I do for you, man," Bruno said, dropping a baggie on the desk. Cowboy scooped it up just as Jimmy Jazz clapped a hand on Bruno's shoulder.

"You're under arrest," he growled. Bruno pulled away and started bouncing around in the lobby like a beach ball.

"Back off, I'm packing!" he squealed and pulled a knife. "The bigger they are — "

"The bigger they are," Jimmy Jazz said. He snatched the knife away from Bruno, throat-punched him, and spun him like a twist toy, pushing him out the front door.

"You have a vacancy, Cowboy," Tony said.

Big Ron was behind the wheel of the Buick, Bernie in the back seat. Jimmy Jazz shoved Bruno in next to him and squeezed in on the other side, making a wimp sandwich. Tony rode shotgun in the front and told Big Ron to get in the middle so Donovan could drive.

"Turn right on Portage, Donnie. We'll drop this turd first," Tony said and as they pulled away, Bruno started to cry. At Memorial Boulevard, Tony had Donovan pull over by the bus depot. He turned toward the back where Bruno was wailing.

"Make him stop," Tony said. Bernie clocked Bruno. "You should have stuck to hawking cheap jewellery to hookers. Check his pockets."

Bernie rummaged through Bruno's pockets.

"Three baggies of pot, two bills in cash," he said.

"Give Donnie the grass, you take one fifty, let Bruno keep fifty. This is your lucky night, bozo. Go inside, buy a one-way bus ticket back to whatever boonie you came from, and never return to Winnipeg."

"What about all my stuff at the hotel?" Bruno asked. Bernie slugged him again.

"Some leave the farm too soon, some too late," Tony said. "You have fingers and toes, a head on your shoulders. You got your stuff. Now, get the hell outta the car."

Bruno bailed and Bernie broke into hysterical laughter. He was even loonier than usual. At least Donovan looked like he was holding it together. But then he started muttering to the car window. Tony had no idea what he was going to do with his brothers. He told Donovan to keep going until they pulled into the driveway of a house on Honeyman.

"Keep the motor running, Don; the rest of you come with me," Tony said. Bernie kicked in the front door and rushed into the house with Tony, Jimmy Jazz, and Big Ron behind him. They all stopped to gawk at the living room painted with stars, moons, and spinning galaxies. On one wall a Minotaur was humping a centaur, Medusa mating with a satyr, other creatures writhing in an orgy with naked nymphs.

They'd caught Prince by surprise. He was covered in paint, lying on a couch and rolling a joint. Billy Triangle lounged in a leather chair, brushing his long blonde hair. He reached for the blade on his belt and Bernie restrained him. Jimmy Jazz jumped on Prince, pinning him. Tony tossed Big Ron a roll of duct tape.

"Make yourself useful, tie their wrists and ankles," he said. Once they were secured Jimmy Jazz bounced Prince in the air, Bernie smacked Billy, and they dragged them out to the Buick.

"Drive back to Portage and go west toward the high-way, Donovan," Tony said after they were all loaded inside. Prince was petrified, but smirking and started droning in the back seat.

"An alien hit squad has arrived on planet road, Billy. Systems spiral within systems, webs inside webs, wheels and cogs grinding against each other. We were magnificent poet-magicians once, Billy; fierce warriors before we submitted to the machine—the bottle, pill, and powder."

"Shut the fuck up!" Bernie shrieked. It only encouraged Prince.

"The nuclear Christ will bathe us in divinity, the atomic furnace nailing angels to the sun."

Bernie angrily tore off a strip of duct tape, slapping it on the pusher's mouth. Prince kept mumbling though and Bernie became hysterical, pummelling him.

"Settle down, little brother," Tony cautioned. It seemed to calm Bernie. Traffic was light on Portage. Prince muttered incoherently behind the duct tape while Winnipeg receded behind them, darkness deepening ahead. At the edge of town, Tony told Donovan to pull over. A bad smell hit the inside of the car.

"Whew!" Bernie exclaimed.

"Who shit themselves?" Tony asked, lighting a cigar. Bernie sniffed the air then punched Billy in the head.

"This one," he said.

"Okay, everyone out," Tony ordered. They started walking into an empty field, dragging Prince and Billy. Tony stopped them when the Buick was a black dot in the distance. The area around them was open, no farmhouse or trees, just flat earth and frozen sky. Bernie giggled as he poured a Gerry can of gasoline on Prince and Billy. But Tony didn't let him light the match. He wanted the pusher to freeze, not burn. Cowboy had given him the idea, telling him how Sawchuk and his cop buddies would snatch an Indian off the street in winter, drive him into the middle of nowhere, and leave him there with no shoes or coat. Some didn't make it back to town or survive the starlight tour. Tony told Bernie to take the duct tape off the pusher's mouth. He wanted to hear him beg. But instead, Prince continued to babble, only faster now.

"I'll never paint that pearl of ice floating in the black sky, a gorgeous celestial orb weeping pale tears."

Tony's eyes went to a bright, cold moon surrounded by dark sky and shimmering streaks of dancing fire. He'd never seen the Northern Lights outside the city. Maybe Sarah would take a trip out with him to see them sometime.

"Take their clothes," Tony said. Billy Triangle whimpered and Bernie cackled as the two pushers were stripped and left in the field naked, huddling together and trying to keep warm. Big Ron drove heading back into the city, hands wrapped tight around the steering wheel, knuckles white, body shaking.

"You okay?" Tony asked.

"Never seen nothing like that," Ron said. Bernie went berserk and bellowed.

"Where you been your whole life, man?"

"Take it fucking easy, Bernie." Tony snapped. Back in Winnipeg, they eighty-sixed the Buick in a lot where kids could jack it. Tony had Buzz pick them up and then drop Donovan and Bernie at the St. James Hotel far from downtown. He was fed up with both brothers. Besides, he had a woman working the bar at the St. James. Maybe Simone could keep an eye on Bernie, let Tony know if things got really bad with him.

The Night Bernie Bender Torched the Trick Shop

What do you want to know about Bernie? Where do I start; the beginning, middle, end? I'm no storyteller. Maybe the night Tony tossed us a few bucks and dumped us at the St. James Hotel. My brother was on the run. A few months earlier he'd escaped from the Stony Mountain Pen. He was giddy, giggling like a loon, not cheerful or relaxed, but driven to be happy, pushed toward it. He was skinny too, edgy. Tony had been keeping him in bennies and taking speed had a tendency to loosen Bernie's tongue, his mouth twitching, words trying to push their way out. I was the only one in the bar who could see his crazy face going full-tilt. Anybody else would be scared shitless or want to scrap him. No in-between with Bernie.

The hotel bar was a desperate little hole; locals sucking back the suds, heat cranked too high, and heavy air strangling shadows, choking off 'Stairway to Heaven' while Bernie played it over and over on the jukebox. Earlier, we had helped big brother take out his competition, Prince and Billy Triangle, who were pushing dope on Tony's territory. We took their clothes and left Prince and his pal in a field far from town. Bernie laughed all the way back to Winnipeg. The old lady swore he was born laughing and slid out giggling. She was what the shrinks called a poor historian. I could tell a lot about my brother by how he laughed; his mood, state of mind. A short, sharp burst was sarcasm; a quiet chuckle, he was pissed, about to pop. Look out then. When we were little, his laugh had been light and full of life. It soured after reform school. Bernie was sixteen and stopped laughing then, talking too, and he loved to talk as much as he loved to laugh. He eventually got his laugh back and found his voice again. By then, we weren't kids.

The last time I saw Bernie was that night; it was in the year of Orwell in a city so bloody cold even Big Brother didn't bother with it. He was eager to talk, almost as if he knew things might go bad when the cops busted him. It was only a matter of time until they did. He leaned in close to me and squeezed my arm.

"The vibe tonight reminded me of my first fire," he said, flicking his lighter. It flared like a flamethrower in the dark. Our waitress came over, told him to stop. He winked at her, his laugh a deep, disarming growl. Bernie was flirting. I tossed her a twenty for the drinks, told her to keep the change. I was flush with a little extra scratch. Tony had settled up with me after I handled a skinner some woman he knew wanted dead for messing with her kid. I threw the goof over the side of the Disraeli Street Bridge. The envelope Tony gave me held an extra five bills. It was a surprise. A dollar usually had to bleed before it left his hands. Bernie was babbling now, telling me he was fifteen and staying out of trouble when he found a job at the Mardi Gras Restaurant.

"Across the street from the Lyceum Theatre," he said. "Fountain in the front window has a freaky clown statue, a harlequin painted crazy colours, and customers toss coins into it for luck; boss donates the cash to the March of Dimes, deducts it from his taxes. I'm good. Keep my paws out. Work like a fiend racing around customers with a cart cleaning tables, the owner, an Ichabod Crane pretzel-man, chasing me through the dining room, arms and legs flapping, screaming at me to go faster. Late one night, I'm setting my last table when this older waitress, about thirty, gives me a hip-bump, says she'll finish for me. Claudette leans over the table, skirt rustling, and I catch sight of the soft, creamy skin just above her nylons and garter. I join the waitresses at the back, all legs and laughter, smoking cigarettes, counting tips, sharing war stories about this guy hitting on them and that jerk stiffing them. They're voluptuous and vivacious, crossing and un-crossing long legs like swinging pendulums. It's sweet torture for a boy of fifteen with only a brother at home. I've had a thing for waitresses ever since."

Bernie guzzled down his drink, ordered another, and gave the waitress a wink when she brought it. Then he went back to babbling.

"The job pays eighty-five cents an hour plus another fifteen cents each waitress shoots me for bussing her tables. I scoop up any leftovers to bring home to you. I hated leaving you alone with Whiskey Jack and the old lady."

Neither of us had ever evicted our parents from our brains. They were lushes, the beerful tearful crying the blues and leaking juices along the ripped seams of their lives. Our four older brothers had escaped before I was born, leaving Bernie at home. The old lady pawned him off on Nana for awhile. She didn't mind. He was company. On Saturday nights she would take him to the corner of Selkirk and Andrews to watch the drunks fight outside the Merchant's Hotel. One time, he saw a guy get kicked in the head so hard his eyeball popped out. But Nana hated when he climbed in her tree and put him on a leash tied to the clothesline. Bernie could run around the yard, just not near the tree. After I popped out, she wouldn't let our parents saddle her with a second kid and sent him back. Whiskey Jack was pissed and put him in charge. So, at the age of six, Bernie became my primary caregiver. He grew into the role and would get excited telling me how our uncle, Just Joe, was teaching him about tools so he could find work fixing cars.

The scene at home was a real trip; the old lady screaming at the houseplants for stealing her air, the old man grabbing the nearest kid to lay a licking on. I was her favourite so most of the time, he left me alone. Bernie wasn't so lucky. Sitting on the floor in front of the television one night, he didn't move out of the way fast enough when Whiskey Jack came home hammered. The old man brought an army boot down, grinding the heel of it into Bernie's hand so hard you could hear bones breaking over his screams. But Bernie seemed happy tonight as he reminisced about the Mardi Gras. He was a born storyteller and had a talent for that sort of thing.

"The law makes all the restaurants where women work late provide them with a ride home at the end of the night. The law doesn't apply to fifteen-year-old boys. Every Friday and Saturday they cut me loose at two AM to make my way back to the North End. I'm wired and detonate out that door with nowhere to go, no way to get there. I often end up at the Princess and Notre Dame Salisbury House where you can grab a cup of coffee or get the shit kicked out of you for looking at somebody wrong. One time, Just Joe staggers in half-cut, looking for a scrap, and he starts to hassle a waitress the regulars like. I get him the hell out of there before he ends up in hospital or worse. He offers me a ride home but cruises the streets instead until he finds two women willing to get into his car for a case of beer in his trunk. He drives us to some dump on Dufferin, leaves me on the couch with a beer, and goes off to a bedroom with them. I fall asleep to the sound of their grunting. When he wakes me, the women are gone. He still doesn't take me home but back to his house. Aunt Willa is waiting with a belt and starts beating the living crap out of him while he runs around, wailing like a pussy."

Bernie started to laugh then cry, choking back tears. This always happened when we talked about Just Joe.

"If I'd only known then what that fucker did to you later, Donnie, I would have killed him right there. I was supposed to be your protector and I screwed up."

Bernie was still in reform school on my eleventh birthday, Aunt Willa visiting family in Ontario. Just Joe picked me up for a sleepover. I was flaked out when he started touching me in a way that felt good but I knew was wrong. I never should've told Bernie when he got out because he went after Just Joe with a crescent wrench, cracked his jaw, broke his nose, and almost tore off an ear. Bernie was finished crying now and started telling his story again.

"One night after work, I head down Princess, hang a left at Logan to cross the Salter Street Bridge. I know I'm back on my own stomping grounds when I get to Selkirk Avenue. Five in the morning, the street is a lonely concrete corridor and my feet echo on the pavement. At the corner of Andrews near the Merchants, a creep crawls out of the shadows, offers me two bits to go into the back lane with him. I run and I keep running till I'm out of breath, can't run no more. Selkirk and McKenzie I see a light turned low in a store window, shadows moving inside. I try the door of the Trick Shop. It opens."

Bernie waved for fresh drinks, tipped our waitress generously, and asked her name.

"Simone," she said, smiling at him before leaving. Bernie started talking again, faster now.

"Neighbourhood kids all go to the Trick Shop for candy, pop, smokes; but it sure is creepy in there at night. Leo sips from a teacup and sits behind a glass counter filled with fireworks and magic tricks. Rows of grinning Halloween masks hang on the wall, staring down like suspects in a grotesque police line-up. Leo's pal, Knobby stands by the door, wearing an old overcoat tied at the waist with a belt. He clings to crutches, balancing on one leg with a plaster cast on the other and bouncing around like a flamingo. He snags a bag of bacon chips off a rack and chows down, complaining they look like deep-fried foreskins. Leo gives me pop, says Knobby thumps his radish all night long and it sounds like he's banging nails into a two-by-four. Knobby starts to whine his mouth is dry. Leo lifts a bottle of booze, offers to lubricate his lips. They're both piss-drunk and crack up. I don't get the joke but laugh. Leo asks me if I'm ready for a real drink. First time I ever tried rye."

Bernie stopped, lit a cigarette, and took a puff before he continued.

"Leo says Knobby ain't been right since his girl dumped him. Crawls ten blocks on his hands and knees to win her back, she tells him it's a stupid thing to do. I get a picture of bozo down on all fours dragging his butt in the dirt. Can't help it and laugh so long and loud, Knobby loses his mind, jerks a crutch over his head, comes at me, hopping on his good leg, screaming at Leo to let him go get the axe and he'll split my skull, bury me in the basement with the rest! Leo says to leave me alone. I'm just a kid. Knobby leans in close to me; eyes glazed and bugging out, grins with black teeth, his breath bad as he growls, old enough to bleed, old enough to butcher. Then he spins around, turns on Leo, calling him a senile reprobate and screaming at him to stop acting holy and righteous. He ain't no man of the cloth no more. Leo doesn't say a word and just sips his whiskey. Knobby is ranting.

"God won't be there when they drop the big one. Best pile all your people in a car, drive into the blast. Better dead than fire racing up and down your body."

Bernie started rubbing his chest. He drained his glass and went to the bar to get refills. He seemed more relaxed when he was talking to Simone, laughing and joking with her. But back at our table, he was serious again.

"Trick Shop becomes a regular stop for me. Beat the Sals. Leo and Knobby are a real hoot, yucking it up and telling jokes, hitting the sauce. I drink pop, sometimes rye. One night I finish work, the boss barks at me in front of everyone, accuses me of stealing food, and fires me. It's a long walk back to the North End. I have no idea how to feed us now. Knobby isn't at the Trick Shop, just Leo. I spill my guts to him and he shoots me a rye, listening all sympathetic, nodding like a fucking bobble-head while I blubber. Then he wraps his big, hairy arm around my shoulder and puts a greasy paw down my pants. I freak out and take off. Why do skinners always come on to us, Donovan? Is it something we say or do, the way we look? Don't matter. I make Leo pay. Every Thursday, he closes early, goes to his Mother's place for supper, and stays the night. I throw a rock through the window, crawl into the Trick Shop. Never noticed before how bad it smells. I snatch a couple cartons of cigarettes to sell Tony, pour gasoline over everything, and light it up. Firecrackers pop. Rockets fly. Masks melt. Whole North End come out to watch the Trick Shop go up. Nothing pulls the neighbourhood together like a good fire, eh. Guess that was when I got the bug."

This time Bernie's laugh had a bitter edge. He finished his story, finished his drink, and left the bar with an arm around Simone's waist. It was the last time I saw him alive. I went back to my room at the Royal Albert Arms Hotel and pulled on a bottle of Jameson until dawn. My mind wouldn't shut off. Memory is just like the old lady, a poor historian, feeding me comfortable lies, fuelling my rage about wrongs, real and imagined. So how do I record what happened without straying from the truth? I can't. The most I can hope for is authenticity, some degree of accuracy in the telling, knowing I will fail.

Bernie didn't become a fire bug torching the Trick Shop. It went back farther. We were still little kids lying in bed awake, listening to Whisky Jack and the old lady party downstairs. She had left her lighter in our room. I showed Bernie my magic trick. Set my tee-shirt on fire. He oohed. I blew it out. He aahed. My brother was older than I was but a follower. He had to try it. Thing was he had a bad cold, camphorated cream rubbed all over his chest. The harder he blew, the bigger the blaze became. He spent six months in hospital with third degree burns and had to have skin grafting. We never talked about it afterward. Time went by and before too long it was like it never happened – until he took his shirt off.

Bernie spent the rest of his life trying to put out that fire. Every time he did though, he had to set it first. So the night Bernie Bender torched the Trick Shop did start something. Everything does. Everything opens into another thing. Beginnings become middles, middles endings, and endings arrive when you stop, stare into the abyss, and laugh like hell, knowing death is just the period at the end of a life sentence.

Four Strong Winds

Sheila was going to be royally pissed. Every day for the last ten, Cowboy had convinced Bob to stay after his shift to help with some chores. It was a little extra cash and this morning Cowboy even bought him a beer. When Donovan and Scott Kostyk joined them, Bob ended up hanging around longer than he'd intended. On his way home now, he was sure he could make it up to Sheila though. He finally had a night off and could spend it with her.

The night before the bar had been the usual disaster area with piles of cigarette butts, chip bags, and broken beer bottles scattered everywhere. But Bob had his system down for doing the job as painlessly as possible. He tackled the hard jobs first—cleaning toilets, mopping floors, and vacuuming the carpet before taking on easier tasks such as wiping down tables and chairs. It was satisfying to watch scummy surfaces come clean as he scrubbed. He believed the work possessed real value, allowing people who looked down on people like him to have a pleasant environment. There wasn't much loose change lying around anywhere. The waitresses had already scooped up any serious cash the drunks dropped and he'd only managed to scrounge together a few dimes, nickels, and pennies, enough for a coffee. But he had a stroke of good fortune while doing the carpet. Under a corner table by the women's washroom, he spied a large brown lump. He carefully rolled it out with a broom in case it turned out to be something unpleasant. It wasn't what he had feared fortunately, but a huge hunk of hashish. When Cowboy came downstairs in the morning, Bob didn't tell him about his find. Soon, he and Sheila were celebrating five years together and the smoke would allow them to celebrate in style.

The curtains were closed when he got home. Sheila wasn't there. Bob sat in the dark living room, wondering where she was. It usually took a crowbar to pry her off the couch. He removed the large bulge pressing against his leg in his pocket and it proved to be a significant piece of real estate. Sheila would be none the wiser if he chipped away at the hash a little. He gathered some provisions — two slices of cold pizza, a jar of Velveeta cheese, crackers, and a beer. He took this feast to the living room on a tray, settled on the floor, and turned on the tube. 'Nightmare Alley' with Tyrone Power and Joan Blondell was just starting. He carved off a small nugget of hash, dropped it in his pipe, lit up, and took a deep toke. Bob hadn't had good smoking dope in ages and savoured it, nibbling on pizza and grooving on the flick. But the movie stretched out too long and he lost interest when the story shifted from carnival spooks and geeks to a hoity-toity society crowd. Banjo Bob turned off the TV and the picture dissolved in seeds of light and jitterbugging stars. He took another hit off the pipe, touching a match to the pellet and drawing a blossom of smoke deep into his lungs, tasting the pungent fragrance on his lips and tongue and the roof of his mouth. He exhaled in the same slow, deliberate fashion he had inhaled and tapped the soft, gray lump of ash into a saucer. Then he lit a thin green candle that radiated shimmering threads of light. It lifted his spirit into the stratosphere and he set more candles ablaze, filling the room with fiery galleons that floated on the air while smoky shadows gyrated on the wall, doing a frenzied voodoo dance. Bob put on Tangerine Dream's 'Firestarter' and turned the volume up. Time dissolved as he strummed Jedidiah, drifting on rhythmic waves of music. Fingers of wind were tickling his face and Bob breathed in the cool, fragrant air. But it was winter. There were no windows open. When he looked up from his banjo, the living room was gone and he was sitting on the ground in a vast plain with the warm earth under his feet. Clouds were skimming across a black sky and the sun bleeding gold at the edge of the horizon.

A ring of large, imposing stones surrounded him like dark sentinels. It was Stonehenge. A sudden loud bellowing broke through the spell's delicate membrane and it fragmented, disintegrating on the living room floor.

"How the hell can you hear anything over that noise?" Sheila shouted, striding over to the stereo and switching it off.

"It's not noise. It's Tangerine Dream. Where you been, babe?" he asked.

"Don't you mean where have you been? You're always bugging me about getting out. So I did. Dave treated me to lunch and a movie. We saw 'The Dresser' — brilliant but depressing. The English are almost as bad as the Russians at being bleak."

"Nice of Greasy Dave to take you gallivanting," Bob said.

"What can I say? He's a genial giant, always bringing over beer, takeout food, and bud."

"He's becoming a fixture on our couch. But hey, you like him, and you never like people."

"You sound jealous, Bob."

"No, not jealous, just a little disappointed. He was supposed to hook me up with his friend at the folk festival and still hasn't."

"Maybe he doesn't want to hurt your feelings."

'What do you mean?"

"Don't tax your brain, Bob. What's this?" Sheila asked, picking the hash up off the floor.

"Found it in the bar. It was supposed to be a surprise for our anniversary."

"Nice," Sheila said appreciatively, sniffing it. The phone startled them and Bob answered. Cowboy's voice was a disembodied, surreal echo. Bob hung up and turned to Sheila.

"Cowboy wants me to watch the front desk for a few hours this evening then stay and clean the bar. It's a bit of a drag. I really wanted to spend my night off with you. But it means an extra twenty bucks in my pocket plus he said he'll spring for a two-four."

"You should go then."

"I hate leaving you alone again."

"I'll be fine. I can amuse myself, Bob. But leave the hash here with me for safekeeping."

Bob was still half-stoned walking downtown and experienced a dizzying array of emotions that gave expression to the night's exquisite splendour. Myriad, cascading images were starting to congregate all around, burrowing into him and hollowing him out, filling him with an incredible sense of well-being. Bob marvelled at the ebony tree branches layered with a silver-blue coat of diamond-encrusted snow and their naked limbs stretching up for a moon they would never reach. Street lamps cast a fine film of light onto twisting, labyrinth-like lanes that were leading him on toward whatever destiny lay ahead. A deep, spiritual epiphany elevated Bob, overwhelming him and eliminating any petty concerns plaguing him. This was damn good hash.

Cowboy was pleased when Bob waltzed into the lobby, blitzed but ready to work.

"Step into my office," he said, gesturing Bob to stand behind the front desk.

"I never worked the desk before, Cowboy."

"Not to worry. Switchboard is patched through to the bar and Velvet will handle any calls. You only need to stand here, look tough, and not let anyone upstairs without a room key. Should be quiet—no band, no cover, no problem."

"No band on a Saturday night?"

"It happens. I'll give you the twenty when I get back later. Your beer is under the counter; just don't crack the case until you get home. I've made this simple for you, Bob. So don't fuck it up. Any questions?"

"I only see a twelve of beer."

"You got good eyes. I couldn't swing a two-four. Anything else?"

"What's the baseball bat for?"

"In case I need to pop one out of the park. I'm gonna boogie, Bob. You be good."

After Cowboy was gone, Bob gazed around the lobby. He'd never been alone there before and an eerie vibe seemed to hang over it. He didn't know what to expect but greeted everyone who came through the door with a big smile. A few tough guys gave him hard looks but they often did in the bar too. He was surprised when a couple of real cuties flirted with him. This was unexpected but not unwelcome. It was quiet for the most part, just as Cowboy had predicted. The night passed without incident and after a few hours of nodding and grinning at people, Bob was bored. It wouldn't hurt to sneak a beer. He didn't have an opener so banged the bottle against the desk, splintering the wood. But the desk was so badly damaged he doubted anyone would notice. The beer was warm but wet and he had a few. Cowboy was late getting back and went straight to bed. Once the bar emptied, Bob started to clean.

Cowboy rolled downstairs early in the morning and cut him loose. It meant Bob could get home early and surprise Sheila, maybe even score a little nookie if he was lucky. He waited for the Wolseley bus at the corner of Notre Dame and Albert with beer bottles clanking in his coat pockets where he had stashed them. The bus driver would never let him board with an open case. His spirits were high and he felt fantastic, leaning against a building with ribbons of colour running up its length. Lion gargoyles glared down from the ledges and he shot them the peace sign as a thin, oyster-hued wedge of light limped across the horizon. But the bus didn't come. Time passed; Bob took off a glove, touching a finger to his nose. It felt like an icicle. The Salisbury House across the street was open. He dashed over for a quick coffee.

A weary-looking waitress with skin the colour of old sheet music and two black treble-clef bags under her eyes scrubbed the grill. Bob poured a coffee and smiled when he paid. She didn't smile back. He took a table by the window to watch for the bus. He'd missed the first at six and the next wasn't due for thirty minutes. At seven forty, he started to worry. He'd nursed his coffee about as long as he could without the waitress kicking him out. Bob grabbed a second cup and a day old copy of the Free Press at the counter then headed back to his booth.

"Refills are fifteen cents," the waitress shouted. He returned to the register and piled all the grungy pennies he'd picked off the barroom floor onto the counter. The waitress tallied them and slid several back.

"Keep it," he said and walked away. He sipped a coffee that had turned rancid in the pot, keeping one eye peeled for the bus while he read Leon Redbone's profile in the paper. There was nothing about any local players. This was typical. It was after eight when Cowboy raced across the street to the Sals, holding his Stetson so it didn't blow off. Inside, he strode to the coffee pot.

"Morning, gorgeous," he said to the waitress.

"That'll be sixty-five cents, Cowboy," she grumbled.

"You may be cranky this morning, but still awfully cute, Kimmy," he said. The waitress sprang a leak and grinned. Cowboy had a knack for turning grumpy souls into songbirds.

"Had a rough night dealing with the drunks and my relief is late," she said. He shot her a buck, waved off the change, and joined Banjo Bob in the booth.

"Can't get enough of us, eh Bob?"

"Waiting for the Wolseley bus"

"Well, you'll wait awhile. It doesn't run on Sundays."

"You're kidding. That means I have to walk home and I'm exhausted."

"Tell you what, here's twenty, take a taxi. Pay me back when you can."

"Thanks, Cowboy," Bob said, tucking the twenty-dollar bill in a pocket, only realizing later after catching a cab at the St Regis Hotel, Cowboy hadn't paid him for the night before. Well, he had the cash now and what was left of the beer. The cab driver had the radio tuned to some easy-listening, turbo-pop, poop-du-jour station. But the taxi was warm and Bob was comfortable. He watched the world drift by the window from the back seat. The early-morning sky had turned to asphalt and street lights strung out like pearls on a necklace hypnotized him as they whizzed past. Bob woke up when the taxi jerked to a stop.

"Is this the place, pal?" the cabbie asked. "Hey, I forgot to turn on the meter. Let's make it an even sawbuck."

Bob paid the driver, stuffing the crinkly ten dollar bill he got back in change into a pocket where he would conveniently forget about it until he found it later and could celebrate his good fortune. Bob was looking forward to seeing his honey and ran up the apartment building stairs. Even with the screwed up buses, he was still home early enough to surprise her. He put his key in the lock, turned it, and pushed. The door only opened partway. Sheila had the chain on. Bob hated being locked out. It brought back too many bad memories. Bob pounded on the door like a bass drum then heard rustling and what sounded like whispers. Sheila took forever getting to the door. She flung it open wide and walked away without a word, a hug, or a morning kiss. Bob took the beer to the kitchen, put four in the fridge, and opened two. When he went into the living room, she'd already assumed her usual position on the couch and was leafing through an issue of Arts Manitoba. She didn't look up. Bob placed a cold beer against her cheek.

"Fuck! What is wrong with you, Bob!" she squealed, snatching the bottle and banging it down on the table beside her. Before he sat down, Bob made sure the cat wasn't squatting in his chair. Sheila continued to ignore him and he sipped his beer, scanning the living room. Books, scratched records, empty beer bottles, dirty dishes, and ashtrays were strewn all over. He could have thrown a hand grenade into the clutter and not made a dent. Then he spotted the guitar case tucked under the couch at Sheila's feet.

Banjo Bob stood up and felt her eyes follow him to the bedroom where he discovered a full complement of ten toes sticking out from under the sheets at the bottom of the bed. He went back to the living room, sat down in his chair again, and removed his toque, tossing it on the floor. He took a deep swallow of his beer. Sheila pulled her dressing gown tight around her throat and lit a cigarette. When she spoke her voice was hoarse from smoking and drinking and fucking his friend. But her words were more an accusation than an admission of guilt.

"What did you expect?" she asked. "How many times did I tell you I don't like being alone when you're working in that fucking firetrap? Say something, Bob! I can't interpret your grunts."

Greasy Dave stumbled into the living room doing up shirt buttons. He grabbed his coat and guitar case. Before leaving, he turned those sad, puppy dog eyes on Bob and mumbled.

"Sorry, man," he said. Funny thing was, Bob believed him. His former buddy shut the door quietly going out.

"Well now I know why they really call him Greasy Dave," Bob said. "Guess I can kiss that friendship goodbye, eh. He never did connect me with his pal at the folk festival."

"You're never gonna play there!" Sheila shouted. "You're tone-deaf!"

Banjo Bob shot to his feet and stood over her, his whole body shaking. Sheila, startled by his sudden aggression, cowered on the couch. When Bob turned to see his raised hand trembling, a deep sigh rocked him. He wasn't sure whether he wanted to hit her or fall to his knees and cry. He ran to the bathroom instead, locking the door and bashing both fists against the wall until they were bleeding and he'd punched holes in the plaster. Then he sat on the toilet seat and wept, only stopping when he had no tears left. He was empty of them, bone dry, his spirit wrung out. He felt nothing. Back in the living room, Sheila was still cringing on the couch. It was his turn to ignore her. He needed time to figure things out. Bob snatched his coat, toque, and Jedidiah, slamming the door going out. He walked to the Wolseley Salisbury House around the corner. Nobody else was inside. He ordered a bowl of beef stew and started plugging quarters into the juke-box to play Neil Young's cover of 'Four Strong Winds' over and over. The Ian Tyson tune was the sweetest, saddest song he'd ever heard, a mournful melody of regret, lamenting the pain of a lost love. It never failed to stretch Bob out on a rack of remorse and heartbreak. He had tried to create some of that same magic in his own songs, longing to catch the beauty, poignancy, and resonance of Tyson's work. He never had.

Maybe Sheila was right. Music moved through him but kept going. It was the story of his life. Everything he ever had was either lost, stolen, or broken. He had remained positive despite this though, resisting any effort to reduce him, weaken his resolve, or crush his spirit. He always believed better times were ahead and refused to yield to the resignation he had witnessed on his mother's face, the despair in the old man's, the desperation of a sister not smart or pretty enough, the struggle of a brother neither gifted nor skilled. Even with this sad family legacy, he managed to maintain his equilibrium and live according to the simple mantra that things would be alright in the end. Sheila complained he had a Pollyanna complex and that the thick-skinned feel too little, the thin-skinned too much. She warned him betrayal came on silent, padded feet to collapse hope. But Bob had never expected her to turn on him like this, believing her more loyal, Greasy Dave a better friend. He fished around in his pockets to find silver for the jukebox and pulled out the gloves she'd given him. He sniffed the leather. It carried him back to the first heady days of the fabulous disaster when Sheila fluttered her eyelash against his in a butterfly kiss. The time together must mean something and maybe their relationship could still be salvaged. They only had to get passed her indiscretion, talk through things, and work it out. Bob's determination was kicking back into gear now. He would continue to make music, play the Winnipeg Folk Festival, and forgive Sheila. He couldn't stay mad at her forever. He didn't realize how long he was in the Sals. It was dark out when he trundled back over to their place. A ragged tangle of apprehension and euphoria filled him as he turned his key in the lock. It didn't work. He examined a shiny new lock, tracing scratches in the wood with a finger. He banged on the door. She didn't answer. He started to pound harder and yell. The caretaker came out of his basement apartment.

"Hey Joe," Bob said. "I can't get inside."

"Sheila had a guy in earlier to change the lock."

"But it's Sunday."

"She told him it was an emergency."

"You gotta spare key?"

"The lease is in her name, Bobby."

"Aw c'mon, man. All my stuff is inside."

"Not my problem. You better split before one of the neighbours calls the cops," Joe said and went back down to the basement. Bob didn't know what else to do so hit the road.

The city was slow clearing the sidewalks in this part of town and he avoided the deep snow by sticking to a narrow footpath tamped out by others. Buildings towered over him, jagged, angular shadows. Bob rambled not sure where to go. He stopped and rested on a bench at the legislative grounds. A sparrow on a tree branch shuddered with the cold while the wind kicked clouds around a dark sky. He had nowhere to stay. His friends were either shacked up or on the street, Howie Hardy on the run, and crashing at Greasy Dave's not in the tarot cards now. Well, at least, he had Jedidiah. It was a good thing he took the banjo everywhere with him. Maybe he could sleep in the bar at the Albert or on the floor in Bertha's Place for a night or two. It was worth a shot. His fingers were fused to the handle of his banjo case by time he got to the hotel.

"Just can't get enough of this joint, eh?" Cowboy said.

"My old lady threw me out."

"Don't tell me you beat her up, Bob."

"Naw man, I don't even know how to make a fist."

"You're in luck. A room just opened up. Bruno, the Midnight Jeweller, is no longer with us. I haven't had a chance to clean it yet and the shitter and shower are down the hall, but it beats the Sally Ann or a park bench. Take the key, get a little shuteye, and we'll talk in the morning. And blow your nose, Bob. You got frozen snot in your moustache."

The room on the fourth floor was down the hall at the back by the fire escape. If there was a fire, Bob could get out fast. In the room, the smell of mildew and urine burned his eyes. He broke a paint seal on the window and cracked it open despite the cold. In the parking lot between the Royal Albert and St. Charles Hotel, two shadows wrestled, either fighting or fucking. On the window ledge he found a green mouldy orange, six Styrofoam cups of frozen pee, and a plastic bag filled with packets of aluminum foil. Banjo Bob dropped the orange and cups of piss over the side, hoping they didn't land on anybody. He brought the plastic bag inside, opened a foil packet, and popped a magic mushroom in his mouth. The chocolate didn't mask the bitter taste and he had to chew around a sore tooth. He counted ten aluminum packets in the bag. They'd keep him stoned a month if he paced himself. Then Bob jumped off the bed, flipped over the mattress, and found eleven more baggies loaded with hash, grass, tabs of acid, and mushrooms. His first impulse was to share the news with Sheila, but the wind quickly went out of him. He was alone again, naturally, in a smelly room in a sleazy hotel. He put the bags back under the mattress, curled up on the bed, and cradled Jedidiah, feeling a familiar emptiness surround him, threading through the universe of the room, touching his heart, and opening a hole in him, knitting a deep melancholy into the isolation and loneliness creeping over him. Eventually, he fell asleep and dreamt of easy travel to other planets.

A sudden, sharp jolt of cold shot through Bob and he shuddered. He was numb, his noodle spongy. Cowboy was standing over him with a sour expression on his face. Bob always thought the desk clerk looked like Lee Van Cleef on steroids. But seeing him through a psilocybin filter now, he realized Cowboy more closely resembled Yosemite Sam on acid.

"I've been banging on your door for ten fucking minutes and was beginning to believe you might be dead in here, Bob. It's good I got a spare key. You need to keep that window shut. The room is freezing. So I talked to Zoltan and he's okay with you being here. Wash up, meet me at the Ox for a brew, and I'll fill you in. First dancer hits the floor at eleven."

"Got nothing else on my agenda, man."

"That's the spirit, bro. Now hurry up."

Bob went down the hall to the washroom and turned on the hot water tap in a sink. A loud howl erupted in one of the showers. Scott Kostyk shoved aside the curtain, looking like a pissed-off lobster. Banjo Bob shrugged.

"Didn't know you lived here, man," he said.

"I don't," Kostyk snapped and closed the curtain, resuming his shower. Bob splashed cold water on his face. He decided after a drink with the desk clerk, he'd call Sheila, tell her about his score, and see if they could sort out this mess. He had nothing to lose. He was in the clover and Cowboy had even called him bro.

Vandal

The racket in the hall was driving Donovan crazy, a steady cacophony of rattling machines and babbling idiots walking by his room, not to mention Siren prattling relentlessly in his brain. Siren always came and went in the past, appearing and disappearing, popping up to catch him off-guard, then slipping off into the void again. In the brief periods when Siren wasn't there, Donovan had a little peace. But now, Siren was stuck in his mirror and there was no rest or break from his singing in a piercing falsetto that drilled right into Donovan's brain.

"If I was a proton and you were a neutron," Siren sang. "Would we matter anyway? Would you have my baby?"

Donovan turned on a radio and cranked the volume. Someone in the next room banged on the wall.

"Shut the fuck up!" Donovan screamed and the loser went back to drinking his ripple.

"Posses of rocketing particles ricochet off the cerebellum," Siren said. "Zing! Zing!"

Donovan raised the radio over his head and was about to throw it across the room when an announcer started reading news. He lowered the radio, sat on the bed, and listened.

"Bernard Bender was arrested last night after a tense standoff with the police. Pulled over for a routine traffic stop, Bernie the 'Blaze' threatened officers with a sawed-off shotgun before being taken into custody. After escaping from Stony Mountain Penitentiary five months ago, he faces new charges, including armed robbery, arson, and manslaughter in connection with a fatal fire in the Exchange District six weeks ago that took three lives."

Donovan hadn't heard from Bernie in a week, not since the night they were drinking at the St. James hotel. Now, he knew why.

The news finished and strands of golden oldies started buzzing in the background, braiding together with Siren's cooing. It wasn't the first time the Bender name had been in the news, but this was different. Bernie was in serious trouble. They would be holding him at the Public Safety Building on Princess Street. Donovan grabbed his coat and headed downstairs. The lobby was empty—no Maggie or Cowboy to slam him with sad eyes, nosy questions, and counterfeit concern. On the street, the air drove an icy spear into Donovan's lungs and helped clear his head. It was four in the afternoon and Loopy Larry's girl was already standing on the corner at Albert and McDermott. Donovan nodded but kept walking. She didn't need him scaring away her johns.

The Public Safety Building elevator had splatters of blood on the ceiling. Donovan doubted civilians would even notice. He rode to the top floor and the door rattled open on a large area filled with desks and wall dividers. He explained who he was there to see and the cop at the counter raised an eyebrow before leading him down a corridor into a hall of steel-plated doors. He stopped at one with the number eleven painted on it and slid open a narrow slot.

"Bender! Visitor! You have ten minutes," he said. Donovan squinted through the slit at Bernie who was bobbing and weaving in the cell with a silly grin on his face, his eyes bruised and his lips puffy. He was still stoned.

"Would have made myself pretty for ya, bro," Bernie said. "But some moron in here before me busted the taps; ain't even any ass-wipe. Makes Stony look good; be glad to get back there."

"So you resisted arrest, Bernie."

"What can I say? I never go down easy. Sawchuk is old school, eh. I deserved the beating he laid on me. I'm just lucky he didn't plant me. I still got a lotta living to do. Word to the wise, bro—no matter how smashed you are, don't point a sawed-off at a cop and tell him you'll blow his fucking head off if he moves. Silly goof grabbed the business end of the barrel and started to wrestle me for it. Good thing it didn't go off — for both of us. I still haven't figured out why they stopped me though. I was doing the speed limit; car was clean, the plates good. It was my girl's car. You remember Simone, waitress I hooked up with at the St. James? Anyway, they nailed me for that fucking fire a few weeks ago. Apparently, I left humongous footprints in freshly fallen snow. Nobody has dogs like me, eh."

Bernie's big feet were a legend; he once beat a kid half to death for calling them pontoons.

"Wolch figures the Crown is gonna go for dangerous offender; may mean a long sentence. I know you hate visiting the folks but I left some vintage leather there. Best you snag it before Whiskey Jack pawns it. Trench coat is worth the trip. You'll look like a rock star in it."

Back on Princess Street, Donovan took a deep breath. Going to see his parents never ended well. They hadn't been to see him while he was in Selkirk. The old lady wrote long loopy letters that made no sense, including a few bucks for the canteen. That was it. Still, collecting Bernie's coat and holding onto it for him was the least he could do for his brother. Donovan walked down William to Main Street.

There were two stretches of no-man's-land cutting the North End off from the rest of Winnipeg. The first, a large expanse of railroad track, extended from the Salter Street Bridge to the Arlington Street Bridge. The second stretch was the Main Drag, a grim landscape with a dozen dreary hotels selling cheap booze to the weaving winos that choked the sidewalks, while gangs of kids with little to lose looked for an easy score. Donovan strode down Main Street like a stealth machine, sticking to the shadows and scanning the street for signs of trouble. Outside the Occidental Hotel, two cops wearing buffalo coats were dragging an unconscious woman to the meat wagon, leaving dark skid marks in the dirty snow. After they'd dumped her into the van, they walked behind it with the doors open wide as they advanced to the next passed-out drunk. The meat wagon would go back and forth between the Main Drag and the drunk-tank for the rest of the night. In front of the Bell Hotel, a couple of kids, strung-out and looking like they hadn't eaten in a long time blocked Donovan's path. The name Bender would mean nothing to them. The bigger of the two had dead eyes, but it was the small one with the mouth.

"Gimme a smoke," he snarled, yanking the pack from Donovan's hands. "Wallet too."

Donovan turned his empty pockets inside out.

"We should kick the shit out of you, fucking white trash." the kid sneered. They wandered away instead to find more profitable prey. The CN underpass was a short, dark tunnel stinking of piss. On the other side, there were fewer hotels and less street action. Donovan kept his guard up anyway. He turned off Main at College, walking to Charles and the building where his parents lived. He stood between the doors and braced himself before he pushed the apartment button. Whiskey Jack's voice crackled through an intercom.

"It's me," Donovan said and the lock snapped open. He took an elevator to the eleventh floor and walked on down a hall as dark and dismal as those at the Albert. He knocked on their door. The old lady screamed at him to come in. He entered the small, gloomy living room where his mother was glowing blue in front of the TV. She waved a glass of gin at him.

"Get in here, you silly bugger. About time you showed up!" she shouted. She was still in a good mood, talking fast, spitting out words the same way Bernie did when he was on speed. Who knew how long this would last. He hadn't seen her in five years and his mother looked different. She was thinner; her hair drab and straw-like, falling out like Nana's had. Old pictures of her had shown a pretty young girl with platinum blonde hair that turned to strawberry later in life.

"Grab a seat!" she shouted. "Your old man is in the can. Where else, eh? Why did you take so long to come see me, Donovan?"

"I was in hospital," he said. Her tone turned from honey to acid.

"Don't play me for stupid," she snarled. "You've been out a whole month. I wouldn't even know if Tony hadn't told me. At least, your big brother is good for something."

He hadn't been there five minutes and his mother was already dragging him into the muck. She pointed at the TV where bombs rained down on Beirut.

"The world has to smarten up," she said. "They sent a man to the moon! You can't get my clothes cleaner than that!"

"Let me turn it off," Donovan said. "There's nothing on but crap."

'Don't you dare touch it, Donnie! PTL Club is on next. The preacher is a hoot, looking like his face hurts when Tammy mangles another tune. All that rot and pretend tickles me and I enjoy watching the thieves, liars, and assholes. They're like my husband and my boys — all except for you. You're different, Donovan. Come give your mum a hug."

He leaned over to hug her just as Whiskey Jack wandered into the living room, shaking a newspaper in triumph and trumpeting his successful trip to the toilet.

"I'm twenty pounds lighter," he announced.

"You're disgusting," Doris said. "Thought you fell in and got flushed into the Red River."

"Well, you can always hope, Dor."

"Say hello to your boy," she said. Whiskey Jack collapsed on the couch, sipped his drink, and rustled his newspaper.

"You hear me!"

"Settle down, Dot."

"Not Dot! Doris! And Doris wants a drink," she said, turning to her son. "How about you?"

She was disappointed to see Donovan decline. Whiskey Jack drained his glass, snatched hers, and went to the kitchen. When he returned, Doris took two lithium and washed them down with her drink.

"Show me," Whiskey Jack said. Doris opened her mouth and wiggled her tongue,

"Satisfied?" she snapped and handed him her empty glass. "Get me another gin."

"You gotta slow down, woman," he said then pointed at Donovan. "Come with me."

Donovan followed him to the kitchen while Whiskey Jack started to brag about being flush with his pensions now.

He pulled a ribbon of cash register tape from his wallet and flashed it at his son, waving it in his face as he flung open kitchen cupboards crammed with cans of stew, chilli con carne, corn, peas, salmon, and sardines. There was white bread, brown bread, and rye; boxes of pasta, rice, and cereal; tins of cookies and cakes and pies, jars of jam and peanut butter. The old man pulled open the fridge, revealing shelves filled with fresh fruit, vegetables, three kinds of cheese, eggs, milk, ice cream, and meat—cold cuts, pork chops, bacon, sausages, a roast, ground beef, a chicken, fucking steaks. The old man was beaming with pride as Donovan fumed. He remembered he and Bernie scrounging for food as kids, scarfing down what they could find, eating uncooked oatmeal from a cardboard tub, sugar sandwiches with stale bread.

"I'm here to collect Bernie's coat," he said. Whiskey Jack's Jekyll kicked over into Hyde.

"Figured something like that. You know your mum is sick, eh. The woman goes through emotions like cigarettes. She's a babbling maniac one minute, a moaning Minnie the next. Doc says she's bipolar, whatever the hell that is. If this keeps up, I'll have to sign her brain away again, maybe for good this time."

"I don't hear my drink being poured!" Doris screeched from the other room. When Whisky Jack and Donovan returned with her gin, she was happy to see her son holding a beer.

"Don't think you're gonna drink it all, Donovan," Whiskey Jack snapped. "He came to get Bernie's coat, Dor. Don't look so surprised. You didn't honestly think he was here to see us."

His mother's eyes were sad and accusing, her mouth a trembling gash. Donovan wanted to collect Bernie's coat and get the hell out before the inevitable outburst but he hated upsetting her. His mother had it tough living with Whiskey Jack. Maybe having a drink with them would help calm her down.

Whiskey Jack led him to a spare room. He didn't turn on a light. Donovan rummaged in a dark closet until he felt the cool leather on his fingers. He pulled the coat from the closet and turned around. His father punched him in the face. Donovan could feel the anger flare first, the fire surging in his veins. Then the cold came, ice flooding into him and quelling the flame. He smiled. It unnerved the old man. When Donovan was just a boy, Whiskey Jack beat him with an army web belt. Donovan never reacted or showed any feeling, no crying, wailing, or screaming, nothing. It frustrated and rattled the old man. It was the same cold that Doris sometimes showed. Back in the living room, she eyed them both.

"Your nose is bleeding, Donnie," she said. "So, how is your brother doing?"

"Bernie? Screws put the boots to him," Donovan said, wiping blood away with a sleeve.

"Serves him right," Whiskey Jack snapped. "Kook knocks over a 'We Jump to the Pump' gas joint then threatens to kill a cop. What's wrong with that boy? What was he thinking?"

"He wasn't thinking, Jack," Doris said. "He never does. Radio says he set a fire killed three people. Did he, Donovan?"

"Well, we are prone to pyromania, Mom."

"You watch your fucking mouth," Whiskey Jack growled.

"No Jack, Donovan is right. We've had a few fires in the family; the first one when he and Bernie were little boys, Bernie burning down the Trick Shop, time I fell asleep with a cigarette in the house on Aikens. Remember the house on Aikens, Jack? You were supposed to buy it for me but never did. I'm happy it wasn't you they arrested, Donovan. You're the best of my boys."

"Are you fucking nuts? What about when he freaked out, broke every single window and mirror in that house you wanted so bad? He's a vandal—a vandal and a killer. None of our other boys ever murdered anyone."

"Not that we know, Jack. Put your teeth in. It's disgusting watching your gums flap."

Whiskey Jack laughed and went into his clown act. The old man always bitched about his wife's volatile nature but he wasn't exactly stabile. He had a chopped-liver face, a mottled nose, and a glass eye he dropped into his drink at the bar when he went to the can. If some drunk came along and was crazy enough to try and swipe his drink, they got a good jolt when they saw Jack's eye staring back at them from the bottom of the glass.

"I have it all, Dor—spectacles, testicles, wallet, and watch," he said, making the sign of the cross, cracking her up.

"Pour me another drink, Jack," she said. He went to the kitchen, this time returning with a glass of booze for each of them and a fresh beer for Donovan. Whiskey Jack and Doris were well lubricated and on the way to being totally drunk. Donovan decided to join them. It was a family tradition that often eased the tension, putting all the anger and bad feelings aside for awhile. The party really got going with the three of them in overdrive. His parents belted out the best hits of two world wars and Whiskey Jack told stories about his army days and his buddy, Gord McKay.

"He went on a big piss-up while his wife was away; sold the fridge, stove, and furniture for a hundred bucks. After he drunk that up, he sold the car and a side of beef he lifted from the sergeant's mess. They busted him back to private for that."

"He had a fancy woman on the side too," Doris said.

"Yeah, well, he kicked the bucket a few years ago. Gord was half-cut, marching down the middle of Portage Avenue when a car honked behind him. So he dropped his pants and wiggled his ass at them. Turned out it was a cop. After they locked him up at the Public Safety Building, they called his wife. She said he could hang himself. So he did."

"He's better off dead, Jack."

"Whatever you say, Dor. Man, we had some good times though. Remember when we got loaded and went to wrestling? Ended up in the ring, scrapping with the wrestlers? They were all wimps. You had to come bail us out, Doris."

"First time I ever saw the inside of a police station," she said. Whiskey Jack had to be up early for work and finally went to bed. Doris stayed up a little longer to talk to Donovan, crying about missing her mother, laughing about how happy she was to see him. Before heading to bed, she told him to sleep on the couch. He waited until they were both snoring, put Bernie's leather coat on over his leather jacket, took the last four beers, and left.

The street was dead at five AM, no sirens or shouting drunks. Donovan decided to take the Salter Street Bridge back downtown anyway. The punks on the Main Drag would be even more desperate now and less discriminating about their prey. As he was tramping across the bridge, he remembered Bernie telling him about going the other way toward the Trick Shop. Bernie was no thinker. After reform school he had snatched purses to feed them, not realizing the woman at the other end of it might need the money and could be hurt trying to hold onto it. Bernie was running with a rough crowd too and they got him into even more trouble. Manfred Krueger stole a car and took Bernie for a joyride that ended with six cop cars chasing them to Portage La Prairie. They came close to being killed when Manfred lost control of the car, almost slamming into a concrete wall at the Rolling Mills. Another time Bernie's buddy borrowed his cool coat, robbed a Seven Eleven. They busted Bernie because of that coat and he did a year in Headingly Jail, not ratting out his pal. Bernie was facing real serious charges now and looking at hard time.

Donovan stopped halfway across the bridge, cracked open a bottle, and drank down icicles of beer. A cold wind blasted in his face as a black shadow burst from its hiding place underneath the bridge. Donovan traced the perfect symmetry of the raven's path as it arced high in the dark sky. Below him railroad tracks coiled in every direction, boxcars banging like thunder while the crews assembled freight trains. Siren was scuttling around on the ground and chasing rats among fragments of broken glass. Donovan saw the skinner's smashed face at his feet. No pity or mercy for his kind. Mess with kids? The fucker deserved to die. Donovan hated how do-gooders always assumed the abused become abusers. The so-called experts were just lazy thinkers, not tracking anyone who didn't show up on their radar. Their shitty little system didn't record those like him who kept what happened to them a secret, healing themselves and getting on with their lives. He polished off his beer, dropped the bottle over the side, and leaned over the bridge, howling into the black night before starting to walk again.

It was light when the Albert came into view. Donovan went straight to his room. He was exhausted, falling asleep right away, wearing Bernie's coat with its leather skin pressing into his own. He woke up late in the day, needing a hot shower to scrub away the residue of visiting his parents the night before. But he couldn't bring himself to take Bernie's coat off and he had to talk to Tony about their brother's situation. He downed a beer and went to the sink to splash cold water on his face. Siren was in the mirror and stuck his tongue out at Donovan, wiggling it like the old lady did sometimes. Donovan went down to the bar and Jimmy Jazz peeled away from Tony's table when Donovan sat there.

"Don't tell me I spooked Jimmy Jazz," he said.

"Very funny, little brother," Tony said. "So you finally went to see the old lady, eh?"

"How do you know?"

"You always get squirrelly after going there. Well, more squirrelly. Besides, Bernie left the leather coat he boosted from Bruno with them. It looks better on you."

"I saw him at the Public Safety Building yesterday. He's still blitzed and in rough shape. Bernie is gonna crash hard when he comes down, despite how positive he usually is."

"The kid is a fuck up," Tony said, taking a pull on his cigar. It was hard to know what he was thinking. Tony never shared his thoughts. But he had a plan. Tony always had a plan. It was something Donovan understood that Bernie and his other brothers never did.

"What happens now, Tony?"

"Wolch can't do much for him now. Crown has what they need to put him away for a long time. He say anything about the fire?"

"Not a word."

"Don't worry about Bernie. I'll take care of him. How you doing, Donnie? Still holding it together without your meds?"

"I'm fine, Tony."

"Good. Get Lawler to boost your Ritalin. It's selling."

"My shrink may be an educated idiot, Tony, but he's not dense."

"Don't worry. He'll do it. So, this Kostyk character you're hanging around with lately, he's always crying in his beer about the fire, taking fucking pictures in the bar. He has to stop."

"We only talk about art and poetry. He's the only person I know besides Banjo Bob who treats me like I have a brain in my head."

"Well, keep your eyes and ears peeled and your mouth shut around him. Beat it before you scare off all my business."

Donovan scanned the bar. Banjo Bob was sitting alone in a corner looking miserable. Bob was like Bernie normally, always putting a positive spin on things no matter how bleak. But he wasn't his normal happy self. Living at the Albert, even for the few days he had, was exacting a toll. The hotel would either corrupt Bob or crush him. Donovan would try to keep his friend safe although there was only so much he could do. Bob brightened when Donovan bought him a beer, but his blue eyes looked like lilies floating in bloody egg-white.

"Appreciate the brew, man," Banjo Bob said. No sooner did Velvet drop their drinks on the table than Itchy Dick showed up.

"Love the tee-shirt, Bob," he said. "Born Again Pagan is so cool, so you."

Dick blew his nose loudly. Banjo Bob exploded.

"Knock it off! You ain't cutting no jazz album!"

"Relax, man. You only got the blues cuz your old lady gave you the boot."

"Maybe you're right. She won't take my calls or nothing. I guess I went with the flow and got flushed. Man, I miss her angel face, the foghorn voice, and boomerang stew she used to feed me, even if I barfed it back up half the time."

"Bummer, Bob," Itchy Dick said. "But hey, things could always be worse. Look at poor Bernie Bender stuck in the can. It's heavy if he did what they said, eh Donovan."

Siren blasted up from a carpet stain, started doing laps on the ceiling, and then crawled into the skylight. Donovan's silence charged the air, seeding it with a dangerous energy the other two could sense. Itchy Dick shut his mouth but Banjo Bob tried to lighten the atmosphere and burst into song. Before long he was leading Itchy Dick and some of the drunks in a rousing chorus of 'Barrett's Privateers'. Donovan decided it was time to leave. Cowboy was in the lobby, holding the phone at arm's length while Zoltan shouted through it at the other end. Siren buzzed around now, studying posters taped to the walls, wailing along with the bums singing the Stan Rogers sea-shanty in the bar. Cowboy cursed and yanked a jack from the switchboard.

"I have worked for tyrants in my time, Donovan, but none as crazy as Zoltan Kisich. He gets on the horn, wants to know if it's busy. I say no. He says fix it. I try to explain I can't run out into the street and haul people in here. He blows a gasket and hollers why not. I tell you, he gets owly when he's doing too much dope. Nice coat, by the way. It looks familiar."

"It belongs to Bernie, my brother. You know — the one your cop buddy beat to a pulp."

"Whoa, slow down, man. Sawchuk ain't my buddy. He's just a dude who shares dirt that I pass on to Tony. Listen, as long as you're hanging around with nothing to do, I need a favour."

"You want me to watch the desk."

"I'll make it worth your while, slip you a few bucks."

"Lemme get something first," Donovan said. He sailed up to his room, returning with the book he'd been trying to read. He squeezed behind the front desk.

"Need to grab a quick drink before I scoot," the desk clerk said, disappearing into the bar. The odd regular straggled in off the street and nodded to Donovan. He didn't acknowledge them and they scurried to the bar or to their room. Then Big Ron showed up. He thumped two large green garbage bags onto the counter.

"Got something for you," he said. He rummaged around in one of the bags and fished out a full-length sheepskin coat.

Donovan was used to drunks and thieves trying to sell him goods at the desk. Sometimes he bought a sweater or watch but never anything with a serial number. Tony had taught him some things.

"Not in the market right now, Ron," he said.

"No, not that, man. You and Cowboy been good, letting me crash here when I had no place to stay. The coat is a thank you gift. I broke into Colin's condo—the creep sweet talked Vera into leaving me. Beat the crap outta the fucker and stole his stuff which I will now sell in the bar. Did you hear about Prince? He lost both legs and a few fingers to frostbite after his little trip outta town. Billy croaked. I still can't wrap my brain around the way we left them. I gotta get out of this town, man. Maybe I'll split when I win the lottery. My old mum didn't leave much when she died besides her birth date. I'll play the numbers on my next ticket. Maybe they'll be lucky. I'm going inside."

Donovan checked out the sheepskin coat after Big Ron was gone. It was worth eight bills easy. The lobby was quiet so he tried to read the book Suzie gave him in the hospital. He and the nurse started talking after he saw her with a copy of 'Beautiful Losers'. Donovan hadn't known anybody of his generation who had read Cohen's novel, let alone hers. But so far he couldn't get into this story about a pathetic jerk wallowing in self-pity, bellyaching about his poor choices in life, and how, if he had it to do all over, he would do better. But at least the book was something to look at besides the puke-green lobby walls and posters for concerts and plays he'd never see. Donovan was a few pages into the book when Darla Jones swept into the lobby. The woman was mischief on a stick with a sweet swivel in her hips and fierce, shining eyes which never failed to fascinate him. She had a warm, confident voice and hands that danced when she spoke.

"Aren't you a little hot wearing a leather coat in here?" she asked.

"No," he said.

"You're just hot then, eh? What are you reading?" Darla asked studying the book. "'Strange Life of Ivan Osokin'.

Russian. Depressing. You see Zoltan? I'm supposed to meet him here."

Before Donovan could answer, the front door groaned open and he gripped the baseball bat Cowboy kept under the counter. Sawchuk rolled up to the desk and towered over Darla.

"Beat it, scrag," he said. "I wanna talk to your boyfriend."

Darla started to protest but then reconsidered and left for the bar. The woman had good instincts. You didn't want to give Sawchuk a reason to remember you. He grinned at Donovan.

"Skinny piece of ass, eh," he said. "But maybe you like them built like little boys."

The pig was trying to provoke him. Donovan didn't bite; he knew the deadeye tango, bait and response, challenge and withhold.

"What can I do for you, officer?" he asked. The cop roared with laughter.

"It was me busted your brother. Bernie squealed like a little mouse when I slammed his nuts in a desk drawer, almost pissed his pants when I hung him by his feet out the window at the Public Safety Building. Some tough guy. Few years before his first stretch at Stony, I chased him through St. John's Park, the two of us slipping and sliding on wet grass. I was about to give him a taste of my service revolver when he jumped in the Red River. Hit the drink like a fucking speed boat. I never seen nobody swim in that scummy water. But I caught him later just like I did now. You Benders are all born to do time, but not Tony eh. He's the BF Skinner of the gutterset, always putting people in boxes — pine, cedar, oak. You see him?"

"No."

"How about Jimmy Jazz?"

"Jimmy Jazz was here but now he's gone."

"What about these two?" Sawchuk asked, dropping two eight-by-tens on the desk, one of Prince, one of Billy Triangle.

"They come around sometimes," Donovan said.

"Not lately I bet," the cop drawled. Cowboy sauntered into the lobby with a glass of rye.

"It's Louis Sawchuk, pride of the Winnipeg Police Pipe Band! How is the kilt hanging, you hunky bugger?"

"Who you calling hunky, halfwit?" the cop growled.

"Not you. Hey, you hear the Russian Bear is back in town? I'm heading over to the Charlie now to pay my respects. Join me. I'm buying."

"You trying to bribe me, Cowboy?"

"Indubitably."

"Well, we better go then."

"What's new?" Cowboy asked the cop, patting him on the back while winking at Donovan.

"Aw, this snot-nosed banker says I need a million bucks to retire. How did he dream up a number like that?"

As they went out the door, Siren soared on the ceiling in dizzying circles while Donovan's mind flipped around like a fish in a boat. He fired 'Ivan Osokin' into the garbage.

"Did you just toss a book in the trash?" Zoltan asked.

"Where did you come from?" Donovan asked.

"I have access to many ways in and out of here. Why you give that book the heave-ho?"

"Couldn't get into it," Donovan said.

"Lemme have a peek," Zoltan said. Donovan dug the book out of the garbage.

"Mind if I hold onto it for awhile?"

"It's all yours."

"What are you doing on the desk? Where's Cowboy?"

"He went to the Charlie."

"The bugger is supposed to be working. Get him on the line," Zoltan said, snatching the receiver away when Donovan got through.

"Be back here in five minutes or I throw all your shit in the street," he said, slamming the phone down. Zoltan was all coked-up and acting zany, starting to rant.

"Don't let Cowboy take advantage of you, Donovan. I know his kind. I lived in the North End too. The kids considered

me a rich guy, called me the candy store, and took my chocolate and cigarettes. I always carried two decks of smokes
though — one for them to take and one for me to keep. When
we moved to a better part of town, the privileged punks there
looked down on me because my parents owned a saloon.
Now look at me. Both those crowds come here to drink. So
who has the last laugh?"

Cowboy was breathing hard when he charged through
the door, his Stetson half off.

"Well, I see my stuff ain't sitting in a snow bank," he said.

"Not yet," Zoltan snarled. "You abandoned your post
again."

"Should I work the front desk or run the bar? I can't do
both. What exactly is my job?"

"Tentative."

"What have you got against me, man?"

"Nothing an eviction notice can't solve. Get behind the
desk, Cowboy. Donovan, wait for me in the café. I'll be right
back. And lose that god-awful fucking coat. You look like a
hood."

Zoltan hustled off to the bar with the tight-assed,
wound-up wiggle he always had when he was stoned. Cowboy settled in behind the front desk and Donovan went into
Bertha's Place. He removed Bernie's coat and hung it on the
back of his chair. He was at the same table as the night he first
saw his brother back on the street. Now Bernie was rotting
in a cell. Zoltan strutted into the café, looking pleased, and
dropped into a chair across from Donovan. Darla came in behind him, stopped in mid-stride when she saw Donovan, then
sat beside Zoltan.

"You two know each other?" Zoltan asked.

"Stop being a jerk," Darla snapped.

"The question was rhetorical."

"Like your love life. Since we're being so cozy, Zoltan,
where is Sarah Grant tonight?"

"Now, you're just being a bitch. Darla can't help herself, Donovan. She's from Toronto."

"You invite me for dinner, he's here?"

"I can't feed my two favourite people? See what Donovan gave me," Zoltan said, holding up the book.

"You aren't going to finish it?" Darla asked Donovan.

"No," he said. "It's too much like real life."

"So, who was that obnoxious character in the lobby?" she asked.

"The creep is a cop," Donovan said. Zoltan went white.

"The police were here? When? Why? What did they want?"

"What they always want," Donovan said. "Information."

"What did you tell them?"

"What I always tell them—nothing. You can relax."

"I have nothing to hide," Zoltan said. Bertha arrived to take their order, smoothing down her apron and treating Zoltan like a rock star. He ordered Gran Marnier for himself, a double scotch for the others.

"Take the premium scotch from my private stock and put it on my tab, Bertha. Darla, I heard you and Fran are performing at that Benefit coming up. I imagine it will be an evening of giggles and garters."

"Not everything is about sex, Zoltan."

"Au contraire, sweet-thighs."

Bertha brought their drinks. Zoltan ordered shrimp and snow peas, Donovan a burger he knew he wouldn't eat. But the scotch was smooth. He could get zonked on Zoltan's liquor.

"Do you have vegetarian?" Darla asked. Bertha looked confused.

"You are what you eat, Darla," Zoltan quipped. The two of them started trading insults, trying to outdo one another with clever comments like it was a parlour game. Donovan couldn't care less about their pretentious wit and didn't listen. He was thinking about Bernie being in jail. When Zoltan snapped his fingers in front of his face, Donovan wanted to break them off.

"I have to stretch my legs," Zoltan said. "We need another round and I need to talk to that bonehead in the lobby about the cops."

Zoltan walked around to Donovan's side of the table, whispered in his ear, and left.

"What was that about?" Darla asked.

"I've been assigned to fascinate you until he returns."

"Think you're up to it?"

"Your eyes are like they're lit by blue fire."

"Oh please, not another poet."

"What you got against poets?"

"Nothing lobotomy can't cure. Are you actually cracking a smile?"

Donovan wanted to let go of his concerns and enjoy this woman's company. Zoltan was shrieking in the lobby and then banged into the café, still shouting.

"I don't pay you to think, Cowboy! If I did, I wouldn't get my money's worth!"

"What's up?" Darla asked as he collapsed in a chair.

"Cowboy is half-cut again, talking rubbish about the police. I am going to fire his ass."

"You say that once a week, Zoltan," she said.

"I mean it this time. And don't you tell him, Donovan. I know you're his confidante."

"Cowboy doesn't have confidantes, just conduits," Donovan said.

"Wow, I am impressed," Zoltan said.

"Because I see through him or because I'm not monosyllabic?"

"Oh please. Don't go commie on me. I can't handle any more proletarian angst. This city is full of it. Forget about the food, let's go somewhere fun. Drink up. But I guess I don't need to tell you, Donovan?"

"No," Donovan said, slamming down the scotch. A few hours later he blew back into the hotel in a rage. Zoltan had dragged them both to the Marble Club where he and Darla continued the brainless banter, while Donovan continued to drink, hoping for a buzz that never came. He'd left when he could no longer handle their yammering. One of the old men from upstairs was hollering at the front desk.

"That wing-nut on days has got to go, Cowboy!"

"What did Maggie do now, Fred?"

"I was sick in my room three days, only left to go down the hall to barf. Three days, not a single soul dropped by to check on me, see how I was doing. I couldn't eat, drink, or smoke. Thought I was going to die alone up there. And if I'd a croaked that silly woman would have been all — oh poor Fred, dead for three days and we didn't know. I should get him a card."

"Getting old ain't for wimps, buddy."

"Ain't that the truth," Fred said.

"I'll talk to Zoltan about her. Hey, you hear Loopy Larry got an eighteen wheeler?"

"Sweet! I miss the road, man," Fred said. "I ain't been inside a semi for years."

"Bullding, I've seen you take them up to your room. Couple times I thought the stairs were gonna collapse under her weight."

"Okay, so I like my women big."

"Grab a drink in the bar then go get some shuteye, Fred. You'll feel better in the morning."

Fred left muttering. Donovan approached the desk and Cowboy studied him while picking a strand of tobacco from his teeth.

"So how you make out with turnip tits?" he asked. "Get your noodle wet?"

"What are you talking about, Cowboy?" Donovan growled.

"Did you dip your wick?"

"Fuck off. I need a bottle."

Cowboy galloped to the bar, returning with rotgut. Donovan snatched it away and headed up to his room, stopping on the stairs to open the bottle and take a slug. Needles of fire tore down his throat. It wasn't Zoltan's high octane fuel but would do the job. Donovan was on a righteous tear. At the top of the landing, the walls were swaying and he almost fell. He took another long pull from the bottle. It steadied him. He stumbled into his room, slamming the door hard to send a message to his neighbours. Donovan collapsed on the bed, sank into a swampy mattress, and tipped the bottle back. Then he stood up again and went to the sink. Siren smiled at him from the mirror.

"Cut the moorings," Siren sang. "Suckling piranha dine on their host, feast on the flesh of fat cynics who no longer sport a lean and hungry look. Shadows now, they drift from a danse macabre to Saturday night disco."

Siren chanted his mantra like a manic jackhammer in Donovan's head and he wanted to tear open his skull and dig Siren out. He swung the bottle at the mirror. It cracked, cutting Siren in two. Donovan punched it and Siren splintered into a million cascading diamonds. He slammed his fist through the window, going at it with both hands and feeling no pain as the sharp shards of glass shredded his skin. He was super-human, tipping the bed, ripping the sheets and the pillow. Donovan broke a chair across the sink and swung a leg at the dangling light-bulb, popping it. He lifted bloody hands above his head and bellowed the Bender holler, screaming "Bernie!"

He woke much later, his joints grinding sandpaper, head only held onto his shoulders by a slender thread of flesh. Broken furniture and glass lay everywhere, ice pellets blowing in through a smashed window. Siren wasn't in the fragments of glass or anywhere else. Donovan stood but his stomach kept moving. He threw up then washed his face in scalding water, burning bruised, broken skin. He found the phone. It still worked and he called the front desk.

"Cowboy," Donovan said. "I need a hand."

Desolation Rose

Dodging Pa's audit cost Zoltan a friend. He'd known Charlie, who Cowboy called Rambo, ever since high school. Over twenty-five years, they'd shared so many things, windsurfing on Lake Winnipeg, wild partying, even a girlfriend or two. When Charlie went through a tough time after his divorce and was down on his luck, Zoltan gave him a job tending bar at the Albert. But the ledger didn't take prisoners. Sacrifices had to be made. His friend had to take the fall. Now, a month after the fact, fingering him for thieving was proving pointless. A few days ago, Pa called from Sarajevo. Tito was dead. Things were better. He and Ma were staying in Yugoslavia, so he was signing the hotel over to Zoltan. After years of Pa hounding him about how bad the business was doing, the Royal Albert Arms Hotel belonged to him. Zoltan could do whatever he wanted with the dump — sell it to someone stupid enough to buy it, drive it into bankruptcy, or just burn the flophouse down for insurance money.

The night before had been another late one and his head was ready to come off. Zoltan was thumbing through Donovan's book, an odd opus with a quirky protagonist. He tossed it on the desk. Maybe he'd take a look at it when his head didn't hurt so much. Trying to get Donovan and Darla together had been a bust. Donovan screwed off in a foul mood and Darla was pissy. Zoltan wasn't sure why it hadn't worked. He'd had success with Scott and Svetlana. Hiring Donovan to work on the front desk wasn't panning out either. Zoltan had hoped it might ease tensions with Tony and the pusher would back off about his debt. But it looked like things might actually be getting worse. Cowboy had told him Tony took Sarah for dinner after her boyfriend croaked. The timing of those two events couldn't be a coincidence. Maybe if he'd dealt with Sarah's problem, he would have been having dinner with her at Dubrovnik's instead. Then the phone rang. All the bills were paid for the week and Tony would have waited to catch him downstairs. So who could it be? Zoltan picked up. Maggie was her anxious self, saying Kostyk was on the line. Zoltan had her patch him through. It only took her three tries to establish the connection.

"Way ahead of you, Kostyk," Zoltan said quickly. "You want a date for a benefit I should never have agreed to host."

"Back out now, we'll both look like assholes, Zoltan."

"You're right. You always are, even when you're wrong. Well, let's do it then. How about the following Friday? Can your pals get their shit together by then?"

"Most of the planning is already done."

They arranged the details and Zoltan got off the phone, glad to tick this off his agenda. It was one less headache. But he still had to rally his remaining brain cells into a cohesive whole to get through the rest of the day. He opened the leather pouch, laid out a few lines of powder, and snorted them. He was ready to do two more when he heard a noise in the hall. He quickly cleared away the coke, went to the door, and swung it open. Cowboy stood there with a sheepish grin, or was it a devious smirk, on his face.

"What are you up to now?" Zoltan asked.

"About six one."

"You're eavesdropping again."

"Man, blow makes you paranoid. I chased Itchy Dick away from your door. Character does more snooping than mooching. Something we need to discuss. It's getting goofy around here. I need some extra muscle to watch the back door at night."

"You have Donovan."

"Still leaves me short."

"What about the night cleaner whatever-the-hell-his-name-is?"

"Banjo Bob is a well-meaning vacuum. No help in a jam. But Jimmy Jazz would be."

"You want me to put Tony Bender's enforcer on staff?"

"Jimmy's okay and you did hire Donovan, after all. He is Tony's brother."

"Donovan is different, doesn't buy into any of the bullshit. Make do with the resources I give you. Speaking of Banjo Bob, what about his room rent?"

"Have a heart, Zoltan. The guy hasn't got any income other than the twenty bucks a night you shoot him."

"He needs to either figure out how to get the cash or fuck off into the sunset with the other freeloaders. I own the Albert now and I have had it with losers ripping me off. I never should've let you run the bar with your harebrained ideas. Playing porno in the bar?"

"Hey, it brought in the booze hounds. The serious drinkers are flocking here now."

"It's driving away my other business! We're just lucky the press hasn't got wind of it yet. All I need is more bad publicity. And, if I catch you spying on me again, you're fired. Get out."

After the desk clerk left, Zoltan did another line of coke and considered his options. Maybe it was possible to restore the Albert's glory days; renovate the rooms and turn it into a boutique hotel; hire funky jazz bands to bring in a better crowd; create cultural events, comedy nights and theatre happenings. Before the fire Sebastian had done that successfully at the Lithium. He could give Bertha the boot, find a chef to offer gourmet dining. Nothing was stopping him. The Albert could become the in place to be again and this prospect excited him. He wanted to share the idea with someone he trusted; someone who would understand his passion, his hopes, and his dreams. He had always been able to talk to Sarah. It had just been lousy timing to try and tell her how he felt when he did. Maybe owning the Albert now and sharing his plans would make a difference, turn things around, and put them on track after so many missteps. After all, where was it written that love is easy? He grabbed his coat and headed out, stopping to buy a single long-stemmed rose. When Sarah came to the door at her mother's house, he pushed the flower on her. Although she accepted it, she had that hurt look she always got when things didn't go her way.

"What are you doing here, Zoltan?"

"We need to talk."

"I have to drive Amy to dance class."

"I only need a few minutes."

"Let me get my coat."

They walked around the block, Sarah turning the rose over in her hands while he babbled at warp speed. He couldn't read her thoughts and didn't know if he was getting through to her. Before long they were standing back in front of the house again. Sarah sighed.

"There was a time when I wondered what kind of partner you would make, Zoltan. But you are not interested in people, just things—your condo, car, clothes, and hotel. I'm glad the Albert is yours now after all the years of waiting. I know how much it means to you and I hope you find whatever it is you're looking for. But it has nothing to do with me. You need to leave me alone; stop calling and coming around. I feel like you're stalking me."

Sarah turned to go inside. Zoltan grabbed her arm and swung her around to face him.

"I know what you and Tony did," he said, spitting the words out.

"You're hurting me," she said, pulling her arm away. Sarah shoved the rose into his chest and stormed into the house. He let the flower fall from between his fingers, allowing it to drop to the ground before he crushed it underfoot. Zoltan didn't start the car right away. He'd been a fool pining away for Sarah. Every single encounter between them had played out along the same sad trajectory. But by totally rejecting him, she'd revealed her inner bitch. Well, his sensitivity had a shelf life. The next time she was lonely, needed someone to talk to about her feelings, he would not be there. She could talk to Tony Bender, assuming he wasn't in prison or dead.

Sarah's mother peeked out from behind a curtain, a little girl at her side. Zoltan turned on the engine of his vintage vehicle and hit the gas. He drove at breakneck speed, buildings flying by in a blur and whipping around a corner, he almost creamed a cyclist wearing an aviator cap. He rolled down his window.

"Who rides a fucking bicycle in February?" Zoltan screamed. He pulled into a quiet cul-de-sac and put the Jag in neutral. He needed to calm his nerves. There was no traffic here, not a soul in sight. Zoltan pushed a cassette into the deck, unzipped the black pouch, and did a line of coke. It didn`t touch him. He did another then threw the Jag into gear. He didn't need Sarah Grant. He had a full tank of gas, Miles Davis on the stereo, and a party waiting at the Albert. His provisions were getting low though. This meant he'd have to deal with Tony Bender.

Juggle Jazz

Darla absolutely adored her apartment with its funky character, spacious sun-lit rooms, and enclosed porch at the back that was an oasis overlooking the Assiniboine River. When she came home from work late, moonbeams would be dancing on the river surface and spilling quicksilver through the windows. On a sunny Saturday morning at the end of February, she was snug under a blanket on the porch, coffee warming her insides while she scanned the Toronto Star. An ad for a cattle call in the entertainment section caught her eye. Toronto Network Theatre needed singers and dancers who could act for Pietro Turnbull's latest musical comedy, 'Tit for Tat'. Pietro's last show had run for two years in Toronto before moving to New York. It was right up her alley; she was back in shape. Three weeks of dancing with Fran had shaken out the cobwebs. Darla decided to send them her CV. Her mind turned to the upcoming Benefit. While offering to perform at the event with Fran had been a spontaneous gesture of concern and would provide an opportunity for them to strut their stuff, it was proving premature. The organizers had announced a date. It was in a week. Darla didn't have enough material yet, just odds and ends; some kickass jazz tapes and one or two comic sketches she'd written. Fran had contributed a few provocative dance moves from her days as a stripper which could be tastefully integrated into their routine. But they had nothing to pull it together, no choreography to give the work a thematic focus. They had a name and Bodacious Bods was sexy enough without pushing the envelope. But that was it. Still, during their last session something intriguing did come to light. They discovered they both could juggle. Maybe that was the answer. Darla went to the closet, dug out her two sets of juggling balls, and dusted them off.

Fran arrived an hour late for their workout but was so charmingly unapologetic it hardly mattered. She explained she was up all night with her new beau. Darla outlined what they had on tap so far as Fran took off her clothes, revealing a black leotard and hot-pink tee-shirt under her jeans and top.

"You're staring, Darla," she said.

"How can I put this politely? Your breasts are so perfect, almost supernaturally buoyant, defying and even mocking gravity."

"Actually, they're unnaturally buoyant. I earned these puppies. Eight years ago I was in a bad car accident, almost died. I underwent a ton of rehab and reconstructive surgery. It took two years to put Humpty Dumpty back together. But I beat the odds staying positive and the plastic surgeon was a real sweetie, blessing me with these bionic boobs, a sad tale with a happy ending."

Darla turned on the stereo and scooped up the red balls while Fran snatched the blue. They started to shimmy and boogie, juggling to Charlie Hayden's 'El Ciego', bodies coiling sensually, coming close together then separating. Darla tossed Fran a red ball. Her partner pitched a blue ball back and it slapped hot and heavy into Darla's hand. They began to fire the balls back and forth rapidly until Fran was holding the red, Darla the blue. Sonny Rollins' racy horn took things up a notch with 'Strode Rode' and they picked up the pace, synchronizing their movements and the flight of the balls to the music's tempo. They were wriggling and bopping; Fran dropped a ball by accident. Darla did likewise by design. Then she lifted a second over her shoulder and let it roll down her back, bumping it with her butt so it joined the first on the floor. Fran followed suit, hitting the ball so hard with her generous hip it took out a table lamp. They collapsed on the floor, giggling and gasping; two weary wantons, slick with sweat and slippery, their shoulders, hips, and thighs lightly touching while a mellow, caressing clarinet oozed 'Blue Horizon'. Darla closed her eyes, letting the music carry her away then felt Fran's long fingers gently touching her cheek and her forehead, brushing damp hair from her face.

"I'm hot," Darla whispered.

"Yes, you are, sweetie."

"Seriously, I'm sweating like a ballerina."

"I don't sweat, Darla. I sparkle. What's this on the stereo now?"

"Miles Davis, 'Kind of Blue'."

"You know your music."

"I was weaned on jazz. My dad has a cigar store but plays drums in a band on weekends."

Fran stood and lifted her hands over her head, swaying to the melody like a lioness basking in the sun, her ivory skin tinted with a delicate, pink pastel, her hair fragrant with lavender. Fran had a good face, wide and open, with bright green eyes and lush lips no surgeon could create. The woman was elemental, fully inhabiting any space she occupied, filling it with an irresistible charm. She was going to be a sensation on stage. Darla was tempted to yield to her desire and the yearning to touch her. But the phone rang and she laughed at the cliché. She turned off the stereo and answered. Fran fled to the bathroom. It was Coil calling again.

After the night they hooked up at the Plaza. Darla had kicked him out. But he'd somehow managed to get her number and began bugging her. He was persistent, eventually persuading her to go out with him. Coil was needy though and became a pest. Then he showed up half-drunk in the middle of the night, banging on her door, hollering like a Brando wannabe. Darla knew that stalkers were more dangerous in stealth mode so let him in, reeking of tobacco and liquor. After discharging his sorry business, he'd lain in bed, blowing sticky gobs of spit on her back, running his fingers through her hair which Darla hated. It was one of the reasons she wore it short. But it didn't matter because she was dumping him the next morning. That was a week ago. Seven days later, he was still harassing her with unwanted phone calls and visits.

While he was ranting on the phone, Darla quietly dropped the receiver to thumb through a thin volume of verse by Neruda sitting on the table. The language of the poet was elegant even in translation and infinitely superior to the dreck Coil penned. He fancied himself a wordsmith and had a tendency to flit back and forth between narcissism and crippling self-doubt. Maybe it was his dismal poetry that had been behind her initial attraction. She'd come home one night to find a poem scratched out in his indecipherable scrawl taped to the door, the work more hysterical than lyrical but a little sweet too.

Fran returned to the living room fully dressed now and Darla was a little disappointed.

"I just peed the Pacific Ocean," Fran said. Darla hung up the phone.

"You ever wake up, wondering what terrible thing you did the night before, then roll over and find out you're lying next to it?"

"A time or two," Fran said laughing. "That reminds me I have a favour to ask. I started to date a drop-dead, gorgeous biker, tall and well-built with long red hair. Means I need to break up with Cowboy. I have no idea how he'll take it. I don't want to hurt his feelings. He's always been good to me. But he is twenty-five years older. I don't want to be his nursemaid. I thought I knew him but Eric has told me stories, scary things Cowboy has done. I don't have very many friends, Darla, especially female ones, and I need a friend now, someone to be there when I tell him. You think you could do that?"

The following day Darla drifted down to the Albert, dreading a confrontation between Fran and Cowboy. Donovan was on the desk. She hadn't seen him since he bailed on her and Zoltan at the Marble Club. She was still angry but he looked so forlorn, an intense energy skimming under the surface of his skin. He was a coiled spring wound too tight; head tilted to the side like he was listening to someone who wasn't there, body twitching as if electrodes were being jammed into him. Darla had only ever experienced such fierceness in a man once before, the Russian dancer who took her virginity when she was seventeen. She could sense something primal was passing between her and Donovan, an understanding beyond language or thought. He was the last of the enigmas. She would have to make the first move. Velvet came out of the bar and placed a drink in front of Donovan.

"Hear anything?" she asked. He shook his head. Velvet squeezed his shoulder and went back into the bar. Donovan drained the glass in a single gulp.

"Something wrong?" Darla asked.

"I'm waiting to hear about my brother," he said. "Cops busted him the other night when we had dinner with Zoltan."

"I just saw Tony in the bar yesterday."

"It's Bernie, my other brother."

"I'm meeting Fran now, but maybe we can grab a coffee some time," she said. Donovan didn't commit and Darla let it slide. Fran wasn't in the bar but all the usual suspects were getting loaded. Itchy Dick was roaming around trying to bum drinks and getting into everyone's business. Banjo Bob sat alone blubbering while Cowboy was holding court at the bar, drinking and joking with his buddies and flirting with any woman who came close. Fran deserved better. Then Scott Kostyk dropped into the chair beside Darla.

"You're performing at our Benefit," he said, his words slurred. "Me too. We'll raise a few bucks to help Sebastian and Terminal Jerks get back on their feet, though finding a new drummer may be problematic, considering theirs died in the fire. And I am not trying to be funny. Oscar was a friend, talented and astute, the only person who ever understood my game of table chess. We were in a booth at the Lithium Café. I picked up an ashtray like this and placed it at an angle to a napkin dispenser like so. Oscar understood right away and made his move, sliding the sugar shaker to a spot threatening the spatial integrity of my coffee cup like this. After that we went into high gear; doing this and this and this, repositioning objects and reconfiguring patterns on the table."

"Hey!" Cowboy barked, waltzing over. "Stop messing with shit on the table. Shoo now."

Kostyk slunk away. Cowboy dropped a drink in front of Darla saying it was on the house.

"Thank you," she said. "Does Zoltan know you're being so generous with his liquor?"

"He took a powder, if you catch my drift. How you doing? Getting a good workout with my lady? If you ever need those sore tootsies massaged, I'm your man, Twinkletoes."

"And where would Fran fit into that scenario?"

"The middle," he said and winked.

"Don't rub that woman the wrong way, Cowboy."

"Rather rub you the right way," he purred, thrusting his hips in Darla's direction. He didn't see Fran standing in the doorway until it was too late. When he did, he muttered he had to relieve Donovan at the desk and tried to give Fran a peck on the cheek. She pulled away.

"Sorry you had to see that," Darla said.

"It's okay," Fran said. "Cowboy can't help himself. He's always liked the ladies. Watching him come on to you will only make this easier. Let's go get it done."

The women had to run a gauntlet of eyes as they left and Cowboy greeting them with a cheerful chirp in the lobby. Again, Fran didn't respond with her usual good humour.

"We need to talk," she said, pointing to Bertha's Place as three bikers entered, blocking the way. Fran's eyes brightened when she saw Eric the Red; Cowboy's narrowed.

"What the fuck are you doing here?" the desk clerk snarled. "You know the deal."

"I'm visiting my old lady, old man," Eric said, throwing an arm around Fran's waist. He bent down to kiss her long and hard. Fran melted. When Cowboy's hand disappeared under the desk Eric released Fran, stepped over, and stood a few inches away from his face.

"I'll ram that baseball bat so far up your ass buckets of blood will pour out, you bleeder."

"Bang me, I'll bang you back, baby," Cowboy snapped. Eric laughed, gave Fran another soulful kiss, whispered in her ear, and left with his friends.

Bertha's was closed and Fran went into the dark café, Cowboy following her. Darla could see them leaning across a table talking, shadows silhouetted by street lights streaming in through a window. She didn't really want to be involved in a sordid little melodrama, but she'd promised Fran and couldn't let her friend deal with this alone. Cowboy's voice was getting loud. He glared at Darla when she entered the café and growled at her.

"This is a private conversation."

"I asked her to be here," Fran said. "I didn't know how you would behave."

"You're fucking a Curb Stomper, Fran!"

"This is what I mean. Listen to you yelling. You're scaring me."

"Eric is a scumbag, never done anything for nobody. He's using you."

Fran didn't answer and it almost seemed Cowboy could sense her slipping away from him. A pinprick of despair opened in him, expanding until it spilled out and he started to cry.

"Don't," Fran said.

"Of all the people passing through this shithole, you're the only one I trust, Fran."

"I know. You remind me of my uncle. Tom Fair was a bachelor his whole life too. I was still a little girl when he would walk all the way from downtown to St. James to have dinner with us. After we ate, he'd stretch out on the couch with me sitting on his chest while he told theatre stories. He was a stagehand at Pantages and met all the greats before they made it big; Chaplin, Keaton, WC Fields. Then he would walk back to his room at the hotel. He died there alone."

"Forget about Eric, Fran. It's better to be an old man's darling than a young man's slave."

"You have that backwards. Better to be a young man's darling than an old man's slave."

"I want to save what we have."

"It's all just feathers and bones now, baby — smoke and ashes."

"Please," he groaned, trying to kiss her. Fran turned away.

"You smell like an ashtray," she said. Cowboy went white. He stood, startling both women and stormed out of the café, slamming the door behind him.

"Poor Cowboy," Fran said. "I told Eric I wanted to handle this myself. He insisted he was worried about me. Isn't that sweet?"

Darla didn't believe leaping from aging barfly to outlaw biker amounted to much progress. But it wasn't her decision. The only two people who understand the chemistry between them are those two people. Love is in the details, desire less discriminating than logic. Cowboy was just like Coil, not knowing when to let go. Some men think they can fix everything; a car, a kitchen appliance, a failed relationship. But they don't understand, it isn't broken; it's over, and all the juggling and the jazz in the world won't repair it.

Jogger Hunt

Scott Kostyk worked in secret, not sharing his painting with anyone. Only Velvet had seen 'Dreaming Dread' when she stumbled onto it the day she visited his gallery — the same day that the cops carted him off to jail. Since then, he had poured everything into the carnivorous canvas, allowing it to consume him wholly with colour speaking to him free of contrivance or conceit. He was grateful that a decade of sterility was done, despite the disturbing possibility it might not have occurred without the Lithium fire. The blaze had rattled him yet ignited something else too, liberating him from stasis and shaking loose lethargy, sparking a fresh energy, rekindling a fire that had lain dormant. Kostyk was lucky to be alive. He could still walk and talk and hold a paint brush. He was also aware of life's capricious nature, the fact things unfolded despite his wishes, wants, needs, and desires. It all went cold in the end, believing otherwise was clinging to denial. Scott was meeting new people who challenged his way of seeing. Donovan and Banjo Bob were artists in their own right, closer to his creative obsession than his former friends. They might not be as refined, but weren't as remote or alienated from the stark clarity of the moment either.

After four weeks of labouring in the throes of delicious derangement and being gripped by an exhilarating fusion of pleasure and terror, he was ready to show his new work. Tonight at the Benefit, he would premiere 'Dreaming Dread', a tribute to Svetlana Bulgakov, his only regret she wouldn't be there to share his resurrection as an artist. Some days her absence was a weight pressing down on him and others when her death still didn't seem real.

But while he was excited at the prospect of showing his painting, Kostyk was anxious too, anticipating a strong reaction. He wasn't sure how well it would be received, whether his friends would love it or loathe it. Still, if nothing else, he was convinced his colleagues would have to acknowledge the accomplishment and recognize the reality he was making art instead of merely pimping it.

Initially, he'd struggled with how to present his painting. The canvas was enormous, too cumbersome to carry over to the Albert even if cut into sections. There was a danger of damage during transportation too, especially in winter. Then, days before the event, a solution hit him. While he despised the medium, the best way to preview his painting was as a multimedia piece, using slides, music, and text. It would still showcase his genius. Fuck false modesty. Kostyk snapped a dozen photos of the painting from different angles and perspectives, some in soft focus, others in sharp relief, adding pictures he took around the Albert and at the scene of the fire. He converted them into slides and arranged them to tell the story of Svetlana's death and his survival. Then he wrote a short, provocative, vital script. He couldn't wait to share his work with the world.

Before leaving the gallery, Kostyk went over the material one last time; sorting through the slides to be sure they were in the right order, checking them for scratches. After this, he loaded them into a knapsack with his script and a tape of the music he wanted to use.

Outside, the air filling his lungs was cold and crisp but fresh, bristling with energy. Frost had hung a silver shroud over everything and the beauty stirred him. This Benefit wasn't just about raising money for Sebastian and Terminal Jerks. The community needed tonight; it was an opportunity to celebrate the lives lost, possibly gain closure, to start the healing process, allowing people to push past their pain.

Walking down Albert Street, Kostyk thought he heard bells. He whipped around, expecting to see Prince sneering at him, Billy Triangle by his side. Neither was there. Billy Triangle was dead and Prince lying in a hospital bed, both legs and hands amputated. He would never again hold a paint brush, assuming he ever had. Kostyk doubted the paintings Prince always bragged about doing even existed. The pusher was a poser with one foot in the art world, the other in Tony Bender's. He didn't have a foot in either now. Scott shuddered. It was a sick thought.

The small crowd milling around in front of the Albert were acolytes of Terminal Jerks, the next young generation, slumming in the gritty part of town, sowing their wild oats before fleeing back to the safety of the suburbs. They didn't deign to acknowledge Scott, had no idea who he was, and couldn't care less. He was just another sorry fossil dragging his decaying ass into the hotel. Kostyk understood how the process of hierarchy worked, with the pantheon of personality placing politicians, captains of industry, athletes, musicians, and actors at the top; poets and painters at the bottom. But performance elevated the lowest forms of life, raising personal stock in the realm of celebrity and generating instant charisma, creating admiration whether warranted or not. Kostyk's current status as a cretin would be reversed by the end of the night with young women sniffing contemptuously at him now congregating around him, casting flirtatious glances his way, clamouring for attention.

Cowboy was fretting at the front desk inside.

"Where are your fucking friends?" he shouted. "We need to get this shindig rolling".

"Not my problem. I'm just performing tonight," Kostyk said, enjoying not being in charge for a change.

"Maybe not your problem, but you and the crown prince made this possible. I was turning away regulars for over an hour. Your pals don't show up soon, I will slap on a cover and throw the doors open."

It wasn't long before Karmin and Sebastian lugged a large wooden table into the lobby and dropped it on the floor. Sebastian placed a cashbox on top and started counting out a float while Karmin arranged items; a rubber stamp, an ink pad, and a placard with photos of Svetlana, Oscar, and Arnold Sinclair, the homeless man in his army uniform. Kostyk wondered where she found the picture. He placed his slides and music tape in front of her. Karmin ignored him. He cleared his throat and she snatched them away.

"Where is Furnace Face?" Kostyk asked. "I thought he was out of hospital."

"He's not coming," Karmin said. "He's so shaken up he's moving back to the country."

"Sorry to hear that," Kostyk said. Karmin raised her eyes to his.

"No, you're not, Scott. You've done nothing but mock and humiliate him from the first day he got into town. I don't know how long I'll hang around. You know, they found a severed hand in the back lane behind the fucking Bate Building last week? No idea how it got there or whose it was. I can't help but think of poor Prince, what he went through almost freezing to death."

The crowd was beginning to come into the lobby. Karmin grabbed her bag and went to the bar. Sebastian sat behind the table, taking twenty dollars from each kid and pressing an ink stamp on their hand before letting them pass. He was all dolled up as his alter ego, Pollyanna Piranha, and dressed in a gold lamé gown with a big bow at the back, fishing tackle earrings, and a blonde beehive wig. He looked like Dusty Springfield on steroids. Kostyk forked over a fifty and waved off the change.

"A small contribution to the cause," he said. Sebastian touched an ink stamp to his wrist. It made Kostyk smile. A few years ago, he, Svetlana, and Karmin had initiated an experimental, multimedia, interdisciplinary stage called Spare Change; it was a venue that allowed artists of every discipline to explore new ideas and take a different direction in their work free of critical comment or conjecture. It was a safe place to fail without risk. Kostyk remembered lying on the floor under a table in the bar at the Albert, plugging and unplugging a cord in a socket to achieve a certain lighting effect as Sylvester Eleven spewed his bad poetry and strummed a stand-up bass he'd fashioned from car parts in art school. A reviewer at the Free Press got wind of what they were doing, showed up, and wrote a scathing review: 'Spare Change, Part Dada Part Dumb'. So Svetlana designed a stamp with 'Dada Dumb' and buttons they sold for a buck apiece.

"Let's get some fresh air before the hordes descend on us," Sebastian said. On the street, he leaned against a brick wall and lit a joint, offering Kostyk a hit.

"No thanks," Kostyk said.

"Right, you don't do drugs. Thanks for the contribution, man. It'll help me to get my new enterprise up and running."

Sebastian pulled a business card from his bra.

"The 'Oh Zone'?" Kostyk asked.

"It was either that or the 'Gee Spot'."

"I believe Pollyanna's tiara may be on too tight,' Kostyk said. Sebastian roared.

"Thanks for that too—my first good laugh since the fire. It's been a nightmare the last few weeks, not just losing the Lithium, but Oscar, Svetlana, Billy, and Prince. You think Prince, in even his wildest acid trip, ever imagined he'd be lying in a bed with both legs chopped off? It's all a little too Jackson Pollock for me."

A pair of drunks staggering down the street laughed and pointed at Sebastian.

"Hey baby," one of them sang out. "Wanna party?"

"We should go inside," Kostyk said. Sebastian tossed his joint in the street and returned to his post at the table. Kostyk went to the bar. It was starting to fill up. The stage was set with lights, amps, and a drum kit for the bands to share. Karmin was fiddling with a tech board by the back wall, cranking the music and turning it down; adjusting the lights onstage, blending blue, green, and red in a kaleidoscope, brightening one area before reducing it to shadows, doing this again in another section. The woman was an artist. Donovan was by the back door, a rockabilly sentry, scanning the bar. They hadn't talked since Bernie Bender's arrest. Kostyk wondered if Donovan knew his brother set the Lithium fire. Itchy Dick was sitting beside Banjo Bob with his head bobbing as he sized up everyone to determine those who might be a soft touch and buy the beer. Kostyk joined them. He didn't want to sit with his artist friends. He preferred to relax and focus on his performance. These two posed no challenge. Banjo Bob seemed more buoyant than he had lately.

"Libations," he shouted, leaning in to Kostyk, lowering his voice. "Listen, you need party supplies, I got the primo stuff — grass, high-grade hash, acid, and mushrooms."

"You know, maybe I should find a quiet place to review my routine," Kostyk said.

"Sure, man," Bob said. "Hey, how come they never asked me to perform? I got my banjo right here ready to go."

"I didn't choose the acts," Kostyk said. He found an empty table to go over his monologue. He hadn't memorized the text and needed to get a good look at it before he read it onstage. It seemed clever enough to hold the audience interest but the real impact would come from the slides of 'Dreaming Dread'. Kostyk was eager to share his powerful, evocative painting, but equally nervous. The energy in the bar was electric, the excitement tangible and growing as the size of the crowd did. But the buzz of conversation was a distraction and Kostyk couldn't concentrate. He would have to wing it when he performed his piece. Writers, painters, and musicians continued to pour into the bar and a clutch of young women paraded like a gaggle of geese, moving with the slightly mincing manner that distinguished them as ballet dancers. His friends were ignoring him. It gave Kostyk time to think and gather his wits.

Zoltan was zonked when he dropped into a chair beside him and began to babble about the sorry state of affairs with his condo, car, business, and love life. In his drunken, coked-up stupor, he had an endless series of complaints. Then he suddenly turned to Kostyk, eyes wide and wild.

"Get out of my head, man. Stop stealing my ideas. I know all your mind-numbing, brain-soaking methods of collecting information. You're a psychic vampire sucking up all my sense impressions, my thoughts, feelings, and desires. But I'm creative too, Scott, and part of the fifth column spying on the bourgeoisie. I'm an undercover anarchist."

Zoltan opened his sports coat to reveal a button with the anarchist 'A'.

"Cute," Kostyk said.

"Don't be such a condescending, hipper-than-thou jerk. Not when I'm being a nice guy. I won't make a single stinking dime tonight. The only good thing about this shindig is it keeps the riffraff out."

Zoltan was still ranting when Fran and Darla joined them. Wolf whistles and foot-stomping went up. The women were dressed in Fosse finery, wearing tailcoats, bowler hats, short shorts, sheer black stockings, and tap shoes with sequins sparkling on their skin and in their hair.

"Buy us a drink, boss," Darla said. Zoltan waved to the bar. Kostyk was surprised Velvet was working. He doubted Zoltan was paying her tonight.

"It's my way of kicking in," she explained. "Besides, someone has to be here. I mean, look at these two. Can you picture either of them serving drinks to this bunch? What did you do to your hair?"

Scott had almost forgotten about his freshly mown buzz cut.

"Decided to chop it off," he said. Velvet passed a hand over his scalp.

"Feels like porcupine quills," she said. "What's everyone having?"

"I'm buying," Zoltan said. After Velvet took their order, Fran leaned past Kostyk to kiss Zoltan's cheek with the clash of perfume and cologne making him dizzy.

"Thank you for the wine," she said. "What you're doing is wonderful."

Zoltan blushed, but before he could come up with a clever comment, Lethal Spit swept over to their table. She wore a black-and-white mini-dress with a single strand of pearls and had a pair of pretties, one male and one female, at her side. It was her turn to dole out kisses, planting one on Fran's cheek first and then Darla's.

"Everywhere you look, damn fine dames," she said. "You two are the opening act. I will introduce you."

When Lethal Spit climbed onstage, Karmin took the houselights down, bringing a spot up on her. She thanked everyone for coming and Zoltan for providing the venue. He stood and took a quick bow to generous applause. Lethal Spit waved her chapbook, saying she dedicated 'Pickled Peter' to the 'Lithium Three'. More applause followed. She read a short poem then asked for a minute of silence. After this, she invited Bodacious Bods up to perform 'Juggle Jazz'.

Fran and Darla sprang onto stage. Karmin turned the spot down, introducing yellow, blue, and red lights. Tendrils of smoky jazz seeped from speakers as the two dancers started to sway sensually, moving rhythmically and juggling in time to a number of tunes. They tossed the balls back and forth between them. It was impressive, better than Kostyk expected. They finished to tumultuous applause, the audience shouting and banging beer bottles on the tables. Flushed and breathless, Fran returned to sit with Kostyk and Zoltan, while Darla bounded through the bar as eager eyes followed her sequined bottom. She strolled over to Donovan by the back door and executed a few quick dance steps before extending her arms in front of him. Donovan nodded as she talked. But he was clearly caught off guard when she leaned forward on her toes and lightly pressed her lips against his. Meanwhile, Fran sipped a glass of white wine as Zoltan complimented her performance. She didn't see Cowboy come up behind her but froze when she felt fingers graze her bare shoulder.

"You two really burned up the place tonight," he said his voice uneasy and awkward.

"Never mind the hooey," Fran barked. She grabbed her coat and crossed to Darla. Donovan opened the back door for her and she left. Cowboy was at a loss and straggled back to the lobby. Kostyk watched all this unfold and didn't hear his name called.

"Earth to Kostyk; beam up, Scotty," Lethal Spit yodelled. The audience started to chant his name. Scott gulped down his drink, ran onto stage, and stumbled over a riser. The crowd erupted. Karmin flicked on the projector. A slide appeared. The audience gasped at Svetlana's face with a fiery

crown painted around her head. Kostyk hit the remote control and another slide, this one of the Public Safety Building
washed over the stage, containing and also blinding him.

"Firing up the neighbours," he cried out and the crowd
groaned. He persevered but the lights were too bright and
reading his script proved too difficult. Kostyk started to stam-
mer, his voice cracking and his throat going dry. Then, it closed
up completely, only letting him croak out the first few words
of his text. He couldn't loosen his vocal cords and started to
panic, hitting the remote control repeatedly in time to the rap-
id, dissonant beating of his heart. The carousel spun, vomiting
up a cascade of jarring images — photos of the burnt-out building that had housed the Lithium, others taken at the Albert,
drawings of stick people running, flames licking at them and
Oscar in an exclamation-pointed coffin. Kostyk's performance
devolved into a disastrous display he desperately wanted to
be over. Finally, he dropped the remote and crept offstage,
slinking back to his table. There was no handclapping or foot-
stomping, just an uneasy, accusing quiet that penetrated his
core. Lethal Spit was onstage, muttering about career suicide
as the audience laughed. Zoltan patted his friend on the back
but it felt more patronizing than comforting and did little to
calm Kostyk's distress. He sat in stony, sullen silence, devastated. He didn't deserve all this ridicule. Lethal Spit started to
perform her piece.

"Runners are a perennial hazard on the city streets,
interfering with traffic and jeopardizing pedestrian safety.
Therefore the city has decided to cull the herd by instituting a
jogger hunt. The Royal Winnipeg Taxidermist Society is offering to stuff jogger heads at a discount."

The crowd was reduced to stitches by her silly presenta-
tion and Kostyk was amazed at how easily they were amused.
Screw them all. He didn't need their approval. His work spoke
for itself. He might not have sequins, long legs, and clever choreography, or Lethal Spit's snarky comments, but his integrity
was intact. He drained Fran's half-glass of wine. Lethal Spit
finished trashing the city's joggers and introduced a poetry
sweatshop while several would-be wordsmiths paraded onto

the stage to recite pathetic dross they had penned for tonight. Terminal Jerks singer, Digger, was the last poet and presented a dismal piece. But when he was done, they gave him a standing ovation. It was all too depressing for Kostyk and he had another drink. Lethal Spit and the Thundering Sighs went onstage and performed a series of rousing numbers as the dance floor detonated with frantic thrashing. After them, the Fried Zucchini Sisters offered a foot-stomping set and following them Apocalypso played a song they wrote and recorded to honour the homeless man who died in the fire. Cassette copies of 'The Steel and the Stone' were being sold with proceeds going to the Salvation Army. The Star Rangers did their punk rock covers of popular Kris Kristofferson tunes, the audience loving their version of 'Silver Tongued Devil'. The music continued with the Royal American Retards and then the Citizens Band from Hell. Darla was back at the table, yanking Zoltan onto the dance floor where he did the spastic monkey. Bob hugged his banjo, waltzing with it while a toasted Sebastian slept at a table, his wig half off and his tiara tilted at an angle. Nobody was talking to Kostyk and he tried to catch Karmin's eye without success. He drank whatever came within reach and when the heat, noise, and smoke were too much for him, he went out to the lobby.

Cowboy nursed a rye and his wounded pride at the front desk. He produced a bottle and a second glass from under the counter, pouring them each a drink. He tossed his back. Kostyk did the same. Cowboy refilled their glasses. This ritual was repeated several times, neither of them speaking. Then Eric the Red and two buddies barged into the lobby. Cowboy flicked a cigarette butt at the biker.

"Don't be a dickhead," Eric snarled. "I wanna see my girl."

"The bitch left in a huff hours ago," Cowboy snapped. The biker laughed.

"I know," he said. "I drove her home, if you get my drift, old man. I bet your boyfriend, Donovan Bender, is still inside though, eh. Don't sweat it. I'm not going in right now. He'll get his, all in good time."

The bikers left the lobby and Cowboy poured another two drinks. Kostyk declined this one, deciding to brave the bar again. It was safer than the lobby. Terminal Jerks had taken the stage to do a final set for the night with Lethal Spit sitting in on drums. As they started, the audience rose as one and gave them a five-minute standing ovation. The always angry pulse of their music was particularly violent tonight and blasted the crowd away. Kostyk bought two doubles and went to see Donovan by the back door. His friend seemed both switched on and off simultaneously when he accepted the glass. He nodded to the door and led Kostyk outside to a dark parking lot behind the Albert. They were sipping their drinks when headlights came on, blinding them.

"I'll fucking kill him!" a voice screamed.

Svetlana was climbing ancient stone stairs in the courtyard of a medieval castle, anxiously sneaking furtive glances behind her as she crept up. Meanwhile the earth slipped away under Kostyk's feet as he floated on the air beside her. At the top of the stairs, high above the earth, another courtyard contained within the walls of a parapet looked out over the countryside below. Svetlana cowered in a corner.

"Why are you scared?" Kostyk asked and she pointed a trembling finger at the two hooded figures lingering in the courtyard, one of them beside the wall, the other sitting on the ledge.

"They're nothing to fear," he said, striding across the courtyard to push the one resting on the parapet over the side. The creature's cowl fell away, revealing a skull on fire and a bony hand that burned Kostyk's wrist as it pulled him over the edge. Scott was a cartoon character as he fell in slow motion, bones raining all around him. He hit the ground, bounced back onto his feet, and walked down Albert Street toward the hotel.

Kostyk was awake now, his pillow soaked in tears. The dreams were getting worse. He was disoriented scanning the room, not much in it besides a bed and side table. He staggered to the mirror. His face was black and blue with deep purple bruises blending into yellow ones. He looked like a poor man's Picasso and hurt in ways he never had before. His lips were puffy, the lower one split, and his left eye was swollen with the bulk of a baseball. A profusion of brawling thoughts rapidly cycled through his brain; the ringing crack of a boot slamming repeatedly into his head, stomach, and between his legs. If Donovan hadn't protected him, he might be dead.

Downstairs, the Albert lobby was deserted and there was no one on the desk. He was just heading out the door when Velvet burst from Bertha's Place, two Styrofoam cups of coffee in her hands. She was wearing a black leather jacket and led Kostyk onto the street. This walk to his gallery was less frenzied than the last they'd taken. Once inside Confidential Exchange, Velvet sat him on the couch and gave him a coffee. He tried to speak but she lightly pressed a finger to lips that still hurt.

"Try to listen for a change," she said. "You have dry blood around your mouth."

Velvet turned on a radio and 'Clair de Lune' filled the room. She went to the sink, wet a cloth with warm water, and washed the blood off his face. Her nearness, the pressure of her hip, and a slight scent of lilac on her skin, allowed him to almost forget his pain. When she finished, she took the half-bottle of wine on his desk, drained the contents, and refilled it with water.

"Your plants need care," she said, picking dead leaves off a fern, watering his Aloe Vera. Kostyk managed to mumble a few words through inflamed lips.

"Why are you doing this?" he asked.

"This beating was just a warning, Scott."

"I guess you know all about it, being a biker's chick."

"Not a biker's chick. I ride solo. When I was little, my uncle would come down from Flin Flon take me for a spin on his chopper. I'd wrap my arms around his waist; feel the wind on my face, hair blowing. I bought my first Harley when

I was eighteen. Being brown is tough in this town, a brown woman tougher, and one on a bike, forget about it. The ya-hoos give you nothing but grief. This one time, I was at a red light with my baby rumbling under me and a yokel in a piss-yellow pick-up pulls up, hollers—how does that big Indian feel between your legs. I tell him my hog is a Harley, lift my boot, and ask how that would feel between his legs. He calls me a few names and fucks off, his goofy grin gone with the green light. Big truck. Small brain."

"Still doesn't explain why your biker buddies attacked me."

"Maybe you're too stupid to be scared; happens to smart people. It's about the company you keep. Donovan Bender is a dangerous dude. Toughest rounders I know walk on eggshells around him, all except for Eric the Red, who may be as crazy as he is."

"I don't understand."

"So, what am I gonna do with you? The hell with it, your plants are good. Come with me."

The Burning Question

Doris was already awake at five AM. But the sudden alarm jolted her into an even higher state of awareness, incinerating every single thought and feeling she had. A DJ all jacked up on caffeine and cigarettes jabbered on the radio. Whiskey Jack hit snooze, rolled over, and started snoring again. Ten minutes later, the obnoxious disc jockey was back, even more fired up than ever and Jack crawled from bed. He wandered half-asleep across the room, dragging his feet on the floor, his slippers scraping like sandpaper on the carpet. In the bathroom, he spit in the sink and took a pee.

"Shut the door!" Doris shouted. Jack slammed it. But she could still hear the clamour of his morning ritual, the grunting and groaning and gargling of phlegm. Doris wanted to kill him. She wouldn't get a moment's rest until he was either out the door or in the ground. Doris tossed her pillow at the squawking radio and missed, instead hitting a bottle that fell and broke, releasing a sweet, nauseating stench of Aqua Velva. Jack came to the door, sniffed, and saw the shattered glass. But he didn't say a word and went back to the bathroom to resume his routine.

Whiskey Jack was banging away on the ironing board, removing every wrinkle in his slacks. He was the last cabdriver to wear a uniform in Winnipeg. It was his trademark along with the immaculate taxi, the clean interior, the washed and waxed exterior. And Jack was particular about the passengers he took too. He refused to take Indians. He would have crapped himself if he knew Doris had a Métis father and Cree granddad. Jack came back into the bedroom to dress. There was no point staying in bed and Doris needed a drink.

She poured an ice-cold gin in the kitchen and carried it to her favourite chair. Whiskey Jack appeared in the doorway dressed in his uniform, a Windsor knot in his tie, hair slicked back with Brylcreem. He didn't look half bad for an old guy. Doris would never tell him that but he knew anyway. She hated how smug he was, how certain about things. It was simpleminded.

"I better go relieve Buzz, see what damage he did to the cab overnight," he said. "I'm still paying for the last ding he put in it."

"You should fire that birdbrain; the bum drinks all your booze."

"Everyone does, Dor," he said. She gulped her gin. "I trust Buzz. He's honest in his way; never stiffs me, delivers booze when I don't wanna, and gives me a shout if he gets a live one on the line."

"You're a two-bit hustler, just like Tony, Jack."

"Don't start, Doris. At least, our oldest comes through for us when we need it, not like your baby boy, your favourite son, the fucking fruitcake."

Doris whipped her glass at Whiskey Jack. He ducked. She snatched a pair of scissors off the table, chased him around the room, lunging at him and missing, taking another swing, almost connecting this time. Jack dropped to his knees, started to beg her not to stick him again. Doris dropped the scissors in disgust and went to make herself another drink. She was half-finished it in the living room when he cautiously came out of the kitchen with her pills and the bottle of gin.

"Go easy on this bottle until I get home with another. And don't forget to take your pills."

After he left, Doris polished off her drink then poured another. It was her life now. Drink, smoke, and watch TV. There was a time before Whiskey Jack when she had a job, hobbies, and even some friends. Nowadays though she was surrounded by a suffocating history — the thirty-ounce beer mug with 'I Dare You' scribbled on it in lipstick-red, the collection of spoons from places she'd never been and would never go; two footstools she made by sewing fabric around large juice cans. But her pride and joy was the three-foot, plaster cherry-boy in a canary-yellow peasant shirt, bright blue pants. The statue had hard, clean lines, finely curved calves, and bare feet with toenails painted crimson. His head was tossed back with a distant, faraway look in his eyes and he had lovely, ripe lips, red as the cherries he held high in one hand but never ate. Her cherry boy was frozen in a state of becoming, a gift from her mother before the custody battle for Donovan.

Something darted in the dark room; a mouse or a rat. The walls started breathing, drawing her into them. Doris wrapped a blanket around her shoulders, refilled her glass, and took two tabs of lithium, washing them down with gin. When did she begin to drink? Whiskey Jack got her started. Living with a legend wasn't easy. Her six sons had the scars to prove it. Her husband had beaten any good out of the boys — three locked in prison so long now she barely remembered what they looked like; Bernie breaking out of the pen then setting that awful fire. Doris knew in her heart Tony put the match in his hand. Her oldest boy had turned into a bastard just like his father. He had been a sweet boy when he was younger, a natural leader taking charge of the little ones, making up games for them. The only son Jack never broke or made cry was Donovan. He always complained giving him a licking was like flogging a corpse. How would he know? Jack didn't have the right kind of brain to understand Dono-van, that the battles his brothers fought on the street he waged in his head. When Donovan hurt someone, it was his mind made him do it, not malice. Doris was close to him at one time. He shared his thoughts with her, no matter how crazy they were and she could tell him about her feelings or lack of them. Donovan had been the last slender thread of light left in her life but he was lost to her now. She saw it in his eyes when he came to collect Bernie's leather coat. He hadn't forgiven her for not visiting him in hospital. She tried to explain in the long letters she wrote him, how she was scared Whiskey Jack would leave her in Selkirk like he had before. She didn't know if he ever read the letters or if he even received them. But it didn't feel like he was ever going to take her back into his life now. There was no point trying to explain anything to anyone anymore. Truth was just a bully, yanking out the last love in her, bruising what little was left of her heart. There are those who become brittle from a lack of love and crack under the strain. But Doris was worn down by its absence, polished to a smooth stone that could sink easily into the cold, deep river, allowing her to drift, unaffected and disconnected, all her feelings locked away forever. It felt good to be numb, to let go and to surrender, to be liberated. She took two more lithium and chased them down with another glass of gin. Then she lit a cigarette, sucking the smoke deep into her lungs while pinches of white and red flame flickered behind heavy eyelids. Doris closed her eyes, entered a room filled with light, and started to sing.

"Daisy, Daisy, I'm half-crazy, all for the love of you..."

City of Ghosts

The Ice Storm

The old lady had really done it this time. She was on the burn unit at Seven Oaks Hospital. It was just like her to set a fire, hardly her first, on the same night a freak ice storm hit. The army had been called out and people were staying in shelters. Freezing rain made the roads hazardous and power lines were down, scattered like sizzling snakes on the streets and sidewalks. Branches sagged under the weight of thick ice with some trees collapsing on houses and cars and others snapping with a sharp report. Buzz hadn't been crazy about coming out in the cab. But he knew better than defy Tony Bender. He loved to get high and wanted to keep all his teeth. The drive, normally ten-minutes, took an hour. Buzz dropped him by the door to the ER. The pusher told him to wait. An ambulance and several cop cars were parked under a concrete canopy and Tony walked to the end of the enclosed area to have a smoke before going to see his mother. He puffed on his cigar and considered the problems piling up for him.

The landlord where Whiskey Jack and the old lady lived was out for blood after seeing the smoke and water damage. Tony would have to hire a lawyer to deal with him, on top of what he was forking over in legal fees to Wolch for handling his brother's case. A week after they iced Prince Bernie was cooling his heels at the Public Safety Building and coming down off bennies. Things could get a little dicey if he started shooting off his mouth about the fire, presenting Tony with a serious problem. He also had to deal with Donovan. The kid handled Sarah's skinner well enough without any backlash, even if bringing the goof's shoes around as a souvenir was bizarre. It was his latest dustup with Eric that troubled Tony though. This never would've happened if he or Jimmy Jazz had been around. At least Donovan had kept his cool when the bikers jumped him behind the Albert the night of the Benefit. He didn't kill anyone this time. Still, it meant Eric the Red was going to keep coming after him. Tony had to end his brother's beef with the biker, a situation that required a far more subtle, discreet touch than the one with Prince. Tony wasn't sending a message now and he didn't want to agitate the Curb Stompers. Maybe he would stash Donovan somewhere safe during the takedown and keep him out of the loop. Then neither cops nor bikers could link him to Eric's disappearance. Sometimes, Tony regretted telling the old lady he would take care of Donovan. But he had the perfect place to park him and getting him out of the way for awhile would give Tony time to sort out Bernie. He and Donovan were tight. Tony stubbed his cigar out against the enclosure wall, stopped at the coffee machine, and then rode an elevator to the fifth floor to deal with yet another family crisis.

The hospital wasn't a quiet place at night with nurses nattering, carts rattling, buzzers and bells going off all the time. The smell of microwave popcorn drifted down the hall from a staffroom along with less pleasant odours — piss, puke, and industrial-strength cleaning products. Tony was tempted to relight his stogie. At a nursing station, a nurse and orderly were flirting and didn't appreciate being interrupted. Tony asked where Doris Bender's room was.

"Visiting hours are over," the nurse said.

"I'm her son," he said. Something in his voice and the way his eyes caught hers convinced the nurse not to argue. She told Tony where to find his mother.

The old lady lay in bed with her hands tied to the rails and bandages covering her face. The smell of burnt flesh brought back the memory of Bernie in the same situation as a kid. Whiskey Jack was sitting beside her, holding her hands, tears streaming down his face. Tony had never seen the old man cry. Doris started to wake up, her breath ragged. A low mewling in her throat made it hard to understand what she said.

"What's that?" Whiskey Jack asked.

"She wants to die," Tony said. The old man touched his wife's arm with a rare tenderness and began to sob.

"Stop blubbering," she croaked. She'd always been tougher. "How long I been here?"

"Two days," Whiskey Jack said. "You burned us out, you crazy old broad. Everything is gone; furniture, clothes, and all the cash I had hid. Doc says you're lucky to be alive. He's upped your lithium to take the edge off for you."

"Tell the asshole to forget about my brain and deal with the pain."

"You're on a morphine drip for that. Once you get your strength back, I'll take you home, Dor, wherever that will be now. I got a surprise. Your son is here."

"Donovan!" she cried out.

"No," Tony said. "Me."

"Oh. Jack, get out. I wanna talk to Tony."

Whiskey Jack left without a fight, another first. Tony filled a cup with water and held the straw to his mother's cracked lips. She sipped the liquid slowly, swallowing it in lumps. Her wheezing sounded like a death rattle.

"Where is he staying?" she asked.

"Crashing in a spare room at my place until we sort things out."

"Aren't you brave," she said. "Make sure you put the toilet paper on the right way or you'll never hear the end of it."

"He'll be good or he'll be gone," Tony said. "I doubt the Sally Ann will appeal to him."

"There's my boy," Doris said. "I need you to do something for me, Tony. In our basement locker, there's a black notebook behind a box of Christmas decorations. Take it to Donovan."

"Don't tell me you're keeping secrets now?"

"None of your business," she said as a coughing fit overcame her. Doris turned her head away and waved him off. Tony took his cue and left. The old man was pacing out in the hall.

"She fell asleep," Tony lied. "We should go."

The cab waiting for them was warm. Whiskey Jack climbed into the back seat and started spilling his guts to Buzz. He just wouldn't shut the hell up.

"Old lady has always been a little crazy, eh; up and down like a toilet seat. But never like this. Says she wants to be cremated so the worms won't eat her. What kind of stupid is that? At least, it's cheaper than a coffin. I'm all tapped out after this fire."

While the old man was talking to Buzz it was for Tony's benefit and less hurt than hint. He was looking for a loan, which Tony would give him. He had Buzz drop the old man at his house then take him to the Albert. The streets were still slick so the cabbie drove carefully. When they arrived, Tony stepped out and skated across the street. Shadows bobbed inside a dark café window; Zoltan's voice boomed loud in the lobby. Cowboy was moping at the front desk.

"You hear that caterwauling? Zeroes come out of the woodwork when Zoltan is on a hoot. He's been a basket case forever, but impossible these days."

The door to Bertha's Place suddenly banged open and Zoltan pranced out into the lobby.

"Ah, the iceman cometh," he said. "I thought I saw you slide in through the door. How you doing, Tony? Is my poor, pitiful minion crying the blues while swilling bile-spiked rye because Fran finally came to her senses and dumped him? He needs to get out more, but not on my dime. I wouldn't invite Cowboy to his own funeral. Still, I did not abandon my dear friends to wrangle wisecracks. Cowboy, fetch more booze before I fire you. Tony, well, you know what I want."

Zoltan went back into the café, Tony to the bar, where only a few desperate drinkers had dared to hazard the ice storm.

"How is your Ma doing?" Jimmy Jazz asked. "I always liked her. She was good to me."

"Go tell Big Ron not to bother playing pool if he can't win," Tony said. Jimmy Jazz did as he was told and took off. So Zoltan was well on the way to losing what marbles he had left. Just a little more leaning, his house of cards would collapse. Velvet brought Tony's scotch and a note from Sarah. She was planning to go to the art gallery next week and could use some company. It was a little good news for a change.

The Pool of Sorrows

Sarah felt small with a hollow sensation coursing through her while she waited on a leather bench in a large lobby with intimidating limestone walls and a high ceiling. It was her first trip to the Winnipeg Art Gallery, a chance to expand her horizons. She was determined to make a fresh start and move in a new direction even if it took her to unfamiliar, possibly hostile territory. She was normally a reserved person and didn't like to put herself on public display, often feeling like people were judging her; sometimes they were. She'd driven by the building before, wondering what the wedge-shaped structure held. The exterior was a triangular slab with no windows and looked like a slice of gray, concrete pie. It could pass for an ancient arrowhead or the prow of a ship. But inside now, the gallery proved to be a disappointment. By the front entrance there was a gift shop for buying cards and trinkets and on a late Thursday afternoon, in the middle of a cold winter, there weren't many people in the place. Auditorium doors were swung open at the other end of a long hallway, revealing well-heeled older women with peacock blue hair mingling with college kids dressed in black. It was hardly the basilica of culture she had imagined but more like a bunker, a mausoleum for hiding art and protecting it from prying eyes, not a means of sharing it. Where did they keep the art anyway? Was it safely stored in a basement vault? The single exception to this dreary atmosphere was a gorgeous, blond-wood banister that swept up a wide staircase, something Sarah would have loved to carve.

Sarah had been hesitant about going to the gallery. She didn't want to go there alone and couldn't find anyone to go with her. Amy was too young and her mother claimed she was too old. Sarah mulled it over for a month before calling Tony Bender. Now, she wondered if that had been a mistake. She still wasn't convinced she could trust him. True, at Dubrovnik's, away from the Albert and the North End, Tony had been a different man, no sign of the dreadful Bender energy so many feared or despised. He was respectful, engaging, and even fun, not crude, lewd, or inappropriate. Sarah recognized his strength and resolve, an ability to make difficult decisions. She could relax in his company and let go of the constant need to be in control with her emotions anchored, available in a way they rarely were. It had been a long time since she had been able to trust her feelings and follow her heart. Failing to accept her intuition in the past had resulted in poor choices, like letting Brad Hunter into her life — into Amy's life. At the start, killing him had been a wild idea she contemplated; the when, where, and how of it. Tony turned theory into practice, rage into action. He kept his word, doing the deed and honouring the agreement they'd made, taking her straight home after dinner. But was his good behaviour just an act? After all, he did commit murder. It was for her, but still. Well, the Winnipeg Art Gallery in the middle of the day was a safe public place to meet him and certainly far less dangerous than a restaurant on Assiniboine after dark.

It surprised Sarah Tony was late. Punctuality had proven to be one of his more admirable traits. He had been early at the Windmill, exactly on time for dinner at Dubrovnik's. She would give him ten more minutes. She needed to tell him anyway about Zoltan appearing unannounced at her mother's door and saying disturbing things about Brad's death. When Tony finally showed up Sarah was ready to read him the riot act. But she sensed a strange crack in his self-confidence, an unsettled edge that hadn't been there before.

"My mother died," he said. "I've been dealing with details, letting people know, talking to the funeral home. Who knew death had so much paperwork? Cropo said they can squeeze us in next week."

"Maybe we should do this another time," Sarah said. She decided not to say anything about Zoltan. It could wait.

"No. Now is good. We're here and it might help take the edge off."

They started walking up the wide staircase with a crowd of school kids close to Amy's age scrambling past them, skipping and jumping, calling out. On the second floor of the art gallery, an enormous skylight with a rooftop garden holding sculptures and plants filled the foyer with sun. The dull stone lobby gave way to exuberant exhibition spaces with vibrant, colourful walls that were not garish but subtle. They enhanced and accentuated images in the paintings, causing them to seem less locked into their frames, instead almost reaching out to touch Sarah.

She carefully examined each exquisite item in the Inuit art collection; delicate and intricate soapstone sculptures, some granite and ivory pieces, with others carved from caribou antlers and bone. There were lithographs and prints and drawings done in both ink and pencil on fabric and paper. It took her breath away and Sarah took her time, immersed in the work before she headed to the next exhibit.

Tony didn't speak as they strolled through the gallery spaces. If Sarah stopped to study a painting, he did too then followed her when she moved to the next display. He was like a puppy or small child. It was endearing yet a little unsettling. This wasn't the man she thought she knew. Tony Bender was the quintessential tough guy. But she sensed a slight, quivering disquiet in him today, some pain leaking out the edges of his cool demeanour. His mother's death was hitting him hard.

The portrait of an eighteenth century merchant caught Sarah's eye. He was well-dressed, wearing an elegant coat and a matching cap trimmed with beaver fur. The large ruffled collar around his neck looked like it was choking him though and the longer she contemplated this canvas the less happy he looked. His angry, troubled eyes were disturbed and disturbing, his sumptuous clothes and fine, plush surroundings suffocating rather than comforting, reducing him to a prisoner consumed by concerns. She turned to Tony. He was preoccupied, so she left him to his thoughts. It wasn't her place to probe or press at this point. She suggested they keep moving with a tilt of her head. He followed her.

The next painting that attracted Sarah was another portrait, this one of a young girl, not much older than Amy. She was attractively dressed in the height of nineteenth century fashion, wearing a pretty outfit with ribbons and bows. She had long black curls, a button nose, and held both hands together in her lap, squeezing her fingers tightly as though they might fly away if she let go. She had a pensive, melancholy look and dark eyes Sarah could feel boring into hers and breaking her heart. Why did the people in these paintings all have such penetrating eyes? Sarah kept staring at the too-worldly face until Tony lightly touched her shoulder. She nodded. She was ready to escape this young girl's accusing gaze. They swept through several galleries filled with magnificent oil paintings. Then Sarah stopped again, drawn to another absorbing work, lingering over it and admiring the way each brushstroke achieved a rich depth of colour, creating a fleshy texture. She could feel the fur of the animals and smell their scent. The four bison grazing on the prairie grass were the last of a large herd Métis hunters led by her great-uncle Cuthbert chased on horseback and shot at from the saddle. The women and children followed behind, cleaning and skinning the carcasses of these magnificent creatures who had sacrificed their lives to feed and clothe the Métis families. No part of the beast was wasted; meat, hair, bones, horns, tails, hooves, teeth, and even tongues served a purpose. The largest bison, nearest to her, at the bottom of the canvas, peered mournfully at some distant point in the gallery as if he sensed his end and the end of his kind; the poverty, misery, and degradation that would descend on those who pursued them across the plain. Sarah shook herself free of the painting's spell and found she was alone. Tony stood beside a reclining bronze sculpture by Henry Moore, studying it with the same intense look he'd had at the Windmill when they first met. His voice came from far away when he spoke.

"What is this — man, woman, whatever — supposed to represent? It's a perfect person above the waist but the bottom looks like someone's crippled insides, torn and twisted in knots, caught in the clutches of a crazy energy, the feet bound by a terrible, restraining weight. Does that even make sense? I don't know."

Sarah had lived in the North End for years, hearing about the awful things the Bender boys did. But she never imagined she would be standing beside the worst of the bunch and listening to him talk like this. Obviously, the death of his mother had released some deep feelings in him and Sarah realized she knew the man's reputation better than the man.

"It does make sense," she mumbled.

"You try to help them," he said. "Give your family money when they're broke and a hand if they need it. But they eat you alive, always wanting more. When do you stop giving, break free from all the emotional blackmail? Both my mother and brother finished at the business end of a match, fire taking them. The old lady's death wasn't exactly unexpected. She was already dead in some ways, her body just catching up to her brain. She and Whiskey Jack so pickled in alcohol it was only a question of which would go first. It was strange seeing them at the hospital, with a recognition passing between them despite the bandages and the burns. It was almost as if they'd found the missing pieces of some puzzle they'd lost ages ago and were reconnecting now for the first time across the years, rediscovering the way they were before I was born. My mother was on a whole whack of drugs, drifting in and out of consciousness, waking up and crying she wanted to die and then that she wanted to live. This 'art' reminds me of that, of her."

Sarah felt an urge to hug him but resisted it, reaching for his hand instead. He instinctively pulled away and then accepted her touch, his cold hand warming quickly in hers. As they walked away from the sculpture, she could feel a stark aloneness vibrating under the surface of his skin.

The decorative arts collection caught Tony's attention. He stopped to admire the craft that had gone into creating the ceramics, glassware, textiles, and metalwork, some dating back to the seventeenth century. When they emerged from this exhibition they came face to face with a work by William Kurelek. In the painting a pond with dead branches floating on the water's surface stood in a clearing surrounded by lush underbrush and thick green foliage. Sarah lost herself in the tranquility of the setting, her mind drifting until someone tapped her on the shoulder. She spun around startled. A security guard smiled at her and then at Tony.

"Look for the two red dots," he said and walked away. Sarah turned back to scan the 'Pool of Sorrows'. Tony spotted the first dot, Sarah the second. They were drops of blood in the palms of a man shrouded by bushes, his arms extended, a crown of thorns on his head. Not particularly religious, Sarah still felt a powerful, undeniable anguish the painting evoked. It was a revelation, just as everything else in her first trip to the art gallery was. It had been an exhilarating afternoon but exhausting and they adjourned to a fourth floor dining room for a late lunch and took a table by a window, where a snow encrusted rooftop outside overlooked Memorial Boulevard. Off in the distance, on the dome of the Legislative Building the statue of the Golden Boy posed like a groom on a wedding cake. The waiter told them jazz bands played on the gallery rooftop in the summertime.

"Maybe we could come sometime," Sarah said and she could swear Tony Bender who was always so cool and in control almost crumbled. This passed quickly. The food was decent and they ate in a silence that wasn't awful or awkward but serene. After they were done, Tony asked her to drop him at the Albert. She almost told him about Zoltan then but didn't.

As they drove away from the Winnipeg Art Gallery, Sarah found herself appreciating the building's stark, severe style, how it actually reflected the immense power of the prairie. She also sensed an unfulfilled yearning in the man beside her. Tony Bender took what he wanted and was used to getting his way, bending people to his will. He was a man capable of murder. But Sarah doubted he had many friends and felt a friend was what he needed most right now. They pulled up in front of the hotel.

"Come into the Albert for a minute," he said.

"I don't want to run into Zoltan," she said finally. "He's been a pest lately, showing up at my mother's house, phoning at all hours, whining about wanting to see me. There is something else. He told me he doesn't believe Brad's death was an accident or suicide and he thinks you and I had something to do with it. Zoltan is drinking too much, doing too much dope. I doubt he would deliberately spill his guts about his suspicions, but it could slip out when he's stoned."

"I'll talk to him," Tony said.

"Don't hurt him. Please."

"Let me see if he's inside. I doubt it at this hour. If he's gone, I'll get you. Someone I want you to meet."

Sarah parked the Dart and Tony was back in a flash. No Zoltan. She went into the Albert with him. The desk clerk at the front was nursing a drink.

"Where's Donovan?" Tony barked. Cowboy pointed at the ceiling. "Get him down here."

The desk clerk fiddled with a sketchy looking switchboard, mumbled, and turned around.

"Done," he said.

"Okay, beat it, Cowboy," Tony ordered and the desk clerk scurried to the bar. This was the Tony Bender Sarah knew. After a thump on the stairs beside the front desk, a door banged open and Donovan Bender fell into the lobby, looking a little crazed. Sarah hadn't seen him in years. He hadn't changed much. He was scruffier with a few more scars, but otherwise the same wired guy with the wild eyes. Back in the old days, Donovan had beaten a kid so bad he needed dental surgery he couldn't afford and the poor bastard walked around with a mouthful of broken teeth for the rest of his life. Donovan didn't attend Isaac Newton the last year of high school and the rumour was that he was in a mental hospital.

"How you doing, man?" Donovan drawled. "No. Don't tell me, Tony. Fact is I don't give a fuck. You're just a carnivore feeding at an open sewer, a trough where the vampires drink cups brimming with blood."

Then he burst into a spasm of giggles, not a happy but tortured sound.

"What are you on, Donovan?" Tony asked.

"Magic mushrooms. Banjo Bob has a stash."

"That's right. Your buddy has been pedaling them in the bar, along with the psychedelics he found in Bruno's room."

"Leave him alone, Tony. He's my friend."

Sarah couldn't imagine anyone talking to Tony Bender this way.

"The old lady is dead, Donovan. Did you go see her in hospital?"

"The night she croaked."

"Funeral is at Cropo's next week. Be there."

"Hey, you're the boss, big brother," Donovan said.

"I want to introduce you—"

"I remember Sarah. She lived on Flora down the street from Nana's house. So you're with Tony now, eh? You have my sympathies."

"Knock it off," Tony snapped. "Don't talk like that when you're dating a ditzy dancer with more boyfriends under her belt than you have scalps."

"It was good to see you, Sarah," Donovan said, spinning around, heading back upstairs.

"I'll walk you to your car," Tony said. At the Dart, he squeezed her hand and apologized for Donovan. Two apologies in one day must be a record for him.

"I'll give you a ride to the funeral if you need one," Sarah said.

"Thank you," he said and then marched back into the hotel with a fierce stride. Sarah drove away, wondering what she was getting into with Tony Bender. But she had to trust her feelings. They were all she had.

Ancient Eyes

Someone had tried to jimmy open the mailbox again, damaging it so badly this time, Darla had to jiggle the key back and forth, almost breaking it off in the lock. The neighbourhood was going downhill fast and wasn't as safe as it had been a few months ago. Last week, she'd come home after work to find a drunk sleeping on the floor in the lobby. The other tenants really had to stop jamming shit into the door to let their deadbeat friends in the building. She had considered moving lately, but the rent was so reasonable, the landlord decent, and there was that porch at the back. Darla collected her mail and climbed the three flights of rickety stairs to her apartment. She threw her coat on the couch, made chamomile tea, and listened to her messages. There was only one from her mother wanting to know when she was coming home for a visit and offering to pay the fare. Darla never accepted money from her parents even when they soft-pedaled it as a loan.

She took her tea to the porch to sort through the mail. Darla wondered if Coil was fiddling with her mailbox. In the month since she dumped him he'd gone from obsequious to obsessive. Ending an affair was never easy. Trying to let the guy down gently only encouraged him to think he could weasel his way back into her good graces. A clean break with no confusing signals was best. Cut the bereft bastard loose and short-circuit the clinging he mistook for love. Darla agreed to meet Coil for lunch at Chopin's today because he promised to return the volume of poetry by Rilke she lent him. The book was a farewell gift from her dance teacher when she left Toronto. Pamela Willow died suddenly last year and Darla hadn't been able to get back for the funeral.

Naturally, lunch had been a disaster with long silences and uncomfortable conversation. When Darla finally told him she was seeing someone, Coil called her a bitch and stormed out, conveniently forgetting he'd promised to pay for lunch. But, at least, she had her Rilke back.

Darla was leafing through a stack of envelopes that were mostly bills when she spotted the bold blue Toronto Network Theatre logo. Her heart pirouetted, leapt high, and landed hard in her throat. She had forgotten about sending them her résumé. Darla took a deep breath and savoured a brief moment of calm before learning if her dreams were about to be realized or crushed. Then she tore open the envelope and scanned the letter contents, pushing past niceties and platitudes to find the inevitable 'we regret'. It wasn't there and she read the letter again more slowly. TNT wanted her to audition on March twenty-first, a week from now. It meant she had to move fast to pack and find plane fare. Zoltan would likely lend it to her.

Darla knew she wasn't leaving Winnipeg for a little while though but for good. It would be hard to let go of some things. She would miss the city, the Royal Albert, the friends she'd made. The news would devastate Fran too. After their successful debut at the Benefit, Bodacious Bods was beginning to secure some offers of work—a gig entertaining at a business function, a second at a private house party. They would have to cancel. She had one other regret. She and Donovan would miss 'Amadeus' at the Manitoba Theatre Centre. They had started dating after the Benefit and actually connected on a visceral level. They talked about art, music, and poetry with an ease that seemed to open him up. Darla felt comfortable in his presence as well, more complete in his company. She knew how this sounded crazy, considering how he was normally with people, who his brothers were. On the surface, Donovan appeared cold and closed down. Darla saw his sweet side though, ancient eyes reflecting lifetimes of experience. His aloof nature wasn't due to any indifference, distress, or distraction. He'd just never learned how to be with others, lacking the self-confidence to get close enough to establish meaningful contact. But this was changing. He was evolving and developing a healthier, happier state of mind. Darla be-lieved she'd had a hand in making this happen. So what ex-actly were these feelings she was experiencing and why were they elevating her spirit into the stratosphere? Maybe it was just what lovers were always going on about. Still, Darla was determined to follow her dreams and she wouldn't be dis-suaded from doing so, no matter how compelling any other concerns might be. She'd talk to Donovan about why she was leaving. Maybe it was possible to preserve what they'd found and keep it alive long distance.

The ambiance in the lobby of the Albert shifted with whoever was working the front desk. Cowboy had a tendency to turn it into a wild-west show where anything could happen and often did. Maggie lent the lobby a befuddled yet kindly charm and Donovan gave it a chilling intensity intimidating troublemakers. But Fran, who was picking up a shift today, generated an accessible atmosphere that allowed her admir-ers to accumulate. They stacked up like airplanes in a holding pattern at the desk, hoping for a chance to engage the god-dess. Fran was generous with these lost souls, gracious and accommodating without a single false note. She was a chame-leon too with an uncanny ability to be transformed by what she wore. In jeans and a tartan shirt, she was a robust, down-to-earth farm girl; in a short, black dress, a sophisticated lady. Today, Fran was fetching in hippie garb, the long, flowing skirt and peasant blouse transforming her into an endearing flower child. She brightened when she saw Darla and a Ro-meo cruising at the front desk backed off, heading to the bar.

"I'm glad you dropped by this aft," Fran said. "I know its short notice but could you work for me tonight? Eric wants to take me to some big bash at the Norlander Hotel and I don't want to disappoint my stud in leather. He's such a doll and always puts a smile on my face. Even Sky likes him and she doesn't usually like anybody I date."

"How is your daughter doing these days?" Darla asked, not wanting to discuss Fran's biker beau. They both knew he'd been involved in a brawl with Donovan at the Benefit. It had nothing to do with them.

"She's in her Cindi Lauper phase now," Fran said, "Wears all the gear and sings 'Girls Just Wanna Have-Fun'. She's pretty good too. Sky is a natural performer."

"Like her mother."

"You're sweet. So, you think you can swing tonight?"

"Of course," Darla said. It was the least she could do, considering her news and she could use the cash. After Fran finished reading the TNT letter, she had a tear in her eye. She stepped out from behind the desk, embraced Darla in a heart-felt hug, and kissed her lightly on the lips.

"Good for you," she said, pulling away.

"It's something I have to do, Fran."

"I know."

"I need to—"

"Be a star."

"Not exactly that. You aren't mad?"

"Why would I be? It's been fantastic working out with you and being back on stage again has been fun. I forgot I knew some of those moves. Besides, I seriously doubt Eric would have ever noticed me if I was still carrying around all that extra weight. I am sad you're leaving, but happy for you."

"Well, I do have to get a part in this play."

"Oh you will. You're talented. I want to see you off at the airport."

"I would love that, Fran. Is Zoltan around?"

"He's upstairs and in a pissy mood. Be careful when you tell him you're leaving."

The door to Zoltan's office was closed and Darla knocked.

"Who is it?" he asked from inside.

"It's Darla."

"Well, come on in then."

"The door is locked, Zoltan."

"Right," he said. A chair scraped. There was a loud bang. Zoltan cursed. "Shit!"

He opened the door and hobbled back to his desk.

"What did you do now?" Darla asked.

"I whacked my fucking shin. Lock the door again. I don't want the riffraff listening around the corner or Cowboy barging in unannounced. What's up, Darla?"

"Read," she said, passing him the letter.

"Good news, bad news. Means I'll be short a waitress. I assume you require airfare."

"I can go standby. It's cheap."

"Fuck standby. You might not get a seat right away and you need to rest for the audition. How much do you need?"

"Figure five hundred should cover the cost."

Darla wasn't surprised when Zoltan wrote out a check for eight. His cynical persona hid a generous nature and his reputation as a money-grubbing slumlord was undeserved. A sharp rap at the door startled them both. Zoltan hollered and Cowboy called back.

"It's me, my lord."

"Get the door, Darla," Zoltan said and when she did, the desk clerk waltzed inside, looking a little too cocky, happier than he'd been since Fran dumped him.

"Why is the door locked, boss? Expecting trouble?"

"Whadda you want, Cowboy?"

"I am going to a party tonight whether you like it or not. The entire planet has been invited, including you. Big Ron Reilly won the lottery, seven-and-a-quarter-million fucking dollars. He's having a wingding at the Norlander with free food and booze. He's rented hotel rooms so we can crash there and sleep it off."

"Why the Norlander, not here?"

"Geez, can't you just be happy for the guy, Zoltan?"

"I don't plan to attend some pimp's party."

"Ron ain't been in that business for months now; never really was to tell the truth."

"Cowboy?"

"Yes, your highness?"

"Get out."

"Yes, your holiness," the desk clerk said, winking at Darla as he left. Zoltan turned his attention back to her.

"So, I guess it was only a matter of time before you escaped the hinterland and hauled your ass back to Hogtown, the center of the known universe."

Zoltan could never resist provoking her about being from Toronto. He claimed it was why she always judged people so quickly. There was truth to this. In the big city you were constantly inundated with sense impressions and competing signals, clashing priorities that compelled you to choose one over the other. You had to be discerning, discriminate between what had value and what didn't. Sometimes, good things got passed over. While in Winnipeg, you could take forever to accept or reject a person or thing and even avoid making a choice altogether. It was definitely more relaxing, but ultimately tedious.

"Just for your edification, Zoltan, we don't call Toronto Hogtown but the Big Smoke."

"I envy you sliding away. Last week, I sat through an absolutely abysmal production of 'Ubu Roi' by Conspiracy Theatre who had cast Randy Wentworth as the King. The man's name sums up his acting ability. Who will I commiserate with now about the miserable state of culture in this town, Darla? You're abandoning me to the philistines."

"There is Deanna Dahl," Darla said. "You've been seeing a lot of her lately."

"Apply a band-aid to a gaping wound? Deanna is not a worthy confidante, Darla. She may be an acrobat in the sack, but is otherwise a witless drone and a slut."

"Don't talk like that, Zoltan. You know better. Besides, the difference between a slut and a stud are two letters of the alphabet."

"That is one of the things I'll miss about you; your ability to turn my clever wisecracks into witty comebacks. But still, the truth can be a blunt cudgel, Darla."

"You need to stop this nonsense. You're doing too much dope, losing weight, and looking burnt-out. Coke is going to kill you, Zoltan."

"Life is gonna kill me. Care for a hit?" he asked, removing a leather pouch from his desk.

"I need to say my goodbyes," she said. "Thanks for the loan. I appreciate it."

"It's not a loan. It's an investment in the arts. Let me know when you're leaving so I can give you a lift to the airport."

Zoltan lowered his head to the desk as Darla was leaving. She was sorry to see her friend wallowing in this blue funk. He'd been indulging too much since Sarah stopped talking to him. Darla had no idea what hold this woman had over him but she definitely had one. She stopped by Donovan's room before going downstairs. She knocked on the door. No answer. Darla hoped she could catch him today. This was her last chance to see him. She had to finish packing, sort things out with her landlord. Stu was a good guy. He loved having creative types as tenants and catered to them. He had a thing for Darla too and would probably be cool with her vacating the premises on such short notice. It wouldn't be hard for him to find someone to rent the place. The digs were decent enough and the neighbourhood still desirable even in decline.

Fran was gone from the front desk now and nobody had replaced her yet. Darla decided to check the bar to see if Donovan was there having a drink. He wasn't, but Tony was; receiving supplicants, dispensing drugs, and doling out rough justice to recalcitrant dopers. Tony Bender was the classic iceman; never giving anything away, showing any emotion, a nervous tic, or a troubled expression. He had the natural narcissism of a predator and a manner yielding nothing but an overarching absence, almost as if he had no soul. He was so different from Donovan. And where was he? Donovan was usually here by now. But he would probably show up at some point in the evening and picking up Fran's shift would provide her with an opportunity to explain what was happening and allow her to say goodbye.

Business wasn't bad in the bar. Still, if Cowboy was right about Big Ron's bash, it would be dead later which was fine with her. Darla could actually enjoy her last night at the Albert and savour the ambiance for a change. Normally, she was working and going crazy taking orders or getting blitzed with Zoltan. Today was different. Darla was stone-cold sober and she could focus completely on her surroundings, observing it in a fresh, filter-free way. Cowboy hadn't left for his party yet and was strutting behind the bar like a potentate without a care in the world. He was gloating as if he had a dirty little secret. Velvet sat on a stool, ignoring him while she read. Darla admired this woman's toughness and appreciated her poise, how she would glide between tables, navigating potential turbulence. Velvet was confident, in control. Nobody messed with her.

But Darla sensed a subtle shift occurring at the hotel. Change was coming to the Albert. It was as if the Lithium fire had dislodged the peaceful coexistence between subcultures, disrupting the delicate balance of an unspoken truce between hoods, hipsters, and artists. Whatever cachet the hotel had enjoyed was slipping away, being overtaken by a malaise. Zoltan's recent excesses only exemplified this; it was reflected in his growing distrust and his paranoia. Darla imagined a dozen different destructive scenarios descending upon the hotel; another fire, a homicidal hood hammering Zoltan so hard he suffered brain damage. This thought both terrified and exhilarated Darla. It lifted her into a rarefied sphere where the heightened energy of risk ruled.

Cowboy muttered to Velvet and nodded at Darla. Velvet put her book into a back pocket, marched over, and placed a Hennessy in front of her.

"I didn't order this," Darla said.

"It's on the house," Velvet said. "I hear you're leaving us."

"Well, that didn't take long to get around."

"Gossip goes through here like shit through a goose. Still, it means I'll get my shifts back."

"What are you reading now?" Darla asked. Velvet handed her the book. "Didn't Donovan give this to Zoltan?"

"And he gave it to me. Enjoy the cognac. I'll bring another when you're done," Velvet said and returned to her stool to continue reading.

The bar usually had three receiving lines. The first in the lobby was where Cowboy would collect cover charge and

Fran starry-eyed beaus, the second at the bar for customers preferring to order drinks directly rather than wait for service, and the last line at Tony's table. But tonight, a fourth was forming. Darla was a woman alone in the bar, a fact which attracted the desperate and hopeful. This began with Banjo Bob staggering over, sitting down, and launching into the story of his life, a sad tale of woe and lost love. Drunks were pretty free with their secrets; he was no exception. Meanwhile, Apocalypso was setting up on stage.

"You like this band?" Bob asked. I don't understand their music but it's cool because I dig their technique. So, sometimes people suck the nice out of you, eh. My old man used to complain I came from a long line of losers on my mother's side. He sent me to a shrink when I was a kid and I spent six months in the crackerjack palace all pumped up on Trifloperazine and Kemadrin pills, eight at breakfast and eight before bedtime. I slept sixteen hours a day and cried constantly for no reason. I've always lived like a monk; no cash, expensive clothes, flashy cars, fancy toys, or house to call my own. I'm just grateful for simple things; a nice meal, a spot to rest my head, and the love of a good woman. That's how it was for me and Sheila. Never had to pretend or play the smooth operator. I just strummed my banjo and let my music soften her hard bits, bring down her decibel level a notch, and refine her rough edges. A song is like a kiss you know; long, slow, and deep. I have music in my soul the way you do dance. You and Fran were hot at that Benefit thingy. Maybe I could back you up some time."

Banjo Bob lifted his instrument from a case and laid it on his knee, leaning forward like a priest listening to a dying man's confession, showing a bald spot on top of his head the size of an ostrich egg. His playing proved to be better than Darla expected, his fingers dancing on the frets and sliding along the strings as he sang a sad melody.

"Hey!" Cowboy bellowed from the bar. "That's enough already with the hurting songs!"

"Jellybelly don't like me much anymore," Bob said. "Nobody cares about nothing; nobody but my buddy, Donovan.

He won't steal your songs, mess with your girl, or crush your spirit."

"You know him well?" Darla asked.

"We met at a poetry workshop years ago. I used to drag Donovan to bookstores and record shops to meet women. Babes loved him. He was like James Dean for poetry chicks. So listen, if you need a little good smoking dope — grass, hash, mushrooms, or acid, see me."

Jimmy Jazz jumped up suddenly and the smile melted off Bob's face. He grabbed his banjo and split as the big man barrelled toward him. After Bob was gone, Jimmy Jazz smiled at Darla.

"Little fat man is on a tear," he said and walked back to Tony's table. Velvet brought her another drink.

"Guess you won't miss the drama around here," she said.

"Have you seen Donovan around lately?" Darla asked and Velvet did something she never did. She sat with a customer.

"Donovan went to see his doctor yesterday and didn't come back. You're working tonight. We'll talk more then."

Velvet stood, briefly rested her hand on Darla's shoulder, and started to walk away.

"Hey, why weren't we friends?" Darla asked and an enigmatic smile crossed Velvet's face.

"You tell me," she said and strolled back to the bar.

Flying on the Ground

"Do you think this top make me look like a tramp?" she asked, holding the blouse between her fingers until it was tight against her chest. Zoltan briefly considered the delicate fabric then shrugged indifferently. He had little to say that would reassure her. The colourful clothing looked good on her. Everything did. Deanna Dahl, while still definitely attractive, was a neurotic mess, terrified of losing her looks, which were naturally fading a little with age although not nearly as precipitously as she feared. Deanna was stunning in her twenties and pursued by all manner of male with musicians, actors, athletes, and men of means flocking to her. Of course, she enjoyed the attention and taken advantage of it. But she continued to hold out for her hero, a gorgeous gallant with an evolved sense of style, well-appointed residence, expensive vintage vehicle, and elegant wardrobe. The man of her dreams would be a high-tech wizard or a marketing genius, a successful entrepreneur or a captain of industry. Above all else, he would be hopelessly devoted to Deanna, giving her whatever her heart desired. But prince charming never arrived, although potential consorts invariably materialized to make promises and raise unrealistic expectations, dream merchants feeding Deanna's fantasies about their incredible future together. When he lost interest and started to ignore her, Deanna would drop into an emotional tailspin.

Zoltan had never been a contender for her affections. He had neither the social weight nor the financial clout. Still, he was flush enough to provide a fallback position between paramours. And far as he was concerned, Deanna was amusing when not obsessed with licking her wounds. Their friendship was fuelled by booze, cocaine, and intermittent sex and only interrupted by the appearance of a new beau. Then, after another inevitable, dramatic breakup, Zoltan would help her pick up the pieces while listening to a distraught Deanna lament. A perpetual disappointment in love bred despair and poisonous cynicism in her. A part-time position as hostess at the Marble Club allowed her to track the spread of STDs through the bar and learn who was infected by who they went home with. She kept Zoltan informed and he was able to avoid risky encounters. It had saved him a trip or two to the clinic. Deanna was primed to party tonight though and after they'd consumed several lines of coke she slipped a hand between his legs.

"Just checking the hardware," she purred. "Or maybe I should say software? Oh, poor boy, it's nowhere."

Zoltan slapped her hand away while Ted and Frieda, who were whooping it up with them, burst into laughter. They were all well-lubricated by now, flinging clever comments back and forth and baiting each other with nasty remarks. It was their idea of fun and despite frequently questionable wit, Zoltan enjoyed it. His pals delivered distraction. He supplied party favours. It took his mind off business at the hotel, Sarah's recent rejection, and the potential threat that Tony Bender posed. They were the only occupants in Bertha's Place now. She'd served them several rounds and was bringing menus, hoping they might buy some food. After a quick perusal, Ted closed his menu.

"Fine dining AND a fast lunch, Zoltan?" he asked. "I think that's pushing the envelope."

"As if you know the difference," Frieda quipped, punching his shoulder. Ted turned to her.

"You have the most beautiful face I've ever seen, Frieda, but you're fat."

Ted had hit his mark with this blunt assessment and Frieda fell silent. Bertha came back out of the kitchen to take their order and left without one. Ted made a big production out of gagging and holding his nose.

"What now?" Zoltan asked.

"The woman needs to learn to lower her arms or how to use deodorant."

After a disappointed Bertha closed, they stayed behind to party in the dark café. Zoltan's stash was low. It meant he had to talk to Tony again.

"If I'm not right back, send out a search party," he said and went to the bar. Jimmy Jazz peeled away from the table when he joined Tony.

"I believe that character is dealing drugs in my bar," Zoltan said and Tony tilted his head toward him, eyes narrowing as he puffed on his cigar.

"Jimmy Jazz just went to top you up, Zoltan. You'll find what you need under the spare tire in your trunk."

Zoltan had no idea how Tony knew what he wanted or how Jimmy Jazz got into his car.

"You hear from Donovan?" he asked. "I've always liked your brother."

"Yeah, he's likeable. Don't be so concerned about Donovan. He thinks too much and lets things eat away at him. Not like you and me, eh, Zoltan. We appreciate the good things in life. But your debt is out of control. You haven't paid me a dime in months."

"Temporary cash crunch," Zoltan said. "This too shall pass."

"You say that. I still don't see a return on my investment. I can fix your financial concerns, Zoltan; clear away what you owe me and generate a serious chunk of change for you, get some real cash flowing into your pocket again."

"We`ve talked about this before, Tony. I will not rent you rooms in the hotel. I got old men living upstairs. They need peace and quiet."

"Your folks didn't do you any favour sticking you with this firetrap. Albert hasn't made a profit in years. Forget about renting rooms. I want to buy your hotel. Don't laugh. I am serious. Think about it. But don't take long. Time is running out. Another thing before you head back to your party. Stop bothering Sarah, calling her, trying to see her. She is out of your life now."

"Sarah is easy on the eyes but hard on the heart as you will soon discover, Tony."

"Jimmy Jazz is back. Go collect your goodies."

Zoltan went to his car and found the cocaine exactly where Tony said it would be. So Tony had found out his folks were giving up their stake in the new world and saddling him with the Albert. The pusher had more pipelines around the hotel than the blue-eyed sheiks in Alberta with Cowboy being the primary one. Zoltan went back to Bertha's Place.

"Ted and Frieda left?" he asked Deanna.

"They got tired of waiting, which just leaves us," she said. After they did a few more lines, Deanna pressed a finger to his lips.

"Stop grinding your teeth," she said. Zoltan drew her finger into his mouth.

"Let's adjourn to my place," he said. When Deanna passed out in his bed, Zoltan couldn't sleep. He kept thinking about Sarah, what he could give her that Tony Bender couldn't. Sure, the pusher probably had some nice things but Zoltan had come by his honestly; well, more honestly. Leonard Cohen's sad music comforted him as the poet chanted, lamenting a mist that left no scars and hotels with paper-thin walls. Zoltan finally fell asleep, listening to 'Sisters of Mercy'. When he woke in the morning, Deanna had left without leaving a trace of being there. Zoltan showered and dressed, resisting the urge to do a line of coke. He had to get to the hotel, count the receipts, and drive Darla to the airport.

The sight of Cowboy loitering at the desk in the lobby irritated him.

"Hung over again, boss?" Cowboy asked and Zoltan exploded.

"Fix the creak in that freaking café door before I fire you."

"I need to find a doohickey for the thingamajig first."

"What's stopping you?"

"I'm doing the best I can on a limited budget, Zoltan."

"Who gave you a budget?"

"Man, you're cranky after a night of carousing. I got something for you," Cowboy said and handed Zoltan an envelope with his name scribbled across the front.

"What is it?"

"Not a clue. I went to the bar for a quick whizz last night, came back, and found it on the front desk."

"This envelope has been opened."

"The glue is shit."

Zoltan examined the contents then waved the note at Cowboy.

"It's anonymous."

"Greek guy, right?" Cowboy quipped.

"What is this list of names supposed to represent?"

"Everyone on it is either dead or missing. Ferret and his cousin speed freaks found stinking up a sty on Sherbrook awhile back. You know what happened to Prince and Billy and we haven't seen the Midnight Jeweller, Eric the Red, Itchy Dick, or Scott Kostyk around lately."

"I saw Itchy Dick in the bar yesterday and I seriously doubt Scott is dead or missing. I have no idea where he's laying low since being beaten down, but he'll turn up."

"The man has made a few enemies."

"None of that explains the note, Cowboy."

"Maybe it's a warning of some kind."

"I haven't got the time or the patience for your nonsense. I catch you snooping in my mail again, you're out of here. Beat it so I can count my cash."

Zoltan drove to Darla's after completing this task. She was packed and ready to leave.

"Here's my key," she said. "Keep what you like, let Fran take what she wants, and give the rest to the Sally Ann. When you're done, leave the key on the kitchen counter for the landlord."

In the car Darla asked Zoltan about Donovan's book.

"Why did you give it to Velvet?"

"I couldn't finish the damn thing. It was too depressing and she reads everything."

"The book belongs to Donovan."

"I don't think he needs it where he is now. Why do you care? You're leaving town."

They found Fran waiting in the airport. Darla checked her bags, and at the departure gate, Fran gave her a long hug, her eyes wet when she pulled away. They always seemed to be moist these days. Darla kissed Zoltan's cheek and it suddenly hit him how much he was going to miss his friend, her irrepressible, positive energy and uplifting spirit. After Darla disappeared behind frosted doors, he and Fran stood staring at them for a long time. Zoltan finally turned toward her.

"Let me buy you a drink," he said. In the airport bar, Zoltan nursed his Gran Marnier while Fran sipped a Brown Cow. Outside the familiar framework of the hotel and his position as boss, they didn't have much to say.

"I don't believe she is coming back," Fran said and Zoltan showed her the apartment key. They agreed to go over to Darla's apartment the following Sunday to sift through her things.

"Would you like to go for coffee sometime?" he asked. Fran smiled with the easy grace of a woman used to such offers.

"I'm seeing someone," she said. Zoltan recalled Eric the Red's name on Cowboy's list.

"Isn't he missing or something?" he asked. Her eyes filled with tears again.

"We were at Big Ron's bash at the Norlander," Fran said, her voice faltering. "Eric went out for a smoke and never came back. I have to go now, Zoltan."

Fran left, not finishing her drink. Zoltan downed his, ordered another, and then went to the bathroom where he did a line of coke. Back at the table, he sipped his drink and ruminated about what was happening in his life, at the Albert. Cowboy's cryptic note could well be a threat and probably from Tony. Zoltan was tired of marinating in squalor, trading quips with the desk clerk, trying to get through long winters, and dealing with frozen faces which never quite thawed out when the warm weather came. So why was he sticking around? Darla got away. Why didn't he?

One thing he would never do was sell Tony Bender his hotel. The pusher would throw out all the old men living upstairs and turn the hotel into a shooting gallery. Maybe Zoltan should go to the police and tell them with what he knew, what he suspected.

The Madman Blues

Little had changed in Selkirk. It was just as insanitized as ever; shit food, indifferent staff, long days, and longer nights; nothing to do aside from playing goofy board games and cribbage or scoping out the other patients. Three months after Donovan's discharge most of the old gang still haunted the hospital halls. A few newbies sulked in the corners, glaring at anyone who came too close. On forensics it wasn't hard to tell genuine head-cases from malingering jailbirds. The spa's regular denizens were usually in legal trouble for some silly reason; shouting at strangers in the street, trying to pay for groceries with poetry, or not taking meds. But cons admitted from the city jail or pen were trying to scam the system to secure an NCR status and beat a heavy beef like murder by convincing a shrink they were crazy. Donovan could have told them how crazy this was if they cared to listen. Not-Criminally-Insane was a life sentence that followed you into the ground. They could haul your ass into hospital for any infraction, real, imagined, or anticipated anytime they wanted, just like Lawler did to him a few days ago. Donovan had been dodging his doctor appointments for three months but Tony kept bugging him to go, get his meds increased. Donovan never should have listened to his brother.

Lawler started his cross-examination with the usual ten questions. Was he taking his meds? How did he feel? Donovan had always beaten the shrink at his mind games, negotiating fastball questions, keeping his answers brief, to the point. The trick to walking a tightrope is not looking down, exhibiting any discomfort, or showing any disquiet. Donovan smiled just enough to satisfy the doctor's suspicions without raising doubts about his state of mind. He apologized, played the penitent patient, and made excuses for missing his appointments. Then Lawler asked about Siren.

Siren had first appeared in this dimension after Just Joe started to diddle Donovan. And, in the beginning, the apparition was a court jester, distracting and teasing him, telling him fantastic stories that took him on trips far from the North End and his family. But then the jokes weren't funny anymore and became biting indictments. That was when Donovan started cutting. They caught him in elementary school and sent him to a shrink. So he had a psych history and when he killed the biker years later, he ended up in Selkirk instead of Stony Mountain. Some hospital staff believed he belonged in prison, not on a psychiatric unit. They studied every move he made and turned one thing into another. If he chose to read a book rather than socialize, he was isolating himself. He was manipulating when he mingled; staying in the background to watch what was happening, he was paranoid; lethargic if sleeping late, manic when wide awake. The inquisitors in lab coats tried to drain his brain. But he never caved, exercising restraint, while not leaving the impression of repressing things. It was a fine balancing act in a facility where good behaviour passed for wellness. In all that time, he never acknowledged Siren's existence. Still, live under constant observation for five years with an orderly monitoring every move you make, whether you're eating, sleeping, or taking a dump, they learn things. So, on this particular Friday afternoon, Lawler was pressing him. Donovan denied hallucinating. It was true. He hadn't seen Siren since he trashed his room at the Albert. Lawler warned him coming to appointments was a condition of his discharge. Then he threw a curveball. He closed Donovan's chart with a thump and handed it to an orderly.

"It's come to my attention you recently had a run-in with the biker you almost killed five years ago. I've been told it was a relatively minor altercation and no one was seriously injured. But it does concern me. I'm admitting you for the weekend to adjust your medication."

So now, Donovan was back in hospital and he knew somehow his brother was responsible. Tony was in tight with the shrink. Arranging an admission on the Ides of March would appeal to his twisted sense of humour. Et-tu-brute, eh brother. But why would Tony do this? What purpose of his did it serve? It didn't make sense.

Down on the locked unit, the nurse took blood and a urine sample. Suzie chatted while she did this, asking him if he'd finished the book she gave him. Donovan lied, saying that he had. It seemed to please her and she said they could talk about it later if he liked. Donovan smiled, knowing he was going to fail the fucking drug screen.

But Lawler kept his word, cutting him loose at the end of the day Monday after increasing his prescription, which would please Tony. Donovan was relieved. He was eager to see Darla. One advantage of Siren's disappearing act was that it made space for her. Darla was taking him out of his head. In the last two weeks, she'd introduced him to new things, opening other worlds to him. When they saw 'The Seventh Seal' at the Winnipeg Art Gallery, the film blew him away. He enjoyed a dance recital by one of her friends and Darla listened to what he said; read what he wrote, and encouraged him to drop the ducktail to let his hair grow out naturally.

At the Albert, Maggie was packing up to go home and slipped away quickly, not looking Donovan in the eye. It didn't surprise him. The woman was apprehensive about absolutely every little thing. In the bar, Jimmy Jazz was at Tony's table facing the door and dealing dope to speed freaks. Tony was probably off starting World War III somewhere. Jimmy nodded at Donovan but gave him a strange look. Something was up. Banjo Bob was parked by the back door, sporting the sheepskin coat Big Ron laid on Donovan. His friend needed a good winter coat, so Donovan gave it to him. Bob was obviously buzzed on more than just booze.

"Good to see you, man. Where the hell you been? We missed ya," he said. Velvet brought Donovan a Jameson, Banjo Bob another beer. Bob handed her a hundred dollar bill and waved off the change. Velvet wasn't impressed.

"Darla isn't working?" Donovan asked.

"She got a part in a play in Toronto and left town, maybe for good," Velvet said.

"Did she leave any contact information?"

"Not with me. Ask Zoltan, maybe Fran knows."

"Go away for a weekend and all the interesting people disappear," Donovan said.

"Hey man," Banjo Bob protested.

"No, you're cool, Bob. But Scott Kostyk hasn't been around lately either."

"You won't see him here anymore," Velvet said.

"Have any idea how to get a hold of him?"

"Not a clue. Something else happened, Donovan," she said. "But Tony should tell you."

Itchy Dick marched into the bar and right over to their table.

"Wait five minutes, the table troll appears," Banjo Bob snapped.

"Hey man," Itchy Dick mumbled. "I got my welfare cheque, could use some mushrooms."

"Well why didn't you say so?"

"I just did, Bobby."

Banjo Bob reached into his instrument case and removed a baggie containing aluminum packets. He extracted one, exchanging it for a twenty. Itchy Dick stuffed the mushroom in a jeans pocket and bolted. The conclusion of this dubious, minor-league drug deal would have been comical were it not dangerous. Tony disposed of Prince for similar shenanigans; Donovan didn't doubt his brother would do the same to his friend. Banjo Bob was a harmless dreamer, just drifting through life and dancing on the edge without a net. Bob wouldn't last long at the Albert if Donovan wasn't there to protect him. He didn't have a killer instinct and would stumble into some predicament he couldn't handle. There was no point in trying to persuade him to abandon the path he was travelling though. Idiot proofing never worked. Brains don`t need it. Idiots don't learn. Banjo Bob pressed a brown paper bag into his hands.

"That's for you, man," he said. "You've been a pal and I had a little luck with this score. I guess my good karma is finally paying off."

Donovan knocked back his Jameson.

"I need another," he muttered.

"Lemme get it," Banjo Bob said and waved to the bar. Fran hustled over with fresh drinks.

"Velvet gone?" Donovan asked.

"She went home. I'm taking over her section."

"You wouldn't happen to have Darla's number in Toronto?" he asked. But Fran slammed his drink down, shot him a dirty look, and left. Back at the bar, she sat on a stool and started to pull on a box of Kleenex. It was odd. Fran was usually the friendliest person in the place.

"She's been like that a couple of days," Bob said.

Cowboy poked his head inside the door and smiled at Fran. She ignored him. He nodded to Donovan, tilting his head toward the lobby. Donovan stuffed Bob's goodies into a coat pocket, downed the last of his drink, and went out to the front. If anyone could put him wise to what the hell was going on around the hotel, it was Cowboy. At the front desk, the man was downright giddy and dancing in his pants.

"Don't mind me," Cowboy said. "I'm still a little blitzed after Big Ron's bash the other night. He won the lottery and invited everyone on the planet, including some he hardly knew to a party. Bugger laid out a real spread, man. We drank and we danced until we dropped. Turned out my old buddy pulled a fast one. While we were having a hoot, he snuck out of town. Didn't tell a soul, say goodbye, or leave a note, nothing. It's too bad. I was gonna hit him up for a loan. I've always dreamed of having a small diner and calling it the Sugar Shack, just a little place to fry a few burgers and brew coffee for folks. Oh well, we had a blast anyway. Sorry you weren't there, but it was probably for the best. Tony took care of Eric the Red, kept you out of it. Nobody can finger you because you were in hospital. Tony had me convince Big Ron to hold his party at the Norlander where the biker would feel safe and he took a long hike off a short pier. Fucker never did learn the diff between alpha and suicidal. But it did blindside poor Frannie. Promise me you won't tell Tony I said anything. Hey, will you do me a favour and watch the desk a few hours? New peeler at the Ox wants my body. She's from Montreal. There's fifty bucks in it for you."

"I'll want the cash up front, Cowboy."

"Don't you trust me?" Cowboy said with a laugh. "No problem, man. So there's a rumour going round Tony plans to buy the Albert. I could handle the whole shooting match for him. Put in a good word for me? Tony listens to you."

After this, Cowboy left the lobby on a cloud. The clown never listened or learned, thinking Donovan had any influence with his brother. He'd find out the hard way. Jimmy Jazz was Tony's right hand and would run the show if his brother did acquire the hotel.

But Donovan sensed something bad had gone down that Cowboy didn't spill. The Albert had always had an edge to it but it was especially intense tonight, almost as if some indiscernible disturbance was undermining what little equilibrium still existed there. Donovan could taste it on his tongue. In the few days he was locked up in the loony bin Darla had left, Kostyk disappeared, and Eric the Red died. Prince was history too. Tony was making a move.

The lobby was quieter after Cowboy was gone. A few regulars straggled in off the street and Donovan held them with his eyes, making them move in slow motion. It got old fast. Then, around eleven o'clock the front door banged open and a woman barged into the lobby with a TV cameraman in tow and they headed for the bar. Donovan bellowed until the walls vibrated. The woman spun around, suddenly his new best friend.

"We're with the local news station and going inside to conduct interviews," she said.

"People come here to drink, not be on TV. You can't take a camera into the bar."

"Well, we can," she insisted. "This is a public place."

"No, it's private property."

"So who's gonna stop us?" the cameraman said. He was big, had a drinker's schnoz. If he wanted to go, Donovan was ready. The talking head was still pushing the soft sell.

"While I certainly understand your concern, there's been a significant development about the arson down the street. Yesterday, the man charged with setting the fire committed suicide in his cell at the Public Safety Building. Now, we know Bernie Bender probably frequented this bar so we want to ask people how they feel about his passing."

"Bernie is dead," Donovan whispered.

"Did you know him? Can I ask you a few questions then?"

"You're trespassing. Get out before I call the cops," he snarled. When the woman shot him a dirty look, Donovan turned toward the switchboard. She shook her head and sighed.

"Let's go, Michael," she said. "This is a waste of time. You teach them their ABCs and they think they run the world."

Sawchuk was sauntering into the lobby as they stormed out.

"Guess you heard, eh," the pig drawled, putting his chubby paw inside a coat pocket and pulling out a cigar. He lit up and a familiar tang hit Donovan like a hammer. His every fibre was fused into a frozen mass that starved his blood of fire.

"Guard found Bernie swinging in his cell," Sawchuk said. "Guess the little bugger couldn't take the heat. Well, it saves the taxpayers a bundle. And no trial means no muss, no fuss, no need to dig up any dirt."

Sawchuk blew a cloud of smoke in Donovan's direction. No reaction. The cop clapped his hands together. There was still nothing. He drilled steely eyes into Donovan's empty ones.

"You're a fucking ghoul, Bender," Sawchuk growled in disgust, turning away and leaving the lobby.

Donovan's brain went into hyper-drive making connections. Bernie was not a quitter. He was carefree with a fierce love for life. Hitting bottom or going through withdrawal in a jail cell would never cause him to hang himself. Someone lent him a hand and now this fucking flatfoot was waving a cigar in his face like a nightstick. Tony didn't share his cigars with anyone except Jimmy Jazz, who didn't smoke them and chewed the stogies down to wet stubs. Tony had pulled some nasty shit in the past, nothing like this. Snuffing Eric and Prince had made perfect sense, but Bernie? Tony used all his brothers yet protected them in his own way. What had changed? It was their old lady. She'd always been the linchpin holding the family together and now it looked like their mother's death had severed the bond for Tony, liberating him of what little connection had survived the years, enabling him to do some things he might never have otherwise. Donovan knew it was his fault. His brother, Bernie, might still be alive if he hadn't gone to see his mother the night she died.

"Hang 'em high," a voice started singing in his brain. Donovan closed his eyes. Siren was floating inside his head. A sudden rap on the desk distracted him and he opened his eyes again. Downtown Tommy was holding out a trembling hand. Donovan hadn't seen the forlorn character since the day he was discharged from hospital three months ago.

"Got a cigarette, shareholder?" the old bum asked, squinting as he went through a mental scrapbook of every soft touch he'd ever tapped in his travels. Then the puzzled gaze turned to dread and he waved a wobbling finger at Donovan.

"Your eyes!" he cried. "I can see the aliens have built an enemy outpost in you!

Siren shrieked. Donovan snapped, flicking his cigarette butt at the drunk. He vaulted over the desk, grabbed him by the throat, and forced him back, banging his body against the front door to open it before firing him headfirst in a snow bank. The bum's skull cracked on the ice.

"Why you do that?" he moaned. Donovan kicked him in the head and Downtown Tommy curled into a ball to protect himself. Donovan kept kicking him, throwing his whole body into it. When a hand pressed into his shoulder, he spun around, fists up.

"Easy brother," Tony said. "Let's go inside and get warm. I'll buy you a drink."

Back in the lobby, Tony directed Donovan to Bertha's Place while he went to the bar. Out on Albert Street, Downtown Tommy had already crawled away, leaving a thin trail of blood behind. Siren was crooning in Donovan's head.

"Who sighs lullabies, through nights that never end; my fickle friend, the summer wind."

Tony returned with a bottle and two glasses, his cigar glowing red in the dark. Donovan wanted to stub it out in his eye. He threw a black notebook on the table.

"The old lady wanted you to have this."

"What?"

"No idea."

"You didn't take a peek?"

"Never had that part of the old lady before why would I want it now? So we need to talk. Your hippie pal needs to stop peddling pot and shit in the bar. I've only let it go so far because he helps keep you on an even keel."

"He isn't a threat to you, Tony."

"You don't make him quit, I will. Get with the program, Donnie. While you were on your little holiday in hospital, I took care of your problem with Eric. That biker won't be putting the boots to anyone anymore."

"I heard about Bernie too, Tony."

"Yeah, it's a shame he lost heart. Bernie was a good soldier; crazy when he was stoned, but dependable. Still, let's face it; he wasn't getting out of the joint any time soon, not with the three bodies on him. Maybe what happened was for the best."

"Sawchuk was just here sucking on one of your cigars and bragging about Bernie's suicide. Our brother trusted you, Tony. He always did what you said."

"Let it go, Donovan. Take one death at a time. The old lady's funeral will be in four days. You be there."

Donovan drained his glass, slammed it down, and left the café. He could feel Tony's eyes boring into him.

His new room on the third floor was brighter and cleaner than the one he'd trashed. There was less action up here too, just old men with broken teeth nursing a bottle in their rooms. He rarely saw another soul, only smelling cigarette smoke and hearing an odd spasm of coughing. He retrieved a bottle of Jameson from where he had it stashed, took a swig, and dumped the contents of Bob's bag onto the bed. His friend had been generous. Donovan counted at least twenty tabs of acid, a whole whack of magic mushrooms. This would do the trick. He opened a foil packet and popped a chocolate-covered mushroom in his mouth, taking a long pull from the bottle. Siren started singing again.

"I don't care what the others say, time has come today."

Donovan went to the mirror. Siren wasn't there so he studied his own face, touching it and searching for traces of the man he had once been. Age was creeping up on him, creasing his flesh with soft folds, carving furrows in it. He was starting to look like his mother. Siren began to spin in his head, a Tasmanian devil droning psychedelic melodies and digging his sharp claws into the spongy mass of Donovan's skull, agitated nerve endings dancing to the music while dogs stoned on rabies and blood barked. Bernie broke off a fence picket to beat the mutts back before helping Donovan with the punks taunting him on the corner of Pritchard. Someone called the cops. They carted Bernie off, leaving Donovan behind. Bernie never complained about being the one they always busted. Why did Tony think he would spill his guts now? Donovan swallowed a second mushroom. It went down easier than the first. An hour later he still didn't feel a thing. He had to accelerate this process and get to the next level. Donovan dropped two tabs of acid and washed them down with whiskey, watching the ribbons of gold flow from the bottle and blast light in his brain. He was rambling in a garden of constellations, while the black ceiling bent into an arc and became a breathing womb. Was it a cliché to climb inside? He cracked open the notebook.

The date on the first page was February ninth, 1964, followed by a letter to a guy named John. Did his mother have a secret lover? Donovan flipped through pages stained with gin and tears, stopping at the last letter in the diary. It was the same day she set herself on fire.

My memory is a jagged mess, John, shifting sands and nagging past. Just back from war, Whiskey Jack was a heap of man straddling his Norton. Family and friends didn't think much of him or understand my attraction. There was a lot of hateful talk like with you and Yoko. But we were both keen to tango and I spit out six boys; Tony, Randall, Jake, Billy, Bernie, and Donovan, all of them lost to me now. You said you were more popular than Jesus and just like they nailed him to a tree that fucking Judas bastard blew you away on the street. I didn't cry the day the music died but something deep inside me froze, put out the fire. I don't feel nothing anymore. Been like that a long while. Everywhere is somewhere, but I'm a real nowhere woman. The hours drag and the years fly. My life is done. I feel it in my bones and the blood I hork up every morning; I can't sleep, eat, or turn off the tap dripping drops in my head as time tick-tocks. I try to keep the lid screwed on tight but I want to smash things, scream until the walls tumble. I waited for Jesus and I waited for you, John. Neither of you came. There is no Jesus, no John; just me, the juice, and Whiskey Jack. He calls me a holy terror sometimes. Nothing holy about this horror show. I don't want to go into the ground and be eaten by worms, makes my skin crawl thinking about it. So I don't think and don't feel, don't do nothing but drink gin, smoke cigarettes, take my lithium, and write you. Goodbye, John. Love Doris.

Donovan slammed the notebook shut and fired it across the room. The old lady had sworn she'd never let anything Beatles in the house before they played Ed Sullivan. But after they were on TV she never spoke of them again. Now Donovan knew why. She'd started writing the letters that very night and had been writing them for twenty years. Well, his mother had her secrets and he had his.

Nobody was around when he got off the elevator at the hospital. He heard voices, dishes clanking down the hall. Donovan didn't recognize her behind the bandages and he pulled them aside. His mother's face was swollen, a mottled, grotesque mask. The tray on the table in front of her bed held a plate with three soft lumps; a gray one, an orange, a green. The mush had spilled on her hospital gown and stained the bandages around her mouth. This was her life now. In the early days, before she started talking about taking the bridge, the old lady had loved to laugh like Bernie and the lines around her eyes would crinkle when she did. She never jumped. She set fires instead. This time she'd come close to finishing the job, but wasn't quite there yet. She needed a little help. A sulphur smell filled his nostrils as he leaned over the hospital bed and kissed his mother's cheek. She sighed, mumbled his name, and didn't fight when he pushed the pillow into her face.

Back in his room at the Albert now, a scream started crawling up from the base of his spine to his throat but he swallowed it back down with gulps of whiskey. Donovan dropped another tab of acid while Siren continued to serenade him.

"Sitting on the dock of the bay; watching the tide roll away. Cut the moorings to ease away from the harbour and escape the dream concentration camps consuming you."

Siren was singing louder and dancing in a dark fire, his head spinning and eyes rolling in the sockets. He lobbed a smile at Donovan and Bernie bounced from the shadows. There wasn't much left after the coroner and the courts were done with him. Donovan gagged, retching sacks of rough air and falling to the floor, thrashing while all of the world's anguish worked its way through him. He couldn't stop crying until he was drenched by a cleansing rain and rose from the floor. His hands were glowing with willowy coils of silver and indigo flowing from his fingers. He wove silk Celtic knots on the air with them as the moon threw high beams into the room, the luminous thread a corridor of light and a ladder he longed to climb. A brilliant sun burst in his brain, cascading needles illuminating him, as he floated above language and outside meaning. There were no answers, no questions. Everything simply was; all the neat theories collapsing constructs no longer propped up by alphabet stickmen or convenient symbols. His molecules were starting to separate now, the spaces between them expanding as events unravelled. Darla's face loomed up in front of him and he fell into her eyes, feeling her warmth. Then she was gone. They used to tell him it was all in his head. But the inside of his head was as real as anywhere else. Donovan flipped the switch. He took Siren's translucent hand and motored off into infinity.

Driving Down Main

When Sarah arrived at the Albert, Tony was pacing outside trailing cigar smoke like an old steam locomotive. It was late afternoon. Zoltan would be long gone by now although Cowboy was peeking out a café window at them. Tony climbed into the Dart and gave her directions to the funeral home.

"How is Donovan doing?" she asked.

"Not bad considering all the drugs they found in his system," Tony said. "He's still floating off in his own world, not responding to anyone or anything. They'll try shock treatment next. It's worked in the past."

Sarah turned at McDermott, went a short block, then left. Driving down Main, even this early in the day, drunks were staggering down the sidewalk. As she went passed the Occidental, she remembered her mother telling her how Poppy had died behind the hotel. Sarah still didn't know where he was buried. She would have to ask her mother. Maybe she would know.

Sarah was confused, pulling up in front of Cropo's. Nine decorative arches arrayed along a stucco façade made the building look less like a funeral home than a restaurant for ribs. She went around to the back and parked under a billboard advertising cars. Sarah had never been to a funeral before and didn't know what to expect. In the reception area, Tony introduced her to some rough looking characters who tried to figure out who she was as they pumped his hand. Sarah wondered which one of them had thrown Brad off the Provencher Bridge. Jimmy Jazz stood in a corner, looking sadder than anyone else. It might have been him. A funeral director with fine silver hair and a face like a polished mask crossed to them. Sarah didn't want to think about why he was wearing so much cologne. He was polite, but in a solemn, practiced way she found condescending. She could feel Tony's body tighten like a crucible and turn his rage into tempered steel. She squeezed his hand and he glanced at her. An understanding passed between them that made the funeral director fidget and excuse himself. Next, a barrel-shaped man in a loud suit bounded over. He looked like a circus clown in a bright blue blazer, green shirt, and yellow tie. Just Joe kissed her hand, trailing spit on her skin. She pulled away but he seemed too dense to catch her disgust. He was one of those people you could never be sure if they were working an angle or just plain stupid.

"Good to see you finally hooked up with a skirt, Tony," he said. "Sorry to hear about the old doll, eh. She was a tough broad when she got wound up, took no flack from nobody. Listen, I never thanked you for getting our stuff back. Cost me a penny or two but was it worth it, made Willa happy too. She would have been here but she has a migraine; either that or a man on the side."

Tony led Sarah away from him and gave her a Kleenex to wipe her hand. The chapel was bright and filled with light. She was expecting something more sombre, dark wood and subtle lighting. An urn stood on a stand beside a podium. At the front, an old man with red, puffy eyes sat by himself. Whiskey Jack didn't seem so tough today. Tony introduced Sarah and his father barely acknowledged her presence. It wasn't hard to read his mind.

"Where's Donovan?" he grunted.

"In hospital," Tony said.

"Blew a gasket again, eh? That didn't take long."

A padre stepped to the podium and started prattling about love, life, death, and God, only mentioning Doris Bender last. He said she was a wonderful woman, a wife, and a mother to six boys. Whiskey Jack wept while Tony stared straight ahead, not flexing a muscle, almost as if his emotions had been flash frozen. The short service finished and a scratchy record of Nat King Cole singing 'Rambling Rose' came through speakers. Then a bagpiper played 'Amazing Grace'. Bagpipes always brought out the Scot in Sarah and she would want to paint herself blue and run naked through the woods.

Everybody looked a little lost afterward. Just Joe loudly announced the ladies at the legion on Salter and Mountain were putting on a spread for them. When Sarah and Tony were climbing into her car, some man shoved a TV camera up to the back window where Whiskey Jack was sitting. Jimmy Jazz came from out of nowhere, grabbed the camera, and smashed it against a wall. As Sarah pulled out of the parking lot, he was pummelling the cameraman. Driving to the legion, she felt Whiskey Jack's eyes burning a hole in the back of her head while he spoke.

"Old lady grew up in Scotland," he grumbled. "Wants her ashes spread in Paisley, I can't afford that."

Sarah dropped them in front of the legion and went to find some parking. They were still out on the street when she came back, Whiskey Jack yelling at Tony.

"You bring a fucking squaw to your mother's funeral!" he shouted. Then he saw Sarah. His face went red and he stomped into the legion.

"We'll go in for just a minute. I need to talk to him," Tony said and Sarah waited inside by the door while Tony spoke to his father. A thick fog of cigarette smoke hung over the ceiling of the legion hall and the smell of beer seemed to be soaked into the walls. It was even more depressing than she'd expected. Some of the people looked like they were almost ready to join Doris Bender in the afterlife. When Tony was done, he crossed to her.

"We can go now," he said. "The old man will spend the night with Just Joe."

Sarah drove Tony to his house on Scotia Street not far from the legion. He asked her in for coffee and she agreed. You have to cut a man some slack on the day he buries his mother. Snowshoes leaned against a wall in the front hall. Sarah couldn't resist touching the damp mesh. Tony had a lovely home with high ceilings, huge rooms, and bookshelves lining the living room walls. Sarah took one book down from a shelf.

"How many of these have you actually read?" she asked and Tony smiled.

"More than you think. Why don't you take that home with you? I think you'll enjoy Louise Erdrich's writing."

Sarah followed Tony and thumbed through the book, while he ground coffee beans and the fresh smell spread through the kitchen. After he'd made them a cup, they went to the living room where he put an album on the stereo. Tony showed her his extensive collection of vinyl records, while Albert King's guitar drifted through strategically placed speakers. He had blues by Muddy Waters, BB King, Solomon Burke, Big Mama Thornton, Mississippi Fred McDowell and the jazz of Miles Davis, Billie Holiday, and Sonny Rollins.

"Whiskey Jack hates my music," Tony said. "He's a simple-minded dunce, doesn't think beyond the lip of a glass. And yes, he is a racist. Don't know how he'll work out living with me. He used to drive the old lady batty."

"Your mother sounds sad. I wish I'd met her. She could have told me what you were like as a little boy."

"She didn't really know me. When I was eleven, lying in bed, I heard screaming, ran down to the kitchen. The old lady was standing over Whiskey Jack with a bread knife, so I snuck up behind her and wrestled the knife away. I think that was when she started hating me; maybe it was before then. She used to tell me I was the destroyer who ruined her body, opening it up to other sons, while Donovan was her redeemer, shutting it down again. Crazy eh?"

"Maybe a little," Sarah said. "I should probably go; I have to pick Amy up from school."

"Thank you for coming to the funeral," he said. "Don't forget to take the book. 'The Plague of Doves' is very good."

It was cold out as Sarah climbed into the Dart and the sky was a heart-breaking blue. The day had been dreary, despite Tony's apparent strength. The truth was that everyone ended up like his mother had; Brad and Poppy too. She had always managed to avoid so much misery and pain by moving on whenever it proved to be necessary.

A week ago, her mother mentioned seeing an available apartment not far from her house. Years earlier, Sarah had resolved to never live in the North End again but took a quick peek at the place to please her mother. It was on Cathedral in a renovated fire-hall and turned out to be absolutely stunning. Were hesitation and caution causing her to miss out on important things? Did she want her legacy to be that she'd locked up all her longing and never really lived? Sarah realized she had to really stop being afraid all the time.

Dance of the Predator

Tony took Sarah on a long trek on the snowshoe trail that ran along the Red River behind his house, showing her the wolf tracks and where deer had nibbled at vegetation. It was a sunny morning and the fresh air stimulating. They were starving by time they got back. She'd brought over stew, leaving it to warm in the oven while they were out. A fragrant aroma spread through the house while Sarah prowled the cupboards and drawers in the kitchen, sifting through cooking utensils, searching for plates and silverware. Tony set the table, opened a bottle of wine, and took her a glass. Sarah lifted the lid off a large casserole dish to let him sniff the contents.

"It's an old stick-to-your-ribs family recipe," she said. "Be careful when you carry the dish into the dining room. It's hot, heavy, and an heirloom from my kookum. So don't drop it."

Tony poured them each another glass of wine as they sat to eat. The stew was delicious with spices detonating in his mouth like firecrackers and the taste and texture of the meat pungent on his tongue.

"It's good," he said.

"I know it's a cliché, but I like to cook," Sarah said. "I enjoy the process of planning meals and prepping them to feed my family, feeling the fibre of the fruit and vegetables and meat on my fingers, the fleshy consistency of kneading dough. This wine is nice. So tell me where your father is. I thought he was staying with you."

"We decided he'd be better off at Just Joe's house. But it didn't take long for him to get on Aunt Willa's nerves and they gave him the boot. He's at the Sally Ann now."

"Then things have come full circle. He put you on the street when you were young. You've done the same to him now."

After they finished eating, they cleared away the dishes, retired to the living room, and spent the rest of the lazy Sunday afternoon drinking wine, listening to music, and talking about the North End; how it had changed, how it hadn't. It was after eight when Sarah left. Tony took her hand at the door and felt its warmth. When she was gone, he poured a cognac and lit a cigar, letting the smoke fill his lungs, luxuriating in the fragrant tang on his lips. The day went well. He hadn't seen Sarah since the funeral a few weeks ago and sharing this delicious meal in her divine company was a pure delight. Tony chuckled. Those weren't words he normally used. He sipped his cognac.

Sarah would complete her carpentry course soon. He'd offer her a loan to get her started in a tough business. She could set up a small shop; build bookcases, desks, tables, and chairs. It was a good investment for him. Things were beginning to look up. The file on the Lithium fire was closed, the cops content they had their man. It was a shame having to put Bernie down, but his brother was headed for a bad end anyway. Tony simply accelerated what was inevitable. And the peace with the Curb Stompers was still intact too. One of their enforcers had helped Jimmy Jazz stuff Eric the Red into a sewer that would serve as a deepfreeze until the spring thaw flushed his body into the Red River, eliminating any stink. Tony had managed to keep Donovan out of it and now he was back where he belonged in the loony bin. Lawler assured Tony his brother would get good care in the secure facility where they were sending him. This was his last good deed for the old lady. Tony Bender believed in happy endings and 1984 was starting to look like a good year. There were still a few loose ends and he was taking care of one of them tonight. Sawchuk had let him know about a loser living at the Albert who wasn't what he pretended to be. Tony rinsed his cup in the sink and called his cab.

A band was making an awful noise at the Albert with kids thrashing around on the dance floor like demented zombies. Let them enjoy their little scene while it lasted. Cowboy was on the desk and looked jumpy. The man was a pimple on the ass of progress and Tony read him like a Louis L'Amour. But this was a three man job. Tony needed muscle now that Big Ron, Bernie, and Donovan were gone. Cowboy almost crapped himself when Jimmy Jazz came out of the bar with a bag of tools. Too bad. He was earning his keep and getting his hands dirty.

"Take us to his room," Tony ordered and Cowboy complied.

The pusher had never been upstairs in the hotel before and the smell almost knocked him over. He lit a cigar. They found Itchy Dick sniffing around in the hall hunting for butts. He shot them a goofy grin. The guy put on a good act. Jimmy Jazz nailed him in the face. Then he and Cowboy dragged him to his room and held him down on the floor while Tony covered his mouth with duct tape. After Tony tied the undercover cop's wrists and ankles, Jimmy Jazz took a huge crescent wrench from the tool bag and whacked Itchy Dick's head so hard it almost came off. The pig passed out. Tony grabbed a cup by the sink, tossed a toothbrush it held in the trash, and turned on the hot water until it was scalding. Then he splashed this in Dick's face. It brought him back to life and he wriggled like a bug burning under a magnifying glass. Jimmy Jazz started to wield the wrench like a baseball bat, swinging wildly at the cop's head while Cowboy watched horrified. Jimmy broke his fingers, snapping them with the wrench.

"Now he won't scratch no more," he said. Tony wrapped a strip of duct tape around Dick's nose and they tied him to the heating radiator. The steam started to hiss as his skin sizzled. The funeral would have to have a closed casket.

Accidentally Like a Martyr

Banjo Bob held his nose running down the hall. Something was rotting somewhere and the smell was especially bad outside Itchy Dick's room. What was he doing in there? In the lobby, Cowboy looked irritated talking to Maggie by the desk. He always seemed to be pissed off about something these days. Being boss was taking a toll on him and he was turning into a real tyrant. But Bob had to tell him about the terrible stink on the fourth floor.

"I know all about it, Bob," Cowboy growled. "But unlike you, I have other things to do. I am not the one with his life in the toilet."

"It's getting hard to breathe up there."

"Jesus, Bob, just back off. I'm going over to the Charlie to enjoy a quiet drink."

Cowboy stormed off. Banjo Bob smiled at Maggie.

"He's not in a very good mood."

"Nobody is these days, Bob."

"Why you so glum, chum?"

"Zoltan wants some rent from you or he's going to kick you out."

"Aw, he's always saying stuff like that."

"He means it this time, I think."

"I'm broke. Cash he gives me for cleaning the bar barely covers my smokes and beer."

Banjo Bob never seemed to have much money, despite selling drugs. He would be rich for a few days, take taxis everywhere, buy rounds in the bar, and tip extravagantly. But then he'd run out of cash and be poor again, a pattern which kept repeating.

"I hate being the one to bug you, Bob, but—" Maggie said then started to choke, gasping for air, her face going gray. She almost keeled over but steadied herself, catching her breath.

"Are you alright?" Bob asked.

"It's Zoltan. He's driving me crazy, always on my case about this, that, and the other thing, screaming and calling me names. I don't know what's got into him lately. He's getting worse."

"You need to relax, live a little, girl. All this stress isn't good for you. I mean, look at me. I could be blue but I stay positive, keep my spirits up. Nothing a drink and a toke don't fix."

"Maybe you could pawn your banjo," she said. Bob was almost angry at her for suggesting this sacrilege but it wasn't her fault. She didn't understand just how much Jedidiah meant to him. And while he didn't have the words to explain it, he had music. Banjo Bob placed his instrument case on the counter and carefully removed the banjo, running his fingers down the smooth neck. Then he started to play it while singing 'Maggie May'. Music flowed through him, cascading in sacred rain and Maggie melted. Her eyes were twinkling and dewy by time the tune was done. She took his hands in hers and squeezed.

"Don't pawn your banjo, Bob," she said. "We'll think of something."

He placed Jedidiah back into the case and flashed Maggie the peace sign.

In the bar, he ordered the single draught he could afford. Fran took her time in bringing it over. Bob didn't have the cash to tip her and the waitress was becoming a bitch anyways. So her bad boy biker dumped her. Fran had to get over her lost love like he had his. Then Sheila barged into his brain, banging bellies and shaking bums with Greasy Dave, body parts raining down in Banjo Bob's head. He had to stop doing so much acid. When he'd moved into the Albert a month ago, it was supposed to be temporary; a place to hang his toque till Sheila took him back. And, as long as she held onto his

stuff, there was hope. But a week ago, he'd spotted Downtown Tommy sporting his sweater with the Nova Scotia flag.
Bob recognized it by the mustard stains. It meant Sheila had
given his things to Goodwill. He was really on his own now.
He nursed his beer. The hotel was becoming a real drag and
the bar depressing with his drinking buddies gone; Donovan,
Scott Kostyk, Itchy Dick, even Cowboy, who wouldn't sit with
him anymore.

Bob was in the can washing his hands at the sink after a beer-laden whizz when he heard the door creak and
caught the whiff of cigar smoke. He spotted Tony Bender in
the mirror behind him by the door. Bob started to turn and a
fist slammed into his face. Blood spurted from his nose. It felt
like it might be broken again. Jimmy Jazz threw him on the
sink and Bob's banjo fell to the floor with a sickening thud. He
reached down to pick it up.

"Leave that fucking thing alone," Tony snarled. "How
many angels can dance on the head of a pin if you're a pinhead? Your days as a pusher are done. Donovan isn't here to
protect you anymore. I'll go easy on you for now because you
were a good friend to him and helped him stay out of trouble.
Collect all the dope in your room and bring it down to Jimmy
Jazz. He'll wait in the parking lot. You have ten minutes."

Bob dashed upstairs, quickly checking Jedidiah for
damage. Fortunately not even a broken string. He gathered
his stash and took it to Jimmy Jazz who grinned and slapped
him on the back like the friendly giant. Bob didn't understand
these people, threatening him one minute, then buddy-buddy
the next. He didn't feel much like going back to the bar after
this and decided to take a constitutional to clear his head. He
went around to the front of the Albert and started to walk,
letting his feet lead him wherever. He'd been warned about
not going down to the Main Drag but as he strolled the street,
what Bob discovered was a lively atmosphere with fascinat-
ing characters laughing and shouting as music poured from
every door. He went into the Occidental Hotel for a drink. It
was a zoo, lit too bright with a bad but enthusiastic band playing too loud and a crowd stepping around a couple making

out in a corner. They were necking and pawing at each other before disappearing under a table. It reminded him of the free-spirited days of the hippie house in Halifax.

When the band took a break, a big native man waved Bob over, poured him a glass of draught from a jug, and pointed at Jedidiah.

"Play me a Patsy Cline," he said. Bob strummed 'I Fall to Pieces' then 'Crazy', the only two Cline tunes he knew. But he had a bunch of Willie, Hank, and Kris Kristofferson songs in his repertoire so played them as his new friend continued to top up his glass. Bob was a hit and a small group gathered around him. The couple that had been horizontal shifted into vertical and danced up a storm. The guy had an arm around his gal in a proprietary manner, not realizing that she was busy scanning the bar for better prospects. Then a fight broke out between her beau and another contender and half the bar joined in the brawl. Bob's big friend lifted their table with its jugs of beer onto the stage. They climbed up, sat down, and drank while they watched the battle royale play out. It was more keystone cops than lethal, the two main antagonists swinging and kicking at each other, missing more than connecting. They fell to the floor and wrestled until the bouncers threw them both out. Meanwhile the woman at the center of this dispute left the bar in the company of a third suitor.

The night became a blur after this, and the next Bob knew he was back on the street again, surrounded by weaving drunks. Through the fog, he became aware of the three boys standing on a corner. They were maybe fifteen or sixteen years old with scarred, emaciated faces; all skin and bones and elbows poking through torn jean jackets. Bob said he had no spare change when they confronted him. One of the kids grinned and punched his buddy's shoulder. Bob stepped forward and a fist landed on his cheek, a second on his nose. He stumbled a little but kept his balance and held onto his banjo. Then one of the kids snatched the case, removed Jedidiah, and jammed the banjo into his groin, pumping his hips, reducing his friends to hysterics. When he snapped off a tuning peg, Banjo Bob went ballistic, bawling and lunging at him. It was too late. The kid lifted the banjo over his head, swung it at a telephone pole, and smashed it. Bob ran into another fist then another and his face filled with stars as he fell to his knees, hitting the pavement so hard something popped. The kids attacked him, one using what was left of his banjo to hit him. Bob believed they'd realize he was no threat and stop beating him if he didn't fight back, forgetting what Cowboy had warned him about. He could always back off, but never back down. It made Bob looked weak so they beat him ruthlessly, hooting and hollering as they put the boots to him, punching and kicking until he was so numb he no longer felt any pain. Eventually, they were either drained or bored because there wasn't much left of him to beat. One of them gave him a good swift kick and they walked away, laughing and slapping each other on the back.

Bob was limp, little more than a soft lump of flesh, and started to crawl on his hands and knees as people stepped around him. A passing stranger booted him hard in the ass, connecting with his tailbone and knocking him flat on his face. Bob climbed back up on all fours and finally made it to a hotel wall that smelled of piss and vomit. He was woozy from both the beating and the booze and threw up. He wasn't sure how long it was before a flashlight shone in his face, two shadows looming behind it.

"What do you think, Derek," one of the cops said. "Drunk tank or ER?"

"ER then the drunk tank," Derek said. They dragged him to a police cruiser, pushing him into the back seat.

"Where's Jedidiah?" Banjo Bob cried out.

"Your buddy took a powder and left you to get a beating."

"I think there were four of them," Bob muttered.

"Now would be a good time to shut your hole," the cop said. Bob looked out the window onto the street at scraps of wood and steel and wire.

"So long, Jedidiah," he said quietly as a melancholy melody heaved up from a dark place in him, a lament, not just for his banjo but for Sheila, Donovan, the Albert, and the city. As the police car pulled away from the curb, Banjo Bob closed his eyes and began to sing.

Chicago North

Wellington Crescent was a winding, tree-lined boulevard with a stretch of parkland beside it that extended down to the Assiniboine River. In April of 1984, this expanse was still a barren sanctuary under snow, yet would soon erupt into a lush, green retreat. Scott Kostyk was taking a long stroll down by the icy water and letting his mind drift. Six weeks after a savage beating behind the Albert the night of the Benefit he'd almost completely healed under Velvet's care. He had no broken bones, the swelling in his face was down, and most of the cuts and bruises were gone. If Donovan Bender hadn't defended him in the parking lot, his injuries might have been far worse. Kostyk wanted to thank his friend but hadn't been back to the hotel since the incident and Velvet was discouraging him from going there. Scott didn't need any convincing. He was still pretty shaken up, his only remaining pain psychic, and he was reluctant to go downtown. Some mornings he woke with his head doing cartwheels and somersaults. After his stroll by the river, Kostyk explored the neighbourhood.

Fort Rouge was a tranquil area with chimes on wide wooden verandas, large, comfortable homes, and green gardens in the backyards that allowed middleclass hippies to grow pot in the summer months. He walked over to Corydon Avenue and the funky little café where he could enjoy a bottomless cup of coffee, catch up on his reading, and pass a few pleasant hours chatting with the owner, Torvald. Velvet had given him a novel to read and 'Strange Life of Ivan Osokin' was strange. But Kostyk wasn't one to give up on a book and dived into it now over his coffee.

"What've you got on the go now?" Torvald asked, topping up his cup.

"PD Ouspensky," Kostyk said, holding the book up.

"Ah, the Slavs," Torvald said. "I prefer Nabokov, with a pinch of Bulgakov for spice. Are you familiar with his novel, 'The Master and Margarita'?"

"No, but my wife, Svetlana, is related to Mikhail."

"Oh, you must read it then. It will tickle your brain."

When Kostyk finally left the Copenhagen Café, it was already dark, another early winter evening in the North Country. Velvet lived in a large Tudor-style building that took up the whole length of a city block on Wellington Crescent. Her apartment, though slightly rundown, was spacious and charming with a warm, homey atmosphere. It had an enormous living room, a dining room, decent kitchen, and three bedrooms. Velvet's bedroom was the largest, overlooking the street with a good view of the river. The second was filled with books and served as a study with an easy chair, a standing lamp, and a small desk Kostyk was using as a drawing table. The third bedroom at the rear of the apartment had been a maid's quarters at the turn of the century and was equipped with a call bell. This was where Kostyk slept on a mattress on the floor. Every afternoon Velvet went to work at the hotel, came home late, and didn't say a single word about the Albert. He never asked. While this respite from his concerns was a welcome relief, it also revealed an unpleasant truth he had refused to face before the Lithium fire. Kostyk preferred art to people. Any guilt about Svetlana's death was less about losing her than an absence of love and his lack of caring.

While Velvet was gone to work, he sat at the reading room desk, staring at a blank sheet of paper and wondering if his ability to draw had deserted him completely. In the last few weeks, he had been trying to sketch her portrait. But Velvet was a difficult subject. Kostyk couldn't seem to create even a simple likeness. How could putting lines on paper catch the growl in her voice, the vibration of Velvet's throaty laughter, or the peculiar habit she had of kneading the carpet with her toes to caress the fabric when she walked barefoot? His poor creative effort was incapable of giving expression to her unassuming, sultry nature; how it hinted at a guarded passion he sensed lurking under the surface of her skin, or the way her dark eyes slipped from playful to soulful to smouldering. Velvet had an ethereal essence he yearned to apprehend through art. It wasn't only a matter of gratitude for her generosity, but something deeper, visceral, and primal. She seemed to possess an uncanny ability to alleviate any affliction tormenting his troubled mind, reducing all his chaotic thought to refuse, allowing him to let go of the hold it had on him. He had never experienced this profound level of comfort before, the ease of being which Velvet had provided. How she managed this was a mystery he was happy to embrace, even if its nature escaped him. In many ways, Velvet was like other women he had been drawn to in his life. And yet, she was different. He was invariably attracted to smart women who shared his tendency to live in their heads, which always ended in a pissing contest to determine who had the greater passion and fiercer conviction, the superior talent. Velvet had a good mind and wasn't shy about sharing her thoughts or opinions. But neither did she dwell on inconsequential, irrelevant abstraction or idle introspection. Her intelligence was intuitive and Kostyk's proximity to it was provoking him to re-evaluate his own processes and priorities.

Returning from the Copenhagen Café now he was determined to get this drawing of Velvet done, to get her likeness down on paper. Frustrated by his failure so far, he feverishly attacked the work, sketching madly, blindly pressing his thumb into a charcoal smear, and pushing it across an emerging forehead, sliding it down the length of a honey-brown throat, transforming it into a shock of black hair. Kostyk suddenly seemed capable of catching traits in her character that had eluded him. Fresh exhilaration flooded him and he finished the drawing quickly. When Velvet came home from work that night, he showed it to her.

"It's yours," he said. She thanked him and slipped the drawing into a dresser drawer. They spent a few hours talking about his day but not hers. Later that night, six weeks after taking him into her home, Velvet took Kostyk into her bed. Afterward they lay together and he touched her arm, lightly running his fingers up and down the length.

"You're intelligent, Velvet. Easy to talk to and fun to be with. But I've never seen you with anyone before. Why is that?"

Velvet didn't respond right away and he waited. When she finally did open up and reply at last, her voice was laced with steel.

"I'm Métis, too brown for some, too white for others. It took forever to find a job in this city. Nobody hires my kind. They say we aren't reliable, won't show up for a shift, and can't be trusted. Zoltan, even with all his issues, is the only person who ever offered me work."

"He says you're his best waitress."

"It's because I work hard but won't work stupid. He likes that."

"You still haven't answered me," he said and Velvet sighed.

"I was fourteen in Grade ten, walking home from school on a warm Friday afternoon. Two white boys started calling me names, describing in detail what they wanted to do to me. I didn't say anything and just headed straight home. I told my mother and she called my uncle. He and a few buddies roared down from Flin Flon on Harleys, flying their colours. Monday morning, they stood beside me outside the school door while other kids filed inside and I pointed out the two culprits, this one and that one. Nobody ever bothered me again after that. I don't take crap from anyone, Scott. You know Winnipeg means muddy waters in Cree? Muddy waters hide secrets. My sister was seventeen when the river took her. They never found her body but didn't look long. Star was just another Indigenous girl gone missing, likely living a dangerous lifestyle, mixing with the wrong people, doing things that precipitated whatever happened to her. That's the thinking. Star was a lean, fine-boned, beautiful girl with delicate features, green sparkling eyes. They say time heals all wounds. But scars remain. I treasure mine. They honour Star, keep her alive inside me. It's like that for you. Wherever you go, whatever you do, you will carry Svetlana with you. She lives in you as Star does me. Maybe that's what I saw in you at the Albert; how you hold onto your pain. You need to stop struggling and embrace it. That's enough talking for now. Get some sleep."

Kostyk woke before her the next morning and made breakfast; scrambled eggs with bacon, toast, and coffee. After they finished eating and were enjoying their coffee, he broached a subject that had been in the back of his mind for days. Kostyk had to deal with outstanding issues. While he refused to be in the business of art anymore, he had poured time and energy into Confidential Exchange and couldn't let the gallery suffer an undignified death.

"There may still be a way to save the gallery," he said. "But it requires an infusion of cash, creative vision, and strong leadership. Sebastian is flush, receiving a decent settlement from the insurance company following the Lithium fire. I am positive that I can persuade him to invest in Confidential Exchange. As for day-to-day operations, Karmin Magis is a determined artist with a formidable intelligence. I need to go down to the Albert to talk to them and maybe see Donovan to express my appreciation for his saving my butt."

"You need to do what you must. I won't try to talk you out of it, although Donovan isn't around anymore. He's gone."

"Where?"

"It doesn't matter. Sit a minute. Something we should do first," Velvet said. She collected various items; a cedar box holding an abalone shell wrapped in fabric, wooden matches, and several leaves of sage. She unfolded the fabric around the shell, lifted the sage from the box, and lit it, allowing it to burn a short while before she blew out the fire. Smoke billowed up. She explained smudging would help heal his mind, body, heart, and spirit, purifying him of negative energy.

"Pull the smoke in to yourself and inhale," she said. "I pass it over your eyes to clear your vision, your mouth so you may speak the truth, and your heart to cleanse it, allowing you to let go of any anger and hate you may have."

When she was done, Velvet pressed the smoking sage into a flower pot filled with earth. Kostyk was putting on his coat at the door when Velvet brought the book.

"So you have something to read on your journey," she said and Kostyk kissed her on the cheek. Velvet smiled, took his face in her hands, and kissed him firmly on the lips.

Outside, the afternoon sky was heavy and gray with the wind kicking around dark clouds. Kostyk's apprehension about taking this trip was tempered by a strong hint of spring in the air. He walked to Corydon and caught a bus that was heading downtown and heaving with boisterous teens going home after school. Clinging to a handrail and jammed up against overheated bodies pressing into him on every side, he was buffeted back and forth with every stop and start. He couldn't breathe and felt claustrophobic. He had to escape this crushing tube of flesh and yanked on a cord. A few kids giggled as an irate driver stopped, his voice crackling through the intercom.

"You only need to ring the bell once," he grumbled. The door whooshed open and when he climbed off, the teenagers on the bus erupted in laughter. He looked around to see where he had landed and was dismayed to learn the bus had only gone a few blocks. He decided to walk the rest of the way to Albert Street.

Standing in front of the Chambers Building, Kostyk realized he was reluctant to go up to the gallery. But it was getting cold and he had to deal with Confidential Exchange. He went inside, expecting the gallery to look like it had the last time he was there. But the place was clean, his plants watered. Velvet was obviously keeping an eye on things. There were no messages on the machine or notes taped to the door nothing to indicate anyone was taking any interest in how he was doing or where he was. Kostyk resisted the relentless, urgent gaze of a particular painting that lurked in a dark corner, sparing himself the indignity of casting his eyes on 'Dreaming Dread'. He had no idea what to do with the damn thing, maybe set it on fire. No, he'd just let Karmin and Sebastian sort it out.

Kostyk didn't know yet what kind of arrangement he could work out with them, whether he'd stay on as a silent partner to earn a percentage on sales or hand over everything for a set price. It was best he talks to Sebastian first, who would be more amenable to the proposal and could help persuade Karmin to participate. Kostyk sat down at his desk and thumbed through his Rolodex only realizing halfway through, as index cards flew by, that the number for the Lithium Café would no longer work.

He was startled by a sudden pounding at the door. Who could it be? Nobody but Velvet knew he was there. Kostyk slipped to the door, where an opaque shadow bobbed in the fractured blue light of the frosted window.

"Open the door or I'll huff and I'll puff and I'll blow your house down!" Zoltan shouted. Kostyk unlocked the door and his old friend scurried inside, taking a swig from a bottle of Gran Marnier and waving an accusing finger at him.

"You have been bad, Kostyk," Zoltan slurred. "This is the second time you've disappeared and not told me where you are. So, you had a beating laid on you. Man up. I mean seriously, the way things are at the Albert these days; I was genuinely worried about you. Good thing Velvet told me you were here when she came into work earlier today and asked me to check up on you. Kudos, by the way, Kostyk; Velvet is a keeper."

"Nice to see you too," Scott said. Zoltan dropped into a chair by the desk and picked up 'Strange Life of Ivan Osokin'.

"This is certainly making the rounds. Donovan dumps it on me; I pass it along to Velvet who always has her nose in a book, now you have it. Grab your coat. I'm buying you dinner."

Out on the street, Zoltan walked fast and Kostyk struggled to keep up as they flew down Portage Avenue toward Hy's Steak Loft on Kennedy. Once they were settled at a table, Zoltan ordered two Gran Marnier, shrimp appetizers, and a bottle of the restaurant's best wine. Then he gulped down both his drink and Kostyk's before turning to the wine. He didn't touch his food when it arrived and started to babble instead. The booze was not only loosening his tongue, but lending a little ballast to his erratic state of mind.

"Turn of the last century, Winnipeg was called Chicago North and the fastest growing city in North America for about fifteen minutes."

"You've shared that particular piece of information about fifty times, Zoltan."

"Christ, I'm not even gone yet and already missing the place. You remember my Jean in the Prairie Little Theatre production of 'Miss Julie'? I was incredible, right? And yet from a lofty perch and the vantage point of his superior critical capacity, Art Cologne claimed my performance was wooden; shallow, fey, and far too precious he said. I recall his exact words."

"Cologne's reviews were always a little arsenic and old lace."

"But equally true is the fact that we hobble giants in the North Country, cut them off at the knees lest they get too big for their britches. Some choose obscurity and some have it thrust upon them; those who know this know and those who don't know don't matter."

"You're not making any sense, Zoltan. You're drunk and you're stoned."

"I am drunk and stoned and perhaps a little ludicrous. But you think too much, Scott; spin these elaborate fantasies about the way things are, the way they should be. However, I will calm your delicate sensibilities and be more direct. Put succinctly, everything has gone to rat-shit since the Lithium fire. People have been hurt, gone missing, and even died. There is a predator at work in these parts and the latest to fall prey to his Machiavellian cunning is Richard Darch."

"Who?"

"Dick Darch, also known as Itchy Dick. Nobody saw him mooching for over a week. The smell by his room got so bad I had Cowboy break down the door. I will never forget what I saw there; half his head was caved in, his body burned black. Word got out quickly courtesy of the usual suspects, killing off what little business I still had. People stopped coming to the bar, some residents moved out. It only takes a single, careless moment of complacency for it all to crash. I am done. I have nothing left to give. I used to worry what would happen to people if I fired them or gave them the boot. But they managed before they came to the Albert. They'll get along when they leave. I sold the whole shooting match; the condo, car, hotel to Tony Bender. He now owns the Albert and I am heading to California in the morning to go into the real estate game with my brother. Here's his business card if you ever get down that way. Glad I caught you before I leave. Let's have another drink, celebrate new beginnings."

It was after three AM when they closed down Hy's and Kostyk walked back along Portage, turning over what his friend had said, trying to absorb it. The city would not be the same without Zoltan. Yet, his selling the hotel mirrored Kostyk's decision to unload the gallery. Maybe it was no accident they were both bailing. He turned off Notre Dame onto Albert where the shops and businesses were all locked down for the night with the shadows of buildings leaning into the road like sentinels guarding the street. How long would they continue to do this?

Kostyk didn't want to disturb Velvet and decided to spend the night at the gallery. She'd be asleep at home and understand he was staying in the company of art he loved to hate to shake off ghosts haunting him. In the morning he went over to the Salisbury House right across the street for breakfast.

The restaurant was buzzing with cheerful chatter and banter, the easy camaraderie of cabbies, cops, and bus drivers on their way to work or just coming off a night shift. He finished his bacon and eggs and lingered over coffee, looking at the cold window where frost had created an elfin script of curling flowers and silver leaves. Down the street, the Royal Albert Arms Hotel seemed almost sedate, as if nothing awful ever happened there. Kostyk guzzled down the last of his coffee and took a walk around to clear his head. On Portage, all the day people were starting to parade in their uniforms; the starched collars and shiny, polished shoes, skirts and high heels. Why did they dress this way in the middle of winter? Scott hadn't showered, shaved, or changed his clothes in twenty-four hours. This rendered him invisible to the indifferent crowd. He headed over to Ellice Avenue where it was quieter with less street traffic.

Central Park, opened in 1893, was smaller than its New York namesake, but it also offered some escape from the chaotic bustle of a busy downtown. When a war whoop went up near the park, Kostyk spotted a short, round man bending over at the curb, oblivious to cars whizzing by him, while he harvested cigarette butts. Banjo Bob Holiday lifted one over his head and did an awkward jig.

"Look what I found, chrome-dome!" he hollered at a man sitting on a snow encrusted bench in the park. Then he saw Kostyk and hobbled over limping.

"How you doing, man," he asked, holding out a hand. "Got any spare change? No? Well, come say hello to my partner anyway."

The other man wore a threadbare jean jacket and John Deere ball cap. He snatched the butt from Bob before passing him a brown paper bag. Kostyk had never before seen Cowboy without his Stetson and when he removed the ball cap to scratch his head, he was mostly bald. He glared at Kostyk, his once steel-gray eyes watery-blue.

"Don't act superior," he growled. "Nobody's more than a paycheque from the street."

Banjo Bob stopped slurping from the bottle.

"Tony Bender gave us the boot," he said. "Fired the whole staff."

"Everyone but that bitch, Velvet," Cowboy muttered.

"Hey, don't sweat it, amigo," Bob chirped. "No point being blue. Spring is just around the corner and we'll sleep in the park and wash in the rain."

"Jumping Judas, you're an irritating jackass," Cowboy snarled.

"I could be miserable too after losing Jedidiah at the Occidental."

"I warned you about drinking in them hotels."

"If Tony evicted you two, what happened to Dono-van?" Kostyk asked.

"They wheeled him out on a gurney. He's catatonic in Selkirk," Cowboy said, grabbing the bottle back from Banjo Bob. They were still arguing over it as Scott left. The Captain's Corner across the street was where he had first connected with Donovan and discovered a street poet with an edgy, authentic voice. Selkirk wasn't far from town. Scott should go visit him, return his book. The bus depot only a few blocks away was a dirty, depressing hole where a security guard patrolled the premises with a nasty looking German shepherd and harassed people. Then when a native woman refused to show him her ticket, he pulled her from her chair and dragged her out the door. Others waiting for a bus acted as if nothing had happened. Kostyk's eyes opened to a side of Winnipeg he'd never seen before, or maybe just chosen not to know.

The ride out to Selkirk was bleak with small patches of green starting to show through the snow. The only other passengers on the bus were an old lady with a fruit basket, probably for a demented husband, and a young woman who went back and forth between reading 'Invitation to a Beheading' and a book on schizophrenia. Kostyk still hadn't completed 'Strange Life of Ivan Osokin' and decided to read more of it before seeing his friend. At a station in Selkirk, the three agreed to share a cab to the hospital. They pulled up in front of an enormous brownstone that had been constructed at the end of the nineteenth century, an elegant edifice with a gorgeous exterior and an inside likely filled with asbestos, mould, and fibreglass. The expansive grounds were covered in snow now but would provide a pleasant place to walk in a few months.

Inside, the others went their way while Kostyk stopped at the reception desk to get directions. The woman behind a security window of tempered glass scrutinized him carefully as she explained a colour-coded legend on the floor. The blue butterflies led to Mood and Anxiety, green to Geriatrics, white to youth, and purple to Schizophrenia. Kostyk followed red ones to Forensics, imagining men in white coats chasing patients down the hall with butterfly nets. At the end of the trail, a steel-framed door of reinforced glass confronted him with three more doors behind it and a security guard in a monitor-filled room between the first two. Kostyk pressed a buzzer. The guard leaned into a microphone.

"Can I help you?" his voice squawked.

"I'm here to see Donovan Bender," Kostyk said.

"Just a minute," the guard said and picked up a phone. When he hung up the young woman who had been on the bus approached from the nursing unit. The guard buzzed her through locked doors that snapped, crackled, and popped. She didn't wear a uniform but had a name tag that identified her as Suzie, RN, her last name covered by a strip of black tape. She either did not remember Kostyk from the bus or pretended she didn't. He explained why he was there a third time.

"You're in luck," she said. "Donovan is doing better these days and can have visitors. But we're in the middle of shift change, so you'll have to wait until after we're done with report."

Kostyk stood outside the door a half hour before a large, beefy orderly was buzzed out and ushered him onto the unit, leading him to a small receiving area beside the guard's office. He instructed him to put his coat, bag, and contents in a locker. Kostyk showed him the book.

"What's this?" the orderly asked.

"It's a book for Donovan," Kostyk said. The orderly skimmed through the pages and then returned it. After he passed a security wand over Kostyk's body, he opened the last doors with an ID badge and let him into the visiting lounge. Kostyk settled at an empty table. Another orderly was positioned in a corner, scanning a magazine with one eye and the room with the other. None of the staff wore a uniform, but it wasn't hard to tell them from patients. Aside from ID, they had better clothes and a subtle, yet definite sense of superiority.

A sign on the wall announced cancellation of the spiritual group and there was a poster with the names of famous people who had suffered from mental illness; Virginia Woolf,

Sylvia Plath, Tennessee Williams, Van Gogh, Hemingway. The poster was clearly intended to provide a positive message for patients but seemed to miss the fact that most of those on the list had either committed suicide or come to some other bad end. A woman with pockmarked skin and a bad perm sat across from a man, her enormous eyes near tears, his angry. Kostyk wasn't sure which was the patient, which the visitor. An emaciated boy who looked barely eighteen was parked on the floor, legs stretched out, arms wrapped around his chest, and his face a tight mask. A middle aged couple studied him with puzzled, worried expressions. Another patient with snow-white hair and cherubic features roamed the room, straightening out chairs and arranging magazines. He wore faded jeans and a wrinkled white shirt. Periodically, he jammed a hand in his pants pocket and stroked himself. When he saw Kostyk was watching him, he made his way over and extended a cool, limp hand. Kostyk took it, grateful it fortunately wasn't the one he favoured for his fondling.

"You're counterculture," the patient said. "It's nice to meet someone who made it through. You know, I'm completely normal except for my voices."

The orderly slammed down his magazine and stood up.

"Stop bothering the visitors," he grumbled.

"Don't bark at me, cretin," the patient snapped back. "He's an empath. He understands."

"You never have visitors and shouldn't even be in here, Stewart."

"How many times I have to tell you that's not my name!"

"You see this?" the orderly said, flexing a bicep. "If you don't behave, I'll throw you over my shoulder and haul your skinny ass down to your room."

Stewart charged him and the orderly yanked a lanyard. A bell gonged and a voice intoned over the PA system.

"Code White. Forensics Level One. Visitors Lounge."

The room quickly filled with orderlies wearing disposable latex gloves. They dragged the patient, kicking and screaming, to the floor, and restrained him, holding his arms and legs. One orderly cradled his head so he didn't bang it against the floor as he flailed. Suzie stood behind the orderlies, holding a med cup in one hand, a small tray with two needles in the other. She stepped forward.

"We can't allow you to assault staff, Stewart," she said.

"Don't call me that!" he howled.

"I have a needle with your name on it, so this can go one of two ways. Take medication orally or by injection. It's your choice."

"You're not scrubbing my brain with fucking poison!" Stewart cried out.

"Hold him, boys," Suzie said and an orderly pulled the patient's pants down to expose his upper buttocks. Suzie jammed a needle in one cheek, a second in the other. The orderly yanked Stewart's pants up again. The others jerked him to his feet and hustled him out as Stewart yelled all the way down the hall. Donovan was waiting outside. The nurse smiled at him when he entered and she nodded to Kostyk.

"Have a nice visit," she said and left.

"It's an achievement upsetting Jesus Two-Two," Donovan said. "He's a woodwork patient and usually just sits in a corner diddling himself."

"You call him Jesus Two-Two?" Kostyk asked.

"There's a second Jesus on the unit now and they argue endlessly about which of them is more divine. Why are you here, Scott? Looking for accommodations? They'll gladly have you."

"I wanted to thank you for saving my ass at the Benefit, see how you're doing."

"Lawler fried my brain and will flash freeze it now then put it in a jar beside his golfing trophies. I'm moving to a more secure facility in a few days."

"You don't belong here, Donovan. You're not crazy."

"Siren has taught me how to live by the acute angle, how to be oblique and slip sideways through space."

Kostyk placed 'Strange Life of Ivan Osokin' on the table.

"I brought you this."

"My boomerang book," Donovan said, pushing it away. "I throw it away; it bounces back. You think you know me because I write poetry, Kostyk? You don't know me, or my brothers. Yes, Bernie set that fucking fire, but Tony put the match in his hand. I'm a Bender too. Look."

Donovan rolled up his long-sleeved shirt to reveal rows of jagged scars running up and down his arm from his wrists to his elbows. The sight was both appalling and alluring to Scott.

"Best go before they keep you for dinner," Donovan said, standing up and walking out. The orderly followed him.

Kostyk sat dumbfounded for a few minutes. He wasn't sure what to think. The visit was too short and he wasn't able to connect with Donovan. Their friendship was over and he would never see Donovan again.

At the locker, he put the book back in his bag. After the oppressive heat of the institutional environment, Kostyk needed fresh air and waited outside for a taxi to take him back to the bus station. He wasn't surprised to learn Tony was responsible for the Lithium fire. And now, this hood had not only gotten away with arson and murder, he owned the Albert too. Kostyk smelled cigar smoke. He turned to find Tony Bender standing behind him.

"Ride back with us," he said. Kostyk followed the pusher to the parking lot reluctantly and was relieved to see Jimmy Jazz wasn't behind the wheel. Tony climbed into the Dart beside the woman who was driving.

"Donovan's friend needs a lift to town," he said.

"Of course," Sarah said "How is your brother?"

"Didn't see Donovan, but spoke to his doctor, left money for the canteen."

"He's fine," Kostyk blurted out. "Clear-headed, coherent, and cogent,"

"Why? What did he say to you?" Tony Bender asked, staring at him in the rear-view mirror.

"Nothing," Kostyk said quickly. "We talked about a book."

"Don't be concerned about my brother," Tony said. "I'll take care of him. I always do."

The woman beside Tony took one hand off the steering wheel to touch his cheek and he leaned in toward her. These simple yet intimate gestures surprised Kostyk. He would never have imagined Tony capable of them. As they drove into Winnipeg, Scott watched prairie roll by the window. The snow in the fields was starting to melt. Soon the farmers would be planting crops and a few months later harvesting them. It all seemed to happen so fast. But maybe that was only in his head. He didn't work the long hours, the days and nights it took to grow grain. He dabbled in oils while Tony Bender sold drugs and Donovan idled away in hospital. None of it came close to the challenges farmers faced. The Dart lurched to a halt. Tony turned to him.

"You get out here," he said. "Stay out of the Albert."

They'd dropped him on the Midtown Bridge and he watched the Dart roar down Donald, no doubt heading toward Tony's recent acquisition. Kostyk started to walk over the bridge and stopped halfway across. Evening was beginning to roll in, salting the sky with stars. The city was quiet, caught in a brief moment of calm before the next outbreak of chaos. It was usually a long time between things happening in Winnipeg; not so much lately. A billboard across the way was announcing a balmy temperature of ten below and the date. It was April eleventh, three months to the day after the Lithium fire. Soon the city would blossom into a paradise of green and gold and he would want to stay. But his friends were all gone one way or the other and much of what he loved about this town was lost or soon would be; places and people disappearing or dying, almost as if, like Zoltan said, some great, predatory bird was swooping down and carrying off pieces of the city in giant claws. Kostyk would miss the smell of lilacs in spring and the trees arching over streets, creating a cool canopy in summer and magnificent ice sculptures in winter. He held his hands to the sky and examined their pale wonder against the approaching darkness, marvelling at the intricate network of sinew and blood, the creases and textures of skin. Three months ago he had almost died. But he was alive now and comfortable in his own body, perhaps for the first time in his life. He realized what he had shared with Donovan wasn't about art but isolation. They were both outsiders among outsiders, on the fringe of the fringe. Yet, alone was only alone until it wasn't anymore. The weight of the book was heavy in his bag and he fished it out. Kostyk flipped through the pages with words, sentences, whole passages flying passed. The Assiniboine River percolated at his feet, the dirty ice cracking and breaking into fragments that fractured and collided, crunching and crushing, forming a wild cubist painting. He lifted the novel over his head and fired it as far as he could in the air. The pages fluttered like tethered wings, the book gliding in a graceful arc before plummeting and landing with an unceremonious thud to sink under the muddy water. He suddenly felt light and started to walk again.

People always said Portage and Main was the windiest corner in North America and if you stood there for fifteen minutes, someone you knew would walk by. It only took ten today before Svetlana was marching across the street, ignoring pedestrian barriers and bleating traffic, twirling a baton and pumping her legs like a majorette. Oscar followed her, beating on a snare drum and behind him, the homeless man playing a tin whistle. The wind blew through canyons of steel and stone as the ragged parade, which included Itchy Dick, Eric the Red, Billy Triangle, Prince, and Bernie Bender, straggled across the wide intersection and disappeared on the other side of Main Street through a crack in time. Velvet was right. Svetlana was inside him now and always would be. It was time for Scott to stop thinking about his feelings and start living them. Time he saw his mother in North Dakota. New Mexico heat would ease any pain in her aching bones; the light was perfect for painting, the wide open spaces ideal for riding a Harley Davidson. When he hit Albert Street, he felt buoyant, despite the obvious signs of progress around him. The Exchange District was being carved into digestible chunks for tourists, with newly installed Victorian-style street lamps and pavement cobbled with interlocking brick.

In the lobby of the Albert, there was no Maggie, Cowboy, or Fran to greet him. The front desk had been ripped out leaving a large, dark stain on the floor and all the posters were stripped from the walls, exposing peeling paint and cracked plaster. The days and nights of drinking with Donovan and Banjo Bob, carousing with Cowboy and Itchy Dick, seemed dreamlike now. Scott wondered what the scene of the Lithium fire would be like. He shook his head. No. He had more pressing business here. A fridge door slammed in the bar. Kostyk went inside to talk to Velvet.

www.ingramcontent.com/pod-product-compliance
Lightning Source LLC
Chambersburg PA
CBHW030801210726
48290CB00002B/377